Wise Phuul

Daniel Stride

Published by Inspired Quill: November 2016

First Edition

Contact the author through their website:
phuulishfellow.wordpress.com

Chief Editor: Sara-Jayne Slack
Cover Design: Venetia Jackson
Typeset in Baskerville

Paperback ISBN: 978-1-908600-59-2
eBook ISBN: 978-1-908600-60-8
Print Edition

Printed in the United Kingdom
1 2 3 4 5 6 7 8 9 10

Inspired Quill Publishing, UK
Business Reg. No. 7592847
www.inspired-quill.com

For Nicky Thomas, Donna Jones, Margi MacMurdo-Reading, Simon Wilson, Peter Wilson, and Mr Black. Without you, I wouldn't be here.

Chapter One

THE CORPSE AT reception was busy. Busy pretending to be busy, Teltö judged, peering at the desktop folder. *Those weather reports are older than me, and it's reading the bloody things upside down.* Still, it was an improvement: last time the lich had polished paperclips for an hour. *Everyone needs a hobby.* Some people liked gardening. Some people counted trains. Madam Venomavat created lifelike office staff. Imperfect, of course, but the flaws only made them more human.

Teltö wished the Undersecretary were as interested in her living visitors. The reception held all the appeal of a backstreet dentist: no seating, except for the undead functionary, and nothing to look at save for the obese potted cactus in the corner. A mauve carpet completed the dreary ensemble. He kicked his heels. He'd trade his entire month's ration dockets for a magazine or newspaper.

Teltö cleared his throat. "Excuse me?"

Pencil in grey hand, the lich scribbled something.

Teltö raised his voice. "Please?"

The lich scribbled something else.

"I'm a living human – class Necromancer, rank underkarl – here to see the Undersecretary?"

The lich slumped forward onto the desk. A bluebottle settled on its head.

Bugger this. Teltö consulted his pocket watch. He'd a double-shift at the Library this afternoon, and this appointment was eating into his lunch break. He needed to grab a cheese roll from the corner bakery too. *I'll come back tomorrow.*

The receptionist jerked up, as if attached to a string.

"Phuul."

Teltö leapt back and thunked into the cactus pot. He cringed, even as he struggled to stop the plant toppling.

The corpse nodded towards the office door.

"The Undersecretary will see you now."

Teltö brushed copper hair from his eyes. He scurried past the corpse and eased the door shut behind him.

A stout, grey-haired, grey-eyed woman in a greyer cardigan looked up from her desk.

"Phuul," she said, "sit."

He hesitated.

"There is a seat. I told you to sit. Now *sit.*"

Teltö Phuul obeyed. Alio Venomavat's office looked much as he remembered it. Bookshelves leaned drunkenly against beige wallpaper; dust trickled onto reports in a dozen tiny waterfalls. Marmalade and malevolent, a feline blob blinked irritably from a corner fortress of velvet cushions.

"Now, Phuul." The Undersecretary toyed with a butterfly-in-amber paperweight. Papers, folders, and a plate of buttered toast graced her desktop. "Thus far, your service in the noble art of necromancy has been the stuff of glorious obscurity, no?"

"I'm but a humble underkarl, Madam Venomavat."

The cat padded over to the fireplace, and sniffed the encrusted soot. That grate grew its own coal deposits: it hadn't worked in years. *Last time this place had a decent blaze,* Teltö mused, *Emperors still ruled the Empire. They ought to burn the building to the ground and start again.*

"Puss, puss."

The cat leapt onto Venomavat's lap, purring like an engine. The Undersecretary scratched behind its ears. For one terrible moment, her face threatened to soften.

"You are twenty-two, Phuul. Twenty-two! Despite your elder sister blazing a trail, you have chosen the path of listless mediocrity."

"I passed the Examination." *She's wearing nail polish. Someone's come into money.*

"Barely." Venomavat let her pet settle. "You've subsisted these past four years as a library clerk. Slaving among the drab and dull, never poking your prodigious nose beyond Qivunako."

Teltö opened his mouth to protest. The Phuuls spent midsummer at a seaside cabin, down at Dyrtölä on the south-east coast. Salt spray and grey waves soaked his childhood memories. *Ah. She means I've never been to the other cities. True.*

"Qivunako is the loveliest city in the Empire."

"Qivunako is a backwater. The smallest and weakest of the Four Cities. Remain here, and your future is assisting some lowly iron mine supervisor. Surely you hunger for greater things? To do your family proud? To escape the towering shadow of Rhea Phuul?"

The towering shadow of someone who thinks the world runs on examination marks. "Not really..."

"False modesty." Venomavat grimaced. An industrial

accident had twisted her mouth muscles years earlier, or so the story went. Teltö believed she was just plain nasty. "Well, Phuul, the Lesser Council and I are giving you a present. Congratulations."

She thrust a paper into Teltö's hands. A travel itinerary. Full of typographical errors and smudges, but a travel itinerary nonetheless. *A river journey along the Nhagivat. Ugh.*

"Yes, Phuul. You'll accompany our very own Master Hova to Kuolinako. He is filling the empty Grand Council seat, and the Lesser Council have designated *you* his Native Assistant."

"But…"

"Your girlfriend works in the Last Capital, no? You'll be delighted to see her again."

Teltö would rather see things at the bottom of ponds. *Where I found her.* "Tuvena and I are no longer together."

"A pity; she seemed a good match for you." Venomavat nodded. "Too good, in fact. Dyrstin gave me updates. Anyway, he works there too, so no doubt he'll show you the ropes."

"I am sure Dyrstin would be a big help." Teltö tapped his foot against a rug that may once have been blue. "But couldn't…"

"No," said the Undersecretary, "we couldn't. You will ensure Hova's home communications remain timely and provide physical aid in mundane tasks. The Master is no longer young."

"But…"

"This is an honour, Phuul," said Venomavat. Her tone suggested nothing of the sort. "Do not disappoint." She shuffled some papers; her eyes drifted to the buttered toast. "You may go."

"Perhaps…"

"No." The Undersecretary reached for a brass hand bell. "Next!"

Teltö trudged from the office, doing the sums of corruption in his head. Even if he gave up black market chocolate and Asrak – and it'd be a cold day in the North before he did that – he'd need months to get enough bribery money together, and he didn't have months. He looked over his shoulder. Madam Venomavat's features were a study in *better you than me* and *sod off, I want to eat my toast in peace.*

The receptionist's face was like a granite slab. "Good news, Phuul?"

"Define good," said Teltö.

• • •

THE SUN WAS sinking behind the Kullio Ranges as he turned into his street. Hungry shadows reached out from the grey-brick terraces, and crept over to where children played with marbles and spiders. The children shouted at each other, carefree and wild. Smoke from the Ironworks drifted across the sky like ink through water, while one by one, drab inhabitants shut drab curtains against the coming night.

Dodging Unut shit on the cobblestones, Teltö hurried. His supervisor had kept him behind at the Library to correct his afternoon's bungling, which meant he was late for dinner. Again. *It's so unfair. The Lesser Council are packing me off to Kuolinako. No wonder I can't concentrate on work.* His worst error had been shelving a former Grand Master's memoirs under crime fiction. *My supervisor has no sense of humour.*

Teltö arrived at the house, and hesitated. He pressed

his nose to the window. *No one in the kitchen. Excellent.* Then the front door opened and his father emerged in his best tweed waistcoat. *Shit.*

The elder Phuul frowned. The once coal-black hair and beard had grown grey, and the man leant heavily on his cane.

"What are you doing?"

"Just admiring the daffodils." Teltö patted the window box. "Don't mind me."

"You're late, again."

"It was a busy day at work, Dad. There was…"

Teltö's father raised his hand. "I've heard. I've also apologised to Widow Saavi for your absence."

Oh shit. It was today. The old woman on the corner had lost her husband to a mining cave-in thirty years ago, and couldn't afford a lich housekeeper to care for her potted rhododendrons and pre-war porcelain dolls. Teltö's parents had badgered him into cleaning the Saavi house once a week.

"As I said…"

"I shall talk with you later. My supervisor from the Ironworks is retiring, and I am already late to the celebration." He pursed his lips. "I have never asked for much, but Father Life, give me a son who is not utterly useless."

He pushed past Teltö and walked off down the street. Feeling his cheeks burning, Teltö climbed the steps.

A dark, pig-tailed head poked around the doorway and grinned at him.

"Don't worry," said Kyrmves. "I kept your dinner warm."

* * *

SMALL AND SPOTLESS, the dining room valued respectability above all. Special-occasion crockery, unused even on special occasions, frowned down from the wall-shelves, as if eating here were a crime. But Teltö Phuul had other things to worry about.

"Well done," said his younger sister, pulling back the sleeves on her academic robe. "A Native Assistant to a Grand Master-elect. I'm so proud."

Kyrmves Phuul meant that sincerely, Teltö knew. She was that sort of person. So infuriating.

He stabbed at his corned beef and potatoes. With his mother on nightshift at the Food Factory and his father out, they had the run of the house.

"It's not an honour, you know."

"Of course it is. You'll meet all *sorts* of people!"

Teltö shook his head. "All sorts of people just itching to do horrible things to me. The Inquisitor General, for instance."

Kyrmves frowned. "But you haven't done anything wrong!"

"What I do doesn't come into it. Here in Qivunako, I'm safe. In Kuolinako? I'm a plaything. And players get bored with playthings."

"Then do something else."

Teltö dropped his fork onto his plate. *Thunk.* "I can't. I don't live in some weird world where a mere underkarl's choices matter."

"Everything matters."

Teltö wanted to shout at her. *You poor little idiot. The world is made of vicious bastards determining how everyone else lives or dies. It's the way it's always been, and the way it'll always be. All us plebs can do is stay out the way.* But he couldn't bring himself to say it. Not to Kyrmves, sweet little Kyrmves with those earnest blue eyes staring at him from across the table. A vintage too good for the world – including him – to sour.

He shrugged. "Three days, then I'll say goodbye to this place for years. I never thought it'd end like this."

"It's not an end. It's a beginning. Like when Rhea got that paper published on Mnoman responses to pain."

Teltö winced. His *other* sister had still not shut up about that damned paper, two years after the event, though now that she'd buggered off to a Mustanako Research Unit, he no longer suffered on a daily basis. *Apart from her bloody letters.* He'd have to open them eventually; the pile under his pillow made sleeping awkward.

Teltö shovelled more potato into his mouth. "She should write a paper on *my* pain. Working for Hova means plenty of data."

Kyrmves poured herself another mug of tea. "Hova isn't that bad."

"He is. It's why the Lesser Council wants rid of him."

"Maybe he's lonely. Never married, has he?"

"No, and any prospective spouse has to be mad." Teltö absently waved his fork. "There's a thought: we marry Hova to a Mnoma. Opposites attract: tall, thin, eccentric alien meets short, pudgy, dull Grand Master-elect. Hova gets a partner, and the Mnoma has the unique sensation of tolerating him. A shame so few Mnomo live here."

His sister snorted. She'd never learned how to laugh normally; an outsider might mistake it for choking, but Teltö knew better.

"Ah," she said, "I shall miss your funny ways. Rhea's good for homework, you for company. Fancy a spider war? We won't have another chance for years!"

A far weaker Necromancer than his sisters, Teltö had learnt long ago not to play at spiders for money. *Except against Dyrstin and arachnophobes.* As Tuvena had said more than once, a Phuul and his bits were easily parted.

"I'm not sure," he began. "I've an awful headache…" *Tuvena said that too. Just not about spider wars.*

"Come on, what sort of odds would you like? I'll give you two Bluetails against a single Yellowtail. No money, just fun."

Generous, but not patronising. How like Kyrmves. The Blues could take more damage, but the Yellows were faster.

Teltö sighed. "Very well."

Kyrmves grinned. "I'll get the spiders. You clear the table." She dashed into the next room, nearly tripping over her robe. Teltö shook his head. *My old school robe. Rhea kept hers.*

He had finished re-shelving the corned beef when Kyrmves returned with a pine box. Picking out three fresh spiders, she placed them gently on the table.

Teltö took his Bluetails to the far end. Mostly black, they were distinguishable by sky blue markings. Kyrmves' Yellowtail looked like a wingless wasp with eight legs and extra hair.

"Ready?" she asked.

Teltö nodded, and concentrated on the small dead brains. Revival of spiders was easy even for most non-Necromancers, creating a gambling game ubiquitous throughout the Empire. But reanimation was just one part. The secret lay in controlling the creatures.

The Bluetails stirred beneath the current of mental energy, and Teltö sent them scuttling towards Kyrmves' Yellow.

The Yellowtail waited until half a millifurlong separated it from the Blues, then dashed through the centre, biting one of Teltö's spiders on the abdomen. Teltö gritted his teeth, and wheeled his Blues around, but Kyrmves' spider was now safely out of range. He looked up at his sister. She smiled serenely back.

"Come on, Teltö. You've got two of them. Coordinate!"

Easy for you to say. He sent one Bluetail chasing after the Yellow, and the other along the table edge. The Yellow feinted, raced across and rammed. Teltö's spider wobbled on the brink, tried to sink its fangs in, but couldn't get into position. It fell off the table. Teltö cursed. *So much for flank attacks.*

Kyrmves snorted. "Where did you learn that manoeuvre?"

Thank Father Life I'm not playing Rhea. I'd never hear the end of it. He concentrated on his remaining Bluetail, and hurtled it towards the Yellow. Kyrmves pulled her spider out the way. The Bluetail whirled and bit. *That's better.* The opposition fled.

"Stand and fight!" muttered Teltö. His Bluetail gave chase. The Yellowtail edged into the centre, until the spiders crouched a millifurlong apart. Teltö tried a diversion: he abruptly shifted his gaze to the door. This often worked against Dyrstin, but failed here. Kyrmves sent her spider in for three solid bites.

"Your Blue is slowing," said his sister. Teltö had to agree. The damage was getting to the Bluetail. He needed to attack, and quickly.

The Bluetail scuttled forward, leaping at the Yellow. It missed. Then Teltö noticed Kyrmves had repositioned her spider near the edge. *Here we go.* The Bluetail moved closer, closer… Teltö rammed. Or tried to: at the last moment, the Yellow drifted left. Carried by momentum, the Bluetail hurtled over the edge.

"Good game." Kyrmves held a Bluetail up to the light, checking damage. "Don't worry. You *are* getting better."

*   *   *

TWELVE DAYS LATER, a dark ship drifted down a dead river in a dead land. The Mää Wastes stretched from the banks of the Nhagivat to the clouded horizon, hills and plains heavy with the decay of centuries. Only a few brave tussocks and thistles stood firm against the encroaching dust. But desert though it was, the Mää Wastes' true terror was its life. As if the land mimicked the necromancy of its rulers, strange insects scuttled beneath grey rocks, while shadows lurked amid the skeletons of ancient trees. And the unseen eyes…

Alone at the ship's prow, the young Necromancer shivered and wondered how many hours still had to pass before they reached Kuolinako. *Probably a few: the air's still breathable.* The mists rising from the depths of the Nhagivat coated Teltö's hair with icy beads; not even Unut furs stopped the chill entering his marrow and stealing the warmth from his soul.

"Oh, for a Qivunako fireside, and a mug of Asrak," Teltö muttered, wiping his nose on his sleeve. Having forgotten to bring handkerchiefs, and unable to borrow one, he needed alternatives. The greatcoat fur tickled his nose and made him sneeze. *Damn you, Hova.*

He glanced down the ship, to where the dead heaved and the living haunted. Mostly crew; the two-dozen or so passengers were staying below deck. Teltö didn't blame them. He'd have ensconced himself on the Common

Room sofas too, under normal circumstances. But the higher-ups were packing him off to the Imperial capital, and while nothing he could do would change that, Teltö had spent several afternoons staying on deck and watching.

On the far riverbank, a sliver of steel caught the setting Sun: a remnant of the Qivunako-Kuolinako railway tracks, unused and forgotten for nigh on half a century. Teltö smiled grimly. Waterway passenger and freight had stood unchallenged even as the years dragged on, and appointments and bribery being what they were, the young man doubted his master would advocate for the restoration of the rail route. Madam Venomavat's nail polish alone testified to that.

Teltö sneezed again, and once more cursed the lack of handkerchiefs. No doubt his superior had stacks among the cargo. The older Necromancer was nothing if not meticulous, though his meticulousness did not apply to anyone Master Hova considered beneath Master Hova. *And that includes his assistant.*

He won't stop at handkerchiefs either. Bloody black-market Asrak prices already burn a hole in my pocket — if he tries to stamp it out like he's promised, how in blazes will I afford it? Why can't he let us drink in peace? It'll take our minds off other shortages for starters. Perhaps Asrak traders engineered Hova's rise as much as the shipping companies. Strongly enforced prohibition jacked up prices, but that wouldn't drive away customers, not in the Viiminian Empire.

"There you are. For an assistant you are most lax."

Teltö leapt to attention. In Imperial society, sycophants survived. "My sincere apologies, Master Hova."

Snowy-headed and porridge-complexioned, Hova

hobbled over. *Tap tap* clacked the infamous black cane, elegantly carved by Tuonakonian artisans, yet as malignant as its master. Teltö eyed it warily. Hova too wore a greatcoat and green scarf, but, befitting his station, his hat was adorned with the white ribbon of the Grand Masters. The furry chimney reached three millifurlongs into the air, majesty turning faintly ridiculous on a man so short and podgy.

The stick lashed out. *Owww!*

"You call me *Master* Hova?" Hova's small black eyes glistened like currants trapped in a stale bun. "Are you forgetting the purpose of this little boat ride? I am of the Great Nine now, and you will address me as *Grand Master*. Not even the Chancellor himself would so presume."

Teltö rubbed his arm. "Sorry, Grand Master Hova." With the investiture ceremony not yet held, the Grand Chancellor *would* make that presumption, not that this son of an Unut cared. Teltö pictured months of fobbing off snubbed officials and wearing his tongue out on stamps, all the while sharing blame as Hova's pettiness added unwanted polish to everyday hardship.

The old man shook his head. "Father Life, the other cities already regard Qivunako as backward and unmannered, and with you even Grand Master Meerm will laugh up his sleeves at me." Hova wagged his stubby forefinger. "On arrival, you shall stay silent, except when I order the contrary. Though I promise duties will leave you no time to think, let alone speak."

An opportunity. "Duties must be carried out, lest our last world crumble," Teltö quoted.

"Saari Ooks, Book Seven, Chapter Fourteen, Verse Thirty-Nine, as definitively translated by Grand Master Ooseman in 7878. Good. You have absorbed some knowledge of the Nine Authors. May you act on that without falling into elementary error: large Kuolinako holds no love for little Qivunako."

"Surely Grand Master Keer is well-respected in Kuolinako?" asked Teltö, meekly.

Hova rolled his doughy face. "Grand Master Keer is the eldest of the Great Nine, and has served the Empire longer than the Grand Chancellor himself. His age commands respect, so much so they forget he is of Qivunako. Enough! I will not discuss high politics with a mere underkarl. The Lesser Council must have been joking when they foisted you on me."

The older man stomped away, the tapping of his cane fading in line with his assistant's blood pressure. Teltö sneezed. *Trust me, Hova, you're not the only one who thinks the Lesser Council was having a good joke.*

• • •

FROM ABOVE CAME shouting and creaking timber. Teltö's eyes flickered open; the low cabin ceiling stared back. *I'm still on that bloody ship.* Scratching fresh fleabites, he rolled out of bed and stretched, taking care not to bump his head. When man and wood fought, wood won.

He yawned, and scooped up his scattered clothing. It needed shaking before wearing. *How sawdust penetrates underwear is beyond me.* The cabin housed a dirty mirror; having checked his ribbon hung as per regulations, and satisfied even Hova couldn't find fault, Teltö climbed over the suitcase barricade, and out. He kicked four heavyset rats pushing his way through the corridor; yesterday he'd seen one perched on a corpse-oarsman's shoulder, daintily nibbling the lich's ear. *A pity Hova isn't scared of rats. It'd almost make this journey worthwhile.*

He slid open the door to the deck; a blanket of thick smoky air stung his nose and throat. He gagged. *So we're near Kuolinako.* Even in the distant south, they knew of the Last Capital, long ago driven below ground by the stench of its own filth. Teltö had heard stories enough about those dark pits and endless mines, and about the cramped, confusing, and short existence of the people who lived in that twilight world of shadows and lamps. Coal ruled the diseased heart of the Viiminian Empire: coal, fumes, and fear. Holding his breath, Teltö looked skywards. A mustard tinge drenched the clouds, set against shades neither truly grey nor truly green.

A crewman wearing a gas-mask and a lumpy grey uniform shuffled over. "You're the Grand Master's assistant?"

Teltö spluttered and nodded.

"You'll need this." She handed Teltö a mask. "We can't have you getting Kuolinako Lung on your very first trip. My uncle died of that. A Shipping Necromancer he was, one of the best."

Teltö pulled it over his face, and breathed relief. Cumbersome as the devices were, they were better than the naked reek of the Last Capital. "Sorry to hear it," he said, half to the woman's face and half to her ample breasts.

"This was his ship. He trained me to help; I was his only family."

If this was his ship, was he fond of rats? Teltö noticed she wore a studded silver ring.

"Is it nice being in the Guild?"

Behind the mask, the crewman's eyes studied him. "What's it to you?"

"I'm just asking," Teltö pleaded. "I'm not an

undercover Inquisitor if that's what you're thinking, and I won't lecture you on social inferiority. I'm just bored, and there's no one else to talk to. If I were Mnoma, I'd be dying."

The woman laughed. "Oh, you've a way with words. Nah, I knew you weren't a shadow-stalker. They're smart."

Teltö bristled. "I'm not?"

"A real Inquisitor would use their time aboard. All you've done is sulk since we left Qivunako."

Drawing himself up to his full height, Teltö puffed out his chest as best he could. "Do you know who I am? One word from me to Hova, and you'll be keel-hauled for impudence."

The crewman shook her head. "Father Life, you are pathetic. Hova hates you, and you know it. Whine to him, and he'll roger you with his cane. You deserve each other."

Hova wasn't exactly Teltö's type. "I…"

"I've work to do. Find someone else to listen to you whinge."

His cheeks were probably red as his hair. She thought she could mock him with impunity? He might tell Hova after all. That fat Unut didn't like underlings, but he liked disrespect even less. A grin crossed Teltö's face. *Yes. That's how he'll see it. The Guild mocking the authority of the Grand Council.*

Tucking the mask under his arm, he returned below. He knew Hova spent mornings doing paperwork over hearty breakfasts; more than once he'd found a stale kipper trapped between council reports. Teltö had never discovered if his master intended them as bookmarks or whether he was saving them for later.

A plump rat begged outside Hova's cabin.

"Shoo," said Teltö. He kicked the rodent, and it scurried away. *If I escape the Black Spot after this, it'll be a bloody miracle.* He tapped on the door.

"Grand Master?"

No answer. He tried a firmer knock.

"Grand Master Hova?"

Still no answer, not even protestations of annoyance. Teltö decided to risk it. He poked his head into the room.

An oasis of luxury, Hova's cabin embodied everything wrong with Imperial society. The newspapers may be full of pleas for belt-tightening in the face of shortages and eternal war reparations, but this shipping company catered to those with fine tastes and the funds to match. Emerald silk curtains enclosed a four-poster feather bed, and bookshelves housed crisp and saucy first editions, some of which Teltö had filched on previous visits.

Where is the old bastard? Teltö stepped inside. And stopped.

Hova lay face-down on the cabin's large green-and-white rug, the shattered remains of a porcelain teacup beside his head. *Oh shit. He's dead. The Inquisitor General will peel my skin for boots.* Dropping the gas-mask, Teltö raced to his superior and heaved him over. Hova groaned, and struggled awake.

The currant-eyes glared up. "Who... are... you?"

The bastard's memory was going. But he was alive. *Thank Father Life.*

"I'm your assistant, Teltö."

"Assistant?" Hova's flushed and flabby face contorted grotesquely. "I... have... no assistant. You are... a spy! Guards!"

Teltö knelt. "No, Grand Master. We're on the ship.

You're ascending to the Grand Council. The Lesser Council sent me with you. Remember?"

"Keer, you traitor!" Hova seized Teltö's throat. "Keer! The treacherous little lapdog!"

What in blazes? I'm not Keer. Get your paws off me. Choking, Teltö tried to pry Hova's hands away, but the crazed fingers tightened. *Help!*

Chapter Two

ABOVE THE GLOBE, a caged cockatiel relished proceedings with malignant glee. Hova's cabin no longer bustled with the inquisitive, but Teltö Phuul still felt unwanted attention.

Mirror in hand, he sprawled across an armchair, and gingerly rubbed his neck, cursing Hova's untrimmed fingernails. Ugly gouges marked throat and jaw.

"Have a nice cup of tea," said the Shipping Necromancer. This one sported a waxed cinnamon moustache and a chin you could stab flies with. "Lucky we found you, eh? Adorably vicious old bastard. Like getting throttled by an angry flour dumpling."

Images of tea turned to visions of shattered crockery, bringing back memories of choking. Teltö put down the mirror and declined queasily.

"Go on," said the Shipping Necromancer. He proffered a tin mug. "It's my special occasion herbal brew from Klem. None of that grotty Principality stuff."

Teltö eyed the brown liquid. "Got anything stronger? Asrak?"

The warmth melted from the Shipper's face. "This is a law-abiding ship," he snapped, chill as the Great Southern Fells. "And don't you forget it."

"I wasn't…"

"The legal stuff's bad enough: I'm not risking my life because of some fool under the influence. But as for the other poison… let me tell you, laddie," he bent to Teltö's ear, "the day I tempt the wrath of the Inquisition will be the day the Nhagivat turns pink."

"My apologies, sir." Teltö felt his cheeks reddening. Upriver from Qivunako, hulls of sunken ships haunted the shallows during dry spells. Teltö knew many of those wrecks could be pinned on Shipping Necromancers' fondness for tipples. *Lovely. I meet the only teetotalling Shipper in the Empire. Though maybe he's just frightened.* The sniffing of shadow-stalkers sobered anyone.

Teltö gave a smile so sheepish it dripped wool.

"Forget I ever mentioned it, sir." He sipped from the mug. Lukewarm and bitter, the tea was hardly special occasion, but Teltö wasn't about to provoke the fellow again. "How's Hova?" Teltö's master had been hauled away, with difficulty, to the ship's physician.

The Shipper slouched against the other armchair. "Last I heard, he was dribbling about the Chancellor and the Guild being out to get him."

"Leather straps?"

The man nodded. "Did Hova have difficulties? Health-wise, I mean."

Apart from chronic humourlessness and an overactive pedantry gland? "He worried about coughing. Always had medicine on hand."

"No, laddie. I meant difficulties here." The Shipper tapped his temple with his forefinger.

"Not that I know of. Why?"

"Master Flourdumpling had better hope like mad he really *is* mad. People claiming Vyrellävek's out to get them end up with Vyrellävek out to get them, and when he gets them, he gets them. If you get my meaning."

Teltö did. Peta Vyrellävek, the Dragon Chancellor, had not outlasted his seven predecessors combined by handing out roses, unless, perhaps, ones laced with arsenic. The notion of Inquisitor General Vöder taking interest in this wasn't pleasant.

"This means I can go home?" *Hova won't need help any more...*

"Whatever gave you that idea?

The idea of staying away from Vöder and friends. "There are some old precedents."

"Which old precedents?"

"That Grand Master who fell into the Venivat, and thought he was a fish?" The Empire had survived eight thousand years. Everything had precedent.

The Shipper toyed with his moustache. "You're a bad liar and a worse Native Assistant, laddie. Duties must be carried out, lest our last world crumble. Your duty is to carry on."

Into the shadows I go. Teltö took another sip. "How far to Kuolinako?"

The man eyed the cabin clock. "We'll enter the Thousand Caves in about three hours. Then another two to the interior port. There'll be people waiting. Your Master Hova is pretty important." The Shipper donned his beaked grey cap. "Sorry, I'm needed elsewhere. Good luck ... what's your name again?"

"Teltö Phuul."

The Shipping Necromancer boomed with laughter.

"Then I'd advise caution. Kuolinako doesn't suffer *Phuuls* gladly."

Teltö tightened his grip on the armrest.

●　●　●

HAVING SQUEEZED A sympathy lunch out of the ship's cook, Teltö wiped the remnants of rye bread and dripping off his chin and strolled down to the cargo hold. A maze of dusty shelves, and stuffed with forgotten junk, the hold took some navigating, but at last he found what he sought: two inert corpses packed like humanoid sardines, and semi-obscured by a fallen tarpaulin. Hova's servants, preanimated to prevent premature rot, though more than two would've been nice.

Teltö dragged the cadavers out of confinement, and sent the reanimation signal flooding into dead cortices. *Rise and shine, you sloths.* The servants stirred, chests rising and falling, and lids rolling back to reveal eyes of milky hue.

The corpses clambered to their feet. *Thank Father Life this isn't an exam.* Why were his always so awkward? Rhea would have them tap-dancing. *Although maybe not. The Guild might complain.* He set the liches to shifting Hova's packaged paraphernalia. The stuff needed to be on deck by arrival.

I need more hands. The Shippers would never let him borrow oarsmen, and living help was out too: the crew and other passengers were busy, and Hova was straitjacketed. If only Kyrmves were here. But she was many a gross-furlong away, learning minutiae by rote.

"Well," he muttered, "if it's only me, so be it." *Probably a quote. Hova could tell me if he weren't mad.* Teltö lifted a box and started towards the door. Halfway there, the bottom fell out, and a series of leather-bound books bounced off his foot, one after the other.

"Bugger."

*   *   *

THE GOODS BULGED against an exterior wall. The servant liches stood blankly nearby; the young man possessed neither the skill nor the inclination to gift them shadow personalities. *Bugger Alio Venomavat.* Teltö sat on a suitcase and rubbed his shins. *The dead are for serving, not playing.* The smog would be nibbling away at the dead lungs, but when these servants wore out, there'd be plenty more where they came from.

The Nhagivat's dull rumble kept him company; its dependable filth ran from the southernmost foothills of the Kullio Ranges to the westerly warmth of the Illuvian Sea. The river would travel many more furlongs and see many more sunsets, but Teltö wouldn't see the sky again, not in Kuolinako. The Capital's chimneys had seen to that.

Barren bluffs stretched into the distance, grey beneath poisonous clouds, while northwards stood a smooth cliff-face, at the bottom of which a cave opened. The yawning gullet swallowed the Nhagivat whole. The ship pressed on, the river carrying it into the underworld, and bit by bit, darkness eclipsed the afternoon haze. *The Thousand Caves,* Teltö mused, as he farewelled natural light. *Where are the other nine hundred and ninety nine?*

Air filters soon made gas masks redundant. Teltö ripped off his and offered silent thanks to whichever forgotten engineer was responsible. Eerie gas-lamps illuminated rock and water, a pleasant change from the Mää Wastes.

"Are you Teltö Phuul?"

He spun around and saw a green man-like figure, over

a centifurlong in height. Stick-thin and monocled, it wore a bottle-green corduroy jacket over a purple waistcoat. A Mnoma, with all the tastelessness of its kind. Teltö frowned. It served him right for not calling into the Common Room to see who to avoid.

"Er, yes," said Teltö, struggling to remember his last Mnoman conversation. As per the diktat of the Nine Authors, the Viiminian Empire had tolerated its other sentient race for thousands of years – but the creatures never became any saner.

"Were you strangled?"

"Um, yes."

"What did it feel like?"

"Painful." Teltö spotted a silk handkerchief in the Mnoma's pocket. "Painful and exhilarating."

The creature opened and shut six-fingered fists. "Exhilarating?"

"A once in a lifetime experience." If that didn't appeal to it, nothing would. With brain chemicals eating their minds if they ever suffered boredom, the Mnomo spent their lives hungering for exotic sensation.

This emerald abomination could barely restrain itself. "Will you strangle me?"

"For a price. I can't strangle just anyone."

"I will give you four silver marks."

All I wanted was the handkerchief. Four silver marks means enough chocolate and liquor to last a month.

"Make it twelve," Teltö said, "and you have a deal." *Yes, Kyrmves, I'm a complete bastard, but that's life. One day you'll see.*

"First, you must strangle. Then I pay."

Teltö feigned a noise of extreme reluctance. But Mnomo never cheated.

"You drive a tough bargain," he said. "Kneel."

The Mnoma knelt. Teltö wrapped his fingers around a neck that felt like a pool cue and was about as substantial. *Careful.* Killing Mnomo was a recognised crime, and the creatures couldn't be reanimated. They had some sort of natural Toast in their veins.

"Ready?"

"Yes, indeed."

Teltö squeezed. Softly at first, then harder. The Mnoma gurgled. Thrusting its head back, it grinned macabrely.

Enough's enough. Teltö released his grip.

The Mnoma stood. "I thank you so much."

"You promised payment."

"Yes, yes." The Mnoma fished into its waistcoat and pulled out a leather pouch, probably of its own making.

"Twelve silver marks," said Teltö.

The Mnoma produced a flat silver ingot and a knife, and dangled them in the air like priceless ornaments. It began scratching the metal.

Teltö's eyebrows arched. "What are you doing?"

"You asked for twelve silver marks. I give you twelve silver marks. See, here are two." The Mnoma thrust the ingot under Teltö's nose. It had scratched, and so marked, the metal twice.

Oh no. "That's not what I meant," said Teltö. "I meant money. Coins."

"I have no coins. I paid them all for the journey to Mustanako."

Teltö looked about. *Damn.* There were too many crewmen. They'd hear the splash if he shoved the creature overboard.

"I am pleased," crooned the Mnoma. "Your statues

are good."

"My statues?" What was it going on about now?

"Your statues," said the Mnoma, pointing. Teltö's gaze followed. Between the lamps, figures graced pedestals cut into the sheer walls of the cave, stone features bathed in amber glow. Teltö recognised famous Chancellors: the ones analysed by centuries of historians and read about by centuries of students.

"Fine work," squeaked the alien. "Human work, not Mnomo. I can tell."

Teltö nodded. "They're human. And old: those pre-date the Mustanako Mutiny."

He indicated a hollow-eyed man weeping into his beard. "See that one? That's Grand Chancellor Yyti. He was our leader during the Nadir, the First Northern War, when the Northerners nearly extinguished us all."

"All?"

"The Empire anyway." Teltö found himself parroting the tomes he'd browsed at the Library. Monitoring shelf-stacking had some benefits, though this tale had passed into legend.

"Yyti stood firm when all seemed lost. The sorry remnants of our people were holed up in Kuolinako, under siege from the Northern forces. The Enemy had just sacked Mustanako, you see, and like the butchers they were, they tried to frighten us into submission."

"How?"

"A lone Northern messenger rode to the upper gates and warned Yyti they would execute three child captives each day. Those bastards weren't bluffing either: they burnt our folk alive to prevent reanimation. Every morning for four years. Flesh roasted black within sight of the Capital, the smell carrying to the nostrils of the defenders even through Kuolinako's chimney smoke. Yet the Chancellor never said a word, never shed a tear, and never surrendered."

A tear rolled down the creature's cheeks. *Sensitive fellow.*

"Then what happened?"

Teltö frowned. *The Mnomo don't value the past, only the present, but how could it not know?* Perhaps it just wanted to hear the story again.

"The Northern leader died, of Kuolinako Lung it's said, though the Enemy camped upwind from the city. Even Northerners have noses. Then his son got called home to deal with rebellion, so the bastards simply packed up and left. When the Imperial messengers ran to tell the Chancellor the good news, they found him sitting quietly in his chair, stone dead. Four years of watching and smelling death every morning, and Yyti never saw his people saved. That's why they show him weeping. The man died of a broken heart."

The Mnoma mopped tears with the handkerchief. "You have given me a bitter draught from the cup of sorrow," it squeaked. "I thank you. Perhaps I shall write an opera about it."

There were a dozen of those. "I'm teary-eyed myself. Any chance you've a spare handkerchief?"

The alien handed him a pink one. Cotton, not silk. *Bugger.*

"Farewell, Teltö Phuul," said the Mnoma. "I thank you again for your kindness." The creature departed sobbing. Teltö stuffed the handkerchief into his pocket. The Mnomo may be generous, but Father Life were they mad.

The ship drifted on, the dark eyes of the past

watching. The crushing weight of years was palpable; the further the journey, the further back the statues went. Soon Teltö saw satirical portraits of early Chancellors, the ones who pretended they served Emperors. He raised an eyebrow. No one these days could get away with giving Vyrellävek scales and a tail.

Chancellors gave way to timeworn images of Kuolinako's Emperors. Once past Gykäkkä and his drooling, gibbering ilk, the older statues bore strange auras of power. Emperor Phyllä XIII with his one arm, Emperor Iilno XLIX, who started a civil war by refusing to name his own son Iilno…

Teltö's spine tingled. These figures, encrusted in eons, were different, alien. To them even Vyrellävek was a thing of no significance, an ant beside a mountain. The Viiminian Empire was an Empire without an Emperor, while beyond the sea the Confederation had an Emperor without an Empire. *Maybe we could trade.*

Lamp-lit darkness became semi-daylight. Teltö squinted; the ship had entered a gigantic cavern topped with a translucent dome; natural or engineered, he could not guess. The Empire had lost such secrets long ago. *So much we once knew.* Pit-mouths peppered high craggy walls. *Like eyes.* Mining was ever-present in the Last Capital, but even so, animal instinct whispered warnings.

Naked of moss, the walls sloped steeply into an interior lake. Fed by the river and fully enclosed by the cavern, the depths looked as lifeless as the surrounding rock. Twin islands stood here too. Jutting out like fangs, their peaks tapered off into spikes, but the sides nearest the other were flattened, such that cliff-faces grinned at each other across a channel. The ship kept to the middle, as though the Empire hinged on it.

Teltö's heart beat faster. *Father Life.* On either island, an enclave revealed a cyclopean statue standing waist-deep in the lake. *They knew how to build back then.* So this was the ancient Empire's last legacy: a memorial to endure until the world itself crumbled. The Father and Mother Eternal, carved into Kuolinako's timeless rock.

Further on gaped yet another hungry cave mouth. There, the Nhagivat would once more become a river. But the ship did not follow the current. The Shipping Necromancers shouted instructions, and the vessel eased towards a harbour on the starboard side. Teltö saw a flotilla of boats and barges, half a dozen piers, and a cluster of stone buildings half-hidden within greenery.

"Master Phuul."

Teltö jumped. *Don't creep up on me.* But at least she was human. Shorter even than Hova, the woman's greatcoat swept the deck. Beneath her pink-ribboned beaked cap, she wore spectacles and a tired expression. She grasped his hand and shook firmly.

"I'm Eriva Phytek. The ship's physician."

Quite the enthusiastic one. "No need to call me 'Master'. I'm just an underkarl." Teltö indicated the ribbon on his hat.

"Sorry. I didn't see it from behind. About your Master Hova, I suspect he's been poisoned."

"Poisoned?" Teltö's blood turned to ice. "Is he going to, um, die?" *Shit.* This was bad. Really, really bad. *And I was stupid enough to try that Shipper's tea…*

"Oh, no. The toxin, for which there are about four possible candidates, has driven him to raving, but wasn't administered in fatal quantities. He's stable now, so I'm handing him over to my onshore colleagues. Pass this note to the Kuolinako authorities." She smiled. "Your Master will be getting the best doctoring in the Empire."

If Teltö wasn't careful, he'd be getting the best torturing in the Empire. Along with most of the people on this ship, Phytek included, and save for the Mnoma, no one would be enjoying it. He skimmed over the surprisingly legible note.

"So he's sleeping?"

"Yes. I dosed him with a sedative in the presence of the Ship's Masters. It'll keep him quiet without masking the poison. He's still strapped down though. Can't be too careful."

"Quite. You've locked your cabin door?"

Phytek dangled a large iron key under his nose. "Phuul," she said, with a touch of weariness, "I may seem like a naïve and gentle scholar, and perhaps I am. But I'm not stupid. We're all dancing on wafer-thin ice here, and I've no intention of falling through."

• • •

"WHAT DO YOU mean 'you won't let me through'?" snapped Teltö. "I've shown you the bloody papers!"

The desk corpse stared. "I have been left explicit instructions about your particular case, Phuul. You and Master Hova may not enter Kuolinako without the requisite Council escort. It is a matter of Imperial Security."

Teltö growled. On arrival, he'd sought to organise a cart, but the Transport officials told him he needed approval from Internal Customs, situated on the far side of the port. Customs refused to grant this until they'd cleared him for entry, so he'd manually moved the luggage with only the help of Hova's dead servants. Teltö Phuul was not pleased.

"They told me there'd be people waiting. It's not my fault they haven't shown up. And Master Hova here," he nudged his sleeping superior with his foot, "needs urgent medical attention."

"None of my affair, Phuul. I have a task to do and I must do it. Duties must be performed…"

"Lest our last world crumble. Yes, yes. The mummified remains of Saari Ooks will be smiling somewhere. But what am I to do?" Teltö gestured at the boxes, and at Hova, still bound and gagged on a stretcher. "I spent ages getting this stuff in. I risked my bloody neck getting Hova down the gangplank. And now you want me to sit around, hoping Kuolinako remembers I exist?"

"Precisely, Phuul. As written in the Book of Tyr, 'Patience is the chief of all virtues in life.'"

As though you'd know: you're dead. Teltö considered making the smug bastard pick its nose. But he resisted the urge; lesser Necromancers meddling with corpses under the control of their superiors seldom ended well.

There was a knock on the door.

"Enter!" said the lich.

A tall and blond young man, adorned with yellow ribbon, green scarf, and a broad grin waltzed into the office. A fellow underkarl from Qivunako.

"Teltö!" The new arrival tucked his fur hat under his arm. "Sorry I'm late. Old Keer's bowels played up this morning, and I spent so long sorting it I clean forgot about you. Anyway, I've a cab for you and Hova, and a cart for your stuff."

Lean and fit, Dyrstin Venomavat hadn't changed much. Only his skin showed the effects of Kuolinako; always fair-complexioned, his angular face now sported a milky hue reminiscent of albinism. Too pale for Teltö's tastes. They needed to send him back to Qivunako for a bit.

Dyrstin grew even more pallid when he noticed Hova. "What in blazes has been going on? Did the old man have a fit?"

"Something like that," said Teltö. "I'll explain later. Dyrstin, now you've decided to grace us with your illustrious presence, please tell my friend you are the escort I need to enter this bloody city!"

The corpse cleared its throat. The reflexes of life were funny things. "Are you acting on the authority of the Grand Council? If so, could I see your documentation?"

Dyrstin manoeuvred around the luggage. Reaching into his greatcoat pocket, he extracted a bag of liquorice sticks, two brass keys, a box of Proth & Proth matches, a packet of Phläx contraceptives – cinnamon-flavoured medium, Teltö noted – a ball of string, a knife, a deck of playing cards, a ration book, a library card, a squarish bottle of lantern oil, some loose copper coinage, and bit of crumpled paper.

"Here we are." Dyrstin smoothed the paper. "Documentation." The corpse grabbed a magnifying glass, and scrutinised the wording as though its unlife depended on it.

"As you can see," said Dyrstin, "Dyrstin Venomavat, Native Assistant to Grand Master Kortek Keer, and acting on the authority of his superior, has come to accompany Hyät Hova and Teltö Phuul into Kuolinako. Any objections?"

"No," said the lich. "Requirements are met. You may go." It duly ticked a box on the form before it.

"I so thank you for your esteemed contribution." Teltö wheeled out his most withering tone. "I don't know what I'd have done without you."

"My pleasure," said the corpse.

Dyrstin just grinned.

*   *   *

TWO UNUT STOOD harnessed to the rough wooden cart, eyes brown and vacant. Teltö glowered. The rest of the Empire considered the shaggy white bovines cute or even cuddly, but he loathed them. If there was one thing Unut could do, it was shit everywhere. Sending some poor karl or underkarl to muck out their stables was an exquisitely southern punishment.

Dyrstin stood on the back of the vehicle, rearranging suitcases with Hova's liches.

"Hova's been poisoned."

Dyrstin nearly dropped a suitcase. "What?!"

"Poisoned. It's driven him mad. On the ship he almost strangled me."

"An irrefutable sign of sanity, if you ask me."

"I'm bloody serious. It took three crewmen to drag him off, and the ship's physician did some tests. Hova thought I was Keer for some reason, though why anyone would want to strangle old Keer is beyond me."

"Ouch," said Dyrstin. "It wouldn't surprise me if Vyrellävek takes an interest in this. The Dragon doesn't like Hova much, but he also doesn't like his Grand Masters poisoned. Or at least poisoned by others," he added, after ensuring no one stood within earshot.

"I can hear the Inquisition sharpening their knives already."

"So what will you do?"

"Pass-the-parcel. Hova's not ascending anywhere, Grand Council or otherwise, so I'll dump him on someone else, then scurry home before Vöder starts measuring me up. Safety first."

"Did the physician say anything else?"

"She gave me a note. Problem is I haven't met anyone in authority yet, with the exception of our mutual friend back there." Teltö nodded towards the customs office.

"It could be worse," said Dyrstin, "at least our plump little Grand Master-elect is going to live. We'll finish loading this cart, then send it off to Hova's new place. I got the address from the Registrar of Building and Housing. Thank Father Life your superior filled in the forms beforehand: what the old bastard lacks in charm, he makes up for in organisation."

"At least if it affects him."

Dyrstin conceded the point. "Meanwhile you, me, and him take the cab to Keer's. We're supposed to be going to Hova's, but my master's live-in medical people are second only to the Dragon's private surgeons. And what's more, I actually trust them."

Teltö jumped up onto the cart and patted the other Necromancer on the back. "Dyrstin Venomavat," he said, grinning, "your Aunt back in Qivunako may be sour as a six-month-old jug of milk, but you're a true friend. Can you assure me of one thing though?"

"What's that?"

"Can you please not be too busy with Keer's bowels the next time I need urgent help?"

Chapter Three

T HE CART RATTLED away down the cobblestone road, the lich servants perched atop the load like gargoyles. Teltö watched it vanish into a side-tunnel. A dozen such shafts pockmarked the lower walls around the interior port, each leading to different sections of the upper city, and after that Kuolinako's mazes multiplied.

Shading his eyes, Teltö stared up again at the monstrous dome. There was something mesmerising about it, the way it bathed everything in a chill, clinical light. *It never rains. There must be an army of dead to water the trees and bushes.* Still, the vegetation around the port seemed healthy; ivy and wisteria vines enveloped Customs, and the garden outside the general store drowned in flowering mint. All surface plants by the looks of it, not the weird modified strains that lived in Kuolinako's underground darkness. Off to Teltö's left, a giant pohutukawa, not yet ablaze with blooms of flame, sprouted from a stony peninsula. *The emblem of Mustanako at the gates of the Last Capital.*

"Are you sure you gave accurate instructions to the

corpse-driver?"

Dyrstin was reading the physician's note, whistling. His deep blue eyes looked amused and relaxed. "Of course. Now stop worrying, stop daydreaming, and come help me with Hova's stretcher."

Teltö obliged, following his friend back into Customs. The dead official sat entrenched behind its bulwark of desk and forms, not lifting a cold finger to help. No instructions meant no action, and duties began and ended with the letter of the law.

"My word," said Dyrstin, backing out the door. "Your little friend's heavy. What were you feeding him?"

"His breakfasts are black market or I'm a Tuonakonian. The perks of being a Grand Master-elect. If I'd been that blatant, someone aboard – probably him – would've had a word to me."

"Hyät Hova using the black market? I'd thought I'd had my share of hypocrisy for the day."

"Hova's got money and status, and food is serious business. The man may not like much, but he likes his vittles. Still, think this is hard? Try getting this down a gangplank by yourself."

Filth encrusted the cab's wheels; black paint splattered the windows and peeled from the sides. The lich driver roosted in its sprung seat awaiting orders. The arrow insignia of the Department of Transport was embroidered on its sable uniform.

"Sorry," said Dyrstin. "Had to get the economy vehicle. Keer's Office insisted."

"This isn't going to work." Teltö bit his lip. "The stretcher won't fit."

They unbound Hova and stuffed the old man onto the cab floor like a bag of oats.

Dyrstin smiled. "Isn't he adorable? Like a little Unut calf."

"Well, he's white-haired and fat," said Teltö. "And he's got stupidity and stubbornness in spades. Though Unut are actually useful."

"True. Imagine spreading Hova-dripping on your toast, or wearing his fur."

Teltö shut and latched the window, enclosing them in what felt like a mobile coffin. Dyrstin slid open the rear hatch, and instructed the driver.

"That's done," said Dyrstin. The lich whipped the Unut and the cab trundled forward. "Next stop, Keer's humble abode. Well, not really humble. He's the longest serving Grand Master, and appearances have to be kept. Also, now we're safe from eavesdroppers, and less concerned with our own appearances, who poisoned Hova?"

"Do I look like a shadow-stalker?"

Dyrstin shrugged. "There must have been some clue."

From somewhere below came a dull thunder. *No. Not thunder: machinery.* The groaning of engines, fuelled by a thousand furnaces and the labour of countless corpses. A world of coal-dust and chains.

Teltö dumped his hat onto his master's chest. If Hova was to be a footrest, he might as well be a hat stand too.

"The poison was probably in his tea. If I had to put marks on it, my guess is Vyrellävek's offing a rival. Hova's pretty ambitious."

Dyrstin nodded. "Though it doesn't seem right. Ambition or no, Hova's the newest of the Great Nine, and has the magnetism of a weta. Why should Vyrellävek fear him?"

"A Shipper said Hova was frothy-mouthed about the

Guild too. Though I doubt it's them. The Qivunako lot's too busy fighting each other to take on the Necro elite." The cab veered into a side-tunnel, the dome's haze gone in an instant. The gas-lamps returned. Teltö fingered his hair, looking at the drowsy bundle on the floor.

"Are you sure the luggage is safe? All Hova's stuff is there, and I need to be squeaky clean. It'd be just my luck if I lost priceless manuscripts, jewels, and pickled organs."

The lamplight turned Dyrstin's face ghostly. He yawned, stretching his long legs as best he could.

"No worries."

"But the cart's unprotected. Suppose my stuff gets requisitioned for the black market?"

Dyrstin laughed. "You poor, naïve little thing. A Qivunakonian bumpkin through and through, aren't you?"

Teltö elbowed him in the ribs. "Spare me the world-weary wisdom. A year ago, you were in my shoes. No Kuolinakonian I've ever met bats an eyelid when people disappear, so why is property off-limits?"

"Everyone," said Dyrstin, adopting a schoolmaster's tone, "from Vyrellävek and Hova down to plebs like us, uses the black market, right?"

"Right." With Asrak outlawed, and most of life's pleasures rationed, few had the willpower or innate austerity to remain entirely on the straight and narrow.

"Well," continued Dyrstin, "if Hova's goods wind up there, certain people will identify them, and those who requisitioned them will wish they hadn't. Qivunako's small and poor enough that everyone's stuff is fair game…"

Teltö nodded. "You get burgled, it's embarrassing, but it's Qivunako so you're not important enough for anyone to care, and your stuff wasn't valuable to start with."

"Precisely. In Kuolinako, egg on the face is unaffordable when you're Hova's level – let alone Vyrellävek's. Messing with the hierarchy could be the pebble that starts the avalanche. So there's an understanding that the bigwigs' stuff is left alone. Or else…" Dyrstin threw his head back and slid a finger across his bone-white throat.

The racket of machinery faded. Soon it was just them and the Unut, plodding along a tunnel without end. Teltö almost preferred the engines.

"But if I'm the one held responsible for egg on Hova's face…"

"Get a bloody grip," snapped Dyrstin. "Your self-pity is getting on my nerves."

"Easy for you!" Teltö fired back. "You're not facing tongs, coals, and Father Life knows what else. I'll bet Keer's diarrhoea is the most stressful thing you've had in the last year."

Dyrstin laughed. "Ah, yes, a year devoid of worry. A year of the shadow-stalkers filing me away. What I've eaten, where I've gone, who I've talked with, who I've slept with. My life condensed into black and white pages, and for all I know, they might come for me tomorrow. Or six months from now. Vyrellävek and his pet Inquisitor General disappear people all the bloody time. But I've learned to live with it, and so will you. Don't like it? Go throw yourself in the Nhagivat."

Teltö snorted. *Under the Dragon's claw.* Dyrstin had changed. Did Kuolinako do this to everyone? Turn good people into ghoulish parodies of themselves?

The lamps soaked the brick-lined tunnel with an ambiance silent and portentous. Pedestrians hurried past, some holding lanterns that bred weird, distorted shadows. Neither Mnoma nor human seemed willing to dawdle. As the cab wobbled deeper into the Imperial Capital, Teltö saw openings where no lights led, where the twilight of Kuolinako surrendered to the void of true night. Memories of the Mää Wastes haunted him; the spaces seemed like holes to another world. He was about to mention this to Dyrstin when the cab halted abruptly.

This wasn't Keer's. "What the…"

"Elevator," said Dyrstin, without emotion.

Grinding screeches emanated from below. Teltö felt the entire cab descending. He frowned. "Special mechanisms or ropes, pulleys, and brute force?"

"Depends," said Dyrstin. "Though since you're going to be disappeared by figures in dark hoods, why bother asking? Face it, Teltö, you're doomed. Dooooooomed."

I'd forgotten what a piece of shit you can be.

* * *

TELTÖ ALIGHTED AND prodded the barred gates. Damp and grainy to the touch, the iron was heavy with rust, and hadn't been cleaned in years. They'd have to tear it down after Keer died: the structure's endurance owed more to stubbornness than functionality. Beyond, a tunnel connected the road with a well-lit grotto. Peering through the moss and iron – more moss than iron – Teltö saw a sprawling three-storied building with ponderous arches and thin, high windows. A fishpond and a gaggle of modified night pines hid in its hulking shadows. Queer blue lanterns hung from the tree branches.

"Stand back," called Dyrstin, extricating himself from the cab. "Oilio's coming."

A dull clanking rang out from the other side. Teltö

backed away, as the gates groaned open. A man stepped out, clutching a crowbar. Teltö stared. *All that, just to open a gate?*

"Venomavat," said Oilio. A black ribbon hung from his fur hat. "Please correct me, but you were taking Grand Master-elect Hova and his Native Assistant to their lodgings, not ours. I shall have to completely rework today's schedule."

"Circumstances change, Oilio. You'd best notify the House physicians that Keer's new-but-venerable colleague needs attention."

Dyrstin beckoned him towards the cab floor.

"Oh dear." Oilio removed his hat and mopped his thinning pate with a handkerchief. Teltö eyed the silk with envy. "This changes matters. The investiture ceremony will have to be delayed, and the Chancellor's Office will not be happy. They run on such a tight timetable, you know. His Excellency insists."

Dyrstin pulled the knife from his pocket, and ran his forefinger along the blunt edge.

"His Excellency will be even unhappier without those physicians. Teltö, assuming you aren't getting strip-searched by shadow-stalkers, please pass the Housemaster that note of yours. Go on, he won't bite. Much."

   •   •   •

TEA, TOAST, BUTTER, and marmalade littered the parlour table. The plates and cups were chipped enamel, but Teltö wasn't complaining.

"This, my friend," said Dyrstin, passing Teltö another slice of carrot cake, "is the life of a Native Assistant. Just don't tell Aunty Alio. Or anyone else. It's amazing how nice people are when they think you have influence. On the other hand, I'm still working out how you talked Oilio into sending *our* liches and supervisors over to Hova's to help with *your* luggage."

"Mam calls it creative laziness. I have a knack for it."

Poor Oilio had turned pale at the ship physician's note, and added more beads of sweat to his copious collection, but the man was competent: Hova was downstairs, undergoing medical attention right now. Some people never turned down tasks if you made it sound urgent.

"Anyway, consider the importance of perks. Take this cake." Dyrstin helped himself to an even larger slice. "Keer just happens to be Vyrellävek's Secretary for Public Nutrition."

"Food," said Teltö, with his mouth full.

"Yes, food. My master, in theory, wields life or death over every Food Factory in the Empire. Your Mam still works at Qivunako's?"

Teltö nodded. He'd have to write to her. *The censors will have a field day.*

"Well," continued Dyrstin, "let's say the Managers curry favour with him. Sometimes with actual curries, though I prefer it when they're sweetening him up."

"Does Keer ever notice you're sampling his gifts?"

"Keer?" Dyrstin arched his eyebrows. "I could distil Asrak next door to his bedroom and he wouldn't notice. He called me by my Granddad's name the other day. Oilio's too busy panicking about his precious schedule – he tugs out whatever hair he has left because the accountant uses the wrong colour ink. Everyone else is either too dead, too busy dusting clocks, or not in a position to care."

Teltö sipped his milky tea. *One day someone just might*

care. The trick with tricks was not to push too far. "And in return you clean up diarrhoea and ensure the old man's rambling letters are sent back to Qivunako. Something tells me that even if things return to normal, Hova won't be as relaxed. He threatened to bury me in paperwork."

"The Hyät Hova we know and love. Can't blame you for poisoning him. I'd be tempted myself."

Teltö threw a napkin. "That," he snapped, "is not the least bit funny."

"Humour is subjective." Dyrstin carried the cake back to the pantry. "Believe me, you'll need it in the Last Capital. It's the only way I survive."

Bastard, thought Teltö, unamused at being the target of his friend's insecurities. He looked around. "Nice house."

"Not only nice, but ancient. Almost as old as Keer himself."

"Ha ha."

"Seriously, it is old. In one of the cellars you can even see scorch marks from the Nadir. Keer's never painted over them. Father Life, those Northerners were vicious bastards, and this house was in the firing line. Drilling weapons and all."

Something bubbled to the front of Teltö's mind. "It's the anniversary of the First Northern War next month, isn't it?"

"It is."

"How does the Dragon intend to celebrate? For want of a better word." How did you describe the five hundredth anniversary of the Viiminian Empire's greatest humiliation?

Dyrstin returned from the pantry. He poured himself some tea. "Ah, Teltö," he said, "you put me in an interesting quandary. The information is confidential, privy only to the Grand Council and Native Assistants."

"But I *am* a Native Assistant!"

Dyrstin smirked. "Why, of course. That's why you'll find out at the next Council meeting."

"Or you can stop being smug, and tell me now."

"I'm not being smug," said the self-satisfied bastard. "Some information is, shall we say, sensitive. When you've seen others dunked for leaking, you learn discretion."

Death Pools, yes, that's it. If you were lucky, you got a trial and a public dipping whilst they read out your confession. If you were unlucky, you disappeared without a trace.

"Point taken," said Teltö, "but it's just you and I, and I'm entitled to the information."

This elicited a sigh from his friend. "Oh, very well. But when Vöder and her henchmen marinate me in concentrated sulphuric, I'll blame you. The Dragon plans a visit to Ilmanako. Did I say Ilmanako? I meant Skeevereet. There'll be formal luncheon with Prince Oym and everything, a grand display of friendship between the Empire and the Principality."

Teltö wrinkled his nose. "That doesn't sound confidential." He buttered some toast, thanking fate for the Secretary for Public Nutrition. "Vyrellävek's always going North. The papers cover his every move. What's one more lunch, even if there are more wines and ribbons?"

"This time the Dragon's broaching war reparations. He's squatting down on his little scaly legs, and begging Oym to forgive our outstanding debt. All fifty-four years' worth. Because everyone knows we in the Viiminian Empire are such lovely neighbours."

Teltö dropped the butter knife. It clunked onto the table. "An end to reparations?" he hissed. "But that means…"

"An end to rationing, yes. Forty-six years since the Fourth Northern War finished, and we still find ourselves starved…"

Teltö nodded towards the pantry. "Starvation is subjective too, is it?"

Dyrstin waved his hand. "Yes, but you and I, and our parents, have grown up knowing nothing but those bloody dockets. Food, clothing, shoes… and all to line the pockets of Oym and his cronies. If Vyrellävek pulls this off, he'll go down as the greatest Chancellor in history, and all coinciding with the five hundredth anniversary of the Nadir."

"Never knew you were such a big Dragon fan."

The other Necromancer took his turn to throw a napkin. "I'm not, you prat. I'm pointing out why Vyrellävek wants this kept confidential. If he succeeds, he's an Imperial hero, and even if you've had your granny disappeared, you'll want to hug the old bastard. If he fails, no one knew about it, so no embarrassment."

Teltö tried to imagine life without rationing. He supposed it would be as if everything were black market, but cheaper and easier to obtain. No more furtive looks over the shoulder every time he bought chocolate.

"But say the Principality's behind the Hova poisoning…"

Dyrstin grimaced. "Yes, there's that. That's the problem with the Northerners: you're never sure who's in charge. Oym is affable enough, but that bloody army of his… It doesn't help that some of our loveable Grand Council members share their belligerence."

"Which ones?" Teltö bit into his toast. He'd added generous dollops of marmalade.

Dyrstin resumed that irritating smile. "You've seen the Lesser Council, back in Qivunako?"

"Of course."

"Imagine a group of people with ten times the power and half the brains, and you wouldn't be far wrong. Let's see…" He started counting off his fingers. "There's Pliil and Yyrtön. Arrogant tossers who hate us mere provincials, and are too young to remember the last war. Think a Fifth Northern War would be a success if only they were in charge, though they'd never dare admit it. Plus Meerm."

"A Mustanakonian wanting war? Isn't the first rule of warfare that their city gets burnt to the ground every time?" Teltö buttered more toast, making all he could of this culinary opportunity. *You lucky bastard, Dyrstin.*

Dyrstin laughed. "Yes, there's that. Nothing like taunting Mustanakonians with it after a few mugs. But Meerm still sulks about the Mutiny. Looking for someone to kick, so he hates those snooty Northerners for undercutting his merchant friends. Also, he thinks Mustanako will see a flood of silver when our brave armies march into Ilmanako. Er, Skeevereet."

"So he thinks we'd win a war?"

"Not only that, but if you let him go on, he'll start talking about knocking down Yyti's Wall, and allowing Mustanakonians to reclaim the lost fields of their forefathers."

Teltö sniggered. "Mad nostalgia. Anyone else trying to get us into war?" He almost looked forward to his first Council meeting.

Dyrstin shook his head. "Just them. On the other side,

there's Sösta. Warden of the Imperial Mint. Dislikes spending money on anything, so you can imagine what she thinks of war. Phermö loves Vyrellävek's peace policy. Home city loyalty, but you never can judge with that accent. Rumi… won't someone think of the children? The man can't take a shit without a lecture. Then you've got the Qivunako contingent…"

"Hova, who's out of action, and Keer, who may be senile, but was on the Council the last time the bombs were dropping."

"Exactly. Adding in the Chancellor himself, it's five-three in favour of sanity, plus Hova, who's too busy getting poisoned to hate anyone. But my esteemed superior has good days. Want to meet him? He'll have finished his afternoon nap, and the old geezer tells great stories. Especially if you like adventures and onions."

"Why not?" Teltö wiped marmalade from his chin. "I wasn't born the last time the old man went back to Qivunako." He smiled. "I suppose it's about time I met my other Grand Council representative. Especially since, you know, I've lived in Qivunako my entire life."

*   *   *

"THIS IS THE drawing room, where Keer spends most of his time these days," said Dyrstin.

They stood in a corridor so thickly carpeted it felt like grass. Keer's art collection graced the panelled walls, together with bronze coat-hooks and crystalline lamps. *Yet they tell us to tighten our belts, the bastards.* Depicting an assortment of scenes ranging from the Nadir to an ice-bound shipwreck off the Great Southern Fells, the watercolours alone were probably worth thousands of marks apiece. Teltö wondered what he'd buy with that sort of money. *Probably the whole of Qivunako. No wonder everyone cuddles up to Keer.*

Greatcoats hung from two hooks. Dyrstin frowned. "Looks like the old man has a visitor. No idea who though. No appointments scheduled."

"Shouldn't we come back later?"

"Nah. Keer's not like Hova. He won't mind." Dyrstin walked on through. Teltö followed, shutting the door behind him.

The interior took Teltö's breath away. Worthy of the court of gibbering Gykäkkä, a crystal chandelier hung from the ceiling, candles like the winter stars. High-backed chairs with stylised leaves ringed an oak table, Tuonakonian by the workmanship. Perfecting the excess, a sky-blue vase rested upon the table. Three irises jutted from its porcelain neck, each petal set with an artist's eye. *Keer probably employs a servant solely to arrange those flowers. Father Life, there's probably an entire greenhouse devoted to growing blooms for this room.*

A coal-fire kept the air cosy, the blood-red embers flickering out one by one. *Five hundred years, and they still don't burn wood in Kuolinako.* Twin armchairs sat beside the hearth. A wrinkled man occupied one, a quilted rug over his lap. He clutched a glass of milk.

"Is that you?" he said. Bald, bespectacled, and owning a bushy white moustache conjoined with side-whiskers, he wore a navy-blue dressing gown over a nightshirt and Unut-fur slippers. Teltö kept his distance. Keer looked harmless, but no one survived seven decades in Imperial Government without having some venom.

"It's me, Grand Master." Dyrstin bowed, feet together, in traditional fashion. "I was checking if you were up. I've brought a friend."

Keer smiled. "How nice. It's so lonely up here sometimes, with only memories for company. But it's certainly a day for visitors. Peta and I were talking about it…"

Peta? Teltö saw Dyrstin's face. *Oh, shit. Of course…*

"Dyrstin Venomavat and Teltö Phuul, I presume?"

There he was, arm slung across a bookshelf. Average height and slender, with a mop of thick grey hair and a face as clean and cold as an icicle. The man whose image stared down from portraits throughout the Empire. His Excellency, Grand Chancellor Peta Vyrellävek, known from the Wall to the Fells as the Dragon.

Chapter Four

THE SEA-GREY EYES left neither Dyrstin nor Teltö. The clock above the marble fireplace ticked onwards.

"Are you, or are you not Dyrstin Venomavat and Teltö Phuul?" said the Grand Chancellor, in a heavy Tuonakonian accent. His tone had neither Hova's bullying impatience, nor Alio Venomavat's barbed malevolence, but rather a cold methodical formality. The bloodless voice of rules-turned-ritual, a sound more machine than man.

Frozen in the middle of Keer's drawing room, Teltö stuttered affirmation. Vyrellävek nodded. If he delighted in causing discomfort, he betrayed no sign. *But they never do.* Vyrellävek was a former Inquisitor General. Those fellows didn't celebrate power; they accepted it as the natural order of things. The Sun rose in the East, water flowed downhill, and the Dragon did what he liked to anyone. It was life, so why gloat?

Flicking a speck of grime from his impeccable cherry cravat, the most powerful man in the Empire settled into a chair embellished with carven images of holly.

"Kortek, if you will permit me a small indulgence, I must make enquiries of these gentlemen." Gently trilling his r, the Dragon might've finished a day's toil in his native city's timberyards.

"Certainly, Peta," said the forgotten old fellow with the milk and the moustache. "I'm sure it's important. A good sort like you wouldn't be asking otherwise. Dyrstin's a good egg too. From a family of good eggs. Why, of all the times I've…"

Vyrellävek smiled with his teeth. They were horribly white. "Thank you, Kortek. I am sure Phuul and Venomavat are upstanding examples of Imperial egginess. Now, Teltö, in your own words, what happened to our beloved Master Hova aboard the *HIHS Naat*?"

He knows about Hova. Perhaps he really was behind it? Teltö wanted to run: back to Qivunako, perhaps, or to some ice cave in the Great Southern Fells, living on fur seals and toothfish for the rest of his days. But terror nailed his feet to the floor. Terror and those pitiless eyes. One could die of frostbite beneath that serpentine stare. Teltö fidgeted with his hair, and the fireplace clock ticked onwards.

Father Life, does the Dragon have mercy? Another voice in Teltö's head whispered. *It doesn't have to be you. There are other suspects.*

His cheeks burning, he spluttered and stumbled. He stared at his bootlaces. But Teltö Phuul did what he had to do. He omitted the Mnoma, but made Eriva Phytek suspiciously knowledgeable of poisons. Dyrstin chameleoned from merely pale to near green.

"Is that everything, Teltö?"

"Yes, Your Excellency." It was none of his business if the Dragon tried to kill Hova. *And I know nothing about any*

Northern Principality visit. Or any war reparations. Nothing!

"My thanks," said Vyrellävek, with glacial warmth. "Honesty is a rare commodity these days." He pulled two envelopes from his waistcoat pocket. "I have something for you."

No one moved.

"Gentlemen, do not waste my time."

Teltö crept forward, taking the envelopes. The eyes were on him all the while.

"Thank you, Your Excellency."

A smile crossed that thin face. It spoke of a predator toying with some weaker beast. "I hope, Teltö, to see more of you. Honest young men are exactly what the Empire needs in these insincere times, and is not the survival of the Empire all that matters?"

Dyrstin had regained sufficient composure to bow; Teltö followed his example.

Vyrellävek turned his shaggy grey head. "Kortek," he said, "I fear I must take my leave of your excellent hospitality. It has been a pleasure, old friend."

Keer inclined his head. "Farewell, Your Excellency."

With one final smile, the Grand Chancellor collected his hat and departed. Shivering and sweating, Teltö watched him go.

"It's so nice to have visitors, is it not?"

Teltö sighed, the spell broken. Ensconced within the soft embrace of his armchair, Keer smiled with senile benevolence. *Or perhaps that's what he wants us to think.*

"Peta is such a decent chap. Did I ever tell you about the time…"

"Good night, Grand Master," said Dyrstin, harsh as a splash of seawater.

"Good night, Dyrstin," said Keer.

Hova would've bit my head off if I'd tried that. The old man's tired eyes concentrated behind the spectacles. "And good night to you, er..."

"Teltö Phuul."

"Phuul. I may have known..."

They fled.

*   *   *

TELTÖ BREATHED A sigh of relief. Here in the parlour, he'd encounter no one scarier than hapless Oilio, or maybe a dead servant. All that time they were talking, and Peta Vyrellävek was standing mere centifurlongs above their heads. He needed to get out of here. Dyrstin slammed and bolted the door. *Too late. The enemy's inside those bloody envelopes.*

"Now where's that clock?" Venomavat muttered.

Teltö frowned. "Which clock?" Wherever it was, he felt an inexplicable lust to smash it, though he wasn't about to venture back into that drawing room any time soon.

Dyrstin picked a small timepiece off a shelf. "Here we are. Come to Dyrstin..." He pawed at the rear chamber like a bee-wolf after honey.

Teltö plopped the missives beside the pot with the cobalt tea-cosy. He eyed them like monstrous spiders. Red Widows, perhaps. Too important to burn, too perilous to open. Depending on their contents, he might prefer the spiders.

"I need a stiff drink."

"Agreed." Dyrstin slid a brass key from the back of the clock. "Asrak?" He raced to a side-cabinet, and fiddled with the lock.

Teltö craned his head around. The cabinet swung

open to reveal a dozen brown bottles in neat rows of three.

"That's quite the stockpile. I thought I'd have to hunt down the local bootlegger."

Dyrstin grinned back. "I *am* the local bootlegger. I said I could run a distillation operation under Keer's bewhiskered nose. Well, here's the evidence." Venomavat conjured a pair of glasses.

Teltö would never regard himself as courageous. He'd never considered himself cowardly either, but silently cursing his luck, he shut his eyes, and tore open an envelope.

"Throw your worst at me, you bastards…. oh dear."

"What does it say?" Dyrstin uncorked a bottle, and poured out the misty contents.

"*Dear Teltö Phuul, underkarl,*" Teltö read. "*In light of the attack on the life of Master Hyät Hova of Qivunako, the Office of the Imperial Inquisition hereby gives notice that you are summoned to its Chambers. Please report to the Tower of the Emperors, level one, at noon this coming Wolfsday. The Office does not wish to subject you to questioning, but this will be reviewed should you choose not to comply with these summons. Best wishes, Inquisitor General Eriva Vöder.*"

Dyrstin sipped his drink. "Sounds like Vöder. I've met her a few times. She's strangely amiable for a woman who presides over the bureaucracy of torture and disappearance. Probably the only Inquisitor General in history to sign letters 'best wishes'."

Teltö opened the other letter. Addressed to Dyrstin, it was otherwise an identical summons.

Dyrstin scowled. "Now that's unfair. I wasn't even on the bloody ship."

"You did tell me about the war reparations."

"Under duress," said Dyrstin. "And they don't know

that. Yet. Though when you were squealing to the Dragon, I'd no idea what you'd spill."

Teltö groped for his own glass. He did need a stiff drink, and more than one. "Because, Venomavat, you were *so* much calmer, standing there so green you looked half-Mnoma. At least you'd met Vyrellävek before. I'd only ever seen his portrait. Still, it could be worse. Whether or not the Dragon's behind Hova's poisoning, he's not stringing us up by our balls just yet. Wolfsday… that gives us four days."

The Asrak burned all the way down. Just what he needed. A few more and he'd be well on the way to sweet oblivion.

Dyrstin narrowed his eyes. "True. And if Vöder or Vyrellävek really wanted us disappeared, they wouldn't have bothered writing."

"They might still find something that interests them, and cook up a story. I know how shadow-stalkers work."

"*I* know how they work," said Dyrstin. "Every week, I walk or take a cab past the Tower."

"Hard not to, it's on every city level." The building was famous even in distant Qivunako. Kuolinakonians used it as a gigantic ruler for measuring depth.

"Not true, actually." Dyrstin finished his own drink. "There are levels beneath, but nice young Qivunakonians shouldn't hear about those. It might give them nightmares."

Venomavat uncorked another bottle, and scowled. "Every time I pass, I see that windowless stone and imagine Vöder sitting in a dark office oiling the machinery of state. Or oiling the machinery of torture. It's all the same to her. But you can't run. They'll come after you, and you'll die screaming. If it weren't for the Toast, they'd bring you back just to kill you again."

Teltö sighed. The initial burn over, the Asrak numbed him pleasantly.

"Bugger it," he said. "We need to stop worrying. Tomorrow's tomorrow, today's today, and I'm not drunk enough. Vöder, Vyrellävek, Keer, and Hova can all get stuffed."

Dyrstin slid the freshly opened bottle along the table. Teltö caught it with his empty hand.

"I tell you what," said Dyrstin, "to take your mind off Vöder, I'll take you to the new play the Mnomo are putting on. I can scrounge us some tickets, no problem."

"Why'd I want to watch a play?" Teltö considered swigging straight from the bottle, but that would be a bit much even here. He refilled his glass.

"Because a bit of fun will do you good? It's a light comedy. Also, think of the audience. It's amazing what 'I'm Native Assistant to Grand Master so-and-so' can do, and you've twice the opportunities I have."

Teltö belched. "And I have twice the standards you do." He downed another glass, and reached for a refill. "Besides, I hate Mnomo. I got a handkerrrrchief off one, but they're all bastarrrrds."

Dyrstin chewed his lip. "I'd forgotten you start doing a Tuonakonian accent when drunk. Better not let the Dragon hear that."

"Ah, buggerrrr Vyrellävek. He can only kill me once. We've drrrrunk the Toast, rrrremember? Badge of office and all, once we've downed it we can't come back!" Teltö started singing:

"A toast to the Toast for keeping me dead,
To stop evil bastarrrds using my head.

With the corrrpses of Guildlings, do what you will:
Us Necrrros are safe, all thanks to this swill.
A toast to the Toast da-dum-da-da-dum…"

Dyrstin tugged away the bottle. "I think, Teltö, you've probably had enough."

"I think, Dyrrrrstin, you've prrrobably got no appresh…appreshiation for song. Fancy a spiderrr warrr? Hehe."

Venomavat suddenly had a grin not unlike Vyrellävek's. But less scary and more fuzzy. He had such a lovely smile.

"For money?"

"Of courrrse. Hehe." *Even worse than I am.*

"Suits me," said Dyrstin. "Now where did I put my spiders?" He dashed out of the room.

Teltö slumped over the table. A wet sensation spread along his arm; he'd dipped his elbow in a puddle of Asrak. He giggled. It seemed so funny, though he couldn't think why.

He settled down, head resting on elbow, and red hair curtaining his eyes. He'd beat Dyrstin, yes he would, and then…

• • •

HE AWOKE TO the cacophonous ringing of the noon gong. Teltö slammed his hands over his ears. *Stop it! Enough!* The Room of the Hours may be floors above, but the bastards might've been hammering away on the table in front of him. He vowed to never, ever suffer a hangover here again. Eleven… twelve. The final peal shuddered through the house, and Teltö lurched to his feet. *Need water. So thirsty.*

Teltö stumbled into the main passageway. The gas-lamps still burned: noon was indistinguishable from midnight. How did Kuolinakonians understand day and night, except as meaningless tradition? Teltö wondered. How did they sleep? Children walked these streets who'd never seen the Sun.

He blundered into two closets before finding the kitchen, where he thrust his face under the tap. Then he threw up in the sink, and spent a good few minutes rinsing away the lingering odour. Where was Dyrstin hiding?

Teltö saw a dark side-chamber. Unable to find the gas-tap, he grabbed a lantern from the kitchen bench. The rusty metal felt rough beneath his fingers. *This'd better be whale oil.* A wizened woman from the mountains, Teltö's great-grandmother used to tell stories of using corpse fat lanterns, and suffering the reek all winter long. She was Old Empire. Keer may be an antiquarian, but he wasn't that extreme, surely? Lit, the lantern didn't smell too vile.

Inside, he found Dyrstin snoozing atop an armchair. Teltö moved closer. Venomavat's legs dangled over the armrest, his two top shirt buttons were undone, and his sleeveless jersey sported an archipelago of stains, yet the blond mane remained immaculate. *Does he do his hair before or after vomiting?*

"Dyrstin, wake up."

No answer. Teltö put the lantern on the floor beside a half-empty bottle, and paused. For reasons lost in the mists of history, someone had rammed a pool cue vertically between wall and chair. *I could see Oilio lancing burglars. Attach a knife and you've a half-decent spear.*

"Wake up, Venomavat," he shouted, prodding his friend in the chest. "Rise and shine!"

Dyrstin groaned and his hand lashed out. Too slow.

"Sod off, Phuul."

"It's noon, Dyrstin. You've work to do."

"Killing you for a start."

No gratitude, Dyrstin? Better me than Vyrellävek. With quarter-past-noon greeted by the inelegant chimes of Venomavat throwing up, Teltö went in search of Oilio.

A lich chambermaid directed him outside. The first decent corpse Teltö had encountered since he set foot in this bloody city. He'd say this for Keer, he kept his dead helpful.

Teltö attained the front door unharangued, and wedged the entrance open with a wilted pot plant. Keer's front door could only be opened from the inside. Standing beneath a crisp cold light, Teltö swept his eyes over the lawn, appreciating the beauty of the night pines and the fishpond shimmering beneath the blue lanterns. A team of liches mulched the rose beds beside the path. *One day, they'll be mulch too. Mother Death would approve.*

He soon saw, or rather heard, the Housemaster shouting at someone. Lower-level servants, presumably. Living ones, or he wouldn't be yelling.

"Housemaster Oilio?"

A bundle of furs and sweat, the Housemaster looked half-hedgehog in the gloom. He swept around as though bitten.

"Who is that?"

"Teltö Phuul, sir. I need your help."

"Just a moment. And they call themselves Deputy Gardening Supervisors…"

The underlings dissolved into the shadows. Oilio nodded his head, and marched briskly back across the lawn.

"Absolutely thankless task." The Housemaster leant his stick against the wall and pulled out a silk handkerchief.

"I can only imagine, sir."

"I would replace them all with liches – so much cheaper, even with registration – but the Grand Master insists they remain on the payroll. If I may be frank, one of his failings is that he never throws anything or anyone out. He has no surviving relatives, you know."

"I'm sure Grand Master Keer appreciates your efforts, sir. Someone must keep the wheels turning."

"No doubt." Oilio mopped his forehead. "Though the Grand Master's appreciation can be somewhat special. He kept my predecessor till she was blind and ninety-nine, and now stores her skeleton in a glass box. Somewhere in the lesser western wine cellar, I think. So tell me, how do you need help?"

Oilio stuffed the handkerchief back into his pocket, and rested his hands on his pot belly. Each digit protruded from the fingerless gloves like a fat pink snail from the shell.

"Is there any word on my master?"

"I believe he still sleeps. I shall enquire after lunch."

"I wish him speedy recovery."

"As do we all."

Teltö adopted his most sycophantic expression. "This is where I need your valuable aid, sir. You see, a Native Assistant's work never finishes. As Saari Ooks so eloquently said, duty must always prevail, and as you provide such an excellent example..."

Oilio grunted. "Thank you. There is too little respect for elders these days. That lazy wastrel Venomavat only mocks my efforts. If he is here at all. He will come to a bad end."

Teltö imagined Dyrstin scrubbing his own vomit. "Oh, I think he's learning laziness doesn't pay." Teltö's mother told him that once. He'd never listened. "But, returning to my own situation, I need to get to Hova's lodgings. I'm but fresh off the boat from Qivunako."

"Eager to start on the hard work, lad?"

"Of course, sir. As a Native Assistant I believe in promptness, punctuality, and diligence." *If the corpses have sorted the luggage, I can put my feet up and enjoy a house all to myself.*

"Excellent. You're asking the right fellow: I'm Kuolinako born, and know this city like the back of my hand."

You're wearing gloves. "Not only that, but I need to write a letter to Qivunako. I must inform the Lesser Council of my master's condition, so they can prepare for the worst."

Oilio beamed. "It's so nice to see young people taking roles seriously. Venomavat does nothing but chase women. He could certainly learn a thing from you."

Teltö smiled. "He could indeed."

*   *   *

THE HOUSEMASTER PROVIDED Teltö with a detailed map, and fifty copper bits for cabs.

"Cabs are the life-blood of this city," opined Oilio. "Wandering away from the main areas is unwise: you will get lost, and that's a worry, even with the map. Kuolinako has nine levels, many dead-end tunnels and forgotten mines, and places as alien as the Moon."

"How do you mean?"

Oilio looked at Teltö in earnest. "I mean places where up is down, down is up, and sideways is simply wrong. At all costs, stay near light. Strange things lurk in the dark places."

"Inquisitors, you mean?"

"Worse. Inquisitors belong here. These things… don't."

Teltö remembered the gaps in the tunnel walls. He nodded.

"By the way, the postal carriage will stop past here in two hours, so if you leave your letter with me, I can post it for you."

"You are a true gentleman, sir."

"One more thing. You'll need one of these." Oilio pulled a lantern from a shelf. "When you're out and about, they're indispensable. Some fools think they can manage with streetlights alone, but Kuolinakonians know better."

Teltö considered the lantern, a standard glass model with a handle clean of rust. "Whale oil?"

Oilio knitted sweat-greased eyebrows. "Yes, Mustanakonian. Expensive, but efficient. Why?"

"No reason…"

•　•　•

HAVING LEFT A politically benign memorandum in Oilio's capable and sweaty hands, Teltö caught a cab into the city. He hoped he'd deciphered those notes accurately. If only Dyrstin had transcribed Hova's address onto something other than a cocktail napkin.

He stopped first at the Income and Rationing Office to register and obtain new dockets. The queue lasted a mere half an hour. *Everyone else got lost.* It was also payday for Native Assistants, so Teltö left the Office rich and happy, the coins clinking in his pocket beside his crisp virgin ration book. He whistled. *I'm going to survive. Bugger the Inquisition.*

Another cab led to his final destination. Expecting a moss-ridden ruin to rival Keer's, Teltö found a sparse utilitarian structure resembling an upturned cardboard box or perhaps a whitewashed tombstone. Square windows stared over a rectangular lawn of browning night grass. Teltö reminded himself to organise a lich gardener. *I can't imagine Hova with this. He's niggles and propriety, not bright and shiny.*

A dead postman had shoved letters under the front door. Teltö held the missives up to the lantern light. Something from the Undersecretarial Office, something from Hova's predecessor... he'd look at them later. He turned on the gas, and wandered through to a medium-sized kitchen. He plopped Oilio's lantern on the table, and rubbed his hands. *Let's take a look.* The cupboards were well-stocked with cutlery, crockery, and other necessities. *Excellent.*

In the corner, a coal bucket stood full to the brim. Teltö lit the range, only then noticing he'd left footprints on the rug. Hova's two lich servants looked at him vacantly. They and Oilio's troop had left him little to do. *Father Life, Oilio's handy. Dyrstin doesn't deserve him. Now for dinner...*

. . .

HAVING DEVOURED A semi-legal helping of mushroom soup with potatoes, onions, and cheese, Teltö curled up in the four poster bed, and considered the Asrak on the dressing table. He'd smuggled a bottle out of Keer's, and it sat tempting him. *If you insist, sir...*

He poured himself water from the decanter, reflecting

on the lives of the Imperial elite. He now understood why Dyrstin never tried getting recalled. *A gambler is our Venomavat. Rich food, feather beds, and all for the small risk of shadow-stalkers spiriting him away.* If Teltö had Keer for a master, he might even feel the same, but with Hova… The silly old Unut caused problems even when comatose.

Teltö yawned. Despite a schedule full of laziness, he'd read through the papers left by Hova's predecessor, and had detected an arse-covering stench right away. Either there were typographical errors, or someone was being creative with the accounts. *Someone who sold the office corpses and pocketed the money.* His own predecessor had left nothing before she'd scuttled off to some Tuonakonian licensing office.

The Asrak hummed an alluring song. Teltö slipped out of bed and padded over to Hova's medicine chest, a lumbering chunk of kauri decorated with serpents. The serpents formed a ring; each devoured its successor's tail. The chest contained bandages, ointment, laudanum, carbolic balls, tweezers… Teltö found a bottle of cough mixture labelled 'Made in Skeevereet' and held it up to the light. The viscous purple liquid seemed harmless. *Asrak goes with everything…*

The result nauseated him. *One myth debunked.* Another glass of water purged the oily taste from his mouth. Turning off the bedside lamp, Teltö nestled between the silk sheets and drifted off to sleep, enveloped in strange dreams.

•　•　•

TELTÖ SAT UP, sweat beading on his face and chest. He turned on the gas-lamp, and grasped for water. Its clean soothing chill spread down his throat. He drew a deep breath and fell back against the pillows. *Only a dream.* Then turned his head.

He screamed. Beside him, milk-white eyes staring at the ceiling, lay one of Hova's liches. *Nightmare necromancy? But I'm only an underkarl!* Teltö leapt from the bed, and crouched, arms thrust out in protection. But the corpse didn't move. *Of course it won't. It's a bloody lich, and you're the only Necromancer in the house. Get it out of here.*

He sent the corpse to the depths of the coal cellar. Teltö threw himself back onto the bed, wondering whether this was a side-effect of the cough medicine. His skin goose-pimpled, Teltö crept towards the room's only exit. The Unut rug caressed his feet like a lover.

Streetlight penetrated a nearby window, bathing the passageway in sombre grey. An amber glow emanating from the stairwell. Teltö returned to the bedroom, relieved. He bolted the door.

Chapter Five

TELTÖ SOURLY EYED the clutter in the sink. He'd made full use of Hova's kitchen, savouring the rich smells of gravy and black market spices all afternoon, but now the congregation of pots, pans, and plates ate up every microfurlong of bench space, and those hardened lardy remnants could blunt pickaxes.

Cleaning-up would have to wait though. Venomavat was dragging him out to the Theatre tonight, and all because of that pool cue business. *Bastard.* Worse, Dyrstin didn't even care about the actual play. He was just cosying up to the producers to resurrect his acting career. *Not quite true. He's also after the girls in the audience.*

Teltö washed and shaved, applied a pungent cologne, then hunted down suitable clothes. Dropping his scarf for an emerald cravat, he donned his good waistcoat: Teltö owned two, but the other carried stains like a war hero carried medals. After spit-and-polishing his shoes and a futile attempt to tame his hair, he took one final look in the mirror, and groaned. The cravat couldn't entirely conceal the throttling, and his thinning face only accentuated the Phuul nose. *Too long without chocolate.*

He hurried out to hail a cab.

"To the Imperial Theatre House," he barked. "And make it quick." The corpse-driver whipped the Unut into motion; Teltö jolted against the seat. He slid the hatch open to glare at the lich. Maybe this one had residual personality. *Like being a complete smart-arse.*

Dyrstin waited outside, hands in pockets. He too sported a cravat and waistcoat.

"Everything sorted?"

Teltö stuffed a handful of bits into the payment box, and jumped down. "Don't mention Hova. Or cabs. I need a holiday."

"As you command, sir," Dyrstin flourished a pair of tickets. "I got these as a bulk deal. Producers like food as much anyone, and as the Native Assistant to the Secretary for Public Nutrition I'm in a unique position to cater to their tastes."

"I take it the Theatre Operators are Mnomo?"

"The managers, producers and actors are mostly human. It's the writers who are the aliens. Let's them be creative in private without making public... spectacles."

The pink and white spires of the Theatre House stretched from street-level to the dim cavern roof. Teltö had expected something grander. So much for the largest wooden structure in the Last Capital. There were larger ones in Qivunako.

The tickets were for the downstairs central area, which afforded a decent view, but meant squeezing past early arrivals. Teltö nudged through the labyrinth of legs, and collapsed into a seat with a sigh. Dyrstin whispered something to a pleasantly plump young woman in the next row. She slapped him.

"Looks like your Native Assistant line isn't working."

"Stop smirking, Teltö. I don't see you having much success either."

"I'm here to watch a bloody play, not to seduce people."

The murmur of a thousand conversations filled the air, amplified by the timber walls. Plebs predominated: underkarl yellow and karl red, with a sprinkling of overkarl black and specialist pink. The rest were Mnomo, or Guildlings, or simply Ordinaries: people without skills who'd escaped the Death Draft and now scratched out livings in other ways. *It must be tough competing against the dead.* Corpses didn't eat or sleep.

Then Teltö saw the balconied tier. *So that's where the elites are.* Velvets, silks, and jewellery distinguished the high-level Guildlings, enough to put the Mnomo to shame. *Flaunting it because they can, while us Necros are forbidden it and no-one else can afford it.* Rising for a better view, Teltö looked for ribbons. There were more pinks and blacks, together with ministerial greens, undermasterly oranges, and masterly purples. But no white ribbons. The Grand Masters were otherwise occupied. Nor was there any sign of the man who wore the blue. *Thank Father Life.*

"Vyrellävek's not here."

Dyrstin twisted his head around. "Yeah. Mind you, the Theatre folk love him. According to some friends of mine, Vyrellävek's a big patron. Says Theatre is the most important of all arts... hold on."

"What is it?"

"Oh, yes, it's definitely her." Dyrstin sighed. "Teltö, Her Vigilance the Inquisitor General is in the audience. That's her. The square woman with the light brown hair."

"Who's she's talking to?" Beside Vöder sat a curly-haired gentleman in blue and yellow silks.

"Sorko, the Dean of the Guild. Wouldn't I like to know what they're talking about?"

A lone drum rumbled like thunder, followed by a trumpet. The crowd hushed and rose for the Imperial anthem. Generations of schoolchildren had parodied those lyrics, shaming a stirring tune, but Teltö wasn't in the mood. He muttered through the first verse, hummed through the second, and settled back into his seat as the final notes died away.

A bearded man in tweed strode onto the stage. "Ladies and gentleman," he began. "It is my delight to present to you the first of our pieces this evening, a new work by the Imperial Theatre Company: a tale of loss and romance set during the Mustanako Mutiny. I give you *The Dragonbone Pipes…*"

"You said this was fluff," Teltö whispered. "The Mutiny is *not* light comedy."

"Yes, yes." Dyrstin flicked his hand. "They've probably got that next."

The curtains drew back, and a Mnoman chorus clustered in front of the stage.

• • •

THE CURTAINS CLOSED. Teltö applauded with the rest: for all the melodrama, the piece was well-acted, with lavish attention to detail. They didn't make the Mutineers baby-eaters either; perhaps they were trying to avoid a Mustanakonian boycott. Some of the crowd wandered out. Dyrstin and Teltö stayed, the former muttering to himself. *Maybe the play upset him. Though he might just be annoyed about not getting laid tonight.* Teltö stretched. Perhaps a night out was a good idea after all.

"Ladies and gentlemen, our next piece is a comedy to warm the hearts of young and old: *The Man Who Married a Hippopotamus!*"

So this was the light relief.

Dyrstin bent towards the ear of the woman in the next row. "Fancy that," he said, "a play about your future husband!" This time he jerked back with sufficient speed. Teltö sniggered, but he could no longer ignore another problem...

"I'm off to the toilet, Dyrstin."

"Thank you, Teltö. I really needed to know that."

Teltö edged through endless legs, suffering grumblings from the rows behind, and went in search of relief. The ushers directed him to a hefty set of double doors. Oak, with stylised trees carved into the wood. Teltö pushed at a door; it didn't budge. Locked? No, he could move it if he put his shoulder into the effort. Once he'd opened it far enough, he slid through, brass waistcoat buttons clinking. The door slammed behind like thunder.

Narrow carpeted stairs, winding one way, then the other, led down to a low-ceilinged passageway, so sparse and undecorated it lacked even the comfort of dust. Teltö trudged onwards as the pressure in his bladder built, his only companions the silent lamps. He looked over his shoulder. The corridor he'd come from looked indistinguishable from that in front. *Where is this place?* He heard a drum overhead. *Must be beneath the stage.*

To his left branched another passageway studded with a succession of doors; signs read 'Necromancers,' 'Guild,' and 'Others' in black block capitals. Teltö scratched his head. *Drinking the Toast makes me qualified, and stops me getting reanimated. It has nothing to do with how I shit.* Aesthetically and functionally, Necro arses were no different from non-

Necro arses, and no amount of snobbery could change that.

Behind 'Necromancer,' he found a grubby office with peeling wallpaper and mauve carpet. A heroically glum lich monitored the otherwise-empty room.

"Can I help?" said the lich.

"I'm looking for a toilet."

"Sorry, Guild members only. Necromancers should inquire in the room labelled as such."

Teltö's eyebrows knitted. "But this is for Necromancers."

"Oh dear," said the corpse. "Someone has switched the signs again. Please switch them back when you leave."

Teltö shook his head, and tried the next room. It was identical.

"Yes?" said the second lich.

"Toilet?" asked Teltö. *The overheads must be ridiculous. The registration costs…*

"Rank?"

About to yell about the clarity of yellow ribbons, Teltö realised he'd left his hat on his seat. *They're distinguishing by rank? These Kuolinakonians are crazy.* "Underkarl."

"The Underkarl toilet lies behind that door," said the corpse. "You may enter."

Teltö bleated brief thanks. He dashed through, and undid his belt, only to stop.

He strode back, fists clenched. "The thing's out of order."

"Yes."

"Is there another I can use? Are any of the others free?"

"They are all free, but you do not have the required rank."

"No one will mind. It's urgent." *I'll rip your head off, you smug bastard. Just because you don't need toilets any more…*

"No. I cannot breach Theatre Policy."

"Suppose," said Teltö, between gritted teeth, "I were a living member of the Theatre staff. Where might I find an appropriate toilet? Purely hypothetically."

"Purely hypothetically: down the stairs at the end of this passage, left, right, left, then the third door on the right. The boiler room has a small facility accessible on the far side."

Teltö fled. He dashed down stairs, his boots scuffing the stone… he found the boiler, with the promised toilet lurking behind vertical pipes. *Such relief.*

Trousers around ankles, he breathed a contented sigh. Rows of cylindrical steel segregated this enclave from the wider room, where a furnace rumbled away like a snoring mechanical dragon. The coals cast a volcanic glow over the walls. *Strange place for a toilet.* But a strange place generally, and hot. He wiped his forehead, his shirt already damp with sweat. The drum thundered again… *but it's coming from beneath my feet, not above.* Of course: he wasn't just hearing the Theatre racket, but also the city level below. *Sodding Kuolinako.*

Teltö was doing up his belt when the door creaked open, and footsteps approached. He cowered out of sight. He wasn't supposed to be here.

"…the orders are tonight," said a hushed male voice, audible over the furnace.

"He's not here though."

"Orders are orders. Besides, after what's been pulled already…."

"Yeah. Imagine the look on Vöder's face."

Teltö peeped between the pipes, and saw two men

with their backs to him. Dressed in black dungarees and bowler hats, one had his hands on his hips. The other gripped a duffle bag.

"That's if Vöder still has a face. The Inquisition will have to analyse what's left for months. But analyse is all they'll do. You can't bring back Necros."

Teltö froze.

"They'll run around like headless chickens." The man chuckled. "Quite the appropriate metaphor for the Empire, eh?"

"Quite. Got the timers?"

The bag holder knelt beside the furnace, and pulled out pliers and wires. As he turned, Teltö caught a glimpse of his face, plain and non-descript in the ruddy light. The fellow owned a thin, sandy beard.

"Pass the cable."

The other man twisted around too. This one was older, with a white beard; he clenched a clay pipe between his teeth. Teltö frowned. Tobacco was expensive. Perhaps this fellow was from Mustanako and visited the Confederation a lot. *Or perhaps they're Northerners.*

"Who do you think will be the new Inquisitor General?"

"Does it matter?"

Teltö suppressed a gasp. *Shit. They're trying to assassinate the Dragon's pet.* Suppose the dungaree-clad assassins found him here, suppose... he eyed the furnace. *They'd dispose of me easily enough. No one would ever know.* He bated his breath, and hoped to Father Life he wouldn't need to sneeze.

The newcomers fiddled with bomb equipment. Teltö sweated in his hiding place. The bastards were not only going to blow up Vöder, but the rest of the audience too. Every man, woman, and Mnoma, sitting upstairs watching a harmless play about a hippopotamus. *Dyrstin's up there. I need to warn them.* And this close to the next city level? The explosion would crack the cavern floor, and send the smoking ruins of the Theatre plummeting…

White Beard grunted. "That should work. An hour hence, this place will be naught but a hole in the ground. Kuolinako's got a few of those." He chuckled gravelly. "That'll teach them for building with wood."

Sandy Beard nodded. "And we'd best be getting out. Hold on, do you smell something?"

The other man sniffed the air. "Vinegar?"

It's that bloody cologne. His heart racing, Teltö looked around for some means of escape, but saw none, save for the far door. Nor did he have any weapon at hand. *Shit, shit, shit.*

"Nah, perfume. You think the actresses have secret rendezvous down here with admirers?"

White Beard cackled. "It's just as likely to be cat piss. You know what they say about the Theatre folk."

Teltö watched them depart. *I have to get out of here.* But he dared not leave his hiding place, not yet. Teltö's shirt grew ever damper with sweat, until it felt plastered to his back. At last, he marshalled his courage, and crept over to the bomb. The men had fastened it to the furnace door. A mass of wires and clocks, the thing ticked menacingly. Teltö licked his dry lips, and reached a hand out, ready to tear it off and smash it into a thousand pieces. Then he stopped. *I might set it off.*

Yes. He had an hour, and there must be someone in authority who'd know how to defuse bombs. He ghosted over to the door, and, heart in mouth, eased it open. Another sound turned his innards to blueberry jelly. *No, Phuul. It's just the Theatre. Let's go.* The brick-lined corridor felt chilly after the boiler, but there was no sign of the men. Teltö slunk back the way he had come. Any moment he expected an explosion or shouts of discovery.

He eased right, into the next corridor. Nothing. Just grey brick walls and granite floor. And the lamps, always the lamps. He brushed a cobweb from the mortar. *So far, so good.* Microfurlong by microfurlong, he crept to safety.

"Bugger, I forgot the pliers. Hold on."

Round the corner came Sandy Beard. Their eyes met.

"Hey, what are you doing?!"

Teltö turned and ran. *Help! They're trying to kill me.* Left led back to the boiler – a dead-end. He sprinted right. The man puffed and swore behind him, but the racket of booted pursuit grew ever louder. *They'll catch me before I find anyone.* And if they caught him… Teltö came to another intersection. Left, no – that led down to Father Life knew where. Right… the stairs back up to the main Theatre!

Teltö's boots clattered over the stone, and up the steps. Suddenly, he remembered the narrow carpeted stairs and the difficult door. They'd catch him before he reached safety. *Shit, shit.* He saw the toilet sign. Inspiration struck. He threw open the door to the mislabelled Necromantic toilets.

The corpse still sat behind the desk, lonely and pedantic.

"How may I help you?"

Heart hammering, Teltö ran to the Underkarl toilet. He dashed inside, and latched the door. *So it's out of order. Doesn't mean I can't use it to hide.*

It was dark, cramped, and smelly as an Unut stable. He huddled down beside the faulty facility, hugging his legs to his chest. His chest felt ready to explode. *Can't breathe too loud.*

"Where is he?" panted a voice. Teltö winced. He'd been just in time.

"Where is whom?"

"A fellow… a fellow ran through here. Where is he?"

"I," said the corpse, "am tasked with ensuring correct utilisation of these facilities. I am not tasked with keeping track of fugitives. Now, what is your rank?"

"My rank?" More heavy breathing. "I'm not a bloody Necro!"

"Then I must ask you to leave. These toilets are for Necromancers only."

"But…"

"If you do not leave, I shall call Theatre Security."

"How, Master Rigamortis?"

"By pushing this switch."

The man cursed loudly. For a moment, Teltö thought they were going to beat down the doors and risk capture. But he heard only muttering, and receding footsteps. The door slammed.

Every moment brought detonation closer. Biting his lip, Teltö undid the latch and peeked out. The man had gone, thank Father Life. Teltö drew a deep breath.

"Thank you," he said to the corpse, as he shook its cold, dead hand. Never had he been so grateful for obstructive bureaucracy. "But where's Security? Push that bloody switch or we'll all end up as confetti."

"Which switch?"

In spite of the circumstances, Teltö grinned. *Your supervisor's a clever bastard.*

•   •   •

BALD AND BLACK bearded, the Theatre Manager sat behind a desk littered with newspapers and scripts. The latter awash in red ink scribbles.

"A bomb in the boiler?" The man rubbed his earring. "Can't say we've had that before; credit for original plotting. What type of bomb is it?"

"One capable of destroying your entire Theatre." Teltö paced the office floor. He picked a thick leather-bound folio off the carpet and dropped it onto the desk. "Along with everything in it!"

The Manager nodded. He rose and dusted off his silk waistcoat, then shuffled over to the corner, where a dirty tartan sofa sprawled against the wall.

"Vaani!" he stomped his shoe thrice. "Get your team together, and sort this out. Dig up your tools too: they've fastened the bomb to the furnace door."

Another man crawled from behind the sofa. Dark haired, unshaven, and broad-shouldered, Vaani looked the sort to crush skulls with his fists.

"Right away, boss," Vaani grunted with the tell-tale pain of the hungover. He pushed past Teltö and slammed the door behind him.

The Manager settled back into his chair with a sigh. "I suppose we must evacuate. A shame. We'll have to wait until next week for the *Post* reviews of my semi-autobiographical *The Man Who Married a Hippopotamus*." The man cocked his head. "Did you read their reviews of our recent productions?"

"Can't say I did," said Teltö.

"Absolutely shocking. No flair or imagination at all. Half cannot write, and the other half will probably scrawl smugly about hippopotami being unmarriageable. Never mind artistic licence, the delightful fudge that sweetens every performance!"

Like a bloody Mnoma. Teltö never understood thespians.

Even Dyrstin had his moments.

"You should also send word to Her Vigilance," Teltö said. *Patience is the chief of all virtues.* "The Inquisition needs to search for the bombers."

The Manager stroked his beard. "Very wise. His Excellency is such a generous patron, I am sure he will want specialists on the case."

When Eriva Vöder herself arrived, Teltö was strangely disappointed. It was hard to feel intimidated by someone with a face like an unpeeled potato. *Dyrstin's right. She's nowhere near as scary as Vyrellävek. Father Life, this woman should be baking muffins for grandchildren, not running a torture regime.*

"So." Vöder flung her hat onto the sofa. "You are Teltö Phuul, the young man who found the bomb?"

"Yes, Your Vigilance."

"Well done. Tell me, what were you doing in the boiler room?"

"I was at the toilet, Your Vigilance."

Vöder frowned at the Manager. "Is this standard?"

"Not in the room per se, Your Vigilance." The Manager's face was a smiling mask. "There are staff toilets adjunct to the main boiler itself. Phuul here was unable to access normal facilities, so went looking for other means of relief."

Vöder returned to Teltö. "So you saw these men?"

"Yes, Your Vigilance."

"Could you describe them?"

To be thought a hero, he must sound the part. He embellished the bombers' malevolence, and told of a deadly cat and mouse game as he'd fled back through the silent corridors. He just had to be careful not to contradict himself. *Cuddly or not, she's still the Inquisitor General.*

"And did they say anything about their intentions or

who sent them?"

Teltö relayed what he'd heard. "I think they were Northerners," he added.

"Thank you," said Vöder. "There may be further questions, but that shall do for now. We shall also question that corpse. With the Theatre's permission."

"Permission granted," said the Manager. *As though he has a choice.*

Vaani returned, a strained look on his face, and a bag under his arm. "I disposed of the bomb, boss." He handed the bag to Vöder.

"Thank you, Vaani," said the Manager. "No sign of the villains?"

"None. Done a runner."

"They will not flee the Inquisition," said Vöder. "My lieutenants will search the area in the coming days. Unfortunately, we must also close the Theatre for the foreseeable future…"

"What?" cried the Manager, rising from his chair. "But that would ruin us!"

"Even so. Public safety is paramount while we search for these gentlemen and their paymasters."

"I shall report this to His Excellency. The Grand Chancellor has always told me how much he enjoys my work…"

Vöder sat the man down with a glance. "The Grand Chancellor delegates matters of public security to my department. He has intervened in your favour in the past, but I would advise against hoping for such this time. Thank you for your cooperation."

There's steel as well as spuds in her spine. The Manager nodded, face turning ashen.

Vöder scooped up her orange-ribboned hat, and

glanced at Teltö. "We shall have need of your assistance. You will hear from us again."

The Manager waited until the door had closed behind her, then put his head in his hands. "Ruined!" he wailed. Vaani crawled back behind the sofa.

Teltö crept from the room strangely pleased. Something was up, plainly, but Vöder made a better friend than foe, and he had until Wolfsday to further cement their unexpected relationship. *I'm still dancing on thin ice, but I'm too necessary to fall through just yet.*

Chapter Six

ARRANGED INTO READ and unread piles, papers carpeted the floor of Hova's drawing room. Teltö had made good progress today, and with Hova still at Keer's, the old man was in no position to object. *Something's up, and I need to find out what.* But so far the letters revealed little. Hova had a contact in Skeevereet, yet the longwinded bastard was writing about exports, imports, cough medicine, and regulations: nothing interesting. Teltö contemplated yet another tied-up bundle. The doorbell rang. *The servants will get it.*

Teltö brushed aside orphaned pieces of string, and plonked himself amid the sofa cushions. Were it not for the daisy wallpaper, he'd almost miss this place. The armchairs were comfier than home, and less stained. The fires were nicer too, and he'd got a cosy blaze going with a stack of decade-old *Doomsday Posts*. The doorbell sounded again, more urgently. *Where are those bloody servants?* He paused. *I locked them in the coal cellar.* Teltö hurried downstairs.

Dyrstin and a woman waited outside. Blond hair

gleamed in the streetlights.

"Teltö!" Venomavat carried three flat boxes, and had wedged a bottle under his arm. "What kept you?"

"Work," snapped Teltö, catching a mix of cologne and illegal liquor. "Who's this?" He jabbed a finger at Dyrstin's companion. *Thin, too thin.*

"A friend of a friend. She's in the Guild." Dyrstin's hand darted over and squeezed a breast.

"And you're both here because…"

"We deserve a celebration after our Theatre exploits."

Our exploits? "I'm busy." He tried slamming the door, but Dyrstin stuck his foot out in time.

"Come on, Teltö. I swiped some custard pies while Oilio's back was turned. You don't want to doom me to the Housemaster's dreaded budget revisions, do you?"

Teltö eyed the pie boxes. Spite warred with gluttony. Gluttony won.

• • •

THE DEAD SPIDERS had been put away for the night, if it could ever be called night in Kuolinako. Teltö had emerged victorious three-to-one, with one no-result after custard splattered over Dyrstin's Yellowtail. The woman had giggled at that, but otherwise stared vacantly at the bundles of letters.

"First Hova, now Vöder." Teltö shook his head, his sense of victory muted. "I feel like a weta caught in an avalanche."

Dyrstin leant back on the sofa, and popped a grape into his mouth. "Ugly but unkillable?"

"You know what I mean." *Those are my grapes, you bastard, and they aren't cheap.* "There's something afoot, and I'll be damned if I'll be someone else's bloody spider. Just for once, I want to do something about it before it happens. Or at least get out the way in time."

"Who cares? Creepy-crawly metaphors aside, you're the fellow who saved Vöder's life. Tomorrow we'll pop along to the Tower, the shadow-stalkers will pat you on the head, and send you home. Which is what you wanted, isn't it?"

"Yes, but that was before. Now... it's more. More than impressing Vöder." He shrugged. "I've thought about this, Dyrstin, and I've realised I'm part of a bigger picture. Waiting until the next assassination won't save me, not when the Powers That Be know who I am. If hiding and running won't work, the only option is to find out what is going on, and prepare." Teltö considered the inane little she-Unut, and wondered what Dyrstin saw in her, other than the obvious.

Dyrstin drummed his fingers on the armrest. "The big picture is of other bigwigs, most like. Pry into the Dragon's schemes if you want, but count me out. I lost all interest in your Hova stuff the moment Vyrellävek walked in my door." He sniffed the air. "Is something burning?"

A sharp smell assaulted Teltö's nostrils. He swept around to see wispy smoke rising from the hearth. *Bugger. I stacked the letters too close to the fire.* He ran over and stamped on the smouldering papers until he'd snuffed the flames. Too late. A dozen letters were near-cinders, and scorch-marks lined the edges of dozens more. Clutching a handkerchief to her face, Dyrstin's friend-of-a-friend fled the room.

Dyrstin picked up a burnt letter. "Please tell me these weren't important."

"Hova will kill me."

"You're in luck. I checked on the fat little Unut

earlier, and he's still unconscious. You'll be back in Qivunako before he notices."

Teltö crumpled a letter. "And it's not as if he had anything important to say in his missives…hold on." He peered at the page, and smoothed it against a wall. Something was there, something dark in the margins. *Words. Hova was using invisible ink.* A chill ran up his spine.

"Teltö, you've gone pale."

"Look," said Teltö. He handed the letter over. "Hova's been a busy boy."

His friend read it and frowned. "I think you're reading too much into this."

"Hova strangled me because he thought I was Keer. Your master knows something. Find out."

Dyrstin returned the paper. "Sorry, Teltö. I'm not getting involved. Your first instincts were right: this whole business is a first class ticket to disappearance. Forget it. It's not safe."

"*Nothing's* safe. We've got to get them, whoever they are, before they get us. Besides, Vöder will help us."

"So you've gone from jumping at every shadow to actively courting danger? Just because the shadow-stalkers are a fact of life doesn't mean you take them to bed with you."

The woman coughed from the doorway. "So you've got that beastly fire out," she chirped, running a hand across a porcelain cheek. "I'm ever so pleased. Is there any Asrak left?"

• • •

HIS HEAD STILL feeling like an Unut had kicked it, Teltö gazed at the dour grey stonework. He stood on the walkway at the very base of the Tower of the Emperors, where the ancient cylindrical structure spread its underground roots. *'Roots' all right. The thing's a bloody tree.* From here the Tower sprouted through nine underground levels to the surface, then a good furlong into the sky, giving unparalleled views over the old city ruins. But no one visited the pinnacle these days, not for fifteen centuries, not since the Grand Council finally wearied of grotesques drooling upon the Imperial throne. Now the Tower housed the Inquisition, and even they were uneasy with living beneath Gykäkkä's walled-up tomb. More than one Inquisitor General had declared the place haunted.

"Come on." A red-eyed and unshaven Dyrstin tugged his elbow. "We don't want to be late."

Daunting chunks of Tuonakonian oak fitted with Qivunakonian ironwork, the doors of the Tower stood open like the arms of Mother Death herself. Built to withstand eternity, those doors had seen Chancellors and even Emperors come and go. But Teltö was immune to their awesome antiquity, feeling more a lich labourer than a Necromancer of the Viiminian Empire. *Give me a glass of water.* Too aggravated for terror, he took his place in the queue and glared at the army of officials who scurried around with briefcases, walking sticks, and papers. Twin chandeliers cast sickly light over the cavernous room.

His turn came; Teltö handed the crumpled summons to the desk corpse. He blinked. Scruffy auburn hair, largish nose, must have been in its early twenties when it fell to the Death Draft... *It's like a bloody mirror. Is this thing really there or does the Inquisition pull this trick with everyone just to mess with their minds?* Teltö struggled to recall whether any recent relatives had failed the Examination and subsequently had their number come up.

"Up those stairs, third door on the left," said the dead

doppelgänger, not recognising the similarity of features. Liches only operated within their instructions, and few Necromancers shared Madam Venomavat's passion for the fineries of small talk.

"Thank you." Teltö shuffled away. *That could have been me.* Just for a moment, the entire Imperial edifice swayed in his mind's eye.

"Papers, please."

Teltö could almost hear Venomavat's teeth grinding.

• • •

"THAT BLOODY RECEPTIONIST might have been your twin," muttered Dyrstin.

Teltö snorted. "I couldn't be that annoying if I tried."

"Don't bet on it."

Teltö tried the doorknob. The office was unlocked. "Hello?"

Candles in jam jars illuminated a whitewashed room that stank pleasantly of strong Northern tea. Someone had shoved cabinets, bookcases, and tables into every corner: too much furniture in too small a space. A living woman Teltö's age scribbled away at a desk on the far side. Of average build, she had strawberry-blonde hair and glasses.

"Teltö Phuul, welcome, I've been expecting you."

Teltö wished he could throw himself into the Nhagivat. Of all the people in all the Empire, it had to be her. "Tuvena," he said. "I suppose it's been a while…"

One ugly little bit of his past, back to haunt him. *Well, not entirely ugly.* Finding someone who enjoyed the seaside and swimming holes had been so sweet, and without her, he'd never have broadened his horizons beyond men. But she changed, and he didn't, and he'd never had a girl before, so didn't know how to react…

"Yes, Phuul, it has," said Tuvena Sytöphin. "Not long enough in my opinion, but clearly Inquisitor General Vöder has a sense of humour. Or perhaps she wants to keep Qivunakonians together. Something we can all be thankful for. Am I right?"

Dyrstin was almost bent double in silent laughter.

"You know, Teltö, when we were in school, I always imagined you failing the Examination." Tuvena left no knife unstabbed. "Afterwards, I often wondered whether you'd found someone to sit it for you."

"Utter Unut shit, and you know it."

"You did tell me you 'didn't want to be another Rhea'. Failing the Examination would've certainly been a point of difference, though I doubt your parents would've approved."

Teltö gritted his teeth. "I passed."

"Perhaps failing might have been for the best. You'd make a wonderful corpse, so useful and handsome. One of our receptionists even looks just like you. But no, you slaved and studied and scraped through, and got yourself all the way to the heady heights of underkarl."

"Enough," snapped Teltö. "Now about why we're here…"

Tuvena smiled. "I know why you're here. Something about attempted poisoning."

"Or perhaps thwarting an attack on the Imperial Theatre House, and saving your boss' life. There's precious little gratitude in you shadow-stalkers, isn't there?"

"The Theatre House investigation is continuing," said Tuvena. "But we are closing in on the Hova poisoner. We took the Grand Master-elect into custody this morning."

"What?!" said Teltö and Dyrstin in unison.

"Standard procedure, though Hova was in the embrace of the Mother when we found him…"

Teltö gripped the desk's edge. "You bastards. Hova was stable. Phytek said so."

Tuvena shooed him back. "She has been saying *many* things. But, yes, your master is dead, and the Wills Office will hunt down surviving relatives. Literally, knowing them. But for the Inquisition, the only question is who is responsible, and this is where you come in."

"Not me," muttered Dyrstin. "I wasn't even on the bloody ship."

"In your case, Venomavat," said Tuvena, considering a pencil, "it's that Asrak operation of yours. The stuff you distil is downright foul."

Now it was Teltö's turn to snigger. Dyrstin scowled. "Someone's been narking."

"Distillation of illegal liquor is serious," said Tuvena. "And you are unquestionably guilty. Poor Phuul here was just in the wrong place at the wrong time."

"Look, Tuvena," snapped Dyrstin, "if you are wanting…"

"I'm not wanting anything. I mean, were I Inquisitor General, I'd be far tougher, but watching you worms squirm provides its own satisfaction." She held up a couple of forms. "Please be so kind as to sign these."

"But these are confessions!" Teltö said, reading over the paper.

"Bright boy," said Tuvena. "No wonder you passed the Examination."

"But I'm innocent!" *Though since when did that matter?*

Tuvena sighed. "I can force you, if you like. The important thing is that you sign those documents. They won't be used, except at last resort. In return for our generosity in keeping your crimes out of the public arena, you and Venomavat are to become informants."

"Narks," said Dyrstin.

"Yes, narks. Your Aunt Alio will be so proud."

"So what do you mean by 'except at last resort'?" asked Teltö.

"Exactly what you think it means. Your confessions remain here, buried, until one of two things happens. The first is that you prove neglectful informers. We work hard here at the Inquisition, and do not tolerate laziness."

Dyrstin raised an eyebrow. "And the second thing?"

"If we are unable to locate those responsible, two ready-made confessions followed by two ready-made executions will be such a relief to Her Vigilance. Vyrellävek likes results."

Teltö gulped, and took the proffered pen. He was buying himself another day.

"Thank you, Phuul. Now you, Venomavat."

Biting his lip, Dyrstin signed. He tossed the quill onto the desk.

"Excellent," said Tuvena. "I shall want regular reports. No fewer than one a week. We all have to do our bit for the Empire, don't we?"

There was a knock on the door. Tuvena looked vaguely disappointed.

"Enter."

The door swung open, revealing a hunchbacked lich. Teltö and Dyrstin let it through. The corpse plopped a folder on Tuvena's desk, rotated on one foot like a macabre marionette, then silently trudged out.

"Have a word with your colleagues," said Teltö. "I'm all for utilitarian liches, but that borders on rudeness."

"Shut it, Phuul," said Tuvena, poring over the

contents of the folder. "Let's see…"

The petulance congealing around Tuvena's mouth would've cheered Teltö any day, but in the circumstances, it presaged good news when he needed it most. *It's the Theatre.*

Tuvena closed the folder, slid open a drawer, and dropped the documents inside. She looked like a cat deprived of its favourite mouse. *Not this time, Tuvena.*

She drew a deep breath. "An execution is in order. Hova's poisoner has been found."

Hold on. Teltö cocked his head. "Who?"

A terrible smile came to Tuvena's lips. "Why, the person who confessed to the crime. You don't think the Inquisition would arrange the execution of anyone innocent, do you?"

Teltö's pushed his hair back from his suddenly clammy forehead. "Who is it?" he heard himself ask.

"A certain Eriva Phytek, ship's physician on the *HIHS Naat*. She confessed late last night. Very late last night, if you take my meaning."

Teltö almost wanted to hug the vile bitch. *I live. The Dragon has his scapegoat.* Conscience mumbled something about Phytek being genial and innocent, but he swept the objections aside.

"So how does this affect me?"

"You are cordially invited to attend the public execution, at ten tomorrow morning. I understand Kuolinako's hours can be disconcerting, but please be there early: we need to sort the distribution of protective equipment."

"Um."

"I said you have been cordially invited," said Tuvena. "You do know what that means, my foolish little Phuul?"

I know what it means. "I'll be there," he mumbled.

"And you, Venomavat, are also invited."

"My pleasure," said Dyrstin. It sounded like he'd rather swallow Unut shit. He wasn't alone.

Tuvena leant back and stretched. The smile returned. "Venomavat, your confession is still current, so get to work on that report. Phuul, the Inquisition hasn't finished with you either. We've got another job for you."

"Which is?"

"Just the thing. As you may be aware, it is the five hundredth anniversary of the Nadir next month. To mark the occasion, His Excellency will journey north to meet Prince Oym."

Teltö nodded. "Letting bygones be bygones, I suppose." *With war reparations in the mix too, though I'm not supposed to know that.*

"Indeed. You will journey with him, passing on whatever you can gather about the political and military situation to our Skeevereet Embassy. I'll send your train tickets in a couple of days. Skeevereet via Mustanako: enjoy the scenery."

Teltö frowned. Clearly Inquisitorial favour carried its own dangers. He'd wanted a gift of a journey home, only to end up sent in the opposite direction.

"But why me? Why not one of your more experienced shadow-stalkers?"

"The official reasons or the real reasons?"

Spoken like a true Kuolinakonian, Tuvena. You have made yourself at home. "Both."

Tuvena sighed. "The Powers That Be have taken an interest in you, Phuul. Father Life alone knows why, but there were two separate memoranda in that folder, one internal and one from the Chancellor's Office. A minister like me is not going to question that sort of clout."

"That's not a reason."

"It is if you work at the Inquisition. I follow orders." *The Kuolinakonian Code.* "Now run along like good little informers, keep watch, and remember: we watch the watchers too." She picked up her hat, flicked off some fluff, and put it down on the 'outgoing mail' tray.

"One more thing, Phuul," she said. "Those boots. Your bootlaces are brown. Under current regulations they should be black. I'll have to confiscate them."

"What?"

"Rules are rules, Phuul. Believe me, it's been a *pleasure.*"

* * *

FILTHY AND SOMEHOW smelling of cat, the cab wobbled back to Hova's. Or the place that'd been Hova's, even though Hova never stayed there. It made Teltö's head hurt.

"Frying pans, fires," said Dyrstin.

Teltö rested his feet against the cab windows, and wriggled his bootless toes. His socks needed darning. "I still don't know why they'd choose me. Northerners tried blowing up the Theatre. Vöder will ensure every second person on the streets of Skeevereet is an Inquisitorial agent, so what use would I be?"

"Perhaps that's the point. Yuck. Is that fungus on the ceiling?"

Teltö squinted. "Make a complaint. Cabs like this are a health hazard."

"Yes, I'll make a complaint, and they'll get round to it next century, if I'm lucky."

"Never mind next century. I'm interested in next

week. You were saying?"

"As I was saying, the current agents will be so busy that extra eyes and ears might be useful. Or maybe the Inquisitor General thinks you're some super-talent for foiling those bombers. You did want to be in the thick of things. Well, here's your chance."

"Not like this. Not jerked around like an Imperial puppet." Teltö sighed. "But I suppose if we weren't puppets, we wouldn't be the Empire. Eight thousand years of obedience to the Nine Authors, and as if that weren't enough, our masters want to give us a remedial lesson tomorrow morning."

The cab halted. Teltö looked out the window as an elevator lifted them a level. "On the bright side, I've survived the Hova crisis. I'd just love to know what exactly the little Unut-turd was cooking up, and what Keer knows. It'd explain why the Dragon offed him."

"Assuming Vyrellävek was behind it," said Dyrstin. "Though that's looking likely. But thinking more about your Northern trip, you've several advantages for a mission like this."

"Like what? I've spent most of my life hiding from shadow-stalkers, not trying to be one."

Dyrstin counted off on his fingers. "You're male."

"Last time I checked anyway. How is that an advantage?"

"The Northerners have that weird patriarchal barbarism. You'd find it much easier to walk around Ilmanako than Tuvena."

"You mean Skeevereet. We lost the war, we lost the right to name the place. Unless you're agitating for a Fifth Northern War?"

"Of course not." Everything looked grey in the dim

light, but Teltö suspected a flush of colour was coming to those pale cheeks. "I'm not a fool."

"I am." *Haha.* "So what are the other reasons?"

"You don't know anything."

"Thank you, Dyrstin. Very profound."

"No, seriously. Necromancy's a capital offence in the Principality, so power isn't important, and you don't know anything about the Inquisition's normal activities north of the Wall, so you can't reveal much if you get caught. You're expendable."

"Tact is such a strong point of yours, isn't it? But this also applies to you. Why not send you instead? Or better yet, why not send us both, so there'll be two extra lots of ears and eyes?"

Dyrstin chuckled. "I've still got Keer, whereas you're free now Hova's carked it. Your late superior won't object to Vöder taking you off his hands for use as an Imperial plaything."

This smug blond bastard needed taken down a peg or three. "I think there's another reason."

"Oh yes?"

"They'll want someone who can do more in Skeevereet than pick up exotic venereal diseases."

"Not funny," said Dyrstin.

"Not funny, yet entirely true, Venomavat."

•   •   •

THE TALE OF Hova's poisoning had spread, fanned by those who saw links with the Theatre. Passing a newsagents, Teltö noticed the *Doomsday Post* trumpeting Phytek's alleged Northern connections. Now a crowd gathered on the filth-strewn cobblestones, and the Inquisition had supplied several wagons' worth of protective equipment. *Never underestimate the number of ghouls and jackals in Kuolinako.*

Teltö squeezed on the gloves, wincing as leather scraped the back of his hand. With gas-mask and cloak, he'd become just another figure waiting for this morning's executions. But if he now looked like everyone else, why did he feel so self-conscious?

"Next," said the lich at the equipment wagon. Teltö moved off to the side.

A hulking wall of rock loomed over him, flat and smooth as glass. Engraved with hieroglyphics and signs of which none now knew the meaning, massive bronze doors were set into it. The doors were closed and locked.

"You know," Teltö whispered to the figure beside him, identical in all ways save height, "I wouldn't mind burying my head under a pillow. Executions still remind me of…"

"Understandable."

"I once overheard Hova saying the Death Pool should be phased out. Since it isn't mentioned in the Nine Authors, the Empire didn't need it."

"Perhaps it's a Qivunakonian thing: we don't have millennia of melting people behind us. Though this is the last Death Pool: industry's got its claws on the others. Keer can remember when there were five in operation. Speaking of Keer, I asked him about Hova last night."

"What happened?"

"I swear, the old geezer turned purple. I half expected steam to come out his ears. Let's say I beat a hasty retreat."

Teltö elbowed his friend. "Here they come."

From the gates of the Tower they came, black cloaked and blue sashed, elite Inquisitors ready to do justice on the enemies of the Empire. Led by a solitary lich bearing gong and mallet, the eight rows of three looked neither left nor right. The crowd receded to let them through. Then came a litter borne by six liches, empty save for a silver tiara atop a cushion. *The Imperial Crown, taken from Gykäkkä fifteen centuries ago.* Teltö had imagined a grandiose thing encrusted with precious stones, but this had a simple conical design and only a single ruby set into the front. *How many poor bastards down the years have been tasked with polishing that?*

Following the litter marched eight more rows of Inquisitors, masked and sashed, boots thudding in time like the ticking of some grotesque clock. At the rear, a single lich clutched a yellowed scroll. The procession halted before the doors, and the leading corpse sounded the gong, a single note ringing through the tunnels. The front row stepped forward and turned. Teltö wondered if Vöder stood in the centre. *You can't recognise anyone in this gear.*

The three Inquisitors approached the doors. One inserted an ornate key into the lock, while the others laid gloved hands upon the brass rings. The mallet struck once more, and the doors swung silently open. Footsteps beating a steady tattoo, the procession moved forward, disappearing row by row into the maw of the chamber. The spectators surged along in the Inquisitors' wake, their own feet an irregular patter against stone.

Here lay the Death Pool, an elliptical lake half a furlong across. Murky waters lapped at the shoreline, and vapours hung above, mitigated only by ancient ventilation. Teltö stood back, thankful for the gas-mask. The cavern resembled a cone; the torch-lit walls curved and sloped towards a point lost somewhere in the overhead darkness.

Two score and eight, the Inquisitors congregated at the edge. The silver-and-ruby tiara gleamed in the torchlight, as it must have done in the days of those cruel and ingenious bastards who first used this place to punish enemies. *How many have died here? The mighty and the low: all forgotten.* The blue-sashed figures bowed, turned to face the lake, and bowed again. *No, not facing. They're faceless, more alien than the Mnomo.*

The scroll-bearer shuffled forward. It unfurled the parchment and read aloud the confessions of those about to die. Teltö frowned. *That corpse is breathing the vapours. That'll eat its lungs in no time.* High necromancy could briefly stop the breathing reflex in reanimated dead, but this corpse drew breath beside the acid itself. Still, plenty more where that came from.

Another mallet blow. Everything and everyone waited.

Scraping, as of rusty chains, came from above. Teltö lifted his head but saw nothing. The screeching grew louder, until finally, a cage descended into the lit area. Iron bars grinned like teeth; and inside were prisoners, bound hand and foot and equipped with gas masks. *They don't want them dying of fumes before their swim.* The prisoners must have been gagged too: there were no screams, even as they threw themselves against the bars.

The cage halted a mere centifurlong above the lake. Teltö tried to recall Phytek's face. Then the gong sounded one final time. A trapdoor opened, and the prisoners fell into the sulphuric waters. No screams, only brief splashes. Teltö couldn't look away. He'd always known of the Pool's existence, but he'd never imagined it like this. *The gulf between knowing and seeing.* At last the ripples subsided.

The scroll-bearer stumbled towards the lake. The

strain on the dead sinews was reaching breaking point. *No good to anybody now.* With one final look at the Crown, it splashed into the shallows. *Shit.* Teltö knew the dead felt no pain, but the sight of the swift-working acid nauseated him.

Still emitting its metallic whine, the cage vanished back into the darkness. The Inquisitors trooped out, followed by the gong-carrier, and the litter-bearers with the precious tiara. Teltö did not remember leaving.

The Inquisitors slammed the doors, shutting the lake in with its secrets. The crowd dispersed like smoke before a wind. But not so Teltö. He stood numb and masked beneath Kuolinako's street lamps, out of place and unmoving. Like beached driftwood at low tide, or some toy soldier left out of its box. He blinked, aware only of his own breathing...

Next he knew, someone was shaking him. Dyrstin's pale face stared down, fair hair free and unusually unruly, and eyes full of concern.

"Take that horrible stuff off and let's go."

Teltö glanced up at the bronze doors, unchanged and ancient, and thought of the prisoners dissolving behind them. They'd got a public death, but disappearances happened all the time: those who simply vanished, as though their lives never were.

Later, walking the shadowed streets in search of a cab, Dyrstin tapped him on the shoulder.

"See the punishment for leaking?"

Teltö shuddered and kept walking.

Chapter Seven

*H*E IS ABOVE *the Death Pool in a cage of his own, unable to scream while faceless figures in black hurl him into a bubbling sulphuric grave. As he falls, he churns his head from side to side, desperate to voice his horror…*

Teltö opened his eyes, and saw only darkness. *Bloody Kuolinako.* The sights and sounds of execution still plagued him; not even abandoning his pursuit of Hova and Keer settled his mind. *I'll be a good little underkarl, I swear.* He'd do exactly as he was told, keep his head down, and with Father Life on his side, he'd make it home intact. Dyrstin was right. Initiative got you killed.

He rolled onto his back, yawning and stretching beneath the smooth sheets. Leaving bed at the whim of a bureaucrat seemed a crime. Just as it'd be a crime to cut up these sheets for black market silk handkerchiefs. *A shame I need the extra coinage.* Teltö fumbled for the gas-lamp, and shoved the decanter aside. The clock read ten to eleven. He flopped back among the pillows in procrastinatory disgust.

The tyranny of time finally forced him up. Once clad

in clean shirt and green cravat, Teltö combed his hair. There was no time to shave.

Downstairs, the liberated liches cleared away dishes. Teltö eyed them nervously. He grabbed Oilio's lantern and his informant report, and hurried out for a cab. First destination, Kuolinako's Undersecretariat.

• • •

RECEPTION WAS BIGGER, noisier, and more disturbing than Qivunako. A long room with a sloping timbered ceiling, it sported an oil portrait of Vyrellävek at one end and a wire cross-hatch at the other, with queues in-between. The cross-hatch segregated the lich officials from the lines of the living, while rows of barbed wire kept the queues orderly. Some of the barbs flaked with dried blood.

One by one, people dealt with the officials, then vanished through one of three exits. The Grand Council employed no designated Undersecretary, but rather a host of generic drudges slaving away for an abstraction. One lich sharpened pencils, another popped envelopes into pigeonholes. *The quick queues of skeleton government. At least there's no doppelgängers.*

The hitherto unthinkable crept into Teltö's brain: he missed Alio Venomavat. For all her beige wallpaper and feline friends, for all that she'd dropped him into this, the Qivunakonian Undersecretary was at least human. Mechanical and inhuman, shorn even of the cosy odours of decay, Kuolinako's Undersecretariat was dead as those who staffed it. *Who runs the Empire: the living or the dead? Vyrellävek or that lich over there, stamping that document?*

Teltö plonked his report on the service-bench. With Phytek blamed for Hova and himself reassigned, he wasn't sure he needed to submit a report, but he'd played safe anyway. He'd even spiced it with allegations of Hova's predecessor defrauding the Mint. Not that Teltö cared whether the fellow had stolen anything, but dredging up retired Grand Masters as Examples amused him. *I wonder whether I've earned a sending home.* Perhaps he was just furthering Tuvena's career. He'd find out soon.

"Your master's papers, Phuul," said one helpful lich, handing him a wad of reports.

Teltö thinned his lips. "My master is dead."

The corpse's chin rose and fell. "Yes."

"Yet I'm still to attend today's Council meeting in my capacity as Native Assistant?"

Once more, the dead head jerked up and down like a drunken puppet. Knowing some high-ranking Necromancers, it might well be. "Yes."

"May I ask why?"

"Yes."

Teltö gripped the wire crosshatch. "Well, why?"

No answer.

"You said I could ask!"

"I said you may ask. That is all."

Teltö walked away with whitening knuckles. He drew a deep breath and skimmed the papers. *Too many pages and I need a magnifying glass.* A nearby grandfather clock neared twenty minutes to noon. He still had time.

•   •   •

THE DRAGON WILL be there, Teltö mused on the cab ride. He studied Oilio's map by lantern. The Grand Council Chambers were situated in a grandiose park two levels from the base of the Tower. *I've been here too long. I'm starting to think like a Kuolinakonian.* The vehicle shuddered to a halt, and he stuffed the map back into his trouser pocket.

Outside, a dark forest stretched into the distance, pockmarked by the quiet glow of hidden lamps.

A gravel walkway ran into the heart of the vegetation. He followed it. The place was an otherworld of blacks and browns, with bursts of green and yellow closer to the lights. Teltö ducked under the overhanging branch of a night pine, the needles like shaggy fur in the gloom. Pushing his own hair back, he pressed on. Modified millennia ago for life without the Sun – the lost science of chemosynthetic conversion, Rhea once called it – thorns and undergrowth spread over strange and twisted rocks. Rata and silver birches kept them company. Still and silent, a pond loomed to his left. Teltö looked no closer.

Housed within a massive marble pyramid, half a furlong on every side, the Grand Council Chambers towered over their wooded confines. Centuries of ivy besieged its walls. Teltö followed the path around. He found an iron door embedded into each side; well-tended specimens of deadly nightshade cast lethal silhouettes upon the gates. The deadly berries hung juicy and innocent in the lamplight. A chill crept through Teltö. *The fruits of Mother Death.*

He approached one of the doors, and held up the lantern for a closer look. Faded hieroglyphics encircled the central brass ring. Cold and ancient. The door creaked open to reveal a narrow path into the heart of the pyramid. Clutching the Council papers like a shield, Teltö entered. He wished someone else were here, even Hova.

The way ended with a lamplit junction. Oak-panelled, another passage ran perpendicular to the first. Shuttering his lantern, Teltö scratched his head. Going left, a further passage branched off to the right. He kept walking, the lamps leading him on, his only companion his own wandering thoughts. *It's never truly dark in Kuolinako. There's shadows, but never night. The stars are as alien as the Sun.* Left sprouted a walkway leading to an exit door, and straight ahead yet another corridor opened on his right.

He soon found it difficult to remember which door he'd originally entered. He stopped and leant against a panelled wall, cursing. Bugger it. He'd wait.

Teltö was idly kicking his boot heels when he heard a door close.

"Hello?" His voice echoed. *Hello…hello…hello…*

"Who is that?" came the reply.

"Teltö Phuul, Native Assistant to Grand Master-elect Hova."

"Hova's dead."

"Yes, but I'm not."

"More's the pity."

Teltö wasn't about to provoke some unknown Kuolinakonian. "Where are you?"

"Here," came the reply. In a lower voice it muttered. "Come on, cretin. How hard is it to find a key?"

"Can you wait for me?" Teltö strode briskly towards the voice. "Grand Master?"

"Find your own way in, you silly little Unut."

Teltö ran. Too late: he arrived to find another empty corridor. *Bugger.* But a key meant a keyhole, and a keyhole meant a door.

"You're not supposed to be here, you know."

Teltö jumped. *Don't creep up on me.* He turned to find a dark-complexioned woman wearing a white ribbon, a yellow cravat and a prim expression. Undisguised wrinkles danced around her mouth and eyes; tied back in a severe bun, her hair held more salt than pepper. *With that face, it's more salt and vinegar.* A female Grand Master from

Mustanako: Suphives Sösta, Warden of the Imperial Mint, and the Dragon's pet miser.

The woman studied him with the tired and dusty expression of a neglected museum exhibit.

"Um," he said. *Nice deferential start.* "Sorry, Grand Master. My name is Teltö Phuul, and I appear to be lost…"

"I can see that. Qivunako is many a gross-furlong that way, lad."

"No, sorry, I meant I am Native Assistant to Grand Master-elect Hova. I'm to attend the Council meeting…"

A pause. For a moment, Teltö feared she thought him a collaborator in Hova's schemes. But he need not have worried. As the hint of a chuckle passed those austere lips, the lines on the woman's face rippled and rearranged in strange ways. *Like dropping stones in a puddle.*

"Quite the pickle," said Sösta. "You, a Native Assistant without a master, and I, a master without a Native Assistant. My poor Tyrtini came down with Black Spot last night and cannot leave his bed."

The Grand Master waved down his reaction. "No fear, he will recover. My physicians caught it in time. I will, of course, deduct the cost of his care from his wages: his sickness was none of my doing, and I warned him to stay off the streets." She lowered her voice. "You would not believe the difficulty in functioning without a Native Assistant."

Teltö held his tongue. Grand Master Sösta smiled, setting off the wrinkles again.

"We had best go in. No point dallying around where we might catch something." She pulled a key-ring from her handbag. "Like jingoism."

The Mustanakonian grasped the lamp beside Teltö's

head. *Click.* A keyhole appeared. *So that's it. But where are Hova's keys? Nobody mentioned this to me.* Sösta selected a key, and inserted it. A twist, a push, and a secret door opened.

In making the inner chamber a perfect hexagon, the Empire's ancient engineers had been accurate to the minutest microfurlong. A large table and a dozen high-backed chairs stood in the centre; a chandelier hung from the ceiling. Five of the walls displayed faded banners. The emblems of the Four Cities: Kuolinako's lancewood, Qivunako's mountain daisy, Tuonako's rock lily, and Mustanako's pohutukawa. Above the entrance, the Imperial banner hung as it had for five hundred years: sable, four eight-pointed stars argent. The bare sixth wall frowned over the room, its absence of adornment incongruous.

A man as blond as he was rotund sat beneath the lancewood. *Dyrstin in thirty years if he doesn't lay off those cakes.* The blue-scarfed Grand Master leafed through his papers making notes, white-ribboned hat at his elbow. Teltö hated to think how much this fellow spent on black market food. Set in a face well-supplied with bushy facial hair, green eyes shone keen and intelligent.

"Greetings, Sösta," he said. Behind him stood a dark young man with a black ribbon and thin features. His Native Assistant.

Sösta inclined her head. "Yyrtön," she said. "You're here early."

Yyrtön smiled. "I'm never early. Or late. Punctuality has gone to pot for too long."

He peered at Teltö's cravat. "Is that the Qivunakonian nincompoop I heard blundering around earlier? You should've left him. Would've taught him decorum."

Sösta shuffled her papers. "Now, now. Everyone blunders in Kuolinako. The newcomers because of your blasted tunnels, and the natives because they're natural blunderers."

"I seem to recall us blundering into your city a couple of centuries ago."

"Calm down, Yyrtön. Else I shall tax cinnamon pastries, and you won't have two bits to rub together."

Yyrtön opened his mouth to reply, only to seemingly think better of it. He returned to annotating papers.

Teltö sheltered behind an empty chair. Bored already, he appraised Yyrtön's Native Assistant. The face disappointed, but the shoulders and chest... *If only he stood up straight, and spent some time in the Sun.* The fellow did not return eye contact. *Oh, I forgot. I'm a yokel with Unut shit under my nails.* Teltö checked his fingers. *Look, it's not Unut shit.*

Two further figures stepped into the room, one a forgettable girl with a red ribbon, watery eyes and freckles, but the other...

Lush dark ringlets streaming past her shoulders, Grand Master Pliil possessed power and beauty, and walked like she knew it. Young for a Grand Master and curvaceous without sliding into Yyrtönian spread, the new arrival modelled a necklace of glittering sapphires. On the Mustanako side, Sösta's wrinkles contorted in a moralising sneer.

The Tuonakonian contingent arrived as a group. *Almost like a family.* Short, with a well-clipped grey beard and a bulbous bald head, Rumi could've been mistaken for one of Keer's favourite onions. Phermö, bespectacled beneath tightly-curled white hair, wore a knitted cardigan and carried a handbag. She smiled at Teltö, who returned the smile with lashings of fake sincerity. He knew the type:

little old ladies so sweet they rotted your teeth, but this was the Grand Council. *What games are you playing, dearie?*

Close behind came another man, his head so devoid of hair it resembled a cue ball with eyebrows. He wore a thin yellow cravat. *Meerm of Mustanako.* Meerm slapped his papers down with such vehemence he set the table wobbling. Watching an inkpot teeter whilst doing nothing to stabilise it, Sösta gave her colleague a chilly nod.

Finally, Dyrstin wheeled in Keer's bath chair. The old man's head slumped on his chest, his spectacles slipping off his nose. Teltö looked at his friend. *Is he asleep?* Venomavat winked.

The seven living Grand Masters seated, the table buzzed with gossip. Everyone had a health complaint or was missing so-and-so's dinner party. The Native Assistants stood silent as corpses. Dyrstin seemed to lapse into extended daydreams. *He's probably thinking about food. Or sex. Or both. Anything but this bloody meeting.* Teltö did his best to remain impassive, not easily: Hova's empty seat drew attention like a magnet.

Peta Vyrellävek entered. From shining black boots to shaggy grey head, the Chancellor had not changed a bit. *Still holding the Empire in his hand, from Yyti's Wall to the southern tundra. He'd wrap his clammy grip around the world if he could.* In the Dragon's wake trod three liches. *Breakfast, lunch, and dinner,* mused Teltö, recalling what mythical dragons ate. Breakfast held Vyrellävek's tall blue-ribboned hat, while Lunch gripped a crystal goblet and a half-full silver decanter. Dinner shut the door, and hobbled over to the table. The corpse pulled out a three-legged stool, and sat with its quill poised like a dagger. *The minute secretary.*

The Grand Chancellor placed the goblet directly beneath the chandelier. He bowed, then poured liquid from the decanter. The water, if it was water, reflected the light, and an eldritch glow spread through the crystal.

Vyrellävek inclined his head. "Father Life and Mother Death," he intoned, "may thy eternal wisdom shine upon this meeting, and preserve the life and health of His Imperial Highness Emperor Gykäkkä IV, long may he reign."

"Long may he reign," muttered the Grand Masters without irony. Teltö wondered if Gykäkkä's deformed brain could have grasped the humour of his perverse immortality. *Dead for fifteen centuries, yet still on our coins, and the Council that murdered him still prays for his health. The daft things you accept as natural until you stare them in the face.*

Vyrellävek returned the decanter to Lunch, and settled beneath the Imperial banner. He wore a carnivorous smile.

"I declare this Grand Council meeting open."

Dinner's quill stabbed at the ink, moving fiendishly fast across the paper. *Faster than any living hand.* The Dragon's eyes dwelt on Hova's empty chair.

"I take it we have no apologies, so moving along … the minutes of the previous meeting."

"One thing." Yyrtön raised his quill. "There is a reference here to Skeevereet. Should that not be Ilmanako… Never mind, I'll talk about it later."

"Thank you, Grand Master," said Vyrellävek. "Now onto the first order of business, the tragic demise of our friend and colleague, Hyät Hova of Qivunako."

"Tragic indeed," interjected Phermö.

"You will have all read Her Vigilance's report," continued the Grand Chancellor. "The finest and sharpest minds in the Inquisition questioned the culprit, with confession and execution following. Punishment oils the machinery of order, as the Nine Authors state, and thus the Empire is cleansed."

"May I propose a vote of thanks to the Inquisitor General?" said Phermö.

"You may," said Vyrellävek. "Seconders?"

"Seconded."

"Söstä seconding. Further discussion? No? All those in favour…"

Ayes hummed gently around the room. *Is Keer voting or snoring?*

"Motion carried," said the Grand Chancellor. "I am sure this recognition of her sterling efforts will warm the heart of Her Vigilance."

"But what of the Theatre bombing?" said Meerm. "Have those perpetrators been caught?"

Vyrellävek's eyebrows lifted. Teltö looked on, partly with the vicarious thrill of watching the Dragon deal with a challenger, and partly with relief. He wasn't the one in the spotlight.

"The Inquisition hunts as we speak. With my personal assistance, I might add."

"They should hunt north," said Meerm. "It's about time we noticed the dagger at our heart."

"There are many enemies to the north," said the Chancellor. Teltö's ears pricked up. "I am sure inquiries will reflect that."

"You mean the Inquisition will turn the tongs on the Principality?" said Meerm, unable to grasp the veiled threat. The Native Assistants exchanged glances. *Look at a bloody map, Meerm. The Principality isn't the only place north of Kuolinako.*

"The Inquisition will do whatever it must. We have had problems in the north before, I believe." *He's talking the*

Mutiny, not the Nadir, you idiot.

"So you still intend to meet Prince Oym?"

Perhaps Grand Masters were more complacent than underkarls. Or perhaps the Mustanakonian thought everyone shared his bellicosity. Either way, Teltö wanted to leap over the table and beat Meerm with his own Council papers.

"Yes, Grand Master, I am. He needs our friendship as we need his."

"But even leaving aside the expense of the journey, and I note Mustanako taxes are once again paying for this, consider the safety. Ten marks says the bombers were in the pay of the Northern Army. That lad over there even saw them at it. You over there…" Meerm waved at Teltö, "they were Northern scum, weren't they?"

The entire room turned on Teltö, who backed into the marble wall. Cold and smooth, the wall lacked so much as a crack.

"Um." Teltö drew a deep breath, and pushed his hair back. "I'm not sure. They didn't really say. They did have dungarees and bowler hats…" *Remind me to do something horrible to Meerm's portrait.*

"Thank you, Phuul," said the Dragon. Teltö relaxed. "The Inquisition continues its efforts, and I for one await the outcome with interest. I have had numerous conversations with Her Vigilance – I am taking an active role in proceedings – and thus far available evidence points to disaffected *domestic* groups." Vyrellävek smiled. "Does that satisfy, Grand Master?"

"Indeed it does, Your Excellency."

Teltö shook his head. *Söstä must be using the Mustanakonian brain quota today.*

"Good," said Vyrellävek. "Moving onto the next item,

the impending anniversary of the Nadir, or as our Northern brethren call it, the Founding. As we discussed last month, I shall be seeking Prince Oym's forgiveness for our outstanding debt arising from the Fourth Northern War. This shall cement positive relations between Skeevereet and Kuolinako."

"Excellent," said Phermö.

"Thank you, Grand Master," said Vyrellävek. "The prospect of our beloved Empire being rescued from this terrible burden fills my heart with joy. While our nation has shown great fortitude – indeed we have now gone twenty-five years without missing a single reparation payment – the demands of rationing have taken their toll on us all."

The Council nodded approval. Yyrtön's chins quivered as he agreed how hard it was to live beneath the tyranny of the dockets.

"But we need a plan if the Prince does not forgive the debt," said Rumi. His accent was weaker than Vyrellävek's, but his voice deeper.

"And your proposal?" asked Vyrellävek.

"If the reparations do not end," said Rumi, "our people will suffer. I say we lighten the load by reducing the fraction of silver in the mark."

"That," said the Dragon, "is a matter for our Warden of the Imperial Mint. Grand Master?"

Sösta visibly squirmed. "I believe it would be more prudent if we all sought to live within our means." She wrinkled her nose at Pliil's necklace, or at least wrinkled her wrinkles.

"Tell that to children who hunger because our wealth goes on reparations," said Rumi. "Reparations for a war that ended before either they or their parents were born."

"Grand Master," said Söstä, "while I sympathise, the Mint is in a long-running struggle with what my staff affectionately name Copper Pirates."

The Dragon nodded. "Please elaborate, Grand Master."

"Criminal elements, who melt down bits for copper, sell the metal for marks, then exchange the marks for bits. Our steady debasement of the bit simply cannot compete with the ever-rising price of copper, and devaluing the mark would make the disappearing bit problem substantially worse."

"Then we drop the ratio of one hundred and thirteen bits to the mark."

Several Grand Masters sat up sharply. *The Dragon had better watch this one.*

Söstä shook her head. "The ratio is set by the Nine Authors. We do not have the authority."

"A hundred and thirteen bits to the mark is what made the Empire great," said Meerm.

Keer's eggshell-thin voice piped up. "It has always been one hundred and thirteen bits to the mark. When I was a lad, it was one hundred and thirteen bits to the mark..."

"Thank you, Kortek," said Rumi, "but returning to the question of authority. Fifteen hundred years ago, the Grand Council walled up the Emperor himself..."

"No," said Vyrellävek, quietly. "I thank you for your contribution, Grand Master." *And watch out for poison in your porridge.* "But there will be no devaluation. Skeevereet would not take kindly to payments in debased marks, and we cannot jeopardise our good relationship."

"I say we don't pay them any marks, debased or otherwise," said Pliil. Her voice lacked the allure of her figure. "Half a century of tribute is quite enough. If Oym is really our friend…"

"The Prince is our friend," said Vyrellävek. "But if we default on our debt, the war drums will beat, and Oym will fall. It is not our interest to provoke a Fifth Northern War."

Pliil whispered something into Yyrtön's ear. The fat man chuckled.

"Has the Dragon lost his teeth?" Yyrtön leant forward. "Is the Grand Chancellor so full of fear, so timid and terrified, that he asks our people to submit to yet more generations of servitude? An honest war may be better than an oppressive peace, and if it falls to me to say what everyone else is thinking, so be it."

Teltö blinked. *Did he just say that?* Dyrstin's own eyes had widened. Söstä had gone pale, Rumi's mouth hung open. Pliil merely sat smirking like a contented cat.

"Treason!" coughed Keer.

"Apologise immediately!" Phermö looked at Vyrellävek. "You cannot let this stand, Your Excellency."

The Dragon rose to his feet. He leant across the table, hands spread like pale spiders. "With respect, Grand Masters," he said, soft and chill. "Some here need to remember their role. The Grand Council serves the Empire, and the Viiminian Empire serves no less than the Father and Mother Eternal. Our mission is sacred, and the disunity that arises from self-important questioning of traditional virtues and traditional authority," his gaze fell upon Yyrtön and Rumi, "cannot help but lead to bloodshed and anarchy. The Empire is immortal, but we are not. All we can do is follow the path laid before us, nipping war and rebellion in the bud. There are enemies out there, always, who would thwart us, but whether they lurk in alleyways or in this very room, they shall be found. And punished. Do you take my meaning, Grand Master?"

"Yes." Yyrtön's chins flushed. "I apologise."

Vyrellävek resumed his seat. "But I digress. I believe it likely Prince Oym will see reason. So unless there are further facets people wish to discuss, we shall now turn to the next agenda item. Mustanakonian import quotas…"

"Far too lax," said Meerm. "If Kuolinako helped its loyal friends in Mustanako, rather than currying favour with the Principality, the Empire would be far healthier."

"Thank you, Grand Master. If I might be permitted to continue…"

For the next two hours, Teltö half-hoped Yyrtön or Meerm would say something else outlandish, if only to break the monotony. They didn't. Meerm jabbed the occasional parochial barb, but Yyrtön kept his eyes glued to his papers. Teltö's legs grew stiff, and it became difficult to suppress yawns as he urged his pocket watch to speed up. Dyrstin stared into space with no more life than a statue.

It finally ended. The Chancellor stood and thanked the Grand Masters, and, making a last ceremonial bow, removed the goblet without spilling a drop. He led the way out, followed by his dead attendants. The remaining Councillors gathered their belongings. Yyrtön scratched his belly.

*   *   *

"HOW DID YOU enjoy the meeting?" asked Dyrstin, as they walked back through the lush vegetation. He gently manoeuvred the bath chair over the gravel. Keer snored within.

"Apart from Yyrtön filling out his own arrest

warrant… long, dull, and dry as a desert." Teltö adjusted his grip on the lanterns. "I wish my predecessor had left something about those bloody things."

"Did she write anything for you?"

"Not a bloody sausage. She ran away from Kuolinako fast as she could. Lucky bitch."

"Ah," said Dyrstin. "There's a story behind that. You see, we were together for a bit. Not one of my more amicable break-ups, I'm afraid."

Teltö contemplated the blades of a passing lancewood. "Father Life, it's good to walk again. Are all meetings like that?"

Dyrstin chuckled. "More fight this time. Yyrtön's got guts, both figuratively and literally. He's whined and thundered before, but never so explicit, and never to the Dragon's face."

"A midnight visit in his future then?"

"Father Life, no. Too stupid to be a threat."

Teltö nodded. "And the moment the Dragon showed his teeth, they all rolled over anyway."

"What did you expect? The man's been Grand Chancellor for a quarter of a century. He knows how to run his Grand Council, and he never, ever makes idle threats."

"I still think those bombers were Northerners," said Teltö. "I just wasn't going to back that pillock Meerm in front of the Dragon."

Dyrstin shrugged. "The Inquisition does what the Inquisition does. It's not like we mere underkarls can question them. You'll be pleased to know I got my first report in."

"How did it go?"

"I reported that Yyrtön was fat. Imagine how much

time they'll spend pouring over that."

Or how much time you'll spend with the Tower's knives. Did you learn nothing from the Death Pool? "Better hope it doesn't come back to bite you."

"Good point. If anyone can come back to bite you, it's Yyrtön. Just ask the pastries."

In spite of himself, Teltö grinned. They sniggered their way along the path.

Chapter Eight

A COAGULATED MASS of black bricks, the Kuolinako Central Railway Station could have been carved from a single, gigantic chunk of coal. Situated below a translucent dome on the topmost level of the underground city, its bulk stretched beside the trains and the tracks like a fireside cat, the modifications of millennia spiking from its roof and sides. Still readjusting to natural light – as natural as light ever got in Kuolinako – Teltö squinted up at the bizarre building, a conglomeration of forgotten architectural crazes. The Railway Station simply engulfed additions into its sooty form, and no matter the effort put into bringing colour to the structure, no matter how inventive the fevered imaginations of drugged Mnoman artists, every green turret and every white archway had long ago darkened to drab and camouflaged grey. But it'd never stopped the dreamers from trying.

A clock tower thrust out from the Station like a coal miner's thumb; shading his eyes, Teltö noted it was two minutes to eleven.

"Enjoy the North," said Dyrstin. "And make sure you

come back alive."

"I'll be back: you have my word."

Other travellers bustled around, packing the platform with noise and aromas. A green ribboned woman wagged a finger at children; behind her, a lich servant carried twin suitcases. Mnoma nattered, and someone was selling roasted chestnuts in small paper bags. In the shadow of the Station, dead newspaper salesmen trumpeted the *Post's* Nadir Anniversary special edition; Teltö bought a copy to read on the journey.

"How long are you stopping off in Mustanako?"

"Two days: the Dragon wants to attend a function." Vyrellävek and his menagerie of officials and guards had left by an earlier train. "Then it's across the border and on to Skeevereet."

The train's whistle shrieked.

"Final boarding for the Eleventy Three to Mustanako."

Teltö shook his friend's hand. "I'd best be going. See you in a month. And sorry for getting you in trouble with Keer."

Dyrstin smiled sadly. "Don't mention it, Teltö." He turned and walked back towards the Station exit. Within moments, he was gone.

Teltö checked his ticket against the massive white 113, and climbed aboard carefully: his suitcase was threatening to explode, and the satchel's strap was broken.

"Fourth Class, sir," said the corpse conductor. "That way."

Teltö eased past bodies, living and dead, in search of the relevant compartment. *Damn cheap Inquisition. Torturers must watch expenses, but Necromancers should travel at least Third Class. We always travelled Third to Dyrtölä. Now I'll be stuck with*

Ordinaries and liches the whole way.

He found his place in the final wagon – a small compartment with a bare floor and two rug-covered benches. *Empty.* Teltö smiled. Far from suffering the prods of Ordinary children, the squeaks of Mnomo, or the glare of a corpse belonging to some show-off in Second Class, peace and quiet beckoned. Just him and the newspaper all the way to Mustanako.

Teltö heaved his suitcase onto the luggage rack. After dumping the satchel and newspaper onto the seat beside, he wriggled back into the soft Unut-fur rug and closed his eyes. The locomotive's whistle wailed once more, and with a motherly chug, the train shuddered into life. He started to doze amid the soothing rattles of the 113.

He heard the compartment door slide open. Teltö opened his lids.

"Oh, hello," said a young woman of nut-brown complexion. With an unbuttoned tweed jacket over a striped shirt, the woman's garb concealed a body that invited a closer look. The bottle-green skirt reached to her ankles. *No ribbon. No Guild ring. An Ordinary.*

The woman stuffed a suitcase and several smaller bags onto the rack. "I wasn't expecting a Necro. The other compartment was full, so I snuck in here. Aren't your types supposed to travel better than Fourth?"

"Long story. My name's Teltö."

"Sufael." She sat opposite. "What takes you to Mustanako?"

"I'm just stopping there briefly. I'm really heading to the Principality. Skeevereet."

"That's a happy coincidence. I work for Mustanako Fisheries and I've been down to discuss new regulations. But I'm from Skeevereet originally. I'm going back to see family.”

“Ah.”

“No need to blush. Northerners are people too, you know, no matter what the *Post* says.”

“Nothing against the Principality, at all...” He obscured the newspaper with the satchel.

The woman laughed. Rich and rolling, the sound reminded Teltö of the sea. “Let me guess: some of your best friends are from the North. No, don’t worry. I’m just pleased to get out of Kuolinako. It gets tiresome pretending to be Mustanakonian. Having to spell my name with a ph feels wrong.”

You’re not the only one pleased to leave. “I’m a Qivunakonian myself.”

“Yes, I noticed the cravat.”

The train entered a tunnel. Night descended, leaving only the rumble of the tracks.

“So,” said the voice in the darkness, “what brings a Qivunakonian to Skeevereet? That’s an awfully long journey.”

“Getting heatstroke is my lifelong ambition.”

Sufael chuckled. “The heat’s not that bad. Just don’t overdose on coffee during cloudless summer days. But really, I’m curious. I’ve never been to Qivunako, though I’d like to go at some point.”

The train climbed an incline.

“I’m on Lesser Council business.”

“Commercial or political?”

“Commercial. I’m investigating the Northern market for Qivunakonian iron.” With Teltö’s father working in the industry, it sounded safe and generic.

“You’re twenty years too late. The North doesn’t need iron. It’s copper we’re after.”

The tunnel spat them out onto the surface, and full daylight flooded the compartment. Teltö rubbed his eyes, and peered out at a sky tinged with the legacy of Kuolinako's chimneys. The train traversed the northerly part of the Mää Wastes, where tree stumps and tussock dotted dusty hills.

"The sky again!" Sufael slung her elbow on the compartment windowsill. *Like a drunk at a pub.* "Kuolinako has a horrible way of making sunlight seem just a dream. Too long in those depths and you forget there's a world outside."

"Some spend their lives down there. For them, the Sun's as alien as the ocean floor."

"Yes, and it's not healthy. You should move the Capital to Mustanako. It's where the people are, and you get light and fresh sea air."

"We can't." Teltö frowned. Even the Mutineers only wanted independence; they didn't want the regalia of central government to follow them.

"Why not?" asked Sufael, a mischievous smile upon her lips.

Teltö shrugged. "Kuolinako's the heart of the Empire, and always will be. It's laid down since ancient times."

"You adjusted from Five Cities to Four easily enough."

"Losing most major wars for five hundred years will do that."

"An honest little underkarl. I've encountered many less realistic. You'd be surprised how many officials here refer to Ilmanako every second breath. One of them even gets her liches into the act."

Teltö recalled Dyrstin's insistent terminology. "Oh, every Imperial citizen hopes one day the North will be restored to the Empire." *And every one of us drinks in the horrors of the Nadir with our Mam's milk.* "It's just most of us don't obsess about it, and those who do tend to be nutters. Personally, I like to take the world as it is."

"Very noble."

"There's no point holding grudges over pipe dreams. You trade with us, we trade with you. Give or take stray letters and words, we mostly speak the same language these days…"

"Ang goor Tuonakonnil reesh."

Teltö chuckled. "Now you're just messing with me. What's that supposed to mean?"

"It's Feleen. The Old Tongue of the North. I only remember the basics from school, but it's still the language of our Church. Anyway, I said 'unless you're from Tuonako.' I think."

Beyond the glass, the midday Sun beat down on the twisted landscape. It grew warm inside the carriage. Sufael pulled off her tweed jacket, and folded it neatly over her lap.

"So tell me," said Teltö, "what made you want to work in the Empire? We're hardly a land of milk and honey. Well, we are, but the milk's stale, and the honey's two servings a month."

"Rationing is a pain," she agreed. "But I want a future. There's nothing for me back home, other than mopping floors and curtseying. Or slaving fourteen hours at Proth & Proth for a rotting jaw and an early grave. For all its faults, the Empire gives women a chance."

"Why wouldn't we?"

Sufael studied him, her merry brown eyes seeking sarcasm. She shook her head. "You are a strange, strange bunch."

Teltö frowned. "How is it strange? Necromantic ability is in your brain, not your genitals. We're not barbarians."

"Yes, you're very civilised." Sufael smiled. "Women treated as equals and a system where merit shines through… not that it does much good if you're a lich."

Teltö had never debated a Northerner before, but he'd heard stories from his father, who'd encountered a whole troop in the pub once. For a good-natured argument, there had been plenty of busted barstools. They held strange ideas up beyond Yyti's Wall.

"Everyone gets the same chance. I mean, it's not much, and we're very big on…" *I have to choose my words carefully. I don't know her.* "… tradition, but it's still something."

"You're missing the point, Teltö. If I'm one of your walking dead, what good does it do me to be on the same footing as the male corpses?"

"The Death Draft is very fair. If you've got skills or ability, you avoid it." He struggled to recall the relevant Nine Authors' quote, but settled for parroting his civics class. "We're far superior to your system of hereditary privilege."

"There's no privilege in the Viiminian Empire? Hah."

"I never said there's no privilege, only that everyone has the same opportunities. If you end up a lich, you're still put to good use."

Sufael gazed out the window. "The opportunities are only there if you have natural ability. No necromantic talent means you're an underling for the rest of your life, and perhaps after."

"There's the Guild."

"Who are still your political and social inferiors, no

matter how much gaudy wealth they accumulate. And every one of them, never mind the Ordinaries, is a potential toy for you after death. But not Necros. No, not the true rulers of the Empire. Why don't you subject yourselves to the same indignity as everyone else?"

"It's not an indignity. Reanimation is a sacred gift from Mother Death."

"A gift many would rather flee from than accept."

"Not without outside help," snapped Teltö. "The Principality sends you back home, in chains, and as for running to the Mountains or Fells… perhaps outlawry seems romantic, but it isn't. If the authorities don't get you, weather and wildlife will. And while you're out there freezing or being eaten, Kuolinako cooks up collective punishments for your friends and family."

"So it's brute force then. You have power over others, so you use it without consequences. Consequences you all-too conveniently escape yourselves through your precious Toast."

It's Tuvena all over again. Sorry, Little Miss Northerner, I'm not letting you wind me up. "The Toast exists for a reason. Without it, nobody would be safe. I could kill and reanimate Vyrellävek."

Sufael gave a snort worthy of Kyrmves. "Good luck getting past the guards."

"I meant hypothetically. I'd then use the powers of his brain to set myself up as the most powerful person in the Empire. Yes, someone stronger could wrest control from me pretty quickly, but I'd just use mirroring to stop that."

"Mirroring?" The woman turned away from the window, and looked across with interest.

"A tactic used in the barbaric days before the Toast. Or so the stories say. It's just theory now. You reanimate two or more Necromancers, the stronger the better, and get them to exert their powers on each other. That stops anybody but really high-level outsiders from tampering."

"It sounds quite clever."

"Yes and no. It led to centuries of civil wars, and scarred landscapes, until the Toast ended reanimation of Necromancers. Some say the Mää Wastes were created that way, and Kuolinako's chimneys merely finished off what survived."

"You did more than wreck the landscape. Ever wondered why the Principality outlaws necromancy?"

"Religion? Your High Priests must've worked out some way to tie necromancy to the Mad God." Strict monotheists, the Northern Church believed in a malignant Creator.

"Religion's just one part of it. I'm not particularly pious, and neither is Oym. The big problem with necromancy is that it stirs up the *uleeveer*."

"The *uleeveer*?"

"I see the term isn't used down south. I suppose you'd translate it as 'the things from outside'. Five centuries after the Wall went up, the Empire still leaves its stain. Swamps and so forth shunned by fish and bird alike, limestone caves with strange screaming echoes."

"Banal superstition."

"Suit yourself, Teltö, but I'd wager there are places around Qivunako you wouldn't venture for all the marks in the Empire."

"The Undersecretarial Office," said Teltö. "But seriously, necromancy is a sacred meeting of Mother Death and Father Life. The Empire's lasted eight thousand years. Shouldn't the *uleeveer* have killed us off already?"

A dull rap on the door stopped further conversation. "Come in," called Teltö and Sufael simultaneously.

A lich wheeled in a trolley laden with a rusting teapot, a kettle, mugs, and a milk-jug. Puzzled by the smell, Teltö peered over the rim of the jug. Bits of curd floated like little icebergs. A circular blue tin labelled 'biscuits' stood open, empty save for crumbs stuck to the bottom.

"Refreshments?" said the corpse.

"No thank you," said Teltö.

"Tea for me," said Sufael. "No milk," she added hastily.

•　•　•

"TELL ME ABOUT Prince Oym," said Teltö. "He sounds interesting." *Hopefully interesting enough to pad a report.*

Sufael drank the dregs of her tea and put the mug on the sill.

"Interesting? No. Sensible, benevolent, and toothless. Oym spends his mornings in bed and his afternoons painting. Your Chancellor's got him in his pocket."

"Your Prince has half the wealth of our Empire in his."

Sufael laughed. "Maybe, maybe not. Money moves in mysterious ways. But a question for you: do you have bears in Qivunako?"

"Pardon?"

"Bears. The big bad-tempered creatures with claws and teeth. I'm writing a poem about one." Her eyes narrowed. "What's the matter, Teltö? You've gone pale."

Teltö thinned his lips. "Sorry. I'd a Great-granny from the villages who never let us name the creature, on pain of the wooden spoon."

Sufael smiled and held up her hands. "No spoon

here."

"I know. It's just funny how these things stay with you. Also, there was Metvet."

"Metvet?"

"Metvet Otsola. A friend from school." *And my first.* "Inquisitive fellow, he always wanted to know everything." *He taught me a few things too.*

"What happened to him?"

"He died."

"Very sad."

Teltö stared out the window. "Yes, a great questioner was our Metvet. One day, he wanted to know what happens when a lich drinks the Toast. A teacher owned a lich-bear she liked to make dance. Too young to legally reanimate humans, Metvet decided he'd animate that to try out his theory."

"This isn't going to end well."

Teltö nodded. "The dead bear ripped open the Toast Chamber, and drank the concoction. Needless to say, it deanimated. The Lesser Council tried Metvet for disrespecting the Toast."

Sufael's eyes widened. "And they found him guilty?"

"The Council gibbeted him in front of the entire school."

Sufael winced. "I can see why bears aren't your cup of tea."

"I needed more than tea. Drank myself into a stupor for a month afterwards, trying to blot out the memory. Wasn't cheap, but it mostly worked. It gets better though: they only took him down last year."

• • •

THE TROLLEY ATTACKED again, still biscuitless, and

Sufael helped herself to more tea. Having escaped the Mää Wastes, and left the Central Uplands behind, the train now cut through the Plains of Ruvia. Teltö saw potato fields, then corn, then wheat, then barley. Orchards of unripened apples stretched beside little rivers. Sufael sipped her drink, and told of life on the Northern coast, of warm sea breezes, and gulls, and boats from the Confederation bearing spices and exotic fruit. She spoke too of Skeevereet's crystal spires and majestic airships, of the Great Lighthouse, and lonely beaches. Teltö listened, enchanted.

"Mustanako is also by the sea," said Sufael, "but it's larger and more serious, and with no crystals or airships. I think you have to experience it for yourself. Visiting as a child, I walked beside the estuary, picking crabs out of the mud or throwing sticks for stray dogs. And the weather: it changes hour by hour, from tempests to utter calm. You get none of that in your filthy crypt of a Capital."

"I'm Qivunakonian. We get exciting variations on rain, frost, hail, and snow."

Sufael finished her tea. "Tell me of yourself, Teltö. Tell me of Qivunako and the south."

"There's lots of ugly old slag heaps from the iron smelters. And that's just the people."

"You can do better than that."

"If you insist…"

He began to describe his own city, nestled among the foothills of the southern Kullio Ranges: a sparse country of Unut and tussock, and thorns and barren windswept rock, a refuge for dark and gnarly woods too old and stubborn to surrender to man or weather. The south was a place of forgotten villages in cold mountain valleys, where the old ways lived not in dusty libraries, but still beat in the hearts of the people. Sufael listened eagerly, and as the story went on, a strange homesickness gripped Teltö; he spoke of the frigid winter sea, of an ocean grey and jealous, of the volcanic rocks that battled the waves. But it was easy to wax whimsical in a warm railway carriage, with a beautiful woman hanging on your every word.

"You know," said Sufael, when silence reigned once more, "we're rather alike, you and I."

Teltö smiled, doubting he was a hidden romantic, but hardly going to contradict her.

The woman looked out the window at the darkening sky. "I love stories. There are any number of rickety old taverns in Mustanako, with travellers telling fireside tales when the lights dim. At home, too many people's idea of a story is alliterative recitation of how men with axes fought monsters. Or each other. Which is pretty much the same thing."

Teltö shrugged. "Plenty of that in the Qivunako Library." A part-time clerk found all sorts of stuff whilst browsing for distracting illustrations. Some of it might even be true.

Sufael's face lit up. "You're a big reader?"

"Let's say I've come across a tome or two in my time," he said, grinning. He'd keep the prosaic truth to himself. The woman liked stories, after all.

*   *   *

TELTÖ PULLED DOWN the wooden bunk bed. Fourth Class meant no mattress or padding, so he spread the seat rug, and added a quilted blanket from the luggage rack. A rolled-up greatcoat served on pillow duty.

"Are you sure you'll be comfortable?" Sufael eyed his effort with undisguised amusement. Easy for her: her luggage contained woollen blanket and bedroll.

"I'll be fine," Teltö lied. "Now let's grab some dinner."

. . .

HE'D NEVER SEEN lines like those in the food carriage. He and Sufael squeezed past a smorgasbord of passengers until they found a gap between the wall and the press of bodies.

"How dare you barge in there," snapped an overkarl with most unfortunate teeth.

Teltö apologised, and vanished back into the crowd. He bumped into the serving table; savoury smells wafted into his nostrils.

The queues took forever, and tastier food had probably been redirected, but Teltö finally found himself with a bowl of lukewarm leek and potato soup, and a slab of rye bread. *A spoon would be nice.* Sufael got a dollop of butter with hers. Teltö wondered whether she'd slipped the staff a bit or ten.

They dipped bread in silence. Then Sufael's face lit up.

"Asti!"

A middle-aged woman in the queue looked around. "Sufael!"

"Small world!"

Work colleagues. Sufael and Asti nattered about fish, while Teltö drank the dregs of his soup. He glanced at the lich ladler, pondering the availability of seconds. He skulked back into line.

No one noticed the reappearance of the red-haired Qivunakonian, and Teltö regained the serving table without difficulty.

"Have you eaten?" asked the lich with the ladle and apron.

Teltö thrust out an empty bowl. "No, sir, I haven't."

"A pity," said the corpse, without pity. "We're all out." It dropped the ladle into the pot, and the spoon struck the bottom with a hollow *thunk*.

*   *   *

THE SUN WOULD still be up back in Qivunako, and in parts of the Great Southern Fells night never fell at this time of year, but in the North things were different. With all else shrouded in grey and black, only the yellow glimmer of the wagon's corpse lantern led the way.

"That was nice," said Sufael.

"What was nice?"

"An old friend of mine from the Department."

He grunted, miffed at the food shortage. *I can't even use the black market for extras.*

They stalked back to the compartment to find the room bathed in the glow of a Full Moon. Another thing he'd missed whilst in the Last Capital.

Teltö ran his hands over the walls. "There's no light."

"That's what you get for Fourth Class." Sufael pulled the curtains. "We'll manage."

Teltö sat on his makeshift bed, and tugged off his boots.

"Good night."

Teltö reflected on the cruelties of life, the hard bunk against his back, while Sufael's snores filled the compartment. The motion of the train finally soothed him to sleep.

Chapter Nine

THE MIDDAY SUN beat down upon the tiled roof of the Mustanako Southern Railway Station. Teltö stood in the shade, savouring the salt tang of the breeze, and watching people mill around the platform. A Mnoma juggled fire sticks amid the adoring faces of a dozen children and the less-adoring faces of three Station personnel.

"So." Sufael palmed the boiled sweet she'd been sucking. "You're in Mustanako for a couple of days?" The Northerner had seen a confectionery vendor when climbing off the train and claimed she simply couldn't resist.

"That's right. Things to do, people to see. One last look at the Empire, then it's onto the Principality…"

"Has the Lesser Council arranged somewhere for you to stay?"

Teltö shook his head. "I'm expected to look after myself until Skeevereet."

"You poor thing. But you know what, there's always rooms available at The Cosy Needle."

"Eh?"

"It's a pub." Sufael stuck the sticky mess back in her mouth and smiled with sanguine innocence.

•   •   •

AFTER THREE WEEKS in the Last Capital, Teltö felt almost naked under the open sky. Late spring had come to Mustanako, and with it clear days and mischievous winds. The gusts billowed through his hair as he followed Sufael into the city; glimpsing himself in an apothecary's window, he did his best to tame the coppery mess.

There were people everywhere, mostly on foot. Necromancers, Guildlings, Ordinaries, and Mnomo clogged the streets, together with Northerners and visitors from all parts of the Confederation. The silent tunnels of Kuolinako had given way to the endless colours, noises, and odours of Mustanako, the largest port in the Empire, and one of the great cities of the world. There were no cabs, and the few carts Teltö saw had ground to a halt, their living drivers shouting while barefoot urchins mounted the vehicles to nab neeps and apples.

"Good afternoon, sir," said a street vendor. "Can I interest you in a new pair of boots?"

Teltö scanned the man's wares. "Sorry, haven't got my Mustanako dockets yet."

The merchant clicked his tongue. "No dockets, no dockets… I am sure I still have something…" He ducked under his stall, and Teltö hurried away. He had better things to spend his hard-earned money on than overpriced factory rejects.

"Fancy a taste of berry cordial, sir?"

A youngish fellow with a beetroot complexion manned the next stall. Three small wooden casks and half a dozen enamel mugs congregated on the table. Teltö moved closer. He wrinkled his nose at the chap's choice of cologne.

"So this is berry cordial?"

"Yes, sir." The merchant mopped sweat with a handkerchief. *Oilio's long-lost cousin.* "Three bits a mug. Very medicinal, and with your choice of blackberry, strawberry, or gooseberry flavours." The man smiled.

Teltö smiled back. He lowered suitcase and satchel, thankful they looked passingly official.

"Can I see your licence?" he asked, the essence of deadpan bureaucrat. A Kuolinakonian lich could not have done better.

The cordial-seller turned a lighter shade of beetroot. "Um, sir…"

"Licence. I take it you *are* licensed?" Teltö drummed his fingers on one of the casks.

"Oh yes." The man thrust out a sweat-smudged paper. Teltö inspected it, his face stern.

"There seems to be some issues here…"

"Take a free mug, with my compliments."

Teltö smirked, and helped himself to a draught of the blackberry. It wasn't half bad, if a bit thin. Sufael leaned against a lamppost at the end of the street.

"So you're in the iron business?" she said, when he caught up.

He shrugged. "Selling iron is thirsty work."

Quieter than the main thoroughfare, the next street meandered past boutique cafés where elite Necromancers and Guildlings sipped drinks beneath the blankness of lich waiters.

"Stop, thief!"

Teltö saw a man chasing a child. The child clutched

several apricots.

"Thief!"

Dirty and of indeterminate gender, the brat weaved around pedestrians and lampposts, slippery as an eel. Teltö stuck his leg out; the thief tripped, and the stolen fruit tumbled onto the cobblestones before rolling into the gutter. Bellowing curses, the man grabbed the urchin by the shirt, and boxed its ears.

"Nobody steals my bloody produce, you hear?"

The man turned to Teltö, and tipped his cap.

"Thank you, sir."

"Don't mention it."

"Bloody little locusts. The Lesser Council is far too soft on truancy if you ask me."

I've found a budding Post *columnist.*

The fellow raged on for several misanthropic minutes, but Teltö barely heard him. He was far too busy suppressing laughter as Sufael collected apricots from the gutter and juggled them behind the vendor's back. She only ever managed two, dropping them all on adding a third.

"One day," she muttered, as the fruit bounced across the cobblestones. Teltö grinned.

The man finally offered them each a clean apricot in thanks. Teltö accepted with gracious impatience. Sufael declined.

• • •

TELTÖ MUNCHED THE fruit, and considered the traffic. Something still seemed wrong.

"There aren't many liches around."

"There's plenty," said Sufael. "Just more living people, and they've got to earn their crust somehow. Who'd want to live in Kuolinako unless you have to?"

"Power hungry albinos with no sense of smell?"

"Very droll. But add in the sailors and other transients, and this is easily the biggest city on the continent. Ah, here we are. Behold the soul of Mustanako."

The so-called soul of Mustanako was a multi-floored establishment. The timbered upper story stuck out over the sandstone lower, propped up by a series of wormhole-ridden supports. Hanging above the main door, a wooden sign rattled in the wind.

"The Cosy Needle," muttered Teltö. "Can't think of many cosy needles myself."

"Here's one for a start." Sufael pushed open the door. Teltö patted down his hair.

After the streets of Mustanako, the quietness of the pub surprised him. A scattering populated the Common Room, three at the bar, and a couple more at tables. In the corner, an aproned woman with a mop hummed an unknown tune, and a Mnoma had passed out atop the piano. In the stone fireplace, a small and desperate coal-blaze struggled to create atmosphere. *But natural light. Too long in Kuolinako.*

The barkeep grinned. He lacked several front teeth, and stored a pencil behind his ear. "Sufael! Good to see you again. How's the poetry going?"

Sufael propped herself up on a stool. "Good thanks, Aarti. I've got a friend with me, and wondered if you had one of your excellent rooms available."

This set off sniggers from the clientèle. "Not like that," snapped Sufael. "He's from Qivunako, and needs somewhere to stay."

The barkeep nodded. "I see the cravat. What brings

you here, lad?"

"Stopping in Mustanako for a bit. I'm heading on to Skeevereet."

"Teltö works for Qivunako Iron," said Sufael.

"Small world," interjected one of the men at the bar, a portly gentleman with short curly hair. "I have a brother who works there."

Teltö smiled. *No more questions.* "So is there a room?"

"There is," said Aarti. "Thirty bits for a friend of Sufael's. I'll waive the bond." He pulled out a leather-bound book, and turned some beer-stained pages. "Name?"

"Teltö Phuul."

Even Sufael sniggered. "Sorry, Teltö," she said, hand over her mouth. With a high and sloping ceiling, the attic room was a mite dusty, but liveable. A lone spider hovered out of reach of all but the most determined broom. Teltö deposited his luggage on the narrow bed, and stopped. Beside the window hung a framed woodcut of Vyrellävek.

Teltö gingerly lifted the woodcut off the hanging nail, and turned the Grand Chancellor's face to the wall. He backed away, heart thumping. *My room, my life.* But what if someone noticed? What if someone reported him? *Phuul, you idiot. Did the Death Pool teach you nothing?* Teltö shook his head. *They wouldn't dunk me for this. Vöder likes me. It's just a joke.* He turned to go. *No one's laughing.*

He reversed the woodcut again.

Grinning like a contented cat, Sufael waited on the landing, arm outstretched against the banister. She'd promised him a surprise.

"First round on me, Teltö."

So the surprise is I'm paying for the second? "Nice," he said, eyes drawn to the curves of her breasts. "I'll have whatever you're having."

Downstairs, he claimed a table whilst Sufael fetched a couple of Myrstä Island Darks. It didn't take long. Teltö sipped his drink. It wasn't Asrak, but the beer was both legal and unrationed, and had a caramel flavour he found pleasant. They weren't even watering it down. A platter accompanied the drinks, piled with toast and dripping.

"So what's the surprise?" Teltö wiped foam from his lip.

"Wait and see." Sufael tried the toast. "Ooh," she made a face. "A bit salty today, methinks."

The Common Room's grandfather clock chimed. No sooner had the sound died than a side door squeaked open. Hunchbacked, and with a snowy neckbeard spreading over a globular belly, a man in an oversized beaked cap limped into the room. His wooden leg thumped against the floorboards.

"Greetings," he declared, easing himself into a fireside chair. Evident age hadn't wearied his voice.

"Who's this?" Teltö whispered.

"The Old Man," said Sufael with a mouth full of toast. "He's a sailor, or was. Now he tells stories and gets fat on free beer. The Needle keeps him as an attraction. Lovely old fellow."

"So he's the pub's pet storyteller?"

The Northern woman shrugged. "You can look at it that way."

"Salutations, fine clientèle," said the Old Man. "Gather round, and you shall hear of my latest adventure." He raised his hand; he wore a tarnished silver ring.

The only adventures old one-leg has had recently is climbing the stairs.

A passing barmaid handed the fellow a handle of beer. "Thank you, lassie," he said, taking a sip and a gentle leer. He sighed contentedly. "Ah, that's better. Now where to begin…"

The story was something about the Sun, stout sticks, and spiders. Utter nonsense every word, though Teltö feigned sufficient interest to keep Sufael happy. She was paying for the drinks, and both beer and bust were definitely worth savouring.

· · ·

THAT EVENING, SUFAEL took Teltö for a walk along Mustanako's sea-wall. The wind had died, leaving only feathered clouds against a burgundy sky. Below sprawled the Nhagivat estuary, where the river emptied into the Illuvian. Shells and seaweed and driftwood and bits of dead squid littered the grey sand. Further towards the south, a grove of pohutukawa lined a cliff-top. Gulls circled overhead.

Teltö looked across at the harbour, where the vessels of a dozen nations assembled in the volcanic shadow of Myrstä Island. He spotted barquentines, and cutters, and trading steamers, and even a pair of archaic longships from the barbaric south-west, dead oarsmen sitting idle in the cool night air. There were also two frigates, the remaining pride of an Imperial Navy forbidden ironclads by punitive peace.

"I told you it's beautiful." Sufael leant against the iron railing. Teltö joined her. Fog drifted in and started to scale the wall.

He watched a rowing boat ease towards one of the steamers. "Did I ever doubt you?"

"Wait until you see the crystal spires of Skeevereet."

"Indeed." Teltö put his arm around her, and drew her close. He nuzzled her.

Forget Tuvena, for once. "So, what are you up to tonight?" *Damn. I sound like Dyrstin.*

Sufael chuckled. "You're very forward considering we only met yesterday. It turns out I've things to do this evening. But we can meet tomorrow. How does nine, at the Needle sound?"

"Sounds good."

"I'll be waiting."

They stood there for some time, locked in a warm embrace as the mists rose to greet them.

•　•　•

HAVING CHECKED THE street map three times, Teltö arrived at a domed brick building with high, narrow windows. If his papers were to be believed, this was the official residence of Mustanako's Governor, the Dragon's Lesser Council equivalent. The four-starred Imperial banner fluttered in the breeze far above, with Mustanako's Pohutukawa flying beneath.

"Your position would be what?" said the guard at the steps. Her face was a collection of scars upon scars, and her nose bent to the left. Teltö decided to not mess with this person.

"Part of His Excellency's entourage. I'm here for the function." *No idea what it's about, but an attaché needs some perks.*

"Can I see your documentation?"

"Hold on…" He fished into his pocket. *Shit. I left it in my other coat.*

"Teltö! Is that you?"

Balancing on high heels, a woman clacked down the

steps towards him. Adorned with orange ribbon, her cherry dress bared arms and shoulders, and complimented smooth red-brown hair. Much make-up had died in vain to disguise the size of her nose.

Teltö frowned. "Rhea?"

He'd known his elder sister lived somewhere in the city, but what was she doing here? *With a new necklace too.*

"Yes, Teltö, it's me." She hugged him. "I only sent the letter last week, and yet here you are. Where's Kyrmves?"

Teltö disguised confusion with a smile. "It's just me."

Rhea frowned. "You came all this way, by yourself?"

"I'm on Council business."

"The Lesser Council is interested in my Engagement Party?"

"Engagement Party?"

"But of course. I wrote all about it. You have been getting my letters, I hope?"

"Oh yes."

"Vaani wanted something special, and with his family large and lavish definitely had to be on the cards. We met at the Research Unit, you know. He was researching modification of cephalopods. And here he is... Vaani, meet my little brother, Teltö."

A slender young man shook Teltö's hand. He wore a blue Kuolinako cravat and an orange ribbon. Beneath a mop of light-brown hair, his face was thin and keen.

"Good to meet you, Teltö. Is this a family visit, or did you get yourself a job as one of my uncle's hangers on?"

Uncle? What uncle? "I'm travelling North in an official capacity."

"So you are working for the old man then. He may jump at shadows, but never let it be said my uncle does not give opportunities to provincials."

"You are…"

"Vaani Vyrellävek, yes. Don't worry about grovelling: we're all equals tonight."

Teltö's jaw dropped. His sister was engaged to the Dragon's nephew?

"Yes," said Rhea, "imagine it." She rubbed her fiancé's shoulder. "Vaani Vyrellävek himself falls for Rhea Phuul. To think I owe it to my published paper."

Rhea prattled on, the lesser Vyrellävek drinking in every word. Teltö stood, blinking dumbly as he tried to comprehend a Vyrellävek falling for a Phuul. Or indeed *anyone* falling for Rhea. That big-nosed, gangly, socially awkward girl whose sole purpose in life was churning out top marks in tests? She'd somehow – somehow – achieved the match of the year too. *The towering shadow of Rhea Phuul. See, Madam Venomavat? I can't escape it, so why try?*

"Come on in, Teltö," his sister concluded. "Help yourself to food. There's plenty to go round: we've got a rationing exemption. Vaani pulled some strings."

Teltö did not need to be told twice.

· · ·

DYRSTIN VENOMAVAT, EAT your heart out. Within ten minutes, Teltö Phuul was stuffing his face with triangular cucumber sandwiches. Held in the cavernous confines of the Governor's Banquet Hall, the function consisted of overdressed Mustanako and Kuolinako elites chattering over costly drinks in costlier glasses. All here to be seen, rather than to attend a mere Engagement Party, yet poor Rhea hadn't realised no one had come for her, or for her outstanding brain. *Silly thing will be poked and prodded and pitied, and kept in a glass jar like one of her specimens.* Say what you like about mediocrity, once Teltö returned to

Qivunako at the end of his trip, his life would at least be his own again – as much as it ever could. Hova, Tuvena, and the rest would be like the Death Pool: nothing more than a bad dream. Rhea? One day, she'd regret being a parrot in a cage, and Teltö planned to tell her he'd told her so.

Not that Rhea seemed to care. Disinclined to chat about Qivunako any longer than necessary, she had promptly vanished back into the crowd of purple, orange, and green ribbons. Teltö didn't mind. It left him more time with the sandwiches on their porcelain trays.

"Cocktail, sir?" said a lich waiter.

The tray bore a selection of drinks Teltö had never heard of, and which on first impression involved a theme of cruelty to olives. No Asrak: this far north they had exotic liquors, and with the wealth on show, who needed illegal and cheap when you had legal and extravagant?

"Thank you," he said, with his mouth full. *If the poor bastards on the dockets could see us now, they'd lynch everyone in the room.*

He peeked over his shoulder lest the elder Vyrellävek manifest unexpectedly. There was no sign of the Grand Chancellor, but another sight caught Teltö's attention. He frowned.

"Tell me, who is that?" He pointed towards the far wall, where a greying woman in a yellow scarf and hair-curlers hurled abuse at a grandfather clock. *She's not Vyrellävek's mother is she? If she were my Mam, they'd lock her away.*

The corpse stared. The other guests gave the woman a wide berth.

"That's the Governor, sir."

• • •

NIGHT HAD FALLEN on Mustanako, but beneath the crystal chandelier, the celebration only grew grander. A log fire kept the air toasty, and amid the haze of perfume and powder, a dozen lich musicians kept the tunes flowing as fast as the wine. With a bow arm showing the stamina only the dead could muster, the lead violinist charmed its audience with melody after melody, cold and dexterous fingers dancing upon the strings with exquisite precision.

"I don't believe we've met."

A plump little man in a silk black waistcoat hovered beside the table. Bespectacled and balding, the man quivered, as though he were a bomb waiting to explode. His brown eyes darted to and fro. Teltö moved to obscure the sandwich tray, and took stock of the fellow's hand. *Silver ring. Guildling.* The Necromancer relaxed. *No one important.*

"Reni Kovo." The man slicked back what was left of his hair.

"Teltö Phuul. And no, we haven't met."

Kovo raised his eyebrows. "Phuul? You are related to Madam Rhea?"

"I'm her brother. Her *only* brother."

"Indeed." The man adjusted his spectacles. "May I have a moment of your time? I have something…"

Teltö folded his arms. "No."

"In that case…"

A shame he's not better looking. "No."

"Then, please, take my card. I wish you a good evening."

The cretin scurried off without a single sandwich. Teltö watched him latch onto fresh prey, then dropped the card on the floor. After a moment's thought, he nudged it under the table.

. . .

PUTTING HIS LATEST glass beside the others, Teltö belched, and reached for the last surviving sandwich. At home he left final helpings to others, as it validated claims he had not eaten the entire meal, but with everyone too dead or too engrossed in political preening to notice, tonight his conscience was clear.

The grandfather clock chimed, and with each chime the Governor struck the timepiece with a rolled-up umbrella. Teltö grimaced. *Bugger, I'm meeting Sufael.* He hunted for his sister. *Look for the nose, look for the nose. There she is.* Rhea had her back to the fireplace. She chatted with a tall hollow-cheeked gentleman in tweed and purple ribbon.

"Sorry, Rhea." Teltö poked his head between them. He felt fat and happy. "I have to go. A splendid party, anyway."

"Who might you be, may I ask?" said the purple ribboned one, as if Teltö were something he'd scraped off his impeccable boots.

Rhea blushed beneath the make-up. "My brother."

"Indeed." The man inspected his pocket watch and strode away without comment.

Doubt flickered over Rhea's face, even the semblance of a frown. But the moment passed, and within seconds the deluded smile returned.

"Give my love to the family," she said, giving her brother a hug. "You're all invited to the wedding. Oh, look, there's the Grand Chancellor himself. Hello, Uncle Peta…"

Teltö snuck out the main doors. Cool but not cold, and smelling of salt, the street air refreshed him as he ghosted past the guard, and into the night. Even at this hour, pedestrians nattered in front of shut coffee houses, and cabs rattled past, some horse-drawn. A Mnoma leant against a lamppost, mangling a sea shanty with an accordion. A clowder of black and ginger cats pawed at its trouser leg.

Teltö considered the cabs, and scratched his head. *Nah, the Needle's not that far, and I need to watch my money.* After a few wrong turns, he got back to the pub.

A wave of warm air and noise greeted him. The Common Room bustled with laughter and the reek of tobacco. At one table, four men hissed in argument over a card game, at another a lone woman scribbled on a notepad. Someone had added fuel to the fire.

Sufael wasn't here yet. Teltö elbowed through to the bar, and ordered a cheap Ruvian Bitter while he waited.

"Here you are, sir," sniffed the bartender. Her red-ringed eyes bespoke recent grief.

"Thank you," said Teltö. "Where's Aarti?"

"You mean my bloody husband?" snapped the woman. She wiped away fresh tears. "Where isn't he? The bastard."

Ah. "Sorry for troubling you, madam."

Feeling his cheeks burning, Teltö darted back into the crowd. He found an empty corner, not far from the piano where a woman thumped out 'The Windy Rocks' and an armada of nautical types sang the rude versions.

Ten minutes passed. Making faces with every sip, Teltö nursed the foul brown brew, and waited for Sufael. Thirty minutes, and he finished his beer. *Where in blazes is she?* Teltö contemplated the empty glass before him, almost tempted to go back for another.

"Can I get you a drink?"

Teltö looked up to see a handsome young man standing over him, dark haired, olive-skinned, and broad shouldered. Not as tall as Dyrstin, this one wore a white shirt with rolled-up sleeves, and a Guild Ring on his finger.

Teltö smiled. "Sure. I'm Teltö, by the way."

"Nieliini. I see you're all the way from Qivunako."

Teltö nodded. "I'm here for my sister's wedding."

The newcomer scratched his chin. "So what'll you be having?"

"A Myrstä Island Dark, thanks," said Teltö. Perhaps he'd be having something else a bit later. He watched the fellow walk over to the bar, and felt himself stirring under the table. It had been a long time, and this Nieliini did have a nice arse.

The man returned with two foaming dark beers. "There you go," he said. "I've just spent six months on a ship transporting spices around the Confederation, and have finally been paid. Ever been that way? No? Well, they're a queer lot up there. Mercenary Necros plying their trade in the endless civil wars, giant snakes, hippopotami…"

Teltö let the sailor ramble on about cults and ship weevils. *Let them talk and they think you're listening.* Everyone loved a listener. Out the corner of his eye, he saw two men in red ribbons whispering in the pianist's ear. They grabbed her shoulder, and led her away. Teltö looked no closer. *Not my business.* Nieliini told of other developments: the Imperial Navy was remodelling its ships, and shipyards were importing skilled labour to cope with demand.

"The North buys all the copper we can dig out, and

we buy all their artisans," was Nieliini's summary, after another beer. "But one thing that's weird: every sailor in Mustanako is abuzz with stories of strange monsters seen off the coast. I don't believe a word of it myself."

Legal closing time came and went, and no one noticed. Teltö cupped his hands around Nieliini's, and smiled.

*   *   *

NIELIINI HAD PULLED the curtains before leaving, and the grey ambiance of late morning drizzle clouded the attic. Raindrops pattered against the window pane. Teltö lolled in bed, hands behind his head, and his nostrils still filled with the pleasant odour of musk. He grinned.

"I hope you enjoyed that," he told the ceiling spider. The arachnid voyeur hadn't moved.

He rolled onto his side and brushed a dark hair from the pillow, reflecting on the taste of the man's tongue. *Tuvena never kissed half as well.* He screwed his face up. *It always comes back to her, doesn't it?* Teltö reached down, and hunted through his pile of clothes until he found his watch. The time closed in on half past ten. The train for Skeevereet left at noon.

Teltö dressed, splashed his face under a tap, and headed downstairs. In the Common Room, he found the woman from the previous night cursing a patron.

"He got what he bloody well deserved."

Teltö scratched his head. He disliked confrontations, especially confusing ones before noon. "Excuse me," he said. "Where's Aarti? I need to sign out."

The patron laughed. "That's what we're fighting about, lad. Aarti had a visit from the shadow-stalkers in the night, and all so his wench could get her hands on the pub and a younger man." He sneered at the woman. "Don't think I haven't seen you."

She spat. "You're already drunk, you silly old fool. Aarti had debts, and lots of them. Is it any wonder he tried something desperate to pay them back?"

"Not what I heard. I heard a certain someone framed him. For smuggling out Draftees on trade ships, or some such. Not that I'm naming names, of course…"

Teltö thinned his lips. "Look, I've got a train to catch. Can I just sign out?" He repressed the chill creeping up his spine. *The Inquisition does what the Inquisition does.*

Aarti's wife sighed, and pushed the register in his direction. "There you go, lad." She flung a pencil; it bounced off the bar and rattled onto the floor. "Go for your life."

Chapter Ten

BLACK BOOTS SLOSHED through puddles. Everyone looked the same in the rain, even the Mnomo, and Mustanako reeked of sweat and must. A neep cart rumbled past, the Unut's fur thick and soggy, and the driver invisible beneath oilskin and wide-brimmed leather hat.

"Teltö!"

"Sufael?" The voice came from somewhere, one crumb of the warm and familiar in a dull and alien world. *There she is. Not disappeared after all.*

"Yes, so sorry." She elbowed through two Mnomo. The creatures squeaked annoyance.

"Detained by work."

He smiled. Better drudgery than the Inquisition. "Not to worry. I'd a pleasant enough time by myself. Something fishy, was it?"

"You could say that."

No laughs at my little joke? "Aarti had a midnight visit from the shadow-stalkers."

"Very sad."

Teltö frowned. "You don't sound surprised."

"I've spent long enough in the Empire to not be surprised at anything."

"Weren't you friends with Aarti?"

"Yes, Teltö, I was. But come on, we've got a train to catch." She pecked him lightly on the cheek. Teltö stopped for a moment, rain beading in his hair. *Sufael loved the Needle.* Shaking his head, he hurried after the inscrutable Northerner.

*   *   *

THE MAN WORE a pinched grimace, as if in search of someone to disapprove of.

"Almost home, love," said the portly woman by the door.

Neither wore rings or ribbons, but resentment hung over the compartment like an invisible blanket. Teltö smiled politely in the woman's direction, but she threw a look that'd sober the most addled drunkard. The husband unfurled today's *Post* and ignored the world.

Teltö rested his elbow on the sill. *Are they angry at us because we're young, or because we're not locals, or because I passed the Examination and they didn't?* With some people it might be all three. He stared out as the train hugged the coastline north. He saw little save fog. Sufael sang softly:

> *The waves are rolling onwards still*
> *In land of foam and mist*
> *So many drown in waters chill*
> *Who've neither loved nor kissed...*

"Shut your trap," snapped the older woman. The man nodded approval without looking up.

No one spoke after that. But for the rumble of the train and the crinkling of the newspaper, glum calm reigned. Teltö wondered what his parents would make of Rhea and Vaani Vyrellävek. They'd love it probably. Another badge to parade around to friends and colleagues; another reason for them to needle him for his 'failures'. If only Rhea had been born normal. His parents might've treated him more as a son and less like some performing sea lion from Dyrtölä. *Sorry, Dad. My sister's the one with the flippers.*

Sufael shut her eyes and leant back into the sheepskin seat rug. She mouthed words to herself; whether from a song or some poem, Teltö couldn't guess.

After an hour, the train weaved inland through hills and pasture. More small towns, one much like another, rustic and ridden with windmills. The windmills stood gaunt and skeletal, unmoving. Then the sour couple got off, which cheered Teltö no end, but Sufael proved no more talkative. By late afternoon, they passed through their first ghost town, where buildings crumbled amid overgrown gardens, and where broken spires and rotting doors stood testimony to the ravages of the Northern wars. A rusted axle wheel lay in a ditch, nearly invisible in waist-high grass. Teltö counted six more abandoned hamlets over the next two hours. At last, the hills flattened into plains of bramble and gorse. If anyone had ever dwelt here, all trace of them had long since vanished into the undergrowth. Twisted fists of rock beckoned at the darkening sky; some resembled animals or malformed teeth.

Then came the Wall. Stone upon stone, it cut through the land like a great grey scar, looming over lush minefields and abandoned military posts. Starting as a queer posthumous monument to Grand Chancellor Yyti, and now controlled by the North, centuries of work from both sides kept it operating. A cluster of buildings lurked in its lengthening shadow.

The train halted. Sufael yawned and stretched.

"Bloody border security," she said. "Every time I go through here, they find a new way of annoying me. It's as if they delight in making a nuisance of themselves."

"They don't employ liches do they?"

"Of course not. We outlaw that, remember?"

"Yes, I know. But for obstructive bureaucracy…"

"Nothing beats an Imperial lich, yes. But the dead don't delight in it. They just do it. In my benighted homeland, the Army runs everything, the borders included. And, well, I've always suspected our boys in blue are compensating for something."

Teltö grabbed his papers, and went in search of the border office. There were two, on either side of the tracks: one for south-bound traffic, and one for north-bound. The Northern one resided in a squat brick building, and divided the arrivals into separate queues for Imperials and Locals.

"Which do you count as?" Teltö whispered.

Sufael chuckled. "Believe it or not, they class me as Imperial these days. Horrible but true."

Beneath an oil portrait of some Northerner – Teltö guessed it was Prince Oym, or at least one of his ancestors – sat a peevish young man with glasses and a dark blue uniform. He had the same brown complexion as Sufael, and a noticeably receding hairline.

The official chewed a pencil as he inspected Teltö's documents.

"You know," said Teltö, "in the Empire we get liches

to do your job."

"There are no liches here." The man reached for a stamp. "Visa approved. Please re-board your train."

Teltö turned to Sufael. "That was easy."

Sufael passed her own documents to the bureaucrat. She sighed.

An official waited for them back at the compartment, this one older, paler, and more solidly built than his desk counterpart. He wore epaulettes on his uniform. The stereotypical Northern soldier, the sort *Post* cartoons skewered every week.

"Any declarable items?"

"Um, no."

"No liquor, liches, or Mnomo this evening?" The fellow twitched his black moustache.

"Sorry, I must have left them in my other coat," Teltö blurted before he could stop himself. He winced at his own stupidity. *You're not dealing with corpses now, you idiot. The less trouble you have, the better your chance of seeing Kyrmves and the rest again.*

"I'll have no cheek, you corpse-buggering rat."

"Mind who you're talking to," said Sufael. "He's with me."

The official turned to the Northern woman. "And you would be of which family, missie? You Prince Oym's long-lost cousin, perhaps, or the daughter of some Count?"

"My father earns his crust keeping the likes of you safe."

"Ha. So did my father, and his father before him. Both my grandfathers died fighting his lot, missie. Brave men they were, doing their duty for their Prince, faith, and country. And not so petty traitors like you could spread your legs for the Enemy and the Mad God."

"I lost relatives too." Sufael's calm was terrible. "But Teltö here has killed no one. Now do your job and leave."

"Disrespectful bitch," snapped the official. "Right, open that luggage and let me see…"

* * *

THE TRAIN HAD stopped for the night, pending track repair. Appreciating Sufael's foresight in buying a lantern in Mustanako, Teltö squeezed the last of his items back into his suitcase. It had taken half an hour to repack after the official had messed with everything.

"What a charming fellow." Teltö heaved his luggage back onto the rack. "As though I smuggle Draft dodgers and Mnomo in my pockets."

Sufael had already climbed into her bedroll. "You provoked him. While I don't defend his rudeness, he was doing his duty. We're very big on that in the North, and smuggling is a problem, never mind security concerns."

"We're big on duty in the Empire too." *Saari Ooks said so.* "But I hardly look a security concern, do I?" *Which is exactly what I am.*

"You look like an Imperial Necromancer. I hope you've brought a change of clothes."

"Of course. I'd swelter in my coat." He sat on the bunk and pulled off his boots and woollen socks. "I've also got an exemption from the ribbon regulations."

"Qivunako Iron must have good connections."

He crawled under the blanket. "You could say that."

"Good enough to organise ribbon exemptions, but not to organise lodgings?"

Teltö hoped the lantern didn't reveal his reddening cheeks. "They assumed I'd look after myself in Mustanako. I've been allowed to stay at our Skeevereet

Embassy."

Sufael chuckled, and shut off the light. The compartment plunged into darkness.

"Oh dear. Not so kind after all."

"How do you mean?"

"Wait and see, Teltö, wait and see."

. . .

JUST AFTER MIDDAY they started moving again, the train rolling onwards through the valleys of the lower North. They were past the shadow of the Wall now, woods and abandoned hamlets giving way to civilisation and fences. Cows and sheep grazed under the watchful eye of men on horseback; Teltö saw several 'Trespassers Shall Be Shot' signs. So these were the fabled Lost Lands. Seeing them now, Teltö wondered if he'd want them back.

The clouds drifted apart, and streams of sunlight broke through. The train crossed a bridge. Beneath, a river ran through a rocky gorge, down towards a lake in the distance.

"Legend says that lake started as a funeral fire-pit during the Founding," said Sufael. "Before the rain swamped it and turned it into a lake. A pretty boring legend if you ask me. Why couldn't it have been the resting place of a giant or dragon?" She pulled out a paper bag. "Biscuits?"

Teltö tried one. "Sorry." He brushed crumbs off his shirtfront. "Too sweet."

"I swear Imperials say that about any candy sweeter than salty liquorice. But you'll have to get used to our ways soon. It's bad manners in the North to criticise offered food."

"I wasn't criticising."

"Lying is another taboo."

"You're messing with me again."

Sufael laughed. "Foiled once more." She munched through another biscuit.

Teltö smiled. Joking aside, he'd have to adjust to Northern ways. They had no Unut up here; the Church regarded them as unclean. *Not far wrong, actually.* Mnomo were considered servants of the Mad God, and were summarily slaughtered. And their views on sex and women… Teltö had laughed at their teacher back in Qivunako when she'd read a Northern list of forbidden acts. Now he was to spend several weeks among people who took that list seriously. *There go half my chances of bedding anyone.*

The train stopped in a series of townships, none screaming distinction from any smallish Imperial town. Then they came to a larger centre whose skyline was cluttered with smokestacks and turrets. Not a true city as defined by the Nine Authors, the North still had a dozen places like it: the satellites of Skeevereet, each with an unpronounceable name. Teltö got off to stretch his legs.

The problem with the Principality is the people, he thought, as he meandered down a main street. He goggled at the clergymen in their head-to-toe sable robes, and wondered whether they were melting in the heat. Those robes would come in handy in a Qivunako winter. Then he spotted a general store and grinned. *Rationing stops at the border.* As he crossed the road in search of a docketless snack, something flew around the corner in a storm of clattering and shouting; Teltö dived backwards to avoid being crushed.

A four horse carriage halted beside him, the animals black and glossy beneath red ostrich plumes. The carriage door sported a crest of two fire-breathing salamanders.

"Dreadfully sorry." A wrinkled man in tweed climbed out, and hastened to where Teltö had landed arse-first on the cobblestones. "No injuries?" he said, offering a hand up.

"Not that I'm aware of," said Teltö. "Sorry, I'm just visiting. From Qivunako." Back on his feet, he rubbed the dust off his trousers.

"An Imperial, eh?" The Northerner looked curious. "Last time I saw an Imperial around here, I shot the blighter for raiding my apple orchard." He chuckled. "Just as well. I later learnt from official channels she was here illegally. Avoiding the Death Draft and all that. Tell me, do you want my coachman whipped? Never let it be said Count Thyorm tolerated incompetent servants."

Teltö looked over at the coachman. A living, cringing coachman with eyes like a beaten cur. *There are no liches here.*

"No, thank you."

"Suit yourself." Thyorm climbed back into the carriage, and delivered a parting salute. "Enjoy the North."

Teltö watched the vehicle disappear down the road. He'd lost his appetite.

●　●　●

COATLESS AND BOOTLESS, he lay with his hands behind his head, staring at the dark ceiling. Tonight had been the last of the food carriage fare, and he wasn't going to miss it. The leek and potato soup held the texture of cat vomit.

The compartment door slid open.

"I've a little present for you, Teltö."

Teltö shielded his eyes from the sudden light. Sufael carried a lantern…and a bottle?

"Here you go." She passed it to him. "Legal Asrak."

Teltö squinted. "Where did you get this?"

Sufael shut the door. "I bought it today, when we stopped in that town. You remember, the one with the bridges? Anyway, since you're keen on the stuff, I thought you might like it. Asrak's much cheaper this side of the border, though hardly anyone drinks it here."

Teltö grinned, and swung his legs around. "No time like now then. Fancy some yourself?"

"I'd love to."

He pulled two mugs from his satchel. "How did you know I liked Asrak?"

Sufael laughed. "I'm good at guessing."

"What's Feleen for 'thank you'?"

"Tes goor Yehi ognash."

"Sounds angry."

Sufael raised her mug. "We were an angry people. 'May you be free from God' was the greatest compliment imaginable, so it doubled as 'thank you.'"

Teltö smiled. The familiar Asrak burn spread through his stomach, along with something else.

"Are you still angry?"

"Want to find out?"

She pressed her lips to his, and as they kissed, he tasted the liquor on her tongue. Desire ignited. He toyed with her shirt buttons, and bared her brassiere. Her hands grabbed his shirt front. Fabric tore; Teltö slipped the ruined garment from his shoulders and flung it into the corner. Soon they lay down on the bed-roll, her body soft and warm against his, her breasts dark and beautiful in the lantern light. His fingers and tongue got to work. Sufael ran her hands through his hair. Her small gasps filled the compartment.

Teltö rode her hard. So much stress, so much anxiety... such sweet release. But even as he thrust, Sufael's legs locked around his hips, an old ghost returned to haunt him. *Tuvena.* Every failure, every inadequacy, Tuvena magnified a thousandfold. That time she'd told him...

"Don't stop."

He blinked, remembering where he was. Sufael was looking up at him, pupils wide and dark. She smiled, and ran her hand over his bare back.

"It's all right, Teltö. It's only us."

He kissed her passionately on the lips, and the unwanted memory dissolved like smoke before a wind. Sufael was right. It was only them, and all the world, all the past, could go hang. *This is happiness*, he thought, rising to his climax, *pure happiness.*

●　●　●

THE DAY DAWNED hot and clear over Skeevereet Station, and a breeze came from the Illuvian. Teltö rolled the sleeves up on the cotton shirt. Softer and lighter than the wools of the coat-bedevilled Empire, the Northern mufti also breathed better, though after last night, he didn't hold out much hope for its longevity. Not that he was complaining.

"Where does your family live?" he asked.

Sufael made way for a robed Churchman. "In the block of flats over there."

She pointed towards a distant tower. One among many, the dark crystal spire sparkled in the morning Sun. Teltö looked closer. What he'd initially taken as surrounding clouds were nothing of the sort.

"Is something the matter, Teltö? You've gone pale."

"The airships."

"What about them?"

Bombs. The rain of death. "They're not… appreciated… in the Empire."

Sufael cocked her head. "The Empire doesn't have airships."

"That we don't have them isn't the problem. It's that you *do*."

* * *

HORSESHIT AND FLIES paved the streets of Skeevereet, Teltö decided, as yet another carriage rolled past. Sufael pointed out this or that Count or Countess, but he'd long ago lost track of the names. He contented himself with nodding.

It's impossible to get lost. Just ask a Churchman for directions. Impervious to the heat, cloaked figures lurked like crows at intersections, no doubt watching for signs of the Mad God. Teltö smiled at one, but got no response. Sufael stopped beside a blossoming magnolia and pointed.

"The Embassy's there," she said. "Two streets straight, then left. You can't miss it, even if you want to."

Teltö smiled. "Thanks. About last night…"

"I'd invite you home, but I have to lay the groundwork with my father. He's a traditionalist."

"Doesn't like Imperials?"

Sufael chuckled. "More that the only good Imperial is a decapitated and burnt Imperial. He wouldn't talk to me for a month after I got my job. My brother's more understanding, but he's away in Klem."

"And your Mam?"

"*Mum.*" Her face fell. "Long story."

They kissed, and Sufael promised to meet up in a few

days. Teltö waved farewell and picked up his luggage. When he looked over his shoulder, the woman was gone.

● ● ●

TELTÖ PEERED THROUGH the iron railings, and groaned. In contrast to the crystal spires, the Imperial Embassy was a monumental maggot of an eyesore. Rusting fire-escapes criss-crossed barred windows and pale grey brick; lacking even the cosy ruinous quality of Keer's, the only thing going for it was endurance. It'd probably been five hundred years between paint jobs.

A walkway lined with dying fuchsias led up to the main entrance, where a solitary guard stood muttering to himself. Teltö approached with caution: the fellow had a rifle slung behind his back.

"Excuse me."

The man sneered down at Teltö, a waste of a pretty face. "Bugger off."

If only. Teltö bit his lip. "I'm on official business," he said, producing the talismanic paperwork.

The guard rolled his eyes. Sea-grey, beneath long lashes. "If you're official, the Empire's really going to pot. Right, in there."

He gestured towards the door.

Teltö turned to head through, but the man grabbed his shoulder and reeled him back.

"New regulations start today. Empty your pockets."

Teltö might've enjoyed a pat-down from such a good-looking fellow, but nothing slew a mood like bad manners and bureaucracy. *Nasty buildings and nastier personnel.* Having finally convinced the man he was not an existential threat, Teltö stuffed his belongings back into his trousers.

Inside, the reek of tobacco struck like a sledgehammer.

It smells like bloody Kuolinako in here. Teltö made towards an ajar door labelled 'reception'.

"Hello?" he spluttered.

A young woman lolled behind a desk, puffing away on a calabash pipe. Blonde, sleek, and shoeless, she kept both feet on the 'out' tray, and wriggled her stockinged toes at him.

"You would be what, exactly?" the woman asked in a bored tone. Her hair cut shortish for the current female fashion, she looked like Dyrstin with breasts. *Not a patch on Sufael's though.* Behind her, the air swirled around stacks of browning newspapers.

"Teltö Phuul…"

"If the name fits, wear it, I suppose." She blew a smoke ring and picked a dagger off the desk. Teltö guessed she used it as a letter opener. "Well, Phuul, what can we do for you?"

"I'm here with His Excellency."

"Can't see him myself. Got him in your pockets?"

Teltö let that one slide. "As part of his entourage, I'm to stay here for the duration."

The receptionist swung her legs down, upending an ashtray.

"By Father Life," she said. With a flick of the wrist, she sent the dagger spinning across the room.

Teltö ducked.

The dagger thudded into a dartboard alongside six others.

"Yes," the woman nodded, "you are serious."

• • •

THE RECEPTIONIST UNDID a latch. "In here."

Calling the room a cupboard would have been

charitable. The air reeked of mildew, and a horrid screeching emanated through the walls. Someone, somewhere, sawed at a violin, badly. A half-full ashtray rested on the pillow.

The woman looked down at Teltö; she had a good millifurlong on him in height. "So you'll be staying here a month." It was not a question.

"Yes." Teltö sighed. "Any chance of seeing the Ambassador this morning?"

"You don't want to see the Ambassador this morning."

He frowned. "Yes, I do."

Another smoke ring. "No, you don't."

"Did I tell you my sister is fiancée to His Excellency's nephew?"

"Try telling someone who cares. You'll want to see the Ambassador this afternoon."

Where do they find these people? "Afternoon it is," he said. "But early would be nice. Is he in a meeting?"

"No." The woman's smirk revealed red gums and yellow teeth. "He's on his nude run. The morning constitutional, he calls it. He'll be back in about two hours."

* * *

A CAFÉ STOOD across from the Embassy. Pleased they accepted Imperial bits and marks, and even happier at not dealing with dockets, Teltö bought coffee and a newspaper. Nearby, a family of four sat in silence, two pigtailed girls eating steaming soup under parental gaze. Teltö settled down at a corner table. One sip of his coffee, and he pushed the drink far to the other side. *We've got rationing.* He screwed up his face. *What's their excuse?* The newspaper featured mostly patriotic propaganda about the anniversary of the Nadir – or as they put it, the Principality's Founding – with something about a new Second Marshal being appointed after the death of the old one. *Ooh. Railway saboteurs apprehended by passing shepherd. Vöder's security strikes again.*

The café's door chimed, and street air gusted into the shop.

"For is it not said," boomed a voice, "that while we are all sad creatures of the Mad God, women are more warped, and so it is only by rejection of their temptations that humanity might become pure?"

Teltö looked up. Two Churchmen were pulling back hoods. Browned by the northern Sun, they both brandished staves; with their robes, beards, and clay pipes, they could have been twins.

"A tempting analysis," said the other. He blew a smoke ring. "But the implications are troublesome. For men are not so malformed, yet it is perversion for men to love one another. Such are the puzzles of He Who Must Be Fought."

Charming fellows. Teltö returned to his paper, and hoped the bookends choked on their coffee.

"Well, well," said the first beardling. "What have we here? A young man with hair of fire."

It's not fire, you prat. It's copper. Now go away. "Can I help you gentlemen?" Teltö asked in his best imitation of Hova's business tone.

"Are you a follower?"

"Not particularly, no."

"A shame. Fire burns the Mad God, and those with such hair are well-suited to fighting Him."

Teltö ground his teeth. While pleased his clothes made

him a passable, if pale, Northerner, their cultural oddities held little appeal.

He reached for his now lukewarm cup. "I'm more interested in drinking my coffee than in fighting Him, thank you." *Even this coffee.*

The Churchmen shook their heads, and buggered off to buy their own refreshments.

Teltö doodled through the crossword puzzle. Too many articles about the Confederation bored him. The letters to the editor were amusing though. Half these men, and they were all men, sounded like they'd never met an Imperial in their lives. *No, we don't love liches.*

"Excuse me, sir."

An aproned man stood over him.

"Yes?"

"You'll have to leave."

Teltö frowned, thinking he'd misheard. "I haven't finished my coffee."

"I can see that, sir." The man nodded apologetically, and scratched his curly black hair. "It's just that Count Groon will arrive in fifteen minutes. He owns this establishment."

"What does that have to do with me? Surely the Count wants people to drink coffee here?"

"Yes, sir. But not when he's around. He likes to use the establishment for relaxation with friends, and doesn't like customers getting the wrong idea."

Teltö pulled out his pocket-watch. He had to get back anyway, and the Ambassador awaited, preferably fully-clothed. He stepped out into the street with the newspaper wedged under his arm. Over at the Embassy, tendrils of smoke drifted from the upper windows. None of the passers-by blinked at it.

Basket in hand, a match-girl leant against the nearest lamppost. Foul breath and swollen jaw told of a life cut short. *Younger than Kyrmves, and she won't see fifteen.* Teltö gave her the remaining coffee, his face locked in a dead smile. *There are no liches here.*

* * *

THE RECEPTIONIST USHERED him upstairs. "He's in here."

Smoke crept from under the door. "Is it safe?"

"Nothing to worry about. You'll be fine so long as you don't mention his bald spot. Marshal Skom did that once; we had to hide the mirrors for a week afterwards."

Teltö ventured inside, hand clamped over mouth. Clouds of smoke drifted around the room, and gathered thickest around the fireplace, where a rotund gentleman with a bucket stood wheezing.

"You there," said the man, in an appropriately foghorn voice. "Have you come about the chimney? I poured water over it. Seems to have worked…"

"No, sir. I'm part of His Excellency's entourage." Teltö coughed. "If I might have a word…"

"You're the Phuul fellow." The Ambassador dropped the bucket; it clanged onto the floor and rolled under the desk. "Most excellent. Would you care to follow me?"

* * *

LINED TO THE rafters with books, and mercifully free of smoke, the study bespoke the sort of comfort a fellow could appreciate. The Ambassador sagged into a padded armchair. Plump, and with greasy grey hair stretching to his shoulders, the man sported a lemon-yellow waistcoat, a blue cravat, and fluffy slippers. There were no necromantic ribbons to be seen.

"I believe," said the Ambassador, somewhat breathlessly, "you sought me earlier? I do apologise. I favour a brisk run in the mornings. Good for the heart."

Teltö perched himself on the edge of the other armchair. "Indeed, sir. I thank you for taking the time out of your busy schedule…"

"Not at all. No need for 'sirs' either. I get enough of that from those bloody Northerners. The polite ones anyway. The more bigoted ones say it too, but they spit it out like a dose of cod liver oil. If there's one thing I can't stand, it's insincerity."

Then why did you end up in diplomacy? "So about my mission." Teltö's inner toady screamed at the lack of 'sir.' "The Tower has made me a temporary attaché for the duration of His Excellency's visit."

"Yes, I've read your file. Very interesting. Brandy?"

A world without rationing. So that's why he sticks around. "Yes, please."

The Ambassador pulled a book from the lowest shelf. He smiled. "A most special volume, this."

The book hid a flask within faux pages. Teltö imagined the pale cheeks of Dyrstin Venomavat turning a covetous green, and received his snifter with impeccable manners.

The man poured one for himself. "I used to be fond of Asrak. Not in polite company, of course, but things are so much more accessible here. Which renders brandy my current poison. Excuse me for a moment."

He crossed to the door, and tested the knob, banging it thrice with his fist.

"Most satisfactory."

The Ambassador removed the key from the lock and

slid it into his waistcoat pocket. He returned to his armchair, where he draped one slippered foot over the other.

"So." The Ambassador sipped his brandy. "You have been enlisted as another set of Imperial ears and eyes?"

"For the duration of His Excellency's visit. I was informed the regular intelligence staff are busy ensuring the Chancellor's personal safety."

The Ambassador studied him with watery grey eyes. "You don't believe that, do you?"

Teltö did his best to look shocked. "Pardon?"

"You're a bright lad, and the reports suggest you have a future. No, don't protest, I know you're only an underkarl. As anyone who's met Nhädiö Meerm knows, brains and rank do not always go together, but do you truly think they'd pick *you* to do Imperial spying?"

My feelings exactly. "It is not my role to question the orders from above. I serve the Empire as best I can." *And in return, they'll send me home. I don't ask for much.*

"It takes years to make a shadow-stalker, Phuul. Whatever you're here for, it's not to pick up something we don't know already."

"So why *am* I here?" Teltö regretted the bald question as soon as it left his mouth.

The man chuckled. "That, my boy, is something I am still trying to figure out. You're no use to us here, so your absence must be useful to someone somewhere else. It's only logical."

He leads me across treacherous ice. "But if my esteemed superiors desired my absence, are there not, um, other avenues of action?"

"Like disappearing you, you mean?" The Ambassador swirled his brandy. "Or sending you home? Where's the fun there? I don't know, my boy. I'm not sure I'll ever know. But I'll say this: your friend the Dragon isn't all-powerful, not by a long shot."

Teltö's brandy snifter froze halfway to his mouth.

"By Father Life, my boy, you look like you've choked on a cat. A plump and fluffy cat at that. But it's true. Even His Excellency must bow to reality. Perhaps it's not that Vyrellävek won't disappear you, but rather that he can't."

"But I'm an underkarl. He's the bloody Dragon."

"Yes, a mere underkarl. Up against Peta Vyrellävek himself. Do you know how our draconic friend achieved his nickname?"

"He eats virgins?"

"Hah, very good. I must remember that. The answer is *I* gave him that name, before he was Chancellor. Before he was Inquisitor General, even. Dragons of myth hoarded power, threw up powerful glamours, and breathed the venom of deception. So it is with Vyrellävek. He has cultivated an image of might, weaving threads of happenstance into the tapestry of legend. He took my little jab and ran with it, believing the moniker would enhance his reputation." A wistful look crossed the jowly face.

"He was right."

"Yes, indeed. But here is the curious thing: even the mighty find themselves caged. Often, the higher the rank, the smaller the cage. And in Vyrellävek's case, he forged the bars himself, back when his reforms turned the Inquisition into the organisation we know and love. The fiends of one's own creation keep many a man awake at night."

Teltö realised what the man was getting at. That even the Dragon lay powerless before the Viiminian Empire's bureaucratic apparatus cheered him, and that necessity favoured his continued existence cheered him even more.

"You'd better hope he never hears about this," said Teltö. "Cage or not, bureaucracy or not, he'd never let you live. As you say, he cares about his reputation."

The Ambassador shook his head. "Even were he listening to us now, I'd wager ten thousand marks he wouldn't do a thing. Disappearing me would upset a delicate balance. The secret of survival, my boy, is not hoping they ignore you. It's in making yourself indispensable. A cat that catches mice may be excused the occasional accident on all but the most elaborately woven rug."

Teltö finished his brandy. The smoky taste lingered on his tongue. "Perhaps he thinks I'm indispensable?"

"The eternal question remains: why? A puzzle more perplexing than any crossword." The Ambassador put down his half-full snifter. "Until further information arises, I'd advise you to continue the charade. You're writing reports?"

"Yes, sir."

"No 'sirs', Phuul," said the Ambassador. "It takes years to make a shadow-stalker, and following orders is the first thing they learn. But let me help your report."

The Ambassador held up his forefinger. "First, despite what you may hear, Oym is not stupid. Nor is he naïve. He is, in fact, highly intelligent, in his own way. But his conception of ruling differs from Vyrellävek's."

"He believes in love, rather than fear?"

"Love?" The Ambassador chuckled. "No. No one loves Oym, not even his wife. Oym believes in not ruling. For him, the task of a Prince is to smile and wave. To paint the perfect Illuvian sunset on the back of budget reports, and compose elegiac poetry during cabinet meetings. He has created a deliberate power vacuum in Skeevereet. There's only one problem."

"People try to fill the vacuum."

"Correct, my boy. But everyone tries to fill it at once, so Oym sits atop the fray like a regal gargoyle. A gargoyle, mind you, not a puppet. He does as he's told, but only after the advice filters through competing interests. So nothing much changes, which makes him happy."

"So how does he keep the Army in check?"

"I've just told you. He uses Vyrellävek to guard them, and vice versa. Look out that window and tell me what you see."

Teltö looked over his shoulder. "That window?"

"What other is there?"

Teltö put his empty snifter down, and got up. Outside, roofs spread towards the horizon, interspersed with dark crystal spires, chimneys, and…

"See the airships?" said the Ambassador. "They're part of the Principality's 42nd Airborne Division. They're getting disbanded, you know. One of Vyrellävek's trophies, what with ship sinkings making Imperial trade routes so vital for Skeevereet. The Army, you may surmise, was furious. Second Marshal Skom used rather non-judicious language to me over that."

Teltö frowned. "Skom's just died, hasn't he?"

"That's the one. Worst case of suicide I can remember. Poor man never learnt the art of indispensability. Anyway, let's say the new Marshal Ventiko is rather more diplomatic."

"Ventiko's an Imperial name."

"Yes, and the North needles him over it. He's prone to overcompensating. But scratch the surface and you'll be surprised. One more thing, can you cook?"

This caught Teltö unawares. "Cook?"

"Yes, cook. I believe you are fond of culinary pursuits?"

"I dabble." Teltö shrugged. "Everyone needs a hobby."

"Good," said the Ambassador. He rubbed his hands. "You see my old chef is no longer with us, and I'm having Ventiko around next week for a little repast. I wondered if you could do the honours? I apologise for short notice, but I do need to make you useful."

Indispensability is the key to survival. "Sure."

"Excellent." The man's eyes sparkled. "I've always said diplomacy begins with the stomach."

Chapter Eleven

G REY SKY AND grey sea, and gulls calling. A rugged beach of rock-strewn sand, and basalt pillars looking like forgotten monsters turned to stone. So far from home, yet so like the memories of Teltö's childhood. But that was another time, another place, and the southern shores of Dyrtölä were cool even in summer. The clouds here could not shield him from the humid heat.

"Behold the Great Lighthouse." Sufael barely sweated. "More fun than dealing with those cretins at the Embassy, right?"

When they'd met at Groon's café that morning, she'd offered to show him around. Teltö imagined this meant Skeevereet city, bars, and docketless shops. Sufael had other ideas.

He stared at the behemoth on its island of rock. "We built it, you know."

"No, you didn't. Neither did your parents, or your grandparents."

"You know what I mean."

"And you know what I mean. Those who built that

Lighthouse are long gone, as far from you as they are from me."

Disinclined to argue, Teltö had an idea. "What are the currents like out there?"

"Pretty tame. Why?"

"Fancy a swim? It took us a good hour to walk here; how about washing off the grime?"

Sufael chuckled. "Sorry, Teltö, brine's a bitch on my skin. And truth be told, I'm not that good a swimmer anyway."

"Suit yourself." He peeled off his shirt. "Look after this for me, will you?"

Boots, socks, trousers, and underwear followed. With the Northern woman's curses fresh in his ears, he bounded into the waves.

It'd been too long. Teltö settled into an easy breaststroke, his limbs finding rhythm as the cool water enveloped his body and washed away the sweat of the day. This was his element, the one thing he'd always beaten Rhea at. *And how I found Tuvena.* One furlong, two furlongs… Stroke by stroke, the Great Lighthouse edged ever closer, until his feet felt the contours of rock. Naked and dripping, he climbed onto the island like some invader from the deep.

A rival to Kuolinako's Tower, the Lighthouse's countless black and white bricks thrust upwards towards the clouds. The circular windows revealed little. Teltö tiptoed around a rock pool, onto a gravel walkway. He followed it.

Someone had screwed a plaque into the door. Teltö wiped away a cobweb, but couldn't make out words. He tried the door handle; flakes of rust came away in his fingers. *We build it, and they leave it to rot.* The path veered off his right, down to a jetty where two rowing boats moored. On the left shore stood a lone pohutukawa. Summer flowers not yet in full flame, the tree stretched twisted branches out over the sea, as if making one last grab at the horizon. *Nothing else here.* With a wave to Sufael, Teltö waded back into the water.

A furlong from land, something brushed his leg. Teltö ducked under, but saw nothing. He swam up and onwards. Then a nudge, and a tug at his ankle jerked him down. *What in blazes?* Had he caught himself in kelp? Twisting, he sought to break free as he sank slowly into the murk.

Teltö clawed at the bind, but its grip only tightened. Then something whipped out to grasp his other leg, and he nearly lost his hold on his breath. The white eyes of a Giant Octopus stared back; his confusion turned to terror. *It's not kelp, it's bloody tentacles.* He struggled, but the suction cups pinned him in place. The creature's mottled body bobbed about, its beak looming closer. *No. Please, not like this.* He sought something to shake the octopus off. But there was nothing, and they sank ever lower. Far below, he made out the sea floor. With pressure building in his lungs, Teltö lashed out. He punched the creature, but his arms moved slowly, as if he dreamt it. He felt so helpless, he could've cried. *Go, you vile horror.* Suddenly, the octopus tore away, and pain like hot knives ran across his skin.

With no time to reflect, Teltö kicked upwards. He carved through the murk, and made towards the precious, life-giving light. He needed to breathe, his chest near bursting... he exploded onto the surface and sucked in lungfuls of air, never so fresh or so sweet. Then he remembered the lurking peril. He ducked under, and saw the dark amorphous form floating below. *Go away.* Teltö fled, stroke after stroke, faster and faster. Any moment he expected tentacles to drag him down, but the creature did not reappear.

He clambered onto the beach, sore and gasping.

"Teltö? What in blazes was that about? You vanished."

Sufael's embrace was warm about his chest. "Attacked," he coughed. "Octopus. Big bloody octopus."

"But we don't get octopodes here. Well, we do, but they're small, harmless and timid."

"This one was big, mean, and trying to kill me." Teltö looked back at the waves. "It should've got me too, but let go for some reason. Something I'm bloody grateful for."

Hands on hips, Sufael shook her head. "So I take it you'll be more careful in future before jumping into strange waters? Ouch, it made a mess of your legs, didn't it?"

Ugly red welts ran along his calves. "It hurt like blazes."

"I bet it did. Come on, get dressed." She handed him his trousers. "We'll head back."

He towelled himself off with his shirt, tying it around his waist until it dried. Trousered and shod, Teltö followed Sufael through the rocky headlands, back to whatever passed for Northern civilisation.

"Couldn't we have gone to the normal beaches? The ones without killer aquatic life?"

"Everyone goes there, and we're not everyone." Sufael's eyes drifted back to his bare chest. "Besides, you wanted to swim, not me."

His reply was dwarfed by a loud crack, and something ricocheted off a rock. *What the...*

Sufael's eyes widened. "Run," she barked. "Quick,

this way, and keep off the sand."

She darted down a pebble slope, across a ledge and into the shadow of an overhanging cliff. Teltö scurried after her. *That was a bullet.* Images of octopodes with rifles flashed through his brain.

Sufael pointed at a small cave mouth. Largely obscured by the cliff, seawater lapped at its entrance. They sloshed through the high-tide foam, and ducked under the low ceiling. A nook to the left proved large enough to accommodate and secluded enough to hide. Together, they huddled in darkness, the wheels of Teltö's mind spinning as the rock pressed cold and hard against his back.

"Did you see them?" he whispered.

"No. I don't know. I don't even know if they're after me or you."

Why would they be after you? Any moment, Teltö expected the scuff of footsteps. He imagined staring down the barrel of a gun, and wondered whether he'd get last words before his brains splattered across the rock. To have escaped the octopus to die in a hole... The phantoms of the imagination were worse than Vyrellävek. With the Dragon you could face the danger. Here, there was nothing to do but wait.

Wait they did. His legs deadened, and the air grew cooler. Sufael waited in silence, her soft breathing a comfort. He put his arm around her. The shirt fabric rubbed against his skin, rough and reassuring. Then his ears caught something.

"Can you hear that?" he whispered.

"Hear what?"

"There's a strange humming in here."

Pause. "I can't hear anything."

The noise faded. Teltö didn't mention it again, but pulled his legs close to his chest.

At last, the Northerner stirred and elbowed him in the ribs. "Let's go."

The sky had grown gloomy, and the tide had receded, leaving a legacy of driftwood and shells. Rubbing life into his legs, Teltö saw no sign of pursuit. *Thank Father Life.*

"Sorry, Teltö." Sufael rubbed her own legs. "I'd no idea our seaside jaunt would be so eventful. So much for enjoying a day off."

Teltö spotted movement on the cliff top. He flinched, but it was only a seagull. "How will we get back to Skeevereet? Whoever they are, they'll be watching the roads."

Sufael snorted. "Even if they are, it won't matter. I know my way around here."

• • •

SLINKING ACROSS FIELDS, the return journey took a good three hours. The clouds were breaking up; by the time they came to the outskirts of Skeevereet, the stars were out. *No different from Qivunako.* Then they crawled out of the final ditch, and Teltö nearly screamed. Black against the shadows, a solitary figure leant against a roadside fence, its hooded head ringed by the light of a nearby warehouse.

"Are you a follower?" the creature intoned. It directed its question at Teltö, not Sufael.

Teltö breathed again. *Only a Churchman. Father Life, they're everywhere. They could give lessons to the bloody Inquisition.*

"Um, no."

The figure pointed. "What depravity were you practising there, down in the ditch?"

Depravity? How did crawling around in darkness aid

the Mad God? Then Teltö realised he hadn't put his shirt back on. Even at this time, the weather was balmy by Qivunakonian standards, and the bloody thing was taking forever to dry.

"We're married," he snapped. Father Life alone knew what these fellows thought of the Ambassador's morning runs. But he put his shirt on after that.

* * *

BARRED BLACK WINDOWS hinted at curtains unpulled for a generation, while the garden plants cast Kuolinakonian silhouettes in the streetlight. If Teltö hadn't known better, he'd have thought the Embassy abandoned. Even the guardsman had vanished. But Teltö did know better, and candlelight flickered upstairs. The gas-lamps were playing up again.

"Good night, Teltö," said Sufael. "Stay close to the Embassy and don't do anything stupid. Also, don't mention what happened today to anyone."

She was giving him orders? Teltö found his objections withering.

"Surely the Ambassador…"

"No one. Look, I'll find out what this was about. Your job is to stay safe."

"I…"

"Safety first, remember." She kissed him and vanished.

* * *

THOUGH HE BAULKED at taking orders from a Northern Ordinary, Teltö spent the next week kicking around the Embassy, and padding his Inquisitorial report with gossip. But mostly, he migrated to the kitchen. The chef-less, docketless kitchen. No one bothered him there: Physsil at reception ate naught but tobacco, and the other staff dissipated on sight. The Ambassador specialised in inviting himself to dinner at official residences, especially ones with good chefs. When here, the fellow contented himself with scrambled eggs and endless pots of industrial strength Northern tea. With a spot of milk.

As for Reqi the guard, Teltö discovered the man's fondness for cheese and gherkin, and sought to use it for advantage. Every day at noon, he trundled down to the front door with a sandwich platter and a glass of iced lemonade, and every day Reqi's frosty exterior melted a little more. The security man even started sharing anecdotes about Northern military foibles, all of which found their way into the report.

"I tell you, Teltö, the North can keep their Rughvneer M6941s and M6969s, and those morons back home can keep their Sämö-Sömö 8289s. There's nothing on the continent as effective as this little beauty."

Rifles all looked the same to Teltö. "What's so special about this one?"

Reqi's eyes never left the weapon. "The F.L.Z. 23X. This thing shouldn't even exist. The Northerners wanted to beef up the M6969's power while switching to a more Imperial style of assembly. As any idiot knows, Kuolinako keeps it simple, so even liches can use the old Sämö-Sömö, but the standard Rughvneer's more complex to take apart. The North always thought it a necessary evil. But, you see, this part slots in here..."

Teltö blinked. "You said this shouldn't even exist."

Reqi paused. "Well, the prototypes failed; Northern conventional wisdom said it couldn't be done. Prince Oym's advisers finally redirected funds elsewhere, and this particular weapon was literally the last off the line. It drifted around as a curiosity before I got my hands on it. Turned out it succeeded where the prototypes had failed, but no one had subjected it to rigorous enough testing to realise. Now it's mine!" He stroked the barrel. "Mine."

Teltö snuck his arm around the guard's waist. "You know, I was wondering if you'd let me hold it." He smiled. "Just the once."

Reqi shoved Teltö away. "You? Don't make me laugh. I'll bet you don't know one end of a Rughvneer from the other."

*   *   *

"DOES HE HAVE interest in anything apart from that bloody gun?" Teltö muttered whilst pottering around with his beloved pans. "If I flirt any harder, I'll burst." It wasn't that Reqi only swung one way, or that he'd gone native with weird Northern ideas; he didn't seem to swing at all. Teltö found it most perplexing.

I'll read up on guns. That should melt him. How hard can disassembling a rifle be? Teltö's stomach rumbled. *I'll start after lunch.* He whipped up a pile of cinnamon toast and added a generous dose of maple syrup. He could do with a drink or two as well, but the alcohol at hand was only fit for cooking, and stocking up would involve leaving the Embassy. *Which I can't do.* Teltö wolfed down the last of the toast and licked the plate clean. Then he went in search of Physsil.

He found the receptionist in the dining room, emptying ashtrays into a rubbish bin. Teltö sneezed.

"Excuse me. Where would I find the gun closet?"

Physsil raised her head, a scalpel intensity in her blue eyes. Teltö flinched. Not for the first time, he wondered where she'd come from and how she'd come to work here. *It can't be the money. She'd make twice as much throwing knives at the circus back home.*

"Reqi send you?"

Teltö shook his head. "I need it for a report. The Empire needs to know this place's capabilities."

"Of course." Physsil sat on the table. "Closet's through there. You might need a crowbar, too. The door's a bit stuck."

"Where do you store the tools?"

"We don't store them. They wander around by themselves."

* * *

THE CLOSET DOOR gave way. Coughing at the dust, Teltö peered inside. The place housed mummified moths, a few dozen pine boxes – bullets presumably – and a gun rack. He tore down the shroud of cobwebs. There was something else too. *Could it be… yes, it's a corpse.* This must have been the lich guard, here to ensure nothing went walkabout, and thankfully on what technically counted as Imperial soil. *The Necro in charge must've left it behind.* Teltö assessed its jaw. *An undecomposed, usable corpse.* Smile turned to broad grin. *No one will mind if I borrow it.*

Teltö sent the lich down to the kitchen on cleaning duty, then lifted a rifle from the rack. He dusted off the barrel. *Probably old. They might not make these any more.* Perhaps it was valuable? Reqi would know. But Reqi would be even more impressed if Teltö could disassemble it before showing him… *There's some old military manuals in the Embassy library.*

Teltö had been to the library a few times now, and knew a short-cut. He ducked through a well-furnished side-office…

Their conversation halted mid-sentence, the important gentlemen looked at him as if he were some club-wielding barbarian from the south-west. Teltö smiled sheepishly.

"There you are," said the Ambassador, recovering first. "Meet Second Marshal Snali Ventiko, Vice-Commander of the Army of the Principality. Marshal, meet Teltö Phuul, our temporary attaché, and renowned chef. He will be cooking this evening's repast."

Oh shit, I forgot it was today. "Pleased to meet you, sir." Teltö bowed. Bald as a ball-bearing, and decked out in a crisp blue uniform with epaulettes, the newcomer towered over the fluffy-slippered diplomat. No wrinkles or folds lined Ventiko's face; the brown skin stretched tight and smooth over the skull beneath.

"Teltö's all the way from Qivunako," added the Ambassador. "What's on the menu, my boy?"

"Beef stew, sir." *My dinner for the next couple of nights. Bastards.*

"Just beef stew?" growled the Marshal. A contemptuous sneer crossed his taught features.

"Seasoned, sir." Regardless of the Ambassador's feelings, circumstances sometimes demanded liberal lashings of honorifics. "And custard pie with wine-steeped plums."

Ventiko shook his head. "I cannot abide alcohol."

Bugger. "Sorry, sir. Make that custard pie with whipped cream."

"Sounds appetising," said the Ambassador. "Feel free to make use of whatever you find in the kitchen." He cocked an eyebrow. "Whatever are you doing with that rifle?"

"I found it, sir," said Teltö. "So I'm putting it back before it causes any damage."

"Excellent, my boy. You'll go far."

"Preferably," said Ventiko, inspecting his nails, "to the bottom of the Illuvian."

The Ambassador chortled. Teltö conjured pleasant images of denting Ventiko's polished skull.

"Very good, sir."

• • •

THE MARSHAL'S SNEER seared in his memory, Teltö grumbled back to the kitchen. *So he's overcompensating. Not just for his Imperial name either.*

Teltö searched the cupboards again, and savoured the possibilities of overdosing the pie with nutmeg. Alas, it'd have to remain a fantasy: Teltö would have to swallow Ventiko if he were to see Qivunako again. Yet while the dutiful part of his brain screamed at him, passive submission felt wrong. Humiliating. This fellow wasn't even an Imperial – he was a Northerner, the traditional enemy. A Northern leader, in fact: perpetrator of plots against the Empire. *If only I can get the bald bastard without hurting him.*

The lich grabbed a mop and attacked the window cobwebs. Seeing it in the light, Teltö realised he'd overestimated preservation. Bits weren't dropping off just yet, but still…

He had it. An ear or two chopped up and mixed with the stew. No one would ever notice.

• • •

EYES DOWNCAST, PHYSSIL ushered him into the office. She'd been twitching all morning, as though fleas were under her skin. Teltö smirked. One person's discomfort was another's delight, and the air downstairs had become breathable ever since he'd hid her tobacco tin in the gun closet. *Nothing personal, Physsil, but I don't want Kuolinako Lung.*

The Ambassador paced the fraying carpet in his slippers. His hair unkempt, the man's bloodshot eyes suggested a difficult night. He sipped desperately at a cup of tea.

"You wanted to see me?" said Teltö, shutting the door.

"Yes, Phuul. I am not amused, not amused at all."

More chimney problems, perhaps. "My condolences."

"The Marshal has fallen ill, and must miss the Anniversary Banquet this coming Doomsday."

"Do we know the cause?" Teltö feigned curiosity as if his life depended on it. It likely did.

"A stomach complaint, I believe. You didn't have any bright ideas, did you?"

Shit, shit, shit. "Bright ideas?" He pushed his hair back.

The Ambassador waved the saucer. "Like putting anything in the pie. Or the stew."

"If there had been any problems with the meal, you would be sick yourself, and the Marshal's physicians would detect any added poisons." Teltö had moved the stew into separate pots, but the Ambassador needn't know that.

"True enough," said the Ambassador, a pinch of Dragon in his watery gaze. "It might just be a coincidence."

"A very unhappy coincidence." Teltö gave a wan smile. "I hope the reputation of the Embassy has not been besmirched."

"Ventiko is not accusing us yet, but if anything is traced back here, the culprit will be dealt with most judiciously. Do you get my meaning, Phuul?"

Teltö nodded. "Loud and clear."

"I do believe poisonings in your presence are not a rarity."

"The Inquisition found and dealt with Hova's poisoner."

"Yes, they did." The Ambassador finished his tea, and propped the cup and saucer atop a desktop folder. "But enough. Prince Oym himself will visit us tonight."

"Another repast?"

"A social call. Oym only eats food he has prepared himself. A habit he picked up from the Chancellor, I believe. I advise keeping yourself scarce."

"But my report…"

"Is coming along nicely with useless information. The Nine Authors did not take counsel with slugs, and neither do I. We do not need useful information from you. Please go."

Teltö bowed, and departed. *Bugger.*

Teltö stepped out into the warm breeze. He tasted salt from the wind blowing in off the Illuvian. *And I can't even enjoy a trip to the beach.*

"Cheese and gherkin again suits me," said Reqi. The F.L.Z. 23X at his feet, the guard leant back in a deckchair, savouring the weather. He'd dispensed with his shirt.

"Sorry," said Teltö. "I'm off for a walk." *Bugger Sufael. If someone guns me down in the street, it's just as likely to be the Ambassador's bunch.*

"Be back soon then." The guardsman smiled. He had a lovely smile when he had a mind to. "Hey," he added, dropping his voice to a whisper, "want to come round to tonight's spider war? Good way to make a few bits on the side."

Teltö stopped short. "You a Necromancer?"

"Me? No. Guild mechanic who got betrayed, dumped into the army, and reassigned. It's a familiar story around here. But I'm no slouch at animating spiders."

"But aren't spider wars banned?"

"Of course. Just like Asrak at home: doesn't stop us expats from doing it. What do you say?"

Teltö still hadn't reassembled the rifle; metallic odds and ends littered the kitchen table. *I need more time. Besides, if it's spider wars, I'm more likely to be bankrupted than bedded.* "I'll give it a miss."

"Suit yourself. But I still want to thank you for the sandwiches, so here's two tickets to Oym's Anniversary Banquet." He pulled a couple of cardboard squares from his hip pocket. "I won them last week, but I've other things on that day. Take a friend if you like."

I could on-sell these. "Very kind of you," said Teltö, shifting his gaze back to Reqi's face.

He headed down the road. Carriages sped along, scattering street urchins and dumping horseshit. A procession of Count such-and-such's household guard trod on each other's heels. And the Church, always the Church, lurked on every corner, and smoked like Kuolinako.

The shops themselves sold little of note, for prices that were. Teltö noticed a pawnbroker's ahead; one of the door-balls was missing. He jiggled the Embassy spoon in his pocket.

•　•　•

THE DOOR SLAMMED behind him. *Meerm wants a war, for this.* There were the carts and cafés, but nothing that'd ever make you want to come back. Skeevereet was a poor man's Mustanako, save for the crystal skyline and the airships circling over its sparse carcass.

Teltö drifted with the crowds, finding himself in an open-air square paved with dull-red brick. Men with briefcases came and went through arches and doorways, or else ate triangular sandwiches alongside squawking seagulls. Beneath a statue of some hero on horseback, three beggars squabbled over a meat pie. Teltö realised where he was. *Victory Square, the Heart of the Principality.*

More lavish than any structure he'd yet seen in the North, a strange building squatted on the far side, enclosed by a perimeter fence. Flags and clock towers graced the roof, while a central spire reached up towards a bitter pinnacle. The Palace of the Prince, restored to glory after its torching during the previous war. In the shadow of the gates, uniformed men paraded in a figure-of-eight pattern around twin three-tiered fountains.

"They must get very bored, doing that."

A man sat on a bench, a wry smile spread across his ageless and strangely familiar features. Brown-faced and brown coated, the fellow rested his hands on an unvarnished walking stick.

"You mean the soldiers?" said Teltö. *Where have I seen him before?*

"Who else? They do it every day too, except when it rains. Scares the seagulls more than the Empire, I'd imagine."

Teltö's mufti notwithstanding, he didn't feel comfortable. "Nice day, isn't it?"

"It is. The problem is keeping it that way. Dark clouds from the North, dark clouds from the South, they come together and make life difficult for us all."

Easy for him to say.

"Though all of this," the man waved his hand at the square, "would make a lovely painting. Oil on canvas, I think."

He doesn't work at the Embassy, does he? Teltö looked over at the Palace. One of the men who'd torched the old one had painted its destruction; the piece now hung in the Qivunako Public Art Gallery.

"I think it's been done."

"I know," said the man. He smiled the smile of a grandmother being taught to suck eggs. "I was thinking something a little less violent than Kloveio. Have you seen his original?"

Few Qivunakonians hadn't. The nightmarish phantasmagoria was a rare point of civic pride, serving as a tourist attraction for the morbid and the Mnomo.

"Not in person," said Teltö. "I've heard about it though."

The man nodded. "You must see it. Beautiful and terrifying, and Kloveio's only work. The poor fellow gibbered away his twilight years in an Imperial lunatic asylum, you know."

"Did he?" They'd never mentioned that on his statue.

"The worst events make the best art. So we must stop good art before it happens, yes?"

"Only if you can control history."

"The purpose of politics, lad, if there is one. Though I often think it's more being in the right place at the right time. For myself, I prefer the easel. It's easier to depict events than create them, and one's work lasts longer." He smiled. "I see Count Alliom walking his dog. I must say hello…"

The man limped away. His left foot twisted inwards as he walked.

.   .   .

"WHAT ARE YOU doing?" hissed a voice. "I told you to stay at the Embassy."

Teltö jumped back from the drapery window. "Believe it or not," he said, "control of my movements falls outside the jurisdiction of Mustanako Fisheries."

Sufael wore a high-necked shirt, buttoned all the way, and a dress that fell to her ankles. Some people, it seemed, were immune to heat. She snorted.

"People want to kill you. People with sniper rifles. Anyone could be waiting round the next corner, and yet you decide to dawdle through the city." She shook her head. "You're insane."

Who in blazes does she think she is? "Perhaps that chap at the beach wanted you instead," said Teltö. "I don't see you hiding out with that Dad of yours."

"Don't bring him into it, you southern bastard. Especially after what your lot did to him."

"'My lot?'" Teltö realised he was shouting. He smiled apologetically at a passer-by. "What do you mean? What's happened?"

Anger flickered in her dark eyes. "He's had his life destroyed."

Teltö blinked. "What, gunman got him too?"

"He's an airship pilot. Thirty years in the 42nd, now redundant because Oym decided to bend over and take it from your oh-so-nice Chancellor. Bloody coward. I mean, at least when they phased out *rulion*, there were humanitarian issues."

"*Rulion?*"

"Stop with the parrot act, Teltö. You know: we used it to make Mustanako glow in the dark. But my father's heartbroken. He loved those contraptions, and has a way with them like no other. Now what? He's too old to learn another trade. I'm having to support him financially…"

"No pension, I'm guessing."

"Not for him. The Commanders look after themselves, but precious little trickles down. Also, the thing about the North, Teltö, something you Imperials can't begin to understand…"

"Thanks."

"It's true, you insensitive prat. You can't understand how humiliating it is for a man to be dependent on his daughter. My father's not only lost his job, he's lost his pride."

Teltö noticed Sufael had red rings around her eyes. He hugged her. "Come on," he said. "Let's have a cup of tea."

Her lip quivered. "Thank you."

•   •   •

THE TEA-ROOM BUSTLED with people. Teltö pushed past a dandy in an opera cape and nearly tripped over a small child.

"If ever there was a creation of the Mad God, it's small children," he muttered, collapsing onto a leather couch.

"Do you think it's safe here? I really…"

"We're fine." Teltö sniffed the tobacco-heavy air. Churchmen lurked in the far corner. "Our gunman waited until we were alone, so I think there's safety in numbers. Now, tell me about your Dad."

Sufael poured out her problems while Teltö reordered tea and lemonade. *Everyone loves a listener.*

"You know what would really cheer you up?"

Sufael finished her drink. "Oym and Vyrellävek's heads on spikes?"

Teltö grinned. "Apart from that."

"Sorry, Teltö. I'm really not in the mood."

"Not that either. Behold," he held out Reqi's tickets. "We can go to the Anniversary Banquet!"

Sufael took one. "Where did you get these? Certain people would kill for them." She frowned. "You didn't kill anyone, did you?"

"No. But Qivunako Iron has good connections."

She smiled. "I'll go with you then. On the condition that we get seats down the back. You'll excuse me for wanting to punch the Powers That Be in the face."

Teltö put his arm around her. "Who could blame you?" He kissed her cheek.

Sufael pulled away. "And only if you stay at the Embassy. I'm not taking a corpse to lunch."

"I understand. I've never met a lich with decent table manners."

Sufael laughed her long rolling laugh, and suddenly everything was right again. Teltö leant across and kissed her full on the lips. For one sweet moment, he forgot about snipers, and Inquisitors, and reports. It was just them, like on the train…

"Creatures of the Mad God," growled a passing Churchman.

Teltö smirked. "Married."

The tea on the table grew cold, but Teltö couldn't have cared less. When closing time came, they wandered hand-in-hand into the lamp-lit street.

*   *   *

SUFAEL FOLLOWED HIM back to the Embassy.

"Be safe," she said as they farewelled among the fuchsias. Reqi was gone, and lights blazed through the barred windows.

"Everything will be fine," said Teltö. He ran his fingers through her black hair; intoxicated by her smell. "I've almost finished my report. Then I can go home."

Sufael grinned. "What report would that be, Phuul?"

Oops. "On how Qivunako Iron can best diversify its markets over the next five years. Nothing important. Well, it is important." He smiled sheepishly. "You understand."

That laugh, again. "Yes, Teltö. I do."

• • •

THE EMBASSY REEKED even worse than normal; Teltö spluttered as he opened the reception door, resolving to call Physsil up on it. *So she found the tin.* But the protests died on his lips.

Half a dozen soldiers lolled around on the floor playing cards. All male, all wearing blue, and all armed and smoking. One sat on Physsil's lap; the woman seemed to be enjoying herself as she raised a half-empty bottle to her lips, and swayed ever so slightly as her new friend's fingers went a-wandering. Teltö glanced at the dartboard. No daggers were in evidence.

"Who in blazes are you?" snapped a man with a chocolate bar. He reached for his Rughvneer M6941.

"Don't mind me," said Teltö. "I just live here." He coughed. *May you all die of Kuolinako Lung, and your throats bleed red.*

"So he does," said Physsil, "for a month. *Hic.* And for the last time, it's Fees-sill, not Fies-sill. I'm an Imperial, not a shit-for-brains Northerner like you lot."

The man on her lap laughed. "So it's Prince O-eem to

you, then?"

"Doesn't work like that," muttered Teltö.

"*Hic.* Right you are, Phuul," said Physsil. "Hah! That's an idea!" She pulled a pencil from her shirt pocket, and scribbled something on the bottle label. "Read that," she said to the Northerner.

He squinted. "Tell-toe?"

Physsil shook her head. "There's a sodding umlaut." She swigged from the bottle. "Why can they not read a sodding Imperial umlaut?"

A door to the right opened, and two figures emerged. One, grey-haired and slippered, the other…

Teltö frowned. *Too short to be Ventiko, and he's got hair.* Wearing a scarlet military uniform, the fellow leant on a stick. His foot twisted inwards. The man from the bench, but now he looked important, very important. Teltö nearly slapped himself.

"So," said the Ambassador, patting Oym on the back, "see you on Doomsday."

"Yes," said the Prince. He seemed untroubled by the malodorous mundungus. "It promises to be delightful. Snali would have loved it, of course. He has a thing for seafood." Dark eyes met Teltö's. "And here is the young gentleman I met earlier who appreciates art."

The Ambassador cocked an eyebrow. "Teltö, my boy, I never knew you for an art connoisseur."

That's because you don't take counsel with slugs. Teltö grinned. He was about to launch into a lecture on Kloveio's use of colour when something at the edge of his vision moved. A tower of newspapers toppled over and buried the soldiers' card game.

"Oh dear." The Ambassador's chins flushed. "We're going to have to give this place a clean-up. Physsil, clean this up."

"*Hic.* Right away," said the receptionist. She pushed her companion off her lap, and giggled hysterically as the poor bastard thumped arse-first onto the floor.

Teltö almost felt embarrassed for the Embassy. *Come on, baldy, show a slug how you deal with a diplomatic incident.* But Oym was no Ventiko. The Prince nudged the black and white avalanche with his stick.

"We really must do this again," he said.

Chapter Twelve

Teltö whistled his way across Victory Square. He'd dusted off his best clothes, including his good waistcoat, and if the cravat identified him as an Imperial, so be it. Today meant bygones-be-bygones, free food and drink, and if all went well, sex afterwards. For once, even his thicket of red hair was behaving. *And I've finished that bloody report. Thank Father Life for Reqi.*

He dallied outside the Palace Gates. Warm westerly winds gusted across the Square and billowed the hair and dresses of passing grandees. Soldiers hurried homeless people along and Guardsmen sneered down from the perimeter wall. No one spared him a glance, let alone took pot-shots.

The clock towers had just chimed ten in the morning when Sufael came running. A dark-grey dress bared her arms.

"Teltö." She rubbed her eyes; she'd clearly been crying again. "I must leave early. Father…"

He pursed his lips. "Come on," he said. "We'll be late."

. . .

OYM HAD A pond in the middle of his grass courtyard, complete with lily pads and a barely readable dedication slab. Unripe plums from the overhanging tree bobbed about in the water, mingling with leaves and twigs.

Teltö knelt at the edge. "I wonder if they get servants to clean it out."

"Every morning," said a voice. "At sunrise."

A man in red velvet and faded yellow sash stood clutching clipboard and pencil. "You are here for the Banquet? Both of you?"

Teltö grinned, and got to his feet. "We're not here for the plums."

"I should hope not. A plum tree has grown here since the Founding. It would offend every true Northerner for an Imperial to so much as touch it."

Teltö opened his mouth, then noticed Sufael's look. He reached for his pocket. "Our tickets."

The man checked his paperwork. A line of hair circumnavigated his otherwise bald scalp; tufts protruded from his temples like goat horns. "I cannot recall seeing you before."

"I'm on temporary appointment."

"I see." The little bastard flicked a white-gloved hand. Teltö took this as permission to continue.

Teltö had no inkling of the way to the Banquet Hall, and Sufael didn't either. Luckily, there were enough well-dressed people who did. Underlings in crimson jackets lined the corridors at regular intervals, noses in the air, and eyes more soulless than the wallpaper. A veritable parade of living wax statues who existed only to serve. *There are no liches here.*

The Hall doors stood open, revealing a room larger

than that of Mustanako's Governor. Stained-glass windows featured a litany of violence: swords, axes, and flames on one side, the crushing of black skeletal forms on the other. *The North isn't big on subtlety.* One window depicted a whirlwind twisting across skulls and parched landscape. A wooden throne and table stood on the far dais, flanked by several lesser seats. All were unoccupied.

Sufael found a place in a back corner. As this put the Dragon at the far end of the Hall, Teltö heartily approved. He settled into his chair.

"Some sort of religious thing?"

"What religious thing?"

Teltö pointed to the embroidered tablecloth. Red runic letters ran from edge to edge.

Sufael reached for the water decanter. The lemon plopped into her glass. "It's the names of the ruling family, together with prayers to give strength in the next world."

"Strength for what?"

"Strength to fight. The Church holds that we'll keep living and dying until He is dead."

"What happens when God is dead?"

Sufael drank. "We'll have some out-of-work Churchmen."

Teltö shuffled his chair closer to the table. "That was some warm hospitality we got at the door. Where does Oym find these people?"

"You're wearing Imperial garb."

"So what? We're here to celebrate five hundred years, aren't we?"

"Goorit reesh, ang goor reesh."

"Pardon?"

"We are, you're not." Sufael stared into space.

Teltö craned his head around. The people who spent

vast sums to look the same as everyone else chattered away at the other tables. Northern elites looked much like Qivunako's, Teltö noticed, only less pale. Further-up, medals glittered in a sea of blue uniforms, while frocked beardlings sat stern and silent in the shadow of the dais.

"Anyone sitting here?"

An old man in blue twirled a droopy white moustache. Pale scars criss-crossed his brown face.

Teltö shook his head. *No medals. Interesting.*

"Thank you." The man lowered himself into a chair. His joints creaked. "Nelim Foorit."

"Teltö. This is Sufael."

Foorit nodded. "Good to meet you. You'll excuse me if I prefer your company to elsewhere in the Hall." He poured himself some water. "So what are your connections to all this?"

"Embassy attaché."

"Permanent or temporary?"

"Temporary."

"So you're here to do something, rather than as punishment."

Teltö felt his cheeks reddening. But Foorit didn't push the issue.

The soldier nodded towards the empty dais. "I haven't attended one of these in years. Skom and friends regarded me as an embarrassment, and you know the modern Army: sheep. I don't know enough about Ventiko, unfortunately. Met him once, but that was years ago."

"What does the Army hold against you?"

"Long story."

A passing Churchman glowered at the old man. "Traitor."

Foorit smiled sadly. "Longer story."

Trumpets sounded. People hushed and got to their feet.

A procession entered from a side door. Decked out in scarlet and silver, Oym himself led the group, a sword at his hip. *But he still uses the cane.* The Dragon dogged his footsteps, greatcoat defying Northern climes. Other dignitaries followed, none of whom Teltö recognised, while the Ambassador brought up the rear, for once not wearing his slippers.

The elites took their places at the High Table. The Prince nodded, and everyone sat.

"Thank you, for your attendance," said Oym. He sounded small and shrill. "Today we mark five centuries of tears and bloodshed."

He waved at the Hall's stained-glass windows.

"But no more. No more shall mothers wail and fathers grieve. No more shall our sons return with bodies mutilated by His will. For today we commence a new chapter in our history, one of peace. His Excellency Peta Vyrellävek, Grand Chancellor of the Viiminian Empire, is here to share this historic moment. Chancellor, would you care to speak a few words?"

The Dragon nodded, and stood. Silent for a moment, he stared out over the guests. Teltö felt the temperature drop.

At last, the Chancellor spoke, and his deep accent reverberated around the Hall.

> *"Bitter was the battle,*
>
> *Bravest lie neath gravestones,*
>
> *Cities age in sieges,*
>
> *Soon brought low by foe-men;*

Trust is put to test and
Tales send mortals wailing,
Dead will bask at dusk while
Deeds are darkness feeding.

So spoke a Northern poet long ago. Hostility, you may gather, is nothing new. I know this myself, coming north during the dying days of the last war with a rifle and muddy uniform. That conflict, as history informs us, was nasty, bloody, and pointless. I shan't trouble you with its horrors. But during our final march back to the Wall, I truly realised that our peoples share a powerful bond. That beneath the hatred, beneath our all-too human flaws, lie nations capable of gratitude and warmth. For there was an ambush, and a scarred-face Northerner stood over me, blood dripping from his bayonet. I expected to die, and if truth be told, the memory haunts me still. But the man offered me his hand, not his steel, and so I lived. He is here today, and once again I thank him for this act of compassion, a bright flicker of trust and hope in a world too-often darkened by treachery and deceit. I therefore speak with complete truth in wishing the Principality a more peaceful and prosperous five hundred years. A toast, then, to Prince Oym, and the North."

"To Prince Oym, and the North!" echoed the crowd.

Vyrellävek sat, amid enthusiastic applause from the nobles and officials, and scattered clapping from the Army and Church. More speeches followed, but Teltö paid little attention. Foorit commanded his full attention.

"You saved Vyrellävek?" *No wonder they hate him.*

Foorit nodded. "That I did. Lean little lad with mangy yellow hair, looked even younger than he was, and dripping blood from a dozen cuts, not to mention terrified out of his wits. I knew the boy was turning my dead mates against me – destroying liches on a battlefield gets messy – but I couldn't do it. So here he is, and here I am. I only escaped court-martial because someone lost the paperwork and everyone else forgot."

"They remembered enough to shun you and take your medals."

"Nah, Vyrellävek came searching when he became your Inquisitor General. Wanted to thank me, but some bastard newspaper got hold of it, and, well, the wife left me, and most of my surviving mates haven't talked to me since. If it weren't for a special pension, I'd have starved. As for the medals, I chucked them. Worthless bloody metal earned in a worthless bloody war. See those preening bastards." He jerked a thumb towards the Army tables. "Not one in ten fought in the war, yet look at their glitter. If it weren't for Vyrellävek, I wouldn't have come."

"But don't you hate him? He's the reason you lost everything."

"I'd do it again. Swatting liches is one thing, but killing boys is another. Sometimes you have to do what's right." Foorit smiled. "Besides, he's lived to give us peace, hasn't he?"

Teltö remembered the Death Pools of Kuolinako. But if loving the Dragon was all Foorit had, he wasn't going to take it away.

"He has."

The first course comprised steamed mussels. Back in the world of rationing, Teltö would've been delighted, but recent experience had refined his tastebuds. A bit too much pepper in the sauce, he decided. Across the table, the old man blew steam from his meal. Teltö dwelt on

Foorit's determination to make a stand for common decency. *He means it too.*

Men in red carried the plates away; Oym rose once more.

"If I may have your attention again, I have several announcements. First, I would like to thank our southern visitors, and in particular the Grand Chancellor. Skeevereet is deep in your debt, Your Excellency. So deep I wish to offer a gift as token of my esteem. All remaining war reparations owed by Kuolinako shall henceforth be forgiven…"

The Dragon's done it. There'll be dancing in the mines of the Last Capital when word gets out. Teltö imagined Vyrellävek's smirk of victory at the next Grand Council meeting. Ration dockets would soon burn throughout the Empire. *I'll save mine. Good toilet paper.*

Someone tapped his shoulder.

"Teltö." Sufael leant so close her mouth brushed his ear. "We have to leave."

His brows knitted. "We? I can meet your Dad another time."

"I'll explain later." She nodded at Foorit. "Sorry, sir, we need to go."

The old man smiled, but Teltö knew those eyes were deep wells of sadness. *Years spent knowing he'll die alone and unmourned, save only for Vyrellävek… it must be like a living death, a self-aware lich.*

"If you want to meet up," said Teltö, "come to the Embassy. I'm here another week."

"Thank you, lad."

• • •

TELTÖ STUMBLED PAST the guards, and out into the

afternoon.

"Sufael, what is this?"

"Quickly," she said. The folds of her dress waving in the wind, she dashed across the Square.

Teltö ran after her. He now regretted all those easy Embassy meals; the stitch in his side hurt like blazes. But she didn't stop until they reached a side-street.

"This had better be good," he panted. "We ran out on a lovely lunch and a lonely old man."

"In here."

Bemused, he followed her into an alleyway. Save for a one-eared cat gnawing a fishbone, they were now alone.

Sufael pushed him up against the wall. "I've lied to you, Teltö."

He frowned. "What? How…"

"I was mulling it over all through the feast. You see, I discovered something. Something important. I know who wants to kill you." Her eyes blazed. "Vyrellävek."

Teltö squirmed against her iron grip. "But if he wanted me dead, the Inquisition…"

"The Inquisition is protecting you." She released him. "I should know: I've been tasked with it. And now I have a decision to make."

She's a shadow-stalker. "But your job in Mustanako, your love of stories…"

"Are genuine. Even Inquisitors have lives." She gave a wistful look, as if remembering her lost innocence. "I did find your Qivunako Iron lie amusing though. I let you keep it because you'd never have come up with a better one."

All my women turn into Tuvena. Teltö straightened his cravat and resolved to stick to men in the future. They were less complicated.

"I have orders, Teltö. Orders to keep you safe until you boarded the train home. Now?" She shook her head. "I'm not sure I can let you go home."

"You're going to kill me?" Teltö flailed around for something to use as a weapon. There was nothing, not even a dustbin lid. "After all we've been through? You cold-blooded bitch!"

Sufael chuckled. "No, Teltö. I'm not going to kill you. The reverse."

"How do you know it's the Dragon anyway?"

"A trade secret. But I now realise why you were sent here. It puzzled us no end. Vyrellävek didn't want to pick a fight with the Tower, so had to get you out of our range. When you turned up dead, he could blame Skeevereet and extract additional concessions."

"So the sniper at the beach…"

Sufael nodded. "In his pay."

Teltö thought it through. "He gave my sister one last look at me during her Engagement Party. How nice. But the Tower wants me alive…will the Inquisition roll over?"

"Not Vöder. You saved her life, and she was ready to send you home – as a newly-minted informant – when the Chancellor made his request. The one remaining mystery is why the Dragon wants you dead."

"Never mind that, how do I get out of here?"

"That's the problem. If I follow orders, I'd take you back to the Banquet, let you board the train, and wave goodbye. Put you down as a successful mission, and a fun fling. Who cares if Vyrellävek and Vöder fight over you afterwards, or if your carriage runs off the rails into a ravine? I've done my duty. Yet…"

"Yet you care about me."

Sufael smiled. "Yes, Teltö, I do. So I had an idea. My

father is heading to see my brother in Klem. He leaves this afternoon, and you need to be with him. You can lie low there."

"But I want to go home. Bury my head under a pillow, and never go further than the Qivunako General Library ever again. And my family…"

"Please, Teltö. Don't make this any harder."

•   •   •

TELTÖ SUPPRESSED TEARS as he changed into his cooler Northern clothes. *I don't want Klem. I want Qivunako.* But in the Empire, when authority came calling, he didn't get to choose. *On the run or not, I'm still a good little underkarl. I'm sorry, Rhea. I shouldn't have mocked your cage. I've got one myself, only less glamorous.* How many years must he spend in exile before he could see his family again? He stuffed the rest of his gear into his suitcase and satchel, and crept down the stairs.

Physsil snored at her desk. Teltö briefly considered waking her. *No.* He couldn't even say goodbye to the Embassy staff, not with the Dragon hunting him. *Which side will the Ambassador take?*

Sick at heart, and with luggage threatening to explode, he dashed after Sufael.

•   •   •

THE FURTHER TELTÖ headed into eastern Skeevereet, the more the city evoked Kuolinako. The crystal-topped tower blocks, office buildings, and shops had been left behind; he now saw a wilderness of billowing chimneys and rumbling machinery. The Principality's industrial heart did not stop even during a national holiday.

Two children sat on the steps of a brick building, their eyes gleaming through their sooty faces. Teltö felt them watching him. *There are no liches here.*

"I hate this part of the city," said Sufael as they reached a crossroads. "I wrote a poem about it as a child. Not a very good one, but I remember being so proud at rhyming mills with hills and choke with smoke."

"Do the workers around here use gas masks?" He'd nearly said living workers.

"No. When the poor bastards keel over, the owners get a fresh trainload from the provinces. Most factories are owned by Counts, so they're just moving underlings around. The Church condemns it, of course."

"Good on the Church."

Sufael raised an eyebrow. "Not really. The Patriarch says this is the work of the Mad God." She waved her hand at the chimneys, the brick, the chains, and the dirt-encrusted windows. "But he's wrong. This is the work of human beings, self-inflicted for generation after generation. The Prince, when he bothers poking his nose beyond balcony or easel, talks of an age of progress. Soon, he says, we'll have lightning at our fingertips. But it won't stop people living and dying in the same old filth. Nothing will truly change."

"Not too different from the Empire then."

She shrugged. "At least the Empire's honest about it."

Teltö chuckled. "That's because we don't have a future, only a past that hangs over us like a ten-tonne boulder. I know you think you're getting ahead by joining the Inquisition, but to misquote the Nine Authors, we're naught but maggots south of the Wall, feasting on what little flesh remains. If you want to be chief parasite, be my guest."

"Feeling more cynical than thou, Teltö?"

"Nothing wrong with being a parasite."

They turned left, past a rusting barbed wire fence, and came to an open space between two abandoned warehouses. A Northern military airship parked on the drab slabs of concrete, looking for all the world like a giant carnivorous slug. The sight raised the ancestral hair on the back of Teltö's neck. Few Imperials had set foot in one, and fewer had lived to tell the tale. Lacking stable access to safe gases, Kuolinako's own experiments had not ended well.

A stout man in blue paced beside the gondola, his pipe-smoke curling into the breeze.

"Sufael." The man's bushy grey moustache twitched. "Who is this?"

"Teltö. I met him in Mustanako."

"This is that Imperial you told me about?"

Sufael waved her hand. "Father, he's a friend, and if you could take him with you…"

"Now you ask." Sufael's father strode towards Teltö, his dark eyes never leaving the Necromancer. "No Imperial scum will board my ship, dead or alive."

"Father, please. He hates Vyrellävek as much as you."

Teltö nodded. "It's true. The old bastard can go hang. I'd throttle him if I could."

The man cocked his head. "Why would that be?"

Think, Phuul. "I've converted to the true faith of the Northern Church. The Inquisition's after me."

Father turned to daughter. "Is this true?"

"Every word."

Sufael's father nodded. "I've never known my little girl to lie." He jabbed his pipe-stem at Teltö's chest. "Well, if Sufael vouches for you, I'll let you aboard. No bloody religious natter though, or off you go."

"I promise, sir." That, at least, was truthful.

. . .

THE SHIP'S MAIN compartment had rows of pine seating behind the controls; decorative yet deadly, two sabres hung between the windows, and someone had pushed several crates of beer against the rear wall. Teltö inspected a bottle; he swiftly replaced the Ruvian Bitter.

"Bunks are that way." Sufael's father indicated the rear door. "Stick your stuff in there, sit down and shut up." He sagged into the pilot's chair and fiddled with the controls.

"Bye, Teltö." The Northern woman ran her hand through his hair. "You were the best assignment I ever had."

One final kiss, before she hurried over to hug her father. Then with nary a wink, she was gone. *The last friendly face for a long time.* Teltö settled onto a bench, and looked out as the propellers hummed into life. He wondered what his mother would think. That he'd been disappeared, most like. He couldn't even get word back to her, not while the Dragon still lived, and that old bastard had ruled the Empire since before Teltö was born. *Sorry, Rhea, but right now I need a dragon slayer for Uncle Peta.*

"We'll be off to Klem soon." Sufael's father did not turn around. "Things to drop off first."

. . .

IT FELT STRANGE looking down on a city. Like a standing at a table with a map, but a map that was vast and alive. The vessel drifted over roads and factories, and still they rose; soon carriages and horses seemed mere insects. Hazy clouds of smoke hovered past the airship windows, until they too were left behind. To Teltö's right, towers of dark crystal sparkled in the Sun, a cluster of black spikes stretching from earth to sky. Eastern Skeevereet spread out like a carpet of chimneys.

Sufael had been right; there was something intoxicating about the world from up here. Behind the dread and destruction these machines wrought lay an unimaginable beauty, a chance to see things anew. *I wonder if Vyrellävek's ever flown. Probably, but he'd miss the wonder. Everyone's an insect to him anyway.* But if they could only conquer hereditary fears, Dyrstin, Kyrmves, Rhea, and the rest would surely love it. A shame the Confederation still embargoed gas exports to the Empire, and no amount of reconciliation could change that.

The smokestacks were soon gone, replaced with the slate roofs and green enclaves of the central city. Victory Square approached, like a red rectangular desert. *The Palace.* The pilot descended, until the airship hovered atop Oym's very roof. *They'll still be eating down there. Dessert, perhaps.* Teltö's mouth watered regretfully. He switched seats for a better view. Then something shiny and cylindrical caught his eye, something metallic falling towards the Palace. Had it broken off the ship? He pressed his nose to the window, in time to see whatever it was shatter amid smoke and light. The light grew brighter, brighter, fierce as the Sun…

The airship lurched, and Teltö was nearly thrown from his seat. He grabbed the bench to steady himself. The bottle crates rattled across the floor; something thudded and crashed in the bunk room. And outside… he blinked. White fire had engulfed the building below, spreading across the roof in an ever-rising tide. Pale and bright in the clear afternoon, the flames clung greedily to the arches of Oym's Palace. *What the...*

"That'll show 'em," said Sufael's father. His eyes blazed.

"But, but..." stammered Teltö. "You've...You could have killed them!"

"I killed them all right. What you saw there, lad, was the very last stockpiles of *rulion*, the rain of death as you Imperials call it. So passes an age."

He shrugged and turned back to the controls. A few switches later, the airship moved away from the wreckage, running towards the north.

From a distance, the devastation became apparent. Masonry snapped like matchsticks, and the inferno devoured the clock towers even as they tottered and fell. Fiery tentacles, silver and deadly, climbed the central spire until it shone over Skeevereet like a colossal candle. Teltö shielded his eyes as a sudden burst eclipsed the Sun itself. Then the glare faded and the spire was once more a grey spike in a clear sky. But only for a moment. A shudder ran through the structure. It crumbled slowly at first, then faster and faster, until with the weight of a falling hill, it collapsed onto the burning Palace. Smoke rose from its fall.

The rain of death. The residue ignited in air, Teltö knew. Those not incinerated would choke in the toxic fumes gathering over Victory Square. This crazy bastard had killed his Prince, the Ambassador... the Dragon. Teltö shuddered. The air had suddenly grown heavy; he felt sweaty beneath the light Northern shirt. *The Dragon's gone. Twenty-five years up in smoke. A new age for the Empire. Perhaps... no, this is too much. This means chaos. Worse than chaos. There'll be a Fifth Northern War.*

"But why?" he heard himself squeak. *The Inquisition had everything covered. They just weren't prepared for madmen.*

Sufael's father snorted. "You want to know why? They took my ship away, the bastards. Thirty-seven years of loyal service, and I'm sent to the slag heap with no thanks and no future. Well, I made sure they have no future either."

Teltö licked his strangely dry lips. "But this'll lead to war."

The man turned. "No problem with that. It's war against the Mad God's Domain. No one's innocent. Not me, not you, and certainly not those bastards back there. The Principality's rotten, the Empire's worse, and long may they smite each other. One man could've changed it, but he betrayed me. There's always betrayal."

He knows something. Teltö kept his voice steady. "Who was this?"

"You wouldn't know him. An Imperial Master from Qivunako with grand plans for revolution, and a new dawn for North and South alike. I never met him, but reading his letters, the genius sparkled. He even sent us money via phoney trade agreements. Then we killed him. Had to. He passed our secrets onto Vyrellävek. The bastard played us like fools."

Teltö had to sit down. *So this is the true assassin. Hova's Skeevereet contact. And Hova wasn't just running guns, he was plotting a bloody revolution. Maybe. But if he's a double agent working for the Chancellor, why did he think the Chancellor was out to get him? No, Keer must have found him out...*

"You've gone white as a sheet, lad. Do you have relatives in Qivunako or something?"

"Um, no. I just read about it. It was that Hova fellow, wasn't it? The poisoning made it to Mustanako's newspapers."

"Aye," said the man. " 'Twas Hova. Slow poisoning with cough medicine did the trick. He was addicted to the stuff. The silly bastard didn't even have a cough."

Teltö had tried that medicine himself. It'd tasted horrible with Asrak. "I also read about a Theatre bombing in Kuolinako…"

"Wasn't us. Have no idea about that one."

Teltö wiped the cold sweat from his brow. "Why are you telling me this?"

"You won't tell anyone. We're riding this out in the Confederation."

There was safety here, Teltö realised, as the airship passed over the terraced houses of northern Skeevereet. He just needed to keep his mouth shut, and he'd spend the next few years in Klem, distant from unfolding catastrophes. An escape. Besides, Vyrellävek had tried to kill him. He owed the Empire nothing.

But there's going to be a war. Sufael? He wasn't sure about her complicity in her father's scheme. But poor silly Rhea, Dyrstin, even Kyrmves and his parents back in Qivunako, their lives were about to be changed forever. He had to get back – and now he *could* get back, with no more Vyrellävek out to off him. *And this mad bastard needs to be dragged to justice.*

The man wasn't about to listen to reason. Teltö needed some other persuasion. His eyes were drawn to the sabres on the wall. Outside historical re-enactment, no one bothered with such things; from what a cousin in the service told him, standard issue bayonets were glorified butter knives, there if one ran out of bullets or intact corpses.

Teltö hesitated. Every moment took him further from

his family, further from doing the right thing. Part of him pleaded to sit down before he killed himself with his own stupidity. *I know nothing about sword-fighting.* But could he ever look his parents in the eye again? *Duties must be carried out lest our last world crumble. What's my duty here?* Life was easier when it was library stamps and Asrak. With a deep sigh, he crept over and reached for a sword.

"I wouldn't do that if I were you."

Teltö jumped. Sufael's father strode towards him, disgust congealing on his face.

"You Imperials are all the same." The man's tone was calm, strangely reminiscent of his daughter. "Blood always tells."

"Turn back." Teltö's firmness disguised his terror. But it was too late to change his mind. He'd have to see this through, to whatever end.

"Hah," said Sufael's father. "Can you pilot an airship?"

Teltö blinked.

"Say you stabbed me with yon sword. What then? You can't pilot. Kill me, and you doom yourself. And for what? The bombs have dropped and the war is on."

"I don't want to kill you," Teltö whimpered. "I want you to turn back."

"Don't think I will."

Teltö pulled down a sabre. "Yes, you will."

Before Teltö could stop him, the man took the other. "Don't think so, somehow. You really are a fool, aren't you? You could've put your feet up in Klem for a few years, but no. It's futile. Absolutely futile."

No one will ever know. Teltö clenched the hilt until his knuckles whitened. Then a face swam before his eyes. Not his parents, not his sisters, not Dyrstin or Sufael. The scarred face of Nelim Foorit, the man who'd lost everything. *And who has just been killed with all the rest.* A sudden calmness settled on him.

Teltö smiled grimly. "Maybe you're right, but sometimes you have to do the right thing."

"Suicide is never right."

"So murder is?"

"Ask the Inquisition. Ask the ashes of your friends and fathers. Don't pretend that every last one of you Imperials isn't swimming in blood. But enough. You've decided to die an unknown hero, and I'm not going to disappoint."

Teltö leapt back as the thrust nearly gutted him. *Father Life, that was quick.* Survival instinct asserting itself, he dashed away, putting a bench between himself and his opponent. He edged back until he felt the wall behind him. His heel kicked against the bottle crate.

The man advanced. "Don't you know? Heroes don't run. They stand and fight."

Teltö lunged wildly, but the pilot parried with ease. The steel bit back, darting towards his face like a pouncing snake. Teltö had no time to block. He threw himself left and went sprawling on the floor. The wind momentarily knocked out of him, he kept his sabre upright, warding off the next attack. But the man only smiled. He flicked his wrist, and suddenly Teltö's blade went spinning away. It ricocheted off the wall and rattled onto a distant bench.

"You don't know much about swords either. A shame. I could've taught you. I used to tutor lads on it…"

I'm about to die. Oh shit, oh shit. Sheer instinct took over. Teltö reached over his shoulder and grasped something cold and smooth. A glass bottle. He threw it.

The beer struck the man's forehead. He staggered back, cursing. Heart in mouth, Teltö threw another, but this one sailed harmlessly past his attacker's ear. It shattered as it landed, sending Ruvian Bitter flooding over the floor. Teltö threw a third beer, which the man dodged, then a fourth. Side-stepping straight into the puddle, Sufael's father lost his footing and tumbled back. His head cracked against a bench. Teltö broke a bottle, and leapt to his feet. He darted towards his groaning foe.

Scraping the jagged glass across the throat was easy. The man lay gasping and bleeding before Teltö realised what he'd done. *I'm a murderer.* The pilot clutched vainly at his severed artery, the red spurting through his fingers. Clouds of blood mingled with puddles of beer. *What have I done?* Teltö retreated, and looked around numbly, somehow expecting the Inquisition to seize his arm and lead him off for punishment. But the shadow-stalkers weren't here. *He's an enemy of the Empire. Is this the right thing?* Life left the dying man, and Teltö could only stand and watch. Droplets of blood trickled from the bottle onto his shoes.

Teltö shut his eyes. "You had it easy, Foorit."

But it wouldn't matter. He couldn't pilot. *I'll give it a go. I can only get myself killed.* There were worse ways to meet the Mother Eternal.

Teltö tiptoed around the blood and beer to the front of the airship. The windows revealed rolling green hills and the Illuvian in the distance. The afternoon Sun illuminated an otherwise pleasant Northern day. But far from in the mood for scenery, Teltö Phuul had other concerns: the controls, a jumble of wires, switches, and buttons. *Where's Reqi when you need him? He's a mechanic, isn't he?* Teltö flipped a switch. Nothing happened. The airship continued drifting over the countryside towards the coast.

Teltö looked back at the body. He didn't want to

gamble on residual knowledge, but still…

The blood-covered lich shambled over. Teltö instructed it to steer back to Skeevereet. It didn't move. Teltö cursed; he needed to make the instructions more specific. *But how to visualise landing? What button, which switch is needed?* He tried again, once more with no response. The lich stood unmoving, with imagined accusation on its face.

Panic rose with each failure. Teltö gritted his teeth and looked out the window. The airship was leaving land behind, and the Illuvian spread out before him, waves rolling across its blue expanse. If he didn't stop, he'd run out to sea and drown. Teltö pulled a lever. Suddenly a high, awful screech rang through the compartment, and the airship swung downwards and sharply to the right.

Frozen at the controls, Teltö hoped against hope that he'd crash into the shallows, and make it out before he either drowned or was incinerated. Then another shape loomed: a black-and-white cylinder upon an island of rock. The Great Lighthouse. Pressing buttons did nothing to alter the collision course.

I'm going to crash into the bloody Lighthouse. Someone help, please help. Teltö threw his hands up, and raced the length of the airship, into the bunk compartment. He rolled under a bed and curled into a ball. *Any moment now.* He buried his face in his hands, as the seconds ticked by.

"Father Life, please…" Tears ran down his cheeks. "I don't ask for much, but please…"

A roar, and heat, as if someone had opened a smelter door. A glass window shattered, tinkling shards falling like hailstones. Teltö shut his eyes. The floor up-ended itself, and he felt himself sliding. He grasped blindly, but could feel nothing. *Am I dead yet?*

Then suddenly he was falling. He spread his arms

instinctively, and opened his eyes just long enough to glimpse a seagull overhead. It squawked at him. *Mocked by a bird: what a way to die.* He held his breath. Any second now...

Teltö crunched into the clutches of the island's pohutukawa. Twigs tore at his skin, and soft, cool leaves brushed his cheek. He slammed his hands over his face. The twisted branches scraped and strained under him like a nest of snakes. Then, suddenly, the tree released him and he splashed into cool water. He felt a vicious knock to the back of his head, and everything went strange. As if his life had skipped a couple of seconds. There were stars too... he sank some way before he regained his senses.

Still groggy, he kicked off his light northern shoes and swam for the surface. He emerged beside a floating wooden door. All around, burning flotsam and jetsam drifted on the waves. *Shit.* Wreathed in fire, the airship crumpled down the side of the Lighthouse; motors and other debris crashed onto the island. *Thank Father Life that was a Northern gasbag.* If it'd been one of the Empire's old models, he'd have been cremated. The wreckage had set the pohutukawa alight too; flames – real ones, not the rich, red flowers – spread hungrily through the upper boughs.

Something landed nearby, and a splash of salt water hit Teltö's face. He made for shore.

Chapter Thirteen

S OFT SAND AND smooth stone met his feet as Teltö staggered onto the beach. In the distance, the conflagration of wreckage rained down upon the sea, basking the Lighthouse in an orange glow; taking with it the remains of the man who'd started the Fifth Northern War, the man Teltö had murdered. The Necromancer groaned. He'd left his luggage on the airship. Now he had stranded himself in an enemy country with no money, no shoes, and a torn shirt. *And blood on my hands.* Teltö banished the thought.

He wrung out his sodden clothes, and hung them over nearby boulders to dry. He'd been lucky overall, he realised, checking himself over. Some minor burns, cuts, scrapes, and bruises, all of which still stung, but it could have been worse. He looked across at the pohutukawa that had saved his life. It burnt like a torch. *Much worse.* Unable to sit still, he paced the sand. From time to time, his eyes scanned the basalt cliffs, lest he renew an old acquaintance, but nothing moved save the gulls. *Whoever you are, you can leave me alone. Vyrellävek's dead, and his secrets died with him.*

The more Teltö thought, the more complicated it became. He'd give anything for his life back in Qivunako: to relax in the armchair; to have his mother run her fingers through his hair, the way she did when he was young; to lose to Kyrmves at spider wars. Without the Dragon, the way south was clear… except it wasn't. How to cross a continent convulsed with war and revolution?

Revolution. Some were not content to live like happy parasites on the Imperial carcass. Some wanted change, and were doing it under Vyrellävek's very nose. *Hyät Hova, revolutionary.* So behind the spite and pedantry, Hova plotted for a better world. It didn't make the bastard any less annoying, and treason was still treason, but for a moment it offered a small and fleeting glimpse at a different life. *A higher-up who cared about something other than himself.* Teltö wondered who else held ideas. Keer knew, that was clear. But given Keer's friendship with Vyrellävek, it wouldn't be collaboration with Hova. More likely, the old man passed information back to the Dragon. *No wonder the pilot suspected double agency. He was right about the leak, wrong about the leaker. He should've poisoned Keer, not Hova.*

But this still left the Theatre bombing. Were multiple groups stirring up mischief south of the Wall? Sufael's father had used the term *we.* Where were the other members of his gang, and what did his daughter know? If she'd been complicit, she'd have come with them. Or maybe not; shadow-stalkers were shadow-stalkers for a reason, and now Teltö had no idea where to find her. *Perhaps for the best. She might resent me killing her Dad.*

Teltö sighed. A throbbing headache was coming on, and he needed to get out of here. He looked out across the water, and the snatches of a song his mother once sang came to mind:

> *From your home to farthest coast*
> *Luck shall smile on them the most*
> *Who make their own first fateful step*
> *And shirk not hardship…*

He'd forgotten the rest, but the catchy tune raised his spirits. He hummed it while the afternoon Sun warmed his bones and the road ahead beckoned. *I need to get back to the Embassy.* Reqi and Physsil seemed his best chance: with fresh clothes and team work, they might all scurry back to the Wall before the North ignited. Once safe in the Empire, Teltö could throw himself under the Tower's protection and use Vöder as his ticket to Qivunako. *Not something I'd have countenanced two months ago.*

His clothes were no longer waterlogged. He donned them and climbed the slope towards the main road, goosebumps dotting his skin beneath the clammy fabric. But before leaving, he looked over at the Lighthouse one final time.

"May you sleep warm in the embrace of the Mother Eternal," Teltö whispered. Overhead, the seagulls circled.

*   *   *

A GINGER CAT toppled a rubbish bin, the clang ringing through the near-deserted suburban street. Everywhere Teltö looked, petite bungalows frowned back through the lengthening shadows. Every curtain had been pulled, every lock fastened. Acrid odours wafted on the breeze, a scent he knew only too well.

Skeevereet was a city in fear.

Blue uniforms rounded the street corner. Teltö leapt

over a picket gate and dived under the nearest rhododendron bush. Twigs raked his back. Peering through the fence, he saw a dozen soldiers with Rughvneer rifles at the ready. *Keep on going, lads, keep on going.* At length, the stomp of boots faded. Teltö crawled from his hiding place and breathed again.

Past the residential ring, and into the city proper, hazy clouds hung over the tower blocks, obscuring the spires. Every second building had burly men testing locks and chains. No one spared Teltö a glance. The few Churchmen he saw kept to themselves. *Even they're afraid.* Teltö passed an alleyway where three hooded figures crouched beside a rubbish bin. *They've had their leaders massacred.*

Coming to a crossroads, he heard gunfire to his left. More people travelled the streets now, but they all hurried the other way – out of the central city. Teltö pushed past a crying child.

Soldiers emerged from a café carrying a kauri table. Half the windows lay shattered, and the men's boots crunched noisily through shards of glass.

"What do you think you're doing?" one snapped at Teltö. "Don't you know there's a roadblock ahead?"

Another chuckled. "You're under martial law now, laddie. I'd slither back up whichever drainpipe you came from."

The Necromancer hurried away down an alley. At least they didn't think him an Imperial.

• • •

TELTÖ STUCK HIS head around the corner and pulled back in frustration. *It's like a deadly game of hide and seek.* He'd have been caught already if that last checkpoint hadn't been so obsessed with a deaf and elderly Northern woman. These bastards brandished rifles at what looked like a couple of shopkeepers.

They're everywhere. Worse, the day was running out, and Teltö only had the vaguest idea of Skeevereet geography. Returning to the Embassy didn't sound such a bright idea now, but it was too late to turn back. *If only Sufael were here.* He pushed hair from his eyes and retreated further into the alley, until he felt a drainpipe press against his back.

Teltö blinked. *A way out.* He spotted a rubbish bin a couple of centifurlongs away. It reeked of fish. Wrinkling his nose, Teltö dragged it over and climbed atop the lid.

Now comes the hard bit. Thank Father Life it's a low roof. He imagined some soldier shoving a gun at his back and demanding identification he didn't have, but he forced himself on. Teltö clambered up the drainpipe and heaved himself over the guttering onto the sloping tiles. He dipped his elbow in fresh seagull shit, but he didn't care. He was safe.

No sooner had he flattened himself against the roof when he heard voices below.

"You hear something?"

"I'm sure I saw something."

"Probably just a cat. What's in here?" Teltö heard an iron clang. "Fish-heads. Yes, a cat."

"Let's go. This place reeks like the Mad God's armpit."

Teltö pressed his face against the tiles; his heart thumped madly. Marshalling courage, he wormed up to a rusted weather-vane. He clutched it and looked over the city. A maze of roofs, steeples, and chimneys spread out beneath the darkening sky. To his left, behind a pair of tower blocks, billowing smoke shrouded central

Skeevereet. *Victory Square.* He perked up. With this macabre compass, he could navigate back to the Embassy.

Minute by minute, furtive rooftop scrambling took him ever southwards. The stars began to appear, granting him the cover of night, while fires burnt at the Army's ever-expanding checkpoints. Teltö watched for the firefly lights of the patrols. Three times, they nearly caught him, and once his fingertips clawed the guttering when soldiers blundered around a corner. Then a scratching sound startled him. He turned to see green eyes. The cat hissed and vanished.

He finally found himself staring at the rear of Count Groon's café. Cross the street, climb a fence, and he'd be outside the Embassy gates. Almost too simple. *What if they've cordoned the place off?* He cursed, realising his entire journey might be for naught. But one thing at a time. He needed a way across.

Barely three centifurlongs away, the Northerners had thrown up a barricade of upturned furniture, and the blue bastards swarmed around it like flies. A body slumped face-down on the cobblestones. Blood pooled around its head and glistened in the watch-fire light. Further along the road, the pin points of lanterns warned against attempt from that direction. A shot sounded, and the Necromancer shuddered.

As Teltö crept back across the roof, a dozen hooded figures turned into the street and approached the barricade. *Churchmen.* He stopped to watch.

A man in blue stood in front of a busted table. "Papers please."

"Who presumes to stop the Most Holy Order on this night of all nights?"

"The 25th Regiment, by order of the Second Marshal.

I must see your papers."

The Churchmen did not even deign to pull back their hoods. "We do not answer to your Marshal. We are the Most Holy Order, and shall this night elect a new Patriarch as we have in synod after synod unbroken since the Founding."

"My orders make no exceptions for the Church."

"Let us through. Your mortal soul is in peril, sir. The Mad God walks tonight."

With the men in blue facing off against the men in black, no one was watching the road, and no one had yet lit the street lamps. Teltö retreated some distance, and around to the right. A park stood opposite, set aside for picnickers in happier times. Several oaks cast their shade far and wide. If he could reach it, he could swing left to the café, then the Embassy.

Heart in mouth, Teltö jumped down onto the cobblestones. No cries of discovery. *Don't run; it'll give you away.* He kept his head down, even as his ears strained for the clatter of booted pursuit. Teltö reached the other side and darted behind a tree trunk.

· · ·

THE COMFORTING UGLINESS of the Embassy reared up. By happy chance, the Northerners hadn't set up a checkpoint outside; Teltö waited for a patrol to pass, then snuck across to the gates. A soft breeze brushed through his tangled hair, carrying the unmistakable whiff of burning.

Reqi had buggered off somewhere. Teltö bit his lip. He of all people wouldn't condemn a man for laziness, but a guard on the door might come in handy this evening. Then something caught his eye, and he looked up. For a moment, a gas-light seemed to flicker in the barred upstairs windows; Reqi had repaired the lamps last week. But a second glance revealed nothing. *The lights are going out from here to the Fells. Will they ever be relit?*

Inside, Physsil slumped over her desk, snoring. She grasped a half-empty Asrak bottle. Teltö moved to shake her awake.

"Errrr, what time is it?" The receptionist blinked pink-rimmed eyes. Twin daggers impaled the desk either side of a paperweight.

"The time doesn't matter," Teltö snapped. "The Dragon's dead, and Prince Oym, and the Ambassador, and Father Life knows who else. Martial law's been declared."

Declared by Ventiko. Too sick to attend. I saved the bastard's life. Teltö might have laughed, but now was not the time to reflect on irony.

"I know." Physsil sat up and stretched. "Asrak?"

He thrust the liquor away. "Not now. Listen. Who else is here?"

"They ran off. Now it's just me. And you."

"Where's Reqi?"

"Out." She yawned cavernously.

"We need to get out of here."

Physsil chuckled. It sounded like a death rattle. "And where will you go, Master Phuul? Home? You have a home. Some aren't so lucky. Some had our homes taken from us. Some had our lives taken from us. There's more than one way to disappear someone." She slumped, and pillowed her head with her elbow. "Go where you will. I've got nothing."

Teltö gritted his teeth. *Think, Phuul, think. You'll need a plan... you'll need fresh Northern garb. Wandering around Skeevereet as an Imperial is a health hazard tonight.* Teltö dashed upstairs to the Ambassador's chambers. He found the doors locked. *Bugger.*

He ran to the tool cupboard and grabbed an axe. Then he attacked the locked door. By the time it gave way, Teltö felt his arms almost ready to drop off. He was lathered in sweat.

"Right," he muttered. He let the axe fall to the floor. "He must have spare clothes somewhere."

The room was small and tamely furnished. A teapot and a half-eaten plate of scrambled eggs perched atop a dirty little bureau. Beside the narrow bed, a dusty bookshelf housed Northern religious tracts. Teltö mentally tipped a hat to the deceased diplomat. The fellow had shown more austerity away from rationing than other officials ever did under the dockets.

Teltö tried a side door and revealed a closet. *Austerity doesn't extend to clothes, does it Mr Ambassador?* There were cloaks and coats, hats and cravats and scarves, shirts and trousers, waistcoats ranging from yellowed fabric so bright it looked almost luminous through to the stygian extremes of funereal black. Accessories for every occasion. There were even seven sets of slippers, each with a label attached for a specific weekday.

Teltö could have spent hours in here. Hunting for the thinnest outfit he could find – no easy task – he at last emerged with a fresh set of clothes. The closet featured a full-length mirror, and he studied himself with approval. His new garb may be oversized and gaudy, and the shoes too pointed for his blistered feet, but the style was Northern, at least.

Teltö dashed to the Main Office. He found the door unlocked, so he poked at the paperwork and reports. A letter mentioning Physsil piqued his interest; it bore the Tower's letterhead. But Teltö had more personal concerns. *What's the next attempt on my life? Another shooting? A rail accident on the way back?* No mention of his name caught his eye; even the letter rack buried no secrets.

The office grandfather clock struck ten, jerking Teltö to his senses. He didn't have time for indulgences.

Some things he would never know.

● ● ●

FORCING LUKEWARM AND fiendishly strong coffee down Physsil's throat didn't help.

"Look," said Teltö, through clenched teeth. "You must know someone who can help."

"People, yes. Help, not a sausage." Physsil gestured around reception. "Why not sit here with me and drink to the end of the world? I'd offer you tobacco, but the tin's missing."

"No thanks," snapped Teltö. "I intend to survive."

Physsil smiled. "Survival, now there's a thought."

The front door slammed. *Hold on, I locked it.* Teltö straightened. Heavy footsteps came down the corridor; grabbing the Asrak from the desk, he crept over to the reception door. He felt ill. Fighting Northerners with glass bottles? He remembered the blood gushing from the throat of Sufael's father. The door swung open. Teltö gripped the bottle tight and lifted it…

Reqi.

"What in blazes is going on?" shouted the guard, his dark hair ruffled and confusion gripping his handsome face. "Someone's kicked a bloody anthill out there."

Teltö lowered the liquor in relief. "Some crazy bastard dropped a bomb on the Anniversary Banquet. The rain of death at that."

Reqi's jaw dropped. "Who did it?"

"I'd bet my grandmother Kuolinako will blame the Northern Army, and that the Army will blame us. Whoever did it took out both Vyrellävek and Oym."

"And our boss," added Physsil. "No more naked runs."

"Oooh," muttered Reqi. "This is bad." He frowned. "Hey, you were there, weren't you? How did you escape?"

"Right place, right time," said Teltö. "Now, how do we get out?" He repressed the urge to shake the fellow by the lapels.

"I know some people. Well, lots of people. I'd never have made it past the checkpoints otherwise. There are plenty of Imperials in Skeevereet. They just keep their heads down."

"Doubly so after this, I'd imagine. Let's go find them."

"Hold on." Reqi waved him back. "I need to collect a few things. Oh, and Physsil," he pulled out a leather pouch, "this is for you." He threw it across the room.

Sitting at her desk, the receptionist caught the pouch with one hand. "Why thank you," she said. "I've been all out too." Physsil grinned her horrible yellow-toothed grin. *Tobacco.*

* * *

TELTÖ PACED THE reception floor. He'd fetched the antique Rughvneer from the gun closet and had dismantled and reassembled it twice, for practice and something to do. But there was still no sign of Reqi. Physsil lit her pipe and puffed away silently. The smoke gathered over her head like a storm cloud.

"Where is he?" Teltö fidgeted with the unopened

bullet box in his pocket.

"Detained by full-length mirror, probably," said Physsil. "Feel free to leave without him."

"I'm not going out there alone." Teltö pointed at the door. "They'll tear me to pieces!"

"But you've that big scary gun." Physsil put her feet on the desk. "You don't know the first thing about firing it, do you?"

Teltö felt his cheeks flushing. "Pardon?"

"That rifle. The one you play with so impressively. You wouldn't actually use it for shooting anything."

"No, but…"

Physsil coughed. "If you were into military history, rather than trying to shag security, you'd know that's an old Lunchbreak Special. Takes so long to reload, the other side can eat lunch while they wait. Well, that and the thing makes a very unique sound. So the other side *know* they can eat lunch while they wait."

Teltö flung the unloaded rifle into the reception's pile of newspapers. He crouched against the wall, head in his hands.

"You know, Phuul," said Physsil, "I might come with you after all. The worst is past, and those who can't go home can at least find a better place to die."

"I treasure your optimism."

"If only you knew."

Reqi thundered down the stairs with a satchel over his shoulder. Decked out in mufti, he'd fixed a bayonet to his F.L.Z. 23X.

"Ready?" said the guard. He considered Teltö for a moment. "I see you've raided the Ambassador's gear."

"He's not going to need it. Reqi," Teltö bit his lip. "I meant to ask. You're Embassy security. Why are you always away?"

Reqi chuckled. "Easy. I'm not needed. Would you loot this place?" He waved his hand at the reception desk and the newspapers. "On second thought, don't answer. Oh, I see you've found yourself a Lunchbreak Special too. Take it along; you might need to club someone to death."

Teltö scowled. "I'll be fine."

Teltö turned off the lamp, and followed the guard to the front door. He smelt Physsil at his shoulder; the woman had departed the desk without murmur. Reqi unbolted the lock and let in the cool night air, clean and refreshing after the mundungun mist. Teltö breathed deeply.

He froze. Restless as night panthers, a dark and hungry crowd gathered in the street. *Oh shit.* Armed with crowbars, axes, and burning torches, the Northerners roared.

"Imperial scum!"

"Servants of the Mad God!"

Teltö backed into the corridor, bumping into Physsil. Reqi lowered his bayonet, and walked out along the path. He raised his palm in supplication.

"It wasn't us," he said, slowly, "so find someone else to lynch. Our Chancellor died too."

Someone threw something: a rock perhaps. It missed the guard's head, and clattered against the exterior wall before vanishing into the fuchsias.

"Do that again," snapped Reqi. "I'll blow your bloody head off. This is *the* F.L.Z. 23X, and don't you forget it."

"Piss off, corpse-buggerer."

The crowd surged forward.

"Stop!" shouted Reqi, lifting his weapon. He fired. From the safety of the doorway, Teltö saw someone's head explode over the pavement. He blinked. He blinked again. *Shit.* Someone else screamed.

"Get back, you idiot!" Teltö shouted. *This'll be a bloody massacre.*

Reqi reloaded and backed towards the door, his rifle levelled at the nearest Northerner.

Someone threw another stone. This one hit Reqi in the face. The guard yelped in pain and flinched away momentarily. As a wave, the mob surged up the walkway.

Teltö slammed and bolted the door. *Suicide is never right,* he argued at his mortified conscience.

"That's what I call ruthless," said Physsil. She struck a match and relit her pipe. For a moment, her sharp chin was illuminated, before darkness returned.

"It was either one of us getting killed or three of us," snapped Teltö, heart racing. "I'll miss the poor bastard as much as you."

"Probably more: I wasn't desperate to get into his drawers. And anyone stupid enough to fire on an angry crowd gets what they deserve. Idiot's put us all in danger. But leaving him to die like that was impressive. You're not a shadow-stalker?"

"No, but I've known a few."

Physsil's chuckle came from the darkness. "So have I."

Thank Father Life for the window bars. Teltö almost forgave whoever built this place. The door would withstand the mob for some time, but sooner or later…

Teltö pushed back his hair. "We need to get out of here."

"So you keep saying. But they'll recognise us the moment we set foot outside."

"Can you knife them?"

"Mobs trump daggers." A lingering scream emanated

from outside. "Fancy rifles too, I expect."

Shit, shit, shit. Hold on. "I might have the answer," Teltö muttered. "Follow me."

* * *

"THEY'LL SEE US leaving," Physsil objected, studying herself in the closet mirror. They'd looted hooded cloaks from the Ambassador's wardrobe, passably similar to Church robes, especially at night. "Why would Churchmen be coming out, rather than going in?"

Teltö raised his hand. He'd tucked a religious tome under his arm. "All shall be revealed. The answer lies in the kitchen."

* * *

PHYSSIL BLEW A smoke ring.

"The Prince could burn you for that. Or whoever changes the new one's nappies."

"No he couldn't." Teltö patted the lich's mutilated head. "I found this one in the gun closet, so it's never left Imperial territory. Technically."

"Interesting." Physsil cocked her head. "What happened to its ear?"

* * *

"SO," REPEATED TELTÖ, more for his benefit than Physsil's. Running straight into an angry mob no longer seemed so clever. "We keep running. They'll be too busy overpowering our friend to worry about a couple of stray clergymen."

"So you say," said the receptionist. She'd pulled her hood down over her face, hiding any traces of femininity.

Teltö refrained from comment. He didn't want a dagger in the eye.

"Ready?"

No answer. Sweat greased Teltö's palms. He imagined Reqi lying bludgeoned to death, or worse. They'd have knives. Crowbars too, and axes. He drew a deep breath.

"Go."

He unbolted the side exit, and dashed into the night, the woman at his heels.

"The Mad God comes, the Mad God walks among us!" Teltö yelled, his terror completely genuine. His panic lent him momentum. He ran up against a mass of bodies; he could almost smell the mood. *It's fear dressed as anger.* His elbows got to work, and he shoved through the first few. Someone grabbed his shoulder; Teltö shook them off. "The Mad God!"

All the while, he kept his mind focussed on the lich shambling down the corridor. *Please let them never have seen a walking corpse before.* He pushed harder into the crowd, but the going grew tougher. An axe handle pressed into his side and he struggled to breathe. *Help!*

"Flee before me, fools," boomed the lich, its voice grotesque as Teltö could make it. It cocked the Lunchbreak Special. "I created you all, and now I return."

The corpse emerged from the door and fired the rifle into the air. Someone screamed, then there was shouting and falling over, and suddenly Teltö was free, but only for a moment before a Northerner bowled into him and knocked him to the grass. Another tripped over him, cursing loudly. There were more screams, and the rustle of people running away through nearby bushes. Teltö clambered to his feet.

"The Mad God," he brayed, pulling his hood down.

Before he knew it, he was through a hedge and sprinting down the cobblestones. Teltö allowed himself a look back. Physsil lurked close behind in her all-concealing cloak. The smoke trailed her like a locomotive.

"Poor lich," said the receptionist when she caught up. No one had chased them. *And no lantern patrols.*

"It died for a good cause." Teltö hugged her. "Well, not 'died', but you know what I mean."

The lights still blazed at the Embassy; visitation from Him hadn't dissuaded the looters entirely. Teltö and Physsil hurried around a corner into an empty side-street. A boarded-up barbers loomed to the left; across the road stood the barred windows of an apothecary. *No alcohol shops to loot. Father Life, I need a drink.*

Teltö looked over his shoulder. "Should we look for Reqi?"

"He's dead."

"I know. I want to see what they did with him."

"Won't do him any good. Nor you. Best find yourself a strapping replacement and forget the whole thing. Oh look…" Physsil knelt and picked an oval object from the gutter. She held it up to the light. Reqi's head, covered in dirt. Blood trailed from an empty eye socket and congealed on the once chiselled chin.

"Someone must have kicked it down the road," mused Physsil. "A shame they spoiled the corpse – you could have sent two liches at them."

"He's done his service." Teltö shook his head. "Let him be."

"My, you have gone native quickly. Next you'll be salivating about reanimation being disrespectful."

It's not disrespect. It's just that he wouldn't be some random lich for me. "Give it here."

He hurried to the picnic park. There were people about now, soldiers included, but with their attention elsewhere. Teltö sniffed the air. *They're burning the Embassy. Bastards.*

He scurried around the oaks, looking for somewhere to bury the guard. Everywhere he tried, the soil proved too tough for finger-digging. Teltö began to sweat. *Sorry, Reqi. I need to get away. I'm sorry it couldn't have ended better.* He propped the head against a tree trunk and ran back to Physsil.

Physsil shoved something at him.

"You'll want this. Keep it as a memory of how he nearly got you killed."

Reqi's F.L.Z. 23X. Still loaded with the dead man's last bullets.

*   *   *

"STOP."

"Don't tell me," said Physsil. "You have an idea."

"No." Teltö tried the doorknob. "I just really need a drink, and this is the first liquor shop I've seen."

"Did I not offer you a drink back at the Embassy?"

The door was locked. Solid oak too. Teltö grimaced, his brain awash with fantasies about the delights to be found on the other side. *I've bloody earned it, and I might not get another chance.* He looked over his shoulder at the silent street. *We're alone. No one will hear us.*

A thrill ran through his gut. "I'm celebrating life, not despair. Stand back."

He cocked the rifle and fired it at the door.

Crack. Teltö jumped. *So that's what it's like to shoot one of these things.*

"Congratulations, Phuul," whispered the voice over

his shoulder. "You've endangered us both, just to put a little hole in a wooden door. Satisfied?"

Teltö peered at the hole. The bullet had passed through about a millifurlong above the doorknob, putting several splinters in the oak. *Is that it?* "I expected more damage."

"I expected someone smarter than Reqi. Can we go?"

• • •

"WHERE TO NOW?" Teltö muttered. He readjusted the rifle under his robes. Bloody awkward, but openly carrying a weapon seemed inadvisable in the circumstances.

They wandered through the silent streets, steering clear of lantern patrols. They hadn't run into any checkpoints yet, or any real Churchmen, but if they couldn't find anywhere by dawn, there'd be trouble.

"Don't ask me. You're the one with the ideas."

A white, long-haired cat sat on the doorstep of a carpentry shop. Physsil reached down and stroked it; the creature purred, content come fire or flood.

Is there anyone who can help us? "Know a shadow-stalker named Sufael?"

"Can't say I do," said Physsil.

Worth a try. Who else… Teltö slapped himself. "I've got it. Ventiko."

"The Marshal? The one you poisoned?"

Bloody gossip. "He might help us."

The cat pricked up its ears, and bounded into the darkness. Physsil stretched. "We are talking about the Vice-Commander of the Army of the Principality? Not some other Ventiko?"

"You'll be surprised." *Or so the Ambassador told me.* "Do you know where he lives?"

"That I do," said Physsil. "But if we're fed to his dogs, I'm blaming you."

Physsil's navigational skills led them past a crystal-spired Church and straight into the checkpoint at the end of the next street. Teltö cursed. He needed a warm, soapy bath and a lie down, not an interrogation; he'd be buggered if he now had to outrun the Northern Army. *And I'm not shooting anything that can shoot back.*

"Papers," said the plump man in blue. He withdrew his clay pipe and yawned. The breeze blew tobacco smoke towards Teltö, who gagged; the fellow smoked a worse brand than Physsil.

"Who obstructs the…" *cough* "… Most Holy Order?" *Cough.*

"For goodness sake," spat the man. "Not again. You bastards are to show identification, or you don't pass."

"Here are our papers." Teltö croaked. He slammed his filched religious tome onto the table. "Repent, oh heretic, lest you gibber for all eternity…" *cough.* "…in the jaws of the Mad God."

"Well spoken."

Teltö jumped. Another hooded figure had materialised beside the barricade.

"Let us through. Your doom is nigh."

A real Churchman. Beneath his hood, Teltö smiled wanly while the new arrival produced a rolled-up scroll. The soldier unsealed and read it, a twitch of anxiety crossing his features. He fiddled with his blue beaked cap.

"Very well. You lot can go through." The soldier returned the paper as though it burnt him.

•   •   •

THE BONA FIDE Churchman had joined them. Physsil

walked slightly ahead. Teltö kept one eye on her, and one eye on their unwelcome companion. His left hand tightened its grip on the hidden rifle.

"So where might you be going, on this night of all nights?"

"We seek Marshal Ventiko," said Teltö. "We have information about today's atrocity."

"Ekki goorin feleet reesh."

He's probably quoting scripture. Or perhaps he's saying hello. What was the phrase Sufael had taught him, the one she'd made him parrot until he could say it without trace of an accent? Something about freedom from God?

"Tes goor Yehi ognash," he replied.

Teltö added a sage nod, relieved when the Northerner didn't pursue the matter.

They travelled in silence through the shadows of Skeevereet, and encountered neither checkpoint nor patrol. It felt like they were the last three people alive.

Finally, the sound of rushing water came to Teltö's ears. The curving road meandered down to a steep ravine with railings on either side. Palatial wooden houses sprawled on the far bank, each trying to outdo the other with gratuitous turrets and wings that led nowhere. *The nobs' part of town.* Teltö glanced into the ravine. Deeper than he'd thought; the stream ran white and angry.

A dozen oaks grew along this side of the water. Lanterns dangled in painted cages from the branches, forming a series of living lampposts. It reminded Teltö of Keer's, but whereas the Grand Master's house was locked in the genteel melancholy of advanced decay, here it felt an affectation of a young and insecure people. *Too arrogant to admit they ape us, too civilised to admit they hate us.* The lanterns illuminated a small arched bridge with white painted railings. Teltö followed Physsil to the crossing, but before either set foot on it, the Churchman darted forward to block the way.

"Brothers, you have yet to tell me your names."

"You did not ask, brother." Teltö eyed Physsil. "Let us cross."

The man raised his hood to reveal a narrow face. The high forehead gleamed like an iceberg.

"But I did ask your names. The most humble novice knows enough of the Old Tongue, brought to these lands at the Founding."

He pushed away Teltö's disguise.

"Teltö Phuul." The man knitted his eyebrows. "They told us of you, and of the prize. Your master was most generous."

Teltö blinked. "What master?!"

"Peta Vyrellävek. Some say we betray our Faith, that we long ago sold our souls for his silver, but no Patriarch would refuse what has flooded North these past years. We could scarcely refuse more, especially if its price was one fewer Necromancer. We thought we had you."

The Dragon's dead, but I've walked into his jaws. Teltö backed away and began to pull out the rifle. The Churchman shook his head.

"The others gave up. Without immediate prospect of lucre, they claimed the orders void. But not I. The Viiminian Empire has a saying. *Duties must be carried out lest our last world crumble.* I would carry out my duty and pursue my reward later. But I never thought to find you so soon..."

Swift as a darting snake, Physsil's arm lashed out. Teltö blinked; the handle of a dagger suddenly quivered in the Churchman's throat. The fellow slumped to the ground, choking and coughing.

"Murder!" Teltö hissed. *Twice in one day, twice the same way.*

"From a certain point of view," said Physsil, leaning over the railing. "Nice long drop. A man could hurt himself falling down there." She jabbed her thumb towards the Churchman. "He wasn't careful. Talking before killing… fatal mistake." She pointed a finger at Teltö's rifle. "You weren't careful. Too slow… another fatal mistake."

From within her cowl, a smoke ring drifted into the night.

•   •   •

WIDE LAWNS BORDERED the tree-lined street. Teltö looked at those lofty windows and imagined the scenes therein. Counts and Countesses quivering in fear and excitement; servants shifting ancestral tables behind thrice-locked doors; grieving cousins recalculating inheritances with a pencil in one hand and a handkerchief in the other. Physsil halted outside a three-storied building. Lights blazed in every window.

"He lives here." She leant against a lamppost. "Give my greetings to Ventiko. And his dogs."

Teltö frowned. "Aren't you coming?"

She shrugged. "Your friend's the chief bigwig now. He'll ensure his visitors are checked. Thoroughly. What do you think will happen when they pat down this simple Churchman and find breasts and daggers?"

They'll find the daggers, not sure about the breasts. "So what will you to do?"

"Survive."

She turned and walked away into the leafy shadows,

not once looking back. Teltö watched her go. Another face he'd never see again. *Too late to turn back.*

He headed to the pillared veranda, where shrubs sprang from twin ceramic pots. A rope descended from the roof. *The doorbell.* He pulled. No sound came, so he tapped on the stained-glass front door. This time, a bearded man in servant's garb opened it.

"The tradesman's entrance is that… oh."

"I need to see Marshal Ventiko. It's an important message from the synod."

"The Marshal is indisposed."

Teltö was almost getting used to living servants. He stepped into the light, allowing the butler to view his hair.

"Would you thwart the foes of the Mad God? Do you serve He Who Must Be Fought?"

"The Marshal's wife thinks so," said the butler. "Very well, come this way. You don't carry weapons?"

Bugger. Teltö handed over the F.L.Z. 23X. and bullet box, consoling himself he had no further use for them.

The butler's eyes bulged. "May I ask what you were doing with this?"

"Protecting myself. The Mad God walks tonight."

"Indeed. Any other weapons? A stray tank of *rulion*, perhaps? A phosphorous grenade or seven?"

"Only the fire of my will."

"Let me make sure." He patted Teltö down, sniffing with evident disgust. "The Marshal does not permit smoking in his house."

"I accede to the Marshal's wishes." *Bloody Physsil.*

The butler led him inside, and up a broad staircase. Pedestals flanked the steps, each with their own porcelain vase. The vases themselves were wide-bottomed, and featured unknown events from Northern history. *An*

Imperial education only goes so far. An oil painting hung at the top of the stairs. Occupying half the wall, it depicted a man in blue shaking hands with a man in green. In the foreground, quills and parchment littered a table, together with a map impaled by four daggers. *Which peace treaty is that?* Teltö mused. *The last one? The one before?* He repressed a snigger. *The next one?*

Then through a side-door and into a passage lined with mirrors. The young man nodded in self-satisfaction at his wild hair. *Yes, I'd pass for a clergyman. Give me a soapbox and I'd pontificate about the Mad God with the best of them.* The nested reflections visually extended the corridor, as if house size were another of Ventiko's insecurities.

At a junction of passages, a wrinkled man in epaulettes inspected a candlestick. He looked at Teltö and jumped.

"Excuse me."

The man skulked away, only to collide with another soldier coming around the corner.

"Oof."

Both tumbled to the carpet.

Teltö raised an eyebrow. "Are they practicing for a pantomime?"

"They're General Staff," said the butler, ushering him another way. "I shan't comment."

'No comment' was fine with Teltö.

The corridor ran up to an imposing set of double doors. An equally imposing set of guards gave Teltö a further pat down, while the butler knocked thrice.

"Second Marshal, a Churchman is here to see you."

"Let him in."

The butler thrust Teltö inside, and slammed the doors. The Necromancer was now alone with a man who held the fate of millions in his hands. *They think I can't kill him without weapons.* Teltö grimaced. *They're right.*

Small and whitewashed, the room contained pine drawers, a coat rack, and a narrow bed, at the foot of which a plump Pomeranian snored wheezily. Ventiko sat sniffing a bowl of soup and dumplings. Clad in nightshirt and cap, his bony form protruded from the sheets like a poker escaped from the hearth.

"Well," he snapped. "What news from the synod? Have our pious friends selected a new Patriarch yet? Please tell me it's one of ours."

"Sir, I come from the Embassy..."

The Marshal's head jerked up. "What? You? I thought you'd disappeared down some rat hole. Where did you find those robes?"

"Um, the Ambassador," said Teltö. *I teeter on a tightrope.* "He mentioned before he died you were not overtly hostile to Imperial interests."

"Why, that blubbery blabbermouth." Ventiko put the soup down. He flexed a skeletal forefinger. "Come."

Teltö moved closer. Ventiko dropped his voice.

"He didn't spread tales about me to anyone else?"

"No," whispered Teltö. "He just compared you with Marshal Skom."

Ventiko cackled. "Skom would have killed to be in my position. In fact, he did. Hah. But there the comparison ends. Whereas my predecessor only dreamt of power, I truly have it within my grasp."

Teltö shuffled back.

"My most loyal troops hold the infant Prince. My enemies are ashes. I could claim Oym's throne for myself, unleash the hordes against leaderless Kuolinako. But I shall not."

For a brief and horrible moment, the skull-face smiled.

"My father was an Imperial, Phuul. Did you know that?"

Teltö glanced at the door. "No, sir."

"He came North during the last war, found a girl, and stayed. I have suffered grief for my Imperial name, and have spent many hours winning over a reluctant people. But while I shall keep the Principality afloat, I cannot betray the shades of my ancestors, not for all the accolades in the North. I mean to lose this war."

Teltö blinked. "Pardon, sir?"

The hollow eyes flickered with annoyance. "I said, I mean to lose this war. I shall ensure the waves of Skeevereet break upon the Kuolinakonian rock."

Is he mad as he sounds? "But if the people suspected betrayal…"

"Those who suspect are no longer here. I mean to be careful, using those with knowledge of the Empire to achieve my design. Now fate sends me one such…"

Oh shit. "Um."

"I trust you are one such?"

The secret of survival is indispensability. "I'll help."

"Good. Should you cease to be useful, or worse, betray me, I shall denounce you for the liar you are, and hand you over to the mercies of the Skeevereet mob. Do I make myself clear?"

"Perfectly, sir."

"I am pleased we have reached an understanding. Any fool can win a war, but it takes artistry to lose one well." The Marshal picked up his soup. "I shall send my troops into Kuolinako's gaping maw."

Chapter Fourteen

TELTÖ FASTENED THE final brass button and evaluated the reflection in the mirror. Kyrmves would say the blue brought out his eyes, or some such; the rest of his family would choke. *There, Rhea. Write a paper on Imperial responses to Northern uniforms.* His own skin crawled at the wrongness, but it couldn't be helped. Survival trumped all, and it had taken both ingenuity and debauchery to get his hands on this gear. Handsome, drunk, and most importantly Teltö's size, the lonely Northern lieutenant had slumbered through the post-coital clothes theft, and would've awakened with no memory, no uniform, and a hangover for the ages. But he wouldn't be too upset. Teltö had left the man's wallet and money.

He rubbed his freshly shaven chin, and crept down the stairs. He'd requisitioned the room on behalf of Ventiko's staff, and while what the staff didn't know wouldn't hurt them, sustaining the lie grew difficult. He'd accidentally used the occasional ä or ö too, which he'd needed to disguise with a hurried cough. *Thank Father Life I'm not Tuonakonian. I'd never hide that accent.*

Below, the landlady mopped the entrance hall.

"Aren't you the pretty one today?" she said. Martial law or no martial law, she'd already stopped supplying brown sugar with his morning porridge.

Teltö mustered a smile for the sarcastic old bitch. "Good morning." He tiptoed around the wet floor. The bucket's water was chocolate-brown.

Outside, a stiff breeze buffeted passers-by. Any moment he expected someone to decry him as an Imperial stooge. *I'm not a stooge. I'm just working for the other side.* But pedestrians shunned the talismanic blue uniform, and Teltö couldn't blame them. The Army had done little to contradict reports of arbitrary arrests. Church bells chimed quarter to the hour. The young man quickened his pace. Ventiko had requested, or rather ordered, his attendance, and the Marshal struck Teltö as the sort who demanded punctuality.

Army Headquarters was an austere blockish building: a thousand and one windows set into tonnes of granite. *The stone was specially imported from the Confederation, if I recall.* Certainly, the architect had little regard for beauty. This could only ever be the home of identical drudges with identical waxed moustaches.

"There are no liches here," Teltö muttered.

He had no sooner chased away expectant seagulls from the steps when he found himself staring up at three unsmiling Security personnel. All wore side-arms on their belts and had rifles slung across their backs. Butterflies twisted in Teltö's gut. He half-expected the bastards to shoot him on sight. *I'd shoot me on sight.*

"Papers," said one.

Teltö handed over his authorisation. Even with the paperwork, he hadn't dared set foot in here without a uniform. Did he look sufficiently Northern? *Clothes maketh the culture.* Well, that at least was sorted – though he drew the line at growing a moustache – and one of these very guards had red hair. Teltö thanked five centuries of intermarriage, and wondered how often Churchmen badgered the poor bastard.

"This says you're Special Forces, answerable only to Ventiko himself."

Teltö pushed back his hair. "That's right. Ask the Vice-Commander if you like. That's his signature there, on the page."

The red-headed guard smiled. "My cousin used to be Special Forces. He told me all about the training you fellows get."

"Good to hear. Very strenuous it is too…"

The guard unslung his rifle. "Any chance you can shoot that seagull over there?"

Teltö looked to where the man pointed. A seagull, perched on the roof of the Army Headquarters: a small bundle of white and grey feathers set against the blue sky. *Father Life, he might as well ask me to hit the bloody Moon.*

"Um, why?"

"That little bugger's been shitting on me all week. I swear it knows what it's doing, too. The Mad God in miniature, if you ask me. It *waits*."

Teltö took the rifle and weighed it in his hands. He recalled the manuals from the Embassy. *A Rughvneer M6941. Same basic design as the Lunchbreak Special, with most of the obvious faults corrected… hold on.*

"I'll tell you what I'll do." Teltö tried to suppress a grin. He knelt, and his fingers got to work on the weapon. Muscle-memory was a wonderful thing, as he knew from his swimming days. Everything snapped together…

"I'll do this."

Before the guards could speak, he'd handed back the rifle, fully reassembled.

"I'll also promise not to tell anyone what you've just asked me. Firing a bullet so close to the Vice-Commander's office window would be court-martial time. Now, let's go see Ventiko, shall we?"

The guard blushed. "Come this way, sir."

Inside, a fresh set of guards patted Teltö down, more thoroughly than Reqi ever had, then led him up a flight of stairs. At the top, a door opened and a fellow with close-cropped white whiskers stormed into the corridor, brows like thunderclouds. Teltö ducked for cover while the man raged past, muttering obscenities.

"In here," said his escort, nudging him towards the open door.

A rolled-out map covered a central table, over which the Marshal's lean form hovered like a weathervane. Stooping slightly, but still a good two heads taller than Teltö, the Vice-Commander of the Northern Army affixed lips to a porcelain teacup. Perched on the map's corners, four further steaming teacups stood to attention, each serving loyally as a paperweight.

"Thank you," Ventiko said, not looking up. "You may leave us."

Security saluted and departed, shutting the door behind. Teltö looked about him. Shelves lined the walls, barren save for three books and a milk jug, while a small side-desk crouched beneath a curtainless window.

"Well, Phuul," said Ventiko, "I see you have gained a uniform. A lieutenant's one at that. Been promoted, have we?"

Teltö felt his cheeks flushing. "I hoped it would garner

less attention, sir."

"Less from the populace, perhaps. More from the officers, who cannot recall Lieutenant Phuul's previous service. But enough. How many liches can the Empire draft into service if the need arises?"

Teltö bit his lip. "Depends, sir. Industry won't like redirections, but they'll tolerate it for the cause. If Kuolinako gets truly desperate, they can extend the Death Draft."

"Such an extension sparked the Mustanako Mutiny, I believe."

"Yes, but if the Empire's survival is at stake..."

"Then we have a variable number of enemies."

Define enemies. Teltö nodded.

Ventiko finished his tea, and swapped his current cup with the north-easterly beverage. He continued drinking.

"Clearly," he said, "to maximise the Empire's defences, we must take the fight to them, correct?"

"I don't follow."

"The more desperate their plight, the more defenders Kuolinako can put into the field. The more liches we face, the tougher it will be for the Principality. Therefore, if we go for the Imperial jugular, the better chance that the North will suffer defeat."

Somewhere, the borders of logic were under siege. "I suppose, sir," Teltö said slowly. "But would it not, um, be less destructive if you kept the Northern forces behind the Wall?"

"The populace demands an offensive war. The atrocities are fresh, and everyone fears an Imperial blockade if the Principality doesn't strike hard and fast."

"But the previous wars..."

"Are past. Imperial forces have a better chance at

home than abroad."

Ventiko commanded an Army he wanted to lose. He wanted to lose because he had Imperial sympathies. But for someone with Imperial sympathies, his bloody flippancy was breath-taking. *So we defend the Viiminian Empire by attacking it?* But then such an invasion improved Teltö's own chances of slipping away. He strangled his objections.

The Marshal moved on to the south-eastern cup, lost in thought. "The Church is unhappy I haven't declared a Holy War. The Patriarch claims censorship. I ask you, what do they expect? They shall submit their publications to my editors, or they shall have no publications. Fetch me that milk."

Teltö breathed easier. Authority was the same the world over: jealous with power, but happy to tolerate anyone who supplied their needs. He'd just passed the jug when the door opened and another officer stalked in carrying a file. This one's lush white sidewhiskers dangled like unfinished knitting, his medallioned uniform a one-man scrap metal yard. *Beware of magnets.*

"Marshal, I..." The officer stopped short. "What is the meaning of this?"

"What is the meaning of what, Colonel Rughvneer?" said Ventiko. He added milk to his tea with the precision of medicine measurements.

"Him." Rughvneer pointed at Teltö's non-medalled chest. "He's an Imperial spy. Why, I'd wager he murdered a man and stole his uniform."

No, just left him satisfied, snoring, and sozzled. Then *I stole his uniform.*

Delicately, Ventiko lowered the jug onto the map. Somewhere in the Illuvian by the looks of it. "How do you know this?"

"He works at their Embassy." Rughvneer's tanned cheeks darkened. "I've seen him skulking. And here he is, in our citadel. He'll see everything. He'll see the map. This is an outrage!"

The Marshal paused. "Lieutenant Phuul is a spy, yes."

What the... A sinking sensation gripped Teltö's stomach. He eyed the door.

But Ventiko hadn't finished. "Our spy." He sipped his tea. "At the Imperial Embassy. Someone betrayed him to the Grand Chancellor. There are so many mysteries floating around right now. When I catch the fellow who neglected to provide security to the Embassy, allowing the street mob to sack the place, there will be a day of reckoning, I assure you. Which reminds me. Weren't you in charge of coordinating checkpoints in that sector, Rughvneer?"

The Colonel's face turned from flushed to beetroot. "An outrageous accusation."

"There will be a thorough investigation."

"Yes, yes. But back to this spy business. If this fellow's ours, why does he have an Imperial name?"

Snali Ventiko coughed quietly.

Rughvneer waved his hand. "Yes, I get it. You sorts are everywhere. Blood and lineage mean nothing any more. But why in damnation don't *I* know about him? Eh? Eh?"

"Lieutenant Phuul is a spy. Not being known about is what they do. But since a Rughvneer will hardly take the word of a Ventiko, I shall show you something. It fell into my hands."

Ventiko crossed to the side desk. He fiddled with a lock and slid open a drawer. He pulled out two scrolls, one of which he thrust at Rughvneer. "Here, Colonel. Please, read this aloud."

Rughvneer frowned. He took the paper and unrolled it. He cleared his throat and read:

Teltö Phuul is our enemy, and possesses knowledge that will prove ruinous if he is allowed to live. He must die, and soon.

"That is the decrypted version," said Ventiko. "From the original," he unrolled the other paper, displaying an ornate seal beneath coded gibberish, "the Grand Chancellor's own personal message. The Imperials learnt of Lieutenant Phuul, and reacted accordingly."

Scowling, Rughvneer threw the message on the table. It bounced off the milk jug, rolled across the Great Southern Fells, and landed on the floor.

"It's a fine mess," said Rughvneer. "Imagine what the Founders would have thought of a chap *with an umlaut* serving our fair nation." He shook his head. "Name means nothing any more."

"Lieutenant," said the Marshal. He did not make eye-contact with Teltö. "The Colonel and I have matters to discuss in private."

Teltö started a bow, and stopped himself. He saluted and left. As he shut the door, he heard Ventiko's voice.

"Good news about your brother, Ereek. I'd heard he was at the banquet, and only learnt the following day that he was on his country estate instead. Happy chance…"

●   ●   ●

TELTÖ LOCKED THE door against his landlady, and drew a deep breath. The Marshal was right: impersonating a Northern Lieutenant carried its own dangers. Sooner or later, there'd be questions, either from Rughvneer, or some other nosy bastard, and that'd be that. He needed to prepare. *When those questions come, I need to answer in triplicate.*

He stared at the freshly-filched copy of Northern military regulations. Tattered and dog-eared though it was, the text held his best chance of survival. *I'll memorise every last sub-clause if I have to.* Teltö smiled. It'd be like reliving his schooldays. *I'm an Imperial. Cramming useless information is what we do.*

The sparse little room sported a clothes rack to go with the bed, desk, chair, and mirror. Having hung up his uniform – he'd a newfound respect for it, seeing as it now kept him alive – Teltö crawled into bed, peeled off his undershirt, and got to work. Propping himself against the pillow, he held the book in one hand, and pencilled notes with the other.

He soon found it all-too similar to school. The various ranks, powers, and obligations, bootlace and medal rules, prohibitions on illicit images, punishments, toilet paper restrictions... the thing could have been written by some faceless bureaucrat in Kuolinako.

He slammed the book down and lay back, staring at the ceiling. He wanted no part in Ventiko's war, or any war at all. Still, if the Marshal launched an invasion, Teltö had to be there, which meant posing as a convincing military officer. Not that he could ever hope to protect anyone: impersonation was his only hope of getting south of the Wall, and then, with luck, to Qivunako. *I wonder what the family are thinking.* And Dyrstin, who'd be having the fun of post-Vyrellävek Kuolinako. The Last Capital would be no more pleasant than Skeevereet.

Teltö's mind drifted to the intercepted message. The Dragon had wanted to kill Teltö because of something he knew. Or something he thought he knew. Did Vyrellävek think Hova had confided in his Native Assistant? Even if he had, why kill the Native Assistant, but not the man himself? *If Vyrellävek was so certain I was involved in Hova's plot, he had no reason to hide it from the Tower. He could've brought Vöder around, Theatre or no Theatre.* The decryption of the Dragon's own messages hardly filled Teltö with confidence. *How in blazes did the Northern military get its hands on this?*

He'd leave the rest of the regulations for another time. He turned the gas-light off and went to sleep. His dreams were troubled.

* * *

"QUITE THE SPINE-TINGLING set of demands."

Teltö nodded. Today, like every day, the Marshal had pumped him on geography, population, buildings, local politics... He'd sung sweetly, but over recent days had slipped from creative guesswork into simply making things up. Fortunately, Ventiko hadn't noticed. Unfortunately...

"Signed by six of the seven living Grand Masters, we see."

"Indeed, sir."

Ventiko poured himself another cup of tea. "We must get it framed."

For someone so loyal to his ancestry, Ventiko was surprisingly chirpy about the Grand Council's ultimatum. The terms contained a laundry list of pettiness, anger, and bombast. The North must surrender the Wall, disband half its military, and quash the punitive terms of the last peace. There was even a requirement that Skeevereet grant preferential trade deals to Imperial merchants. *Meerm's doing.*

"Um, sir," said Teltö, "can't you possibly enter into dialogue with Kuolinako? To avert war, I mean."

"Never try to stop the unstoppable, Lieutenant Phuul," said Ventiko. "You saw the papers' reaction when news of the Northern Embassy in Kuolinako filtered through. Headlines baying for blood."

Something scratched at the door. The Marshal let in the expectant Pomeranian, which greeted its master with a little yelp. It wanted its midday walk.

"The populace desires war," continued Ventiko, scratching behind his pet's ears. "Our duty is to obey the public's wishes. Otherwise they shall find someone else, someone less desiring of a satisfactory outcome, and we shall dangle from the nearest lamppost."

Teltö cleared away the tea tray and said nothing. At least he'd finished the regulations.

●　●　●

FROM ALCOVES AND nooks, scruffy paperboys bearing the last legal newspaper in the North screeched the news. The ultimatum had expired at midnight, and Skeevereet and Kuolinako were again at war.

Citizenry had laboured for days to clear the rubble from Victory Square, but since eight o'clock this morning men with guns had directed civilians elsewhere. Today, the heart of the Principality was awash in blue. Demonstrating to the world it feared neither foe nor weather, the Army assembled in force, ranks upon ranks of men unflinching while rain streamed down oilskins and dripped off helmets. Beside them stood the skeletal remnants of the Palace, twisted with silent agony. Teltö looked over at the charred timber and collapsed spires. *Oym wanted something less violent. If only he'd known. If only anybody had known.*

He backed further under the overhanging roof. As

part of the Second Marshal's staff, Teltö was not expected to stand in formation, so he and Ventiko's various other underlings had scrambled for shelter. That at least was a crumb of comfort; the sheer size of the Northern military had already ruined Teltö's morning. *And they've got the satellite towns too.* The Empire had the larger populace; it didn't seem fair that the Principality's battalions could keep level pegging with Kuolinako. Skeevereet's draft must have cast its net wide.

"Here comes the 42nd," said the fellow at his elbow. "They've been reinstated."

Darker than even the darkest clouds, the horde of airships hovered over the Square. Teltö flinched. *Things just keep getting uglier.*

"I read that the Empire has been secretly developing airships of its own," continued the man. "The one that dropped the bomb was one of theirs."

"Nah," said another, "The Empire's still screwed by the gas embargo. Imperial agents hijacked one of ours."

"Do you think they'll bring back *rulion* too?" Teltö asked. He imagined the rain of death over Qivunako. His great-grandmother had told him of the bunkers during the last war, of a friend whose eyes melted and eyebrows flamed. *And we're far to the South. Get out of Mustanako now, you bastards, before you glow in the dark.*

"*Rulion?* The fire stuff?" The first staffer looked at Teltö quizzically. "They phased that out twenty years ago. Oym – the late Oym, blessed be his name – had the manufacturing equipment destroyed and everything. It'd take years to bring it back." He shrugged. "Not to worry. There's always the phosphorous grenades. They *burn*."

Morning ticked away. Dispensing with an umbrella, Ventiko strolled up and down the ranks. Teltö could spot him easily; the Second Marshal walked head and shoulders above all but a handful of troops. None knew the callous calculation going on in that hairless head. *I shall send them into the maw of Kuolinako.* Teltö wondered how the men would react. Still, this was the Enemy. They needed to die. *Foorit would say otherwise. Foorit would see boys with mothers and sisters and lives still to live.* But the old man had been incinerated, and the decency he'd suffered for had burned with him, along with the life work of the Dragon. *Sorry, Vyrellävek, I outlived you, and sacred mission or not, I'm now watching a mobilisation sworn to destroy your immortal Empire.*

The rain never ceased, but at least it wasn't cold. The staffers prattled on about sniffles, and office politics, and former girlfriends. Teltö kept aloof, even when prodded about the Marshal's growing eccentricities. *You mean he was normal to start with?* Ventiko finally completed his inspection. Teltö trailed the staff back to Headquarters; the Marshal no doubt desired his daily dosage of inside information.

"Not today, Lieutenant," said Ventiko, on regaining the foyer. He stripped off his oilskin and handed it to a blond underling. "It's almost noon. Come back tomorrow."

He wants to walk his dog. One of them anyway. Teltö trudged off into the rain. He kicked a puddle at a paperboy to cheer himself up.

• • •

TELTÖ PUSHED OPEN the study door. From within came the crisp patter of turning pages and the scratching of a pencil.

"Um, sir?"

Hunched over a notebook, Ventiko faded into the beige armchair, his expression tight and humourless. He draped one booted foot over the other and did not look up from his scribbling.

"Lieutenant Phuul. We have not requested your presence."

"Correct, sir."

"Then why are you here?"

"About the landing idea, sir. Are you sure it's wise?"

"Wise, Phuul, and necessary."

"But the Imperial Navy lacks ironclads, sir. You would kill more Northerners taking an overland route to Mustanako, and do less damage to the Empire."

Ventiko turned a page. "There is no overland route. The railway lines have been sabotaged. And we do recall your claim that Kuolinako has spent significant funds on its Navy."

"Yes, but…"

"Do not interrupt, Lieutenant. Knowing Vyrellävek, we are talking funds well spent. So a seaborne attack not only satisfies Northern desire for immediate retribution, but also plays to these new Imperial strengths. A march through bracken-choked minefields – your overland route – would raise suspicions, and undermine our authority. Would you prefer Second Marshal Ereek Rughvneer?"

"No, sir."

"Good. This audience is over."

Anti-airship guns are easier to manage on land, he thought, shutting the door behind him. But Teltö wasn't raising this new objection. His survival hinged on keeping the Marshal happy.

He ghosted down past Security and outside. On the

lowest step, a fair-haired functionary sat peeling an apple. Something about the face drew Teltö's gaze. He looked closer. The underling's teeth gripped a calabash pipe.

Stepping over stray apple peel, Teltö bent down. "Physsil," he whispered, "is that you?"

Physsil wiped the knife on her trouser leg, and put it back in her pocket. "Well spotted, Lieutenant Phuul."

Her hair trimmed into a definitively masculine style, she wore a uniform several sizes too large. The bagginess well-disguised her figure.

"What are you doing here?" *Surviving.*

"Working."

"As an Army Fruit Peeler?"

Physsil put her pipe down, and bit into an apple slice. Her hideous yellow teeth munched away like a clockwork toy. "Don't you know the military is the only way to get ahead in the North? But yes, I'm on a break and Ventiko hates smokers. Especially indoors."

"But you're female."

"You've noticed." She finished the slice, and jerked a thumb back at Headquarters. "They haven't. Padding around the waist works wonders. Funny thing is I still get lusty looks from the big bad staffers. Most of 'em guilty as they are sultry: Northmen have weird ideas about sex. Terrified they're fancying another man."

Teltö recalled the source of his uniform. Now he thought about it, the fellow did look the self-loathing type; it'd been hard enough finding someone of appropriate tastes, with the Church looking over everyone's shoulder. *He had a nice set of thighs though.* "Liquor's the antidote, but you don't want them discovering the contents of your trousers."

Physsil nodded. "Doing the voice is bad enough." She

let fly with an impressive baritone. "Reporting for duty, sir!" She coughed wheezily. "Have you got over Reqi yet?"

Teltö frowned. "I suppose…"

"Good. There ain't nothing more pathetic than unrequited lust. He wasn't into men, you see. Or women either. When he did accept dinner invites from star-struck Northern ladies, they got confused fast. Often asked me whether they'd offended him." Physsil smirked. "If the girl annoyed me enough, I'd say he hated her dress. Poor thing would change her entire wardrobe to please him. I laughed myself silly."

"Did he know you were doing this?"

"Does it matter? Reqi didn't care. He only gave a shit about his gun and his own reflection. But he liked the attention enough to let the admirers keep trying. Wined and dined every week, and no one ever called him up on playing truant from his job. Bastard."

An open carriage rolled past, pulled by twin horses with white socks and blue plumes. Teltö eyed the monocled man in the back seat. Count Sergev Rughvneer, unless he was mistaken. *Perhaps the wealthiest man on the continent, and about to become even wealthier.* The elder brother of the Colonel commanded a host of munitions factories, and according to rumour had concluded lucrative supply contracts with the Northern war machine – contracts that exempted Rughvneer's workers from the draft. There were also rumours about the Count's role in undermining the F.L.Z project. *For Northerners, everything is personal. Who needs the Inquisition when you've got family honour?*

Teltö watched the vehicle and its illustrious occupant rounded a bend. "Ventiko had better watch his back." *No, Snali. Your enemies aren't all ashes.*

Physsil chewed another apple slice. "What gives you that idea, Lieutenant?"

Is that sarcasm? "Count Sergev could lever in his little brother as Vice-Commander. He's got the wealth, he's got the clout. The fellow makes the North's weaponry; he can surely break someone like Ventiko."

"Ventiko has the little Prince in his possession. Armed guards round the clock. He ain't going anywhere."

"Suppose there's an accident? I get the feeling that what the Count wants, he gets."

"You think the Count wants his insufferable little brother lording it over him?"

Teltö frowned. "But he's family. That means everything to Northerners."

"So it does, but brothers are rivals, and Sergev's already done Ereek a favour or three. It may interest you that as of last night Ventiko promoted Colonel Sidewhiskers to Major-General, for sterling service in not getting incinerated at banquets."

Teltö cocked his head. He'd heard nothing about any promotions. From his experience, Ventiko absorbed information, but never dispensed it.

"How do you know that?"

Physsil smirked. "Habits of a lifetime, Lieutenant."

A lifetime I know nothing about. "I think Ventiko's going dotty."

"Everyone's dotty around here."

"He's taken to using the Imperial 'we'."

"Skom did that too. But I'll admit the power is going to his bald head. The silly bastard's allowing female airship pilots."

Now she's showing off. "Why?"

"Wants more women in the military, and had to start

somewhere. Where will it end?" Physsil spat out an apple pip. "Next they'll legalise necromancy and beg Kuolinako to take them back."

· · ·

CHATTING TO PHYSSIL became a ritual for Teltö, even when Ventiko wasn't dragging him along to tea parties. One day, they sat on a bench in the shade of an elderly beech. An afternoon breeze descended from the north. Summer had arrived in Skeevereet, and with it days where the Sun hammered all but the hardiest salamander into sweaty lethargy.

"So they're landing just off Mustanako," said Teltö. It'd been an interesting morning audience with the Marshal. So much strategy; a shame Ventiko hadn't told him where the airships were raiding. "Then it'll be a two pronged assault from land and sea. Or so they think. Ventiko's taking personal command of the landing force."

Physsil yawned. "He doesn't want the Army under another man."

More like he doesn't want anyone messing up his lost war. Teltö had kept Ventiko's secret, instead spinning a tale that painted himself as the architect of the North's demise. Physsil hadn't questioned his story, but didn't look impressed either.

He wiped sweat from his face with a cotton handkerchief. "Meanwhile, *Major-General* Rughvneer's garrisoning the Wall."

"He won't like that. No glory. Nothing that makes Sergev sit up and take notice. Not even any medals, unless there's one for sitting on your arse. Knowing the brass around here though, there probably is."

A certain breed of low-level functionary lived to

second guess superiors. Teltö wondered if the woman had Venomavat ancestry.

"He's not stuck on his arse altogether. He's been put in charge of supply lines, and what have you."

"Just so long as he's out of Skeevereet. No one wants Major-General Sidewhiskers spraying his scent round the Capital without supervision. He might get ideas." "I'm going with the Marshal, incidentally. If there's going to be an epic military disaster, it should be a well-supervised military disaster."

Physsil nodded. "Good for you."

"Need to keep an eye on him, in case he has ideas of his own."

In truth, he'd talked Ventiko around after claiming to have taken a good hard look at coastal ramparts. Sufael's ramparts, rather than Mustanako's, but there had been no need for specifics.

There was a pause. Overhead, the leaves rustled. "Are you coming?" Teltö asked.

"No," said Physsil.

He frowned. "You're staying here? I can smuggle you aboard, then once we've screwed over the Northerners, we can both slink off into the countryside, easy as pie."

Physsil coughed. "I can't go back. No home, remember?"

Like getting blood from a sodding stone. Teltö realised how little he knew about her.

"Why? Is it something you've done?"

"Everyone's done something. You should know that by now. But put it this way, Phuul: if you ever ask again, I'll make you a eunuch." A dagger slid into her hand. "So don't ask."

The last Teltö saw, she was walking back up the steps,

her hair shining in the Northern Sun.

• • •

THE DAY OF departure dawned warm and drizzling. Teltö prowled the main deck of the freshly renamed *Prince Oym*, mulling over his impending sea journey. He'd have company, at least, and lots of it; the mountainous troop ships, each holding over two thousand men apiece, seemed virtual floating islands. But size wasn't everything. *Prince Oym* itself was a sturdy little ironclad, well-equipped with guns. Could Ventiko send this lot to the bottom of the Illuvian? Teltö hadn't dared ask. Only yesterday the Marshal had flung a teacup at Rughvneer. *Side-whiskers dodged; I mightn't be so lucky.*

Teltö leant against the railing, and watched the end of the farewell ceremony. He repressed a yawn. Church, Army, and Nobility, Skeevereet's triple estate, huddled together in mutual antipathy on the quayside, while a brass band beat out the Principality's anthem. Ponderous and sober, the tune fit the granite faces of the Church leadership. The Supreme Commander of the Northern Army, a plump babe of two, squatted on a makeshift throne; moustachioed men in blue held a tarpaulin over their little Prince.

Farewell, Physsil and Reqi. Farewell, Sufael. Teltö remembered the woman's rich laugh, her love of words, the way she'd tasted that night on the train. *And what would she think of me now?* Could she understand what her father had become? Shadow-stalkers weren't stupid, but wilful blindness was a funny thing. Teltö imagined Rhea or Kyrmves starting a war. Would he run to the authorities, or simply run? *Thank Father Life, I've never had to make that choice.*

The dreary anthem concluded, and a man in a white cowl stepped forward. He raised his staff in a gesture towards the sky and shouted Feleen at the ships. *The Old Tongue of the North. Five centuries, and they call it old.* To Teltö's ear, the language only ever grated. Once or twice, he found himself catching something he thought he recognised, but otherwise it sounded like a stream of gibberish. Worse, angry gibberish: a succession of hate-filled themes condensed into words. *The way the North thinks, the fellow's probably delivering a blessing.*

Then they were off, and the shoreline drifted away, grey expanse fading into white.

• • •

HOURS PASSED. FOG followed the armada south along the coast. Teltö poked his nose into the galley, then retreated to his cabin amid curses. *What is it with Northerners and sugarless porridge?* Before leaving Skeevereet, he'd pushed a porridge-related letter under his landlady's door. What the missive lacked in politeness, it made up for in sincerity.

A two-bunker, his cabin wasn't far from the boiler. Engines rattled through the walls, and with only the barred window on the door for ventilation, the air felt like a steam bath. *At least I have it to myself.* Teltö sat on the lower bunk, and was pulling off his boots and socks when the door opened. A Churchman walked in with a knapsack.

"Hello," said the cleric. He pulled back his hood. The thick greying beard didn't disguise the double chin. "My name's Welleorm. Chaplain. Are you a follower by any chance?"

Teltö tensed. "I'm Phuul," he said, never taking his

eyes off the man's face. His sweat-slick fingers reached for his pocket revolver. "Special Forces Lieutenant. Sorry, I'm not religious."

Welleorm betrayed no recognition. He shrugged, and threw his knapsack on the other bunk. "No worries. Though you do have the hair for it."

"So people keep telling me." Teltö breathed again. *Not an assassin.*

"You're a Special Forces Lieutenant?"

"Yes, Welleorm, I am. Fetch me a rifle, and you'll wish you hadn't."

"Don't get tetchy: I believe you. Never had much time for guns myself, though I know the basics."

The man doffed his cloak, and began unpacking. Teltö lay back, and shut his eyes. This lasted all of five minutes before he felt Welleorm shaking him.

"What?" he snapped.

The Chaplain proffered a tobacco tin. The lid featured lewd and impossible scenes involving mermaids.

"Fancy a pipe to break the cabin in?"

"I don't smoke."

Welleorm rummaged in his satchel, and pulled out a deck of playing cards. "A hand or two of My Fair Lady with a ten-bit start?"

Teltö frowned. "My Fair Lady? Don't you mean…" He stopped himself. *Northerners don't call it Black Nykövä, you idiot.* "I mean, I don't have any money." Not technically true; he'd collected bits and pieces in an old sock, but the Chaplain needn't know that.

"My word, Phuul. You are a boring fellow."

"Just fighting the Mad God in my own way."

Welleorm's mouth twisted. "I've always thought the best way to fight Him is to enjoy ourselves, but each to his own. Judging by the Asrak under your bed, I'd have thought you more interesting."

Teltö jerked up. He bumped his skull against the upper bunk. "Owww."

"Here, try this ointment."

Teltö rubbed his scalp, and eyed the flat blue tin. "Does it keep the swelling down?"

The other man shrugged. "I don't know. I've just found it."

• • •

THE DAYS DRAGGED on. Bunking with a Churchman proved less worrying than Teltö had feared. He even warmed to his new companion, snores and smoke-fumes notwithstanding. Welleorm couldn't half sing after a few drinks, though his favourite lubricant was a vile mixture of cold Northern coffee and Asrak. Teltö had traded the latter ingredient for a sweet amber brandy.

"You didn't hear this from me," said the Chaplain one afternoon. He'd uncorked a fresh bottle, and sat cross-legged on the floor, puffing away on his briar pipe. "But the new Patriarch's a prick. He's no silver swallower, but he's the next worst thing."

Shirtless and shoeless in the cabin's heat, Teltö lay on the bunk and studied his cards. "Silver swallower?"

"Yes, silver swallower." Welleorm's face grew hard. "A bastard cleric who does odd jobs for the Empire in return for a mark or three. Imagine – Northern Clergymen bought and sold by the Mad God! I've promised to cut the throats of any I find, and damn the consequences."

"Understandable," said Teltö. "So what's wrong with the new Patriarch?"

"Likes to bully and dominate. That's not what the Church is about. Threes."

Could have fooled me. "Go fish."

The man picked up a card, and knocked his empty glass over.

"The last one was even worse. It's all leadership does these days, force their tastes onto everyone else. I mean, we're all creations of the Mad God, right?"

"Right. Sevens."

"Go fish. Anyway, since we're His creations, we must rise above Him, right? To thwart Him by being decent and happy, and suffering through whatever He throws at us."

"Ever heard of a fellow named Nelim Foorit?"

"The traitor who sold us out during the last war? What's he got to do with it? Nines."

"Oh, nothing. Here you go."

"The Church should get back to building a better world, not clamping down on anything the Patriarch of the day dislikes. Twos."

"Go fish."

"Mark my words, chocolate will be next."

"What about Asrak? Sevens."

"Go fish. Nah, the new Patriarch's mistress drinks the stuff by the bucketful."

They did it to themselves, Teltö decided. A hierarchy of prejudice where the poor bastards at the bottom were the only ones with a clue. With a smirk, he nudged the seven into his hand and declared victory.

•　•　•

THE NEXT DAY, the fog had gone, replaced by clear skies and choppy seas. The fleet swung to the starboard, rounding the massive headland of Cape Valarauko, or as the Northerners named it, Cape Stinky. In one of the Northern Wars, either the second or the third, an Imperial General had marched living troops through there, thinking it easier than fighting through the Wall. If Teltö recalled correctly, the troops returned the favour by throwing her into a lava lake.

"I've seen it up close," said Welleorm. He and Teltö had wandered out to the poop deck for some fresh air. No crew about: just them and a line of three guns. The artillery gleamed in the late morning Sun.

"Really?" asked Teltö queasily. He'd felt nauseous since breakfast.

Welleorm nodded. "Never again. Never had the stomach nor the nose for rotten eggs, though I've got the stomach for most things." He chuckled, and patted his prodigious paunch. The cloak somehow only accentuated it. "Ever been to Kuolinako?"

"Can't say I have."

"Lucky thing. Oh look," the man pointed. "A geyser. A big one."

Teltö squinted. The coastline was hazy, but atop an outreaching cliff, a thin dark line could be seen.

"Kuolinako's man-made," said Welleorm. "Cape Stinky reeks like the Mad God's arse, and that's entirely natural. All geysers and broken crust and pools of boiling mud. Streams of lava too. The place glows at night."

A most unfortunate turn of phrase with a war on. A cool south-westerly ruffling his hair, Teltö considered the barren cliffs in silence. The place couldn't be called dead. For something to have died, it must have once been alive – one could not have the Mother without the Father – and Cape Valarauko had never been born. It had been a No

Man's Land before the Nadir, and would outlast them all, churning itself up till the world itself crumbled.

"What were you doing there?" Teltö steadied himself on a railing. Brush-strokes from the ship's recent paint-job ran all the way along.

"Cartography. I did maps before I joined the Church, and the bloody Army wanted to detail the Cape. Every pit, every crevasse, the sort of coverage you can't get from the air." Welleorm shrugged. "We trudged out there, me and our gang of a dozen. At first it wasn't so bad; one smart-arse – might have been me, actually – joked about geyser roulette to spice things up. Became less funny after a while. We lost three to muddy explosions before they called the expedition off. Then, on the way back, came number four. That was the fellow who convinced me to join the Church: had half his face burnt off and died moments before we got him to safety. I was too slow with the ice-pack." The Chaplain paused, staring blankly across the water. "So much for our mighty Army. This was peacetime. The Imperials must have laughed themselves silly."

A gull swooped past, gliding over the waves. Teltö gritted his teeth. The squawking gave him a headache.

"You still don't look well, lad. Perhaps you should go back to bed."

"I'm fine."

"No, you're not." Welleorm grabbed Teltö's shoulder, and led him towards the stairs. "I've always said you Special Forces types are softies…"

Bile surging up his throat, Teltö twisted away from the man's clutches and rushed back to the edge. He had to keep it in, keep his mouth clenched… too late.

"Sorry, sorry…" Hands on knees, he retched out the

remains of his breakfast over the *Prince Oym's* nearest poop-deck gun.

The Chaplain helped him up. "You, Phuul, are definitely going back to bed. Quickly now, you don't want Ventiko to see what you've done to his toy cannon."

*   *   *

TELTÖ KEPT TO his bunk, the sheet pulled over his head. The Marshal would kill him, he decided, or at least make him spend eternity cleaning the gun with a toothbrush.

"Wake up, Phuul."

He peeled back the covers; he'd grown used to their stickiness.

The Chaplain knelt beside the bed, clutching a flask. "I've brought water."

Teltö sat up, and nodded thanks. The cool liquid cleared his head, and washed the taste of bile from his throat. "So does Ventiko know…"

Welleorm grinned. "No. Nor will he. I cleaned the worst off myself, and a sudden squall did the rest. Who'd have thought? Blue skies to grey in half an hour. We're in Imperial waters now. You know, Phuul, I've meant to ask. Your surname…"

Teltö wiped sweat from his brow. "My family moved after the last war. Legally."

"Ah." The man nodded. "Yes, I thought you were a bit pale for a pure Northerner. What's your given name?"

"Teltö." He saw Welleorm's expression, and added "after my grandfather." *Truth makes the best lie.*

"With a name like that, I'll bet you find standard-model typewriters a pain. Still, I can't judge. I've an aunt in Mustanako with one of those umlaut-laden monstrosities too. She taught me how to pronounce the bloody things."

"I've relatives in Mustanako myself."

"Really? Mind you, it works for the other side too. Most Imperials have Northern blood somewhere. Either that or they're some inbred knuckle-dragger from Qivunako."

Teltö curled his lips. "Quite."

• • •

TELTÖ YAWNED AND rubbed his eyes. *The next day already.* The seasickness had worn off, but the blanket of warm air still stifled him, and his stomach felt like a hollow pit. He climbed out of bed and stretched. Welleorm had gone, Father Life knew where, but the man had left the top off the tobacco tin, and the individual leaves had escaped over the top-bunk pillow. Teltö shrugged, and located his underwear.

He was reaching for his trousers when the world turned upside down. The floor suddenly upended itself, tipping him over violently. *What the...* Teltö slammed against the far wall, and yelped when another drunken roll threw him onto his arse. The tobacco tin clunked onto the floor, contents spilling everywhere. A half-empty bottle rolled past his outstretched hand, the lid thankfully screwed on.

Teltö struggled to his feet, the grogginess of sleep banished in an instant.

"What's happening?!" he shouted.

It was as if he were inside a snow globe, and some monstrous child were shaking it. He clutched the bunk to steady himself while the ship shuddered again.

"Welleorm, where are you?!"

Teltö judged it safe to let go, and dashed to the door,

the tobacco rough beneath his bare feet.

He ran through the corridor and up the steps, still in his underwear. He heard roars and shouting. Someone screamed. *It can't be airships. The Empire doesn't have them.* Teltö arrived on deck to find the world in tumult.

Oh shit. The Illuvian frothed like a boiling pot atop a range. Geysers of salt spray erupted from all sides, splattering the deck alongside the early-morning drizzle. The hissing foam ran over the timbers, over Teltö's feet, and up to his ankles, as all about him wide-eyed crewmen and soldiers hung on for dear life. The ship rolled again; Teltö grabbed some wet rope to save himself from sliding across and over the edge.

The water needling his bare skin, Teltö stumbled to his feet, and over to the railing. He pushed past the sailors, and stared out over the waves. He blinked. Not a dream, but a waking nightmare. A troop ship foundered off the starboard side. Massive grey-green tentacles enveloped its hull.

Teltö shook his head. "This isn't happening. What is it?"

The man beside him clung on like a limpet. "Some creature of the Mad God's devising. I'd say it's a squid, but the thing's big as a whale. Bigger."

The Northerners attacked the creature with axes and fire. Neither had any effect; three sailors hacking at one tentacle were suddenly brushed into the sea when another whipped past them. The monster tightened its grip, clenching itself against the side of the ship. Even over the roar of the Illuvian, Teltö heard the snapping timbers. Windows shattered, and there must have been an explosion in the boiler because orange flame erupted through the portholes, sending smoke into the foam-flecked air. The despairing crewmen leapt overboard to be swallowed by the waves.

Something else was down there. Huge and mottled, eyes milky, the head of the creature drifted amid the destruction. Teltö remembered the octopus that day beside the Lighthouse. Compared with that, this was a mountain next to a pebble. What sorcery or science had conjured it from the depths of the Illuvian? He gazed mesmerised at the blank eyes, and realisation came. The beast was dead, animated by necromancy. *So that's Vyrellävek's secret.* Prohibited from building ironclads, the Admiralty had bred squid-things for weapons, giant sea beasts capable of withstanding anything humanity could throw at them.

"What's the matter, fools?" A harsh voice cut through the blanket of terror. Ventiko charged over, his rage so indomitable that the ship itself ceased to rock and seemed to lie cowed.

The Marshal accosted a crewman, and threw him bodily onto the deck. "Don't stand there," he bellowed. "Fire the guns. Aim for the head."

"But sir," whimpered the sailor, "we might hit the troop ship."

"We don't care about the troop ship. It's doomed. We must save the *Prince Oym.*"

The man got to his feet, and with his terrified crewmates, set to work loading the ship's artillery. Ventiko folded his arms, his face seized by raw determination. The hollow eyes drifted to Teltö.

"Phuul."

Teltö backed away, too late. The cold fingers grabbed his shoulder, and tugged him to the far side, away from the sailors. The young man winced at the vice-like grip. *He could snap my neck like a matchstick.*

"Is there something you've hidden from us, *Phuul?*"

"No, sir."

"This is Kuolinako's doing, isn't it? Lich squids?"

"I think so, sir."

The Marshal slapped Teltö. A short *clap*, followed by stinging pain.

"Either you lie or your knowledge of Imperial forces is useless. We have had enough."

Teltö rubbed his cheek. "But, sir, they're destroying the Northerners. Isn't that what you wanted?"

"What we want," said Ventiko, "is you gone."

"I can help… I can interfere with the Necromantic link… perhaps." *For all the good that'd do. Like trying to stop the bloody tide. They'll have hundreds of Necros coordinating this.*

Ventiko scowled. "Filthy little liar."

The Marshal wrapped his arms around Teltö's torso. Teltö struggled, helpless as a rag doll. With a fluid motion, Ventiko lifted him into the air and speared him over the railing. The next thing Teltö knew, the white foam rushed to seize him…

He splashed into the sea.

The water was bracing but not freezing. He kicked himself up to the surface, and spluttered as a wave crashed over his head. But there were no squids on this side, no tentacles to crush the life out of him, no blank white eyes larger than his body… Teltö swam blindly away from the listing ship. He'd gone about half a furlong before he regained control of himself.

Treading water, he peered towards the eastern horizon and could just make out the outline of the shore, dim and pencil-thin beyond the turbulent sea. Teltö's heart sank. He'd back his swimming against anyone in

Qivunako, but Father Life, that was a long way, even without monsters to evade. His countrymen would be lurking out of sight, controlling their beasts beyond the range of the Northern guns. Artillery still thundered across the water.

To his left, a smaller wooden vessel snapped apart, its mast tumbling into the churning waves. The squids were reducing the Northern fleet to firewood, and neither soldier nor sailor nor even Ventiko's iron will could stop them. An overcrowded lifeboat wallowed in the swells. Teltö started to make towards it, only to spot a better solution. A stray plank bobbed on the waves not ten centifurlongs away. He paddled over, and embraced it, hugging it to his body like a lover. He shut his eyes and clung on while the world collapsed around him.

Chapter Fifteen

Father Life alone knew how long he drifted. Idly aware the currents dragged him away from the squids, Teltö Phuul didn't care. His world had become the rolling of the waves, the spatter of salt water against his lips, the soft rain on his skin... so long as his fingers clutched the life-giving wood, he was safe. From time to time, something brushed his leg, and he kicked it away. Nothing could come between him and his plank.

So when Teltö found himself sinking, it startled him into wakefulness. *What in blazes?* Something tugged him down. He let go of the plank, and dove under the surface. A hand clasped his shoulder. Teltö struggled up, and saw a man in a soaked blue uniform grabbing at him.

"Get away." The black beard dripped into the sea. "Get away."

Teltö shook his head, and treaded water. "No," he spat. "Find your own plank. Mine."

He tried to shove the Northerner aside, but the man had his powerful arm wrapped around the plank. Teltö got a palm in the face.

"Get away."

Teltö clawed at the wood with his fingernails. A wave smashed over them, blinding the Necromancer with a torrent of water and knocking the breath from his lungs.

"Bugger off."

The plank sank beneath their combined weight, dunking Teltö once again. He pushed away in panic. *There's only room for one.*

Then the Northerner pulled a knife. "Come closer," he shouted. Beneath his dark brows, his eyes blazed like hot coals. "I'll gut you like a haddock. Come on, you bastard. Try me."

He means it. Defeated and sick at heart, Teltö pushed away into the waves.

*   *   *

HE SWAM FOR a long time, hoping to find floating debris: a mast, perhaps, or even an empty apple barrel. None came.

"Help!" Teltö whimpered. "Help!"

In all the steel-grey sea, only the gulls heard him.

Teltö struggled on through the swells, stroke after steady stroke. Pride fuelled him, the knowledge of his skill in the water, and the shame if he failed now. *Come on, Phuul. Remember Dyrtölä? If you can swim to the Far Rocks on the eve of your sixteenth birthday, you can bloody well do this.* But that had been different. Then, the sea had been his friend and ally, almost a second home, and his triumph had never been in doubt. Today, every passing wave sapped his strength.

Numbness spread through his limbs. He stopped noticing the cold, and it grew harder to battle the waves, or even keep his head above water. By the time an arm came down and tugged him aboard, Teltö was barely aware of it.

* * *

"LOST YOUR UNIFORM, eh?" said Welleorm.

Squished among damp survivors in the lifeboat, Teltö shivered. "Thank Fa..." *Wrong religion, Phuul.* He disguised his error with a wheezy cough.

He pushed sea-soaked hair from his eyes. "Someone tried to drown me."

The Chaplain chuckled. "Are you sure he didn't succeed? I swear, if it weren't for that mane of yours, we'd have missed you altogether."

About to relay how Ventiko had tossed him overboard, Teltö stopped. *My word against the Vice-Commander?* At best, Ventiko would scoff, and out him as an Imperial. At worst...

"It was *my* plank, curse him." He shivered again, more violently this time. His teeth chattered like a child's rattle. The lifeboat bobbed on the waves; Teltö's stomach lurched each time the little vessel rolled, and the oarsmen grunted and cursed.

"Your plank? How so?"

Teltö squinted through the drizzle. The shoreline loomed closer, dark and hazy with mist. *Safety. We've left the carnage behind.*

"I found it first. He grabbed it from me, and left me to die."

"So if he'd found it first, you'd have drowned rather than fought?"

"No, but..." Teltö tried to calm his teeth, but failed.

"Let him be, Phuul. Necessity makes monsters of us all. Here, have some of this." The man handed him a pewter hip flask. "It'll cheer you up."

Teltö fumbled it. Cursing, he unscrewed the top. *Asrak. Sweet Asrak.*

"Here now," said Welleorm. "Not all of it."

•   •   •

TELTÖ AWOKE TO the gentle crackle of wood burning and the aroma of cooking meat. He blinked, struggling to remember where he was, or how he'd come to have this thumping headache. He was warm though; someone had wrapped him naked in thick woollen blankets, and piled him atop a bedroll with rolled-up greatcoats.

He groggily sat up and rubbed sleep from his eyes. He lay inside a tent, that much he knew, and his mouth watered. *Sausages. Pork, I think.* Stomach rumbling, he crawled outside.

Chin resting on fist, Welleorm slouched beside a small camp fire. He prodded the contents of a frying pan. Never had Teltö seen him so drawn and weary; bags had developed under his eyes, and the robe over his uniform looked torn and mud-stained. A tankard of something brown rested on the grass by his feet.

Welleorm swatted a sandfly. Then his eyes met Teltö's and a smile spread across his face like the Sun emerging from behind a cloud.

"You live!"

The tongs clattered into the pan. Suddenly, Teltö found himself in a crushing embrace. The man reeked of ale and stale sweat, but so genuine was the elation, so snow-white and innocent the feeling, it was impossible to be annoyed.

Welleorm released his grip, and Teltö could breathe again.

The Chaplain rescued the tongs. "Never do that to me again, Phuul. Never!"

"What…" Teltö eyed the sausages, so plump and juicy. *They need breadcrumbs, but I'll eat them as is. All of them.*

"You turned delirious, you silly bugger. You rambled on about a dead man with no head, and another spouting blood like a fountain, and something about a floating castle of death. There must have been an Imperial ship near, because our drowned troops rose to the surface, and…"

"Attacked?"

Welleorm shook his head. "That's the strangest thing. If they'd attacked, we wouldn't have made it. They *sang* to us. And you were babbling and slurring like a madman. The fellows in the boat wanted to push you overboard, but I stopped them. Once we made land, I took you to the nearest Army physician. He wasn't happy with me. Nearly shot me, in fact."

Teltö pulled his legs up against his chest. "Why?"

The Chaplain shrugged. "You'd floated in the Illuvian too long. Giving you Asrak wasn't one of my better notions. But you made it. You've been asleep for two days, drifting in and out of a God-sent fever. I watched over you all that time. The least I could do."

Welleorm had done more than that. He'd also located a fresh-if-bulky uniform, socks, undershirt, and underwear. Teltö crawled back into the tent, and dressed. He'd shrunk several notches on his belt. He imagined greeting Kyrmves like this. *My, what a nice uniform you've got, Teltö.*

Teltö set to work on the sausages. The juice ran down his chin, and he had to restrain himself from gorging it all at once.

Welleorm nodded. "You'll probably want to know the

fate of the Expeditionary Force."

"Squid salad?"

A sandfly landed on Welleorm's trouser leg. He squashed it. "Got you, you little godling!" He smiled. "Where was I?"

"Sea-monsters and Ventiko's incredible matchstick navy?"

"Oh yes. The *Prince Oym* is at the bottom of the Illuvian, but the critters finally let us be. Not killed, mind you, but it gave us time for a getaway. The Marshal ordered the surviving fleet eastwards. After half a day, we stumbled across a natural harbour. And here we are." He waved his hand. "The weather cleared last night, and there's a freshwater lake inland. We've been bloody lucky."

Yes, the Marshal was quite attentive during my geography lesson. "What about food? Surely…"

"The food and armaments were almost untouched. Every single packhorse and mule made it too. Ventiko thinks he can re-establish supply lines to the Wall."

"So he's not retreating north?" Teltö looked over at the tents and camp fires. *The war continues…*

"Depends on what Rughvneer's doing with logistics. Airships come and go. All we can do is wait, and burn corpses." Welleorm shook his head. "I'd forgotten how unnerving necromancy can be."

●　●　●

THE HARBOUR WAS at least scenic. Ripe blackberry bushes and conifer groves stretched into the distance, while the beach itself sported rich red sand. All day long, playful blue waves toyed with the anchored Northern ships. Any other time, Teltö would've spent hours diving and mucking around in the water, but he was still too stiff and sore for such exertions. He limited himself to limping errands for the Chaplain.

That evening, he squatted beside the campfire and finished the stale biscuits he'd scavenged. Welleorm had disappeared off to administer blessings, or whatever the fellow did when he wasn't smoking, drinking, or gambling. Which was a relief; the cleric made a fine friend so long as one didn't overdose on him: the tobacco smells rivalled Physsil's, and Teltö was convinced he cheated at cards. Not to mention the sniggering about buggery. *Don't worry, Welleorm. Your arse is safe from me. I have standards.* A handsome Private walked past. *And standards or not, I'm not about to get into trouble.*

Teltö contented himself with mentally undressing the soldier until the man disappeared among the other tents, which at this hour were less hives of activity and more gathering points for shared boredom. With dinnertime over, the Northern forces mulled around distractedly. *I'm on Imperial soil. If I were to sneak off...* He shook his head. *I don't know the land, and I'm still too sick to try.* It was a long way to Qivunako.

But more than escape gnawed at his mind. This afternoon, he'd heard snatches of other doings. Rughvneer had kept supplies flowing, while the engineers were well-advanced in repairing the railway tracks. Ventiko himself had organised garrisons for the ghost towns between here and the Wall. The Second Marshal may or may not have been mad, but the bastard could've been doing a better job at losing the war. *I shall send them into the maw of Kuolinako. He must be trying to choke us.*

Teltö stared into the flames. With every passing hour, the possibility Ventiko had lied grew more and more real.

That the Marshal had played others for fools was scant comfort when Teltö remembered how much he'd fed the bald bastard. *I can't even call Ventiko a traitor. He's the de facto ruler of the North. Humiliating the Empire is his job description.*

Teltö put out the fire, and crawled into bed. After tossing and turning for about an hour, he rose and donned his uniform. Perhaps a walk would settle his nerves. Outside, a thousand footprints had crushed the grass into mud, and the food wagon had gouged an ugly trail in the soft earth. Teltö followed it. The encampment sat on a broad plain several furlongs inland from the harbour; sporadic conifers and other trees dotted the landscape like sentinels, grey and foreboding in the moonlight. The night air reeked of sweat and tobacco.

A tussock-covered knoll loomed to his left, whence came light and sounds of celebration. Keeping always to the shadows, Teltö drifted closer. Half a dozen soldiers clustered around a fire. One toasted Dear Old Snali, the Hero of the Hour, while another weaved a thrilling tale of lifeboat survival over something alcoholic. *Probably grog.* Teltö smiled. He couldn't begrudge them pride in defeat. The Empire had Yyti, after all.

Hands in pockets, Teltö wandered away into the dark. One by one, campfires exhausted themselves until just he and the trees were left. The breeze rustled the branches above. *The winds of home. If only I could float on them all the way to Qivunako. In one of those vile airships, perhaps. Sufael could write a poem about it.*

Something gripped his shoulder. Teltö jumped, daydreams shattered. *Don't creep up on me.*

"Where do you think you're going?"

A man stood silhouetted against the gloom. Teltö squinted; he made out a rifle.

"Thinking of deserting, sunshine?"

I've found the perimeter. "Sorry. Wasn't thinking."

"Then start. Guard duty's tough enough without having to keep fools in the right place."

So much for escape. Mumbling apologies, Teltö hurried back the way he'd come. After a quick stop at the latrines – the smell was worthy of the Mad God – he wove his way back to Welleorm's still-empty tent. Teltö bundled himself in blankets. He was still staring at the canvas roof when the light of dawn spread through the camp.

* * *

CLOUDS GATHERED, AND by midday a shale sky hung over the sea. The Illuvian slept uneasily; its boisterous foam raced up the wine-dark beach, dumping driftwood and kelp at the feet of the Northerners. More ghastly gifts were left too; and the men who scoured the sands were not seeking shells or treasure. All morning, victims of the squid attack had washed up along the foreshore, pale and bloated, and all morning, the survivors had dragged the drowned to the fire-pit beyond the far sand-dune. Smoke and smells of cooking meat wafted on the breeze.

One corpse sprawled at Teltö's feet, limbs protruding like some blubbery starfish. Teltö prodded it with a stick. His stomach rumbled; somehow he couldn't look at the bodies without imaging them glazed in honey and served with vegetables. Out of season vegetables, worth impoverishing yourself on the black market for…

"Oy! What do you think you're doing?"

Teltö dropped his stick on spotting the insignia. "Just checking for signs of life, sir."

The Captain ran a hand through close-cropped ginger hair, as if checking for lice. "They're dead, you idiot. For the fire-pit only."

"As you say, sir."

"Which regiment are you with, and who is your superior officer?"

"Special, sir."

"One of the Vice-Commander's pets? Weren't you lot supposed to be meeting with him?"

"Sorry, sir. I meant I *felt* my regiment was special. I'm with the 113th, and my superior officer was Reetle, sir." Name-tags on washed-up clothing were a wonderful thing.

"Reetle drowned."

"Yes, sir. And what a truly special man he was. I haven't been reassigned, sir."

"I swear everyone's bloody paperwork was eaten by the squids. Right, let's get this one to the bonfire before it rots." The man shuddered. "Or put to other uses. My uncle was killed twice in the last war, if you get my meaning."

To reanimate the corpse at Teltö's feet, if only for an unnerving cough or the twitch of a smile, proved sorely tempting. Once, Teltö would've done it without a thought, to put the fear of God into this Northern cretin. Now, survival trumped satisfaction, but perhaps he could get the best of both worlds...

"Look," pointed Teltö. "One of those corpses moved. Just behind you."

The Captain screeched like a train whistle as he swept around. "Where?" he barked, colour draining from his face. "Where is it?"

"Sorry, sir. My imagination. A trick of the light." Teltö smiled and clapped his hands together. "Right then, let's move this waxen load of lard."

• • •

THE NEXT DAY, the rain started. Big fat Unut-loving rain, the sort that beat down like a thousand thousand tiny hammers. Or in Teltö's case, the sort that found the hole in the tent canvas, and dripped directly onto his nose. He awoke with a curse, lurching bolt upright in the darkness. Drip after bloody drip landed on his head, and rolled down his face and chest.

"You'd think we were in bloody Tuonako." He shoved his blanket to the far side of the tent. Welleorm was still absent. *No snores.*

For hours, Teltö listened to the infernal patter on the canvas. When dawn came, he reached for his undershirt, groggy and grumpy. Yet also determined. Those hours lying awake had given him ideas. Teltö Phuul had a plan.

• • •

THE WIZENED CREATURE peered out from behind large spectacles. Keeker, the Quartermaster of the 113th: half those Teltö talked to called him a couple of biscuits short of a snack, the others called him mad. But he presided over the regimental cooking, and Teltö had not been idle.

"So you're Lieutenant Phuul?" Keeker nibbled at dirty fingernails. "Who did you serve under?"

Behind the Quartermaster, a young man wearing a scarf and an expression of indecisive angst sheltered under an overhanging tarpaulin. Two bags of potatoes leant against his legs; he'd piled peeled ones in a bucket.

"With respect, sir," said the scarf-wearer. He waved a potato peeler, whilst dodging the leaks in the tarpaulin. "It's whom."

"What?" snapped Keeker. His simian features

wrinkled.

"Whom did you serve under, sir."

Keeker's overlong arms flailed. "What does it matter who I served under, you blue-blooded blue-brained idiot. What matters is who *he* served under."

"I served under Reetle, sir." Teltö glanced out at the rain. "He was a casualty. Squid fodder."

"And you have been reassigned to…"

"No one yet, sir. The Powers That Be have more important things to worry about than common muckers like me." Teltö smiled. "Wrong surname, sir."

Keeker nodded in evident approval. The information gathering had paid off.

"Yes," said the Quartermaster. "Bloody toffs think they're so much better than the rest of us – keep your mouth shut, Sergeant. Anyway, Phuul – can you cook?"

"With my eyes shut, sir."

The man chuckled, if indeed Keeker could be called a man. "A useful skill round here. Almost as useful as no sense of smell. Right then, you're on. Come back in an hour and we'll sort your weaponry: Rughvneer M6941 and Lono revolver. You know, the standard. This here is Sergeant Speer – would be Private if there were any justice in the world, but there ain't."

Speer nodded politely. Too politely. *Someone's got a bit of breeding.*

• • •

THE NECROMANCER WHISTLED through the camp, ignoring the rain sneaking down the back of his shirt. The plan had been brilliant. In one stroke, he'd protected himself from awkward questions, and virtually booked his ticket home. If Ventiko marched on Mustanako, Teltö could tag along until they hit somewhere recognisable, and then scurry off into the undergrowth. The cherry on top? As regimental cook, he'd control his own bloody food.

Mug in hand, Welleorm waited for him back at the tent.

"Phuul," he said, swaying against the pole. His breath reeked of ale, and maybe something stronger. "Some news. I've travelled hither and yon with Rughvneer's bunch…"

Teltö ducked out of the rain, and plopped himself on a rolled-up coat. "So that's where you've been. By all accounts, we're heading south in a couple of days."

"The main force is; I'm not. They're shifting me to one of the garrisons. I figured that since you're Special Forces, and the paperwork's a mess…"

"Not Special Forces. They've reassigned me to the 113th as a cook."

Welleorm's face fell. "So you'll go south with the rest." He collapsed onto a pillow. "God is cruel. So bloody cruel." He crawled into a ball and burst into tears.

He saved my life and thinks it all for nothing. Teltö patted the poor fellow. "I'll be fine."

.   .   .

WELLEORM REALLY HAD been worse for wear, but the weather went a long way to sobering him up. The next day, Teltö helped him pack, ready for the air journey north.

"Are you sure you don't need the tent, Phuul? It'll probably piss down the whole way."

Teltö looked at the rain, which fell heavy and relentless. Water trickled off his borrowed oilskin. "Quite sure." A drop scored a direct hit on Teltö's nose; he wiped it away with a grunt. "I'll find a replacement."

"Stay safe, then. If you get yourself killed, I'll ask the Imperials to bring you back just so I can kill you again."

If only he knew. They shook hands. From the gondola door, a man in blue waved, and held up a watch. The Chaplain seemed to treat punctuality as the work of He Who Must Be Fought.

Teltö smiled. "Perhaps we'll meet again."

"The Mad God should be so kind."

With a final salute, Welleorm boarded the airship. Teltö shuffled back, and the propellers began to hum. *Sufael must have stood like this when she farewelled me.* The craft lifted into the grey sky, terrible and majestic. Once it had reached altitude, it hung suspended for a moment. Then it swung around like a weathervane to face the north. Teltö watched until it disappeared over the forested hills.

He didn't need Welleorm's tent, true enough. The man had done enough for him already. But he did need…

"Oy!"

The bespectacled little squirt dropped the crate.

"Yes, sir?"

Teltö puffed out his chest, and strode over to the cowering Private. He circled the man, face frozen in what he hoped was a sufficiently intimidating sneer.

"Which regiment, Private?"

The fellow's oil-skin was long as Teltö's, which meant it reached to the ankles on him. "The 113th, sir." He blinked through fogged-up glasses. "Please don't hurt me, please."

Perfect. "I must warn you that the current state of your uniform violates three separate provisions of Provisional Regulation 214D. As a superior officer…"

The fellow fell to his knees. "No, no, please don't. Not

a court-martial, please. I'll do anything."

A shame he's not better looking. "I need to inspect your tent."

A few more well-placed threats from Lieutenant Phuul, laced with appeals to obscure regulations, and Teltö had somewhere to sleep. This tent had enough space, even when shared, though the tear in one corner allowed in cool air and infernal rainwater. Not that Teltö complained; wet Northern summers held little terror for a Qivunakonian, and he planted his bedroll well away from the leak.

That evening, the order came through. They'd march at dawn.

*   *   *

MIST AND DRIZZLE harried the march south. Wrapped in oilskin and unseasonable scarf, and burdened by rifle and pack, Teltö concentrated on keeping one foot in front of the other. The conifers gave way to grass, and then the grass turned to mud. Every day, the mud encrusted itself on his boots and trouser legs; he soon gave up even pretending to clean them. But every step took Teltö closer to Qivunako and closer to home, a thought he treasured through the dark and lonely nights that followed.

"I want every pot and pan accounted for, Phuul," Keeker told him one day during dinner preparation. "That's good metal we're talking. Good metal, you hear me?"

Teltö did not look up from the potatoes. "Yes, sir."

"If we lose a pot, we'll need to find another one. That takes time, Phuul."

Teltö reached into the bucket beside him, and grabbed a grubby spud. *Father Life, who washed this one? Was*

Speer asleep? "Yes, sir."

The Quartermaster poked the overhead tarpaulin with a stick. Water splashed close to Teltö's left boot. "Do you want to be the one responsible for losing good metal?"

Teltö visualised good metal inserting itself into Keeker. "No, sir."

"You drive them too hard," said a new voice. "Too much harshness, and before you know it, they'll want to kill you more than the enemy."

Teltö looked up to see a lean and monocled gentleman of middle-years. Grass and mud-stains peppered the man's blue uniform; he carried a book under his arm.

Keeker subsided. "As you say, sir," he grunted. "Phuul! By the Mad God and all His monstrosities, what are you doing?"

Teltö jumped. "Pardon, sir? I was merely peeling potatoes, sir. As you ordered, sir."

Keeker poked Teltö's chest with his stick. "And in what part of the regulations do potatoes trump your Regimental Chief?"

Shit. "Sorry, sir. I didn't recognise him, sir. I don't think we've met, sir."

"You served under Reetle, but haven't met the Chief?"

Shit. Shit. Shit. "I was only recently transferred, sir. Sorry, sir."

Keeker nodded. "Well, then. Phuul, meet Colonel Frevorum Groon. He's Regimental Chief of the 113th. To me he's the boss, to you he's the bloody Prince..."

"Goodness, no," said Groon. "I'm not even a Count. I would never claim Princeship."

Keeker visibly winced. "It's a figure of speech, sir."

"Oh, sorry." Groon smiled. "Carry on." He removed his monocle and wiped it with a handkerchief. "I see Lieutenant Phuul is of Imperial extraction."

Teltö thinned his lips. *Best tread carefully.* "My family moved after the last war, sir. Legally, sir."

"Indeed. You must tell me all about it at my little card game tonight."

Teltö grimaced. "My apologies, sir. I have duties…" He eyed Keeker.

"Nonsense," said Groon. "You have no duties this evening. The Quartermaster shall find someone else to wear your shoes, as it were."

"If you say so, sir," said Keeker.

Bugger.

•   •   •

GROON'S PRIVATE ENCAMPMENT stood on the summit of a small hill. *Someone wants to escape the mud. If I were a toff, I'd do the same.* The rain had stopped, for now, but angry cumulonimbus obscured the setting Sun. Teltö wondered if he'd get back to his tent before the skies opened. Halfway up the slope, he hit a mud patch. His right boot skidded out from under him, and he grabbed a clump of grass as a lifeline. Teltö yelped and sucked his fingers. Serrated toitoi: razor grass.

With stakes and tarpaulin, the Colonel had created a dry outdoors area. Teltö saw that the place overlooked a lake. The surrounding toitoi were in flower; the shaggy white blooms blew gently in the evening breeze. *Very pretty.* Teltö winced. *Very painful.*

"So pleased you could make it," said Groon. He readjusted a lit oil lantern. "Please, Lieutenant, take a seat. Don't worry about sirs and titles. We're all friends."

A collapsible table and chairs had been laid out beneath the tarpaulin. Teltö slid into the nearest seat. "How in blazes did you get all this up here?" He peered closer at the lantern in front of him. *Made in Kuolinako. Hah.*

Groon smiled. "The same way anything is ever done, Lieutenant. With servants. Oh, you've cut your hand." He tut-tutted. "I did tell the suppliers we ought to have more gloves."

Teltö gritted his teeth. "Bloody toitoi. Have you got any disinfectant and bandages?"

"Somewhere." Groon shook his head. "Alas, my servants are out fetching dinner. But we'll survive, won't we?" He patted Teltö's shoulder.

"I suppose. You said you were having a card game…"

"Yes, Lieutenant, I did. My card games are quite popular. I'm particularly fond of Black Nykövä, but my enthusiasm exceeds my talent…"

Teltö frowned. "Black Nykövä? You mean My Fair Lady…"

"I mean what I mean, Lieutenant. Silver now and again is nice, but lucre has never driven me." He smiled. "I have other motivations, and it is no accident we are alone tonight."

"Pardon?"

"I have waited a long time for this."

Teltö pulled his Lono revolver and pointed it at Groon. "You're one of them." He backed out into the night, where drizzle had started falling again. "Father Life, you bastards don't give up, do you?"

Groon stared. "Lieutenant, what on earth are you doing?"

Teltö cocked the Lono. "You're trying to kill me." *One of the Dragon's minions. Like the silver swallowers.*

"It would appear you are trying to kill *me*. Quite why, I cannot fathom. Now put down your weapon, and we can discuss this like gentlemen."

Teltö paused. Groon had not actually threatened him. Perhaps he had leapt to conclusions? *In which case I've just pointed a gun at a superior officer. Which means firing squad…*

"Lieutenant, you are not merely of Imperial extraction; you *are* an Imperial." Groon placed a small pine box on the table. "Which is why I need you. Please sit, and I shall explain."

Teltö edged forward. Was this Ventiko all over again? Still, he had to trust Groon; shooting the fellow would see him arrested and shot. *I'll hear him out.*

"Good lad." Groon opened the box. "Now observe."

Teltö looked inside. He blinked. *Spiders? He's excited about a bunch of bloody Yellowtails?* Then, as one, the spider legs twitched. They scuttled out onto the table, and ran round and round the lantern's base.

"Hold on," Teltö began. "These are dead spiders…"

"Yes, the spiders are dead." said Groon. "Animated by my own necromantic powers!"

Teltö scratched his head. Stray water droplets fell onto the table. "But you're a Northerner. You're forbidden from doing this. Father Life, you're forbidden from *learning* this!"

Groon nodded. "Yet I have learned this. I can *read*, Lieutenant, and the Empire has many useful libraries. I would consider myself a reasonable practitioner in spider wars, were I only able to find someone to compete against."

"You're wanting a spider war partner?" Teltö spluttered.

"No, Lieutenant, I am looking to move on from

spiders. Spiders are a trifle, a diversion. I would learn the secret at the heart of the Viiminian Empire. I want to animate *men*."

Maybe I should shoot him. "An unauthorised Necromancer? Kuolinako and Skeevereet would drop everything to purge you."

"I know, Lieutenant. Hence the dead-ends. But I ask you: why should I be left in ignorance because I was unfortunate enough to be born on one side of Yyti's Wall, rather than the other? Why am I so different from you?"

"But…" Teltö recalled Ventiko's explanation to Rughvneer. "What makes you think I'm an Imperial at all? I might be pretending. A spy who weeds out traitors."

"Lieutenant, my cousin owns a café opposite the Embassy. I know a surprising amount about goings-on…" Groon tapped his fingers. "A red-haired Necromancer named Phuul worked as an Imperial attaché. A red-haired Necromancer named Phuul attended the Anniversary Banquet, and had the good fortune to leave early. And now a red-haired man named Phuul has joined my regiment. I believe the simplest explanation is the best one, and, dare I say, a spy would be put to other, better, uses. A spy would not draw premature attention to himself by preferring the Imperial *toitoi* to the Northern *flayer's weed*…"

"I was gaining your confidence."

"Then why query *my* use of an Imperial term? Why lure me from the path, only to shoo me back? And then there is your death threat. Either you are utterly irrational or you fear unmasking. Observation suggests the latter. You, Lieutenant, are a Necromancer."

Bugger. "And you want me to teach you."

"Correct, Lieutenant. Between your existing duties in

the kitchen tent, if it isn't too much trouble. You will find me a most dutiful student. There will be a reward too, I promise."

Teltö jerked up. "A reward?"

"Silver, books, anything you please. I even have a servant who will meet your baser needs, should you be that way inclined." Groon chuckled. "I did try it myself once, back when I was eager to experience absolutely everything Imperial. But no, xenophilia will only go so far."

Teaching necromancy to the North? If the shadow-stalkers find out, they'll disappear the entire Phuul family. But I'll never get a better chance to escape.

"Silver, and you let me go?"

Groon removed his monocle and wiped it. "Let you go where, Lieutenant?"

"Home."

Chapter Sixteen

Save for Rhea, Frevorum Groon knew more about the history and theory of necromancy than anyone Teltö had ever met.

"I find Saari Ooks criminally underrated as a thinker," said the Colonel one evening within his private tent. A Yellowtail spider crawled across his palm. "Did I tell you I have the complete and annotated Nine Authors at home? The definitive Ooseman translation?"

"Yes." Teltö collapsed onto a bundle of Unut-fur blankets. *You've told me thirteen times.* "But while political philosophy has uses…"

Groon often used terms Teltö had either forgotten or else never learned. Worse, when Teltö resorted to analogies to communicate ideas, his student analysed them literally, to the point of absurdity. For all Groon's intelligence and conscientiousness, it was like learning to cook solely through memorising recipe books.

"This isn't working." Teltö rubbed his eyes and yawned. Groon's lessons on top of his existing kitchen duties left him perpetually exhausted.

"I detect frustration," said the Colonel. "The sentiment is mutual."

"What we really need is something to practice on."

Groon blinked. "A human corpse, you mean?"

No. I mean a bloody Unut. "I take it you don't have any lying around?"

"Not as a rule, no. Alas, I lack the options of the Empire, with its convenient Death Draft, or, going back in history, the ability to wage war to obtain fresh... material."

Teltö relived the conversation on the way back to his own tent. *We're heading to a bloody warzone, Groon. You'll soon have all the material you need.* Teltö knew he needed to escape before then. Could he convince Groon that he'd already done his best to teach him what he knew? *I'll drop the silver request if he'll just let me go.* Unless the Colonel's affable demeanour hid other motives. After his Ventiko experience, Teltö felt a lingering fear. The only thing worse than Northerners with necromancy would be Northerners with the Toast...

No. Unlike Ventiko, Groon could only ever be a lonely eccentric. Lonely eccentrics were no match for the power of institutions. *The Church would see it as complete surrender to the Mad God, and in their own way, they'd be right.* The Principality had defined itself against its southern neighbour for five centuries: a blip in the history of the Viiminian Empire, but all the Northerners and their ancestors had ever known. *They'd no longer be the North any more. They'd be little more than an Imperial province with an odd language.* Teltö smiled, as he opened his tent. *No need for that. We've already got Tuonako.*

•　•　•

AFTER SEVERAL DAYS of trudging through the rain, the muddy grass gave way to rolling hills choked with gorse and blackberry. Teltö nabbed liberal handfuls of berries, for the first time in his life pleased to purge the taste of his own cooking from his mouth.

"You know," said the little snoring bastard from his tent; Teltö had nicknamed him Private Saw, his true name being unpronounceable Northern gibberish, "blackberries are good for your health. Them, and nuts. I like nuts."

"You're in the right place then," Teltö murmured, as they followed the well-worn trail through the bushes. Never mind evening necromancy lessons, Army Cooking was just wrong. No appreciation for taste, texture, or aroma, just getting bland muck into bowls fast as humanly possible. *I'm wasted here. They'd be better off getting liches to do it. Perhaps Groon has the right idea.* He grabbed another berry and scowled.

Suddenly, Saw tripped and fell; his spectacles plopped into the mud.

"Help," screeched the Private. He clawed at the ground. "Something's got my leg…"

Teltö squatted onto his haunches, thinking the man had stepped on some forgotten rabbit trap. Then his eyes widened. A grey hand gripped Saw's ankle, dragging him into the blackberry. *A lich. There are Necromancers around.*

Teltö didn't hesitate. He ducked into the bush, braving the thorns that grabbed at his hair and uniform. Where was the bloody thing? He heard Saw's yelp. He shoved back brambles to let in light. Then he saw it. White eyes in a grey face; a shadowy hand crept towards Saw's throat. *Right, you bastard.* Teltö cleared his mind, and reached out to the dead brain, probing the mental chains that linked it to its master. He sensed a more powerful

Necromancer than himself controlled the lich, but the control was distant and divided. *They'll think it's an error.* Biting his lip, Teltö ordered the lich to release its captive. For a moment the grip eased… Someone shoved him out the way. Teltö tumbled onto his arse. The soft mud squelched beneath him; a chill seeped through his trousers. *Shit.* He heard a gunshot, and flinched. Looking around, he saw another soldier, slinging a Rughvneer M6941 over his shoulder.

"Sorry," panted the new arrival. "We've been having problems with these things all along the line. Spread the word, keep a good lookout, and keep your rifle ready. There might be more."

Teltö nodded. The man ran off. He helped Saw to his feet, wincing at the odour coming from the Private's trousers.

"It had me, it had me," whimpered Saw.

Teltö patted him on the back, and returned the glasses. "Not any more. Come on, we're lagging."

From over the next hill, he heard another scream. *Father Life, they're only corpses.* Teltö ran panting through the bushes, and up the slope. *Another gunshot.* He reached the summit, sweat running down his face.

Three men sprawled on a barren patch off to the left. *No,* Teltö corrected himself: *two men and a lich.* He picked his way over the blood-slicked grass. A high calibre weapon had blown off half the lich's skull, scattering bits of brain into the nearby bushes; the body had fallen face-down, to Teltö's relief. Its hand still clutched a bloodied knife.

The two soldiers lay strewn like rag dolls. One face-down, the other on his back with his arm across his face. *Like at the beach.* Teltö grimaced. *But I'm less hungry now.* He bent over the latter, and pulled away the arm.

Groon.

"Colonel!"

Groon's chest and stomach sported multiple wounds; blood drenched the front of his uniform.

"Colonel!" Teltö shook the fellow. *Don't die, you poor silly bastard. You're my ticket out of here.*

Groon coughed and opened his eyes. "Afternoon, Lieutenant." Blood dripped from his mouth. "I'll cancel our lesson tonight. Not feeling my best. Stabbed."

"Don't move, sir," said Teltö. "You'll be fine, sir."

"Please, Lieutenant. My mistake. I thought… a chance for practical work. Then it jumped my poor servant. Cut his throat." He nodded at the other man, only a centifurlong away. More coughing, more blood. "Then it spitted me like a roast pigeon. Shot the blighter. Too late…"

"Colonel, sir. About our agreement?"

"No time, Lieutenant. I suppose I'll reanimate. Most annoying. Imperial Necromancers have the Toast to protect them, but what do I have?" Groon smiled. "I know what I have."

"Sir?"

Groon lifted a silver-inlaid revolver. His hand shook. "Look away, Lieutenant. I'll deal with my servant too. Only proper."

Teltö stood numbly, and walked back to the path, not looking back. He heard a gunshot.

Private Saw came running up the hill. The blackberry bushes reached chest-height on him.

"Did you get it, sir?" he panted. "You destroyed it, please tell me you destroyed it."

What do I tell him?

Teltö silently shoved Saw away, and kept moving.

Another shot sounded in the mid-afternoon.

*   *   *

ALL DAY, WHEN he least expected it, Teltö found himself reliving the crack of Groon's last gunshot. Night was worse. Teltö's role as regimental cook excused him from guard duty, which meant hours of pot-scrubbing gave way to hours of staring up at a dark canvas ceiling, hours full of rumination, guilt, and fear.

"May he lie safe in the arms of the Mother Eternal," Teltö muttered to the darkness, when Saw was out. Whether the Mother heard him, Teltö couldn't decide.

He found himself yelling at Saw for anything and everything, and especially for snoring. Saw himself looked in bad shape. After his experience with the liches, the little Private jumped at every shadow.

"There's things out there, I tell you," he said, arriving back at the tent one night. "Things you can't see, but they're there. I've never been the religious type, but you can feel the Mad God walking. The Empire gives me the creeps."

Teltö sat up and yawned. "Indeed."

"I want to thank you for diving in to rescue me. What you did was so brave I don't know how you managed it. Walking corpses… it's all so unnatural and terrifying."

"It's just a matter of practice. And if the Empire scares you so much, bugger off to the Confederation. The far side, so I can't hear you snore." Teltö bid an irritated good night, and pulled his blanket tight about him. He still couldn't sleep.

But one day, Saw didn't come back. The march continued; no one noticed or cared when Teltö pointed out his absence.

"These things happen," Keeker had said. "Get those potatoes peeled, Lieutenant. Sharpish."

"But, sir." Teltö gritted his teeth. "A man has vanished."

"Someone disappears in the Empire? Colour me shocked. Now finish those god-sent spuds."

Teltö could only shrug. That night he rummaged through Saw's possessions. He discovered a half-written letter, a blank diary, and a box of milk chocolates. *Mother Death, I can't remember his real name, but keep him safe. Tell him I'm sorry for yelling at him. I'm sorry for everything.* Teltö allocated himself a couple of blocks a day in memory of the Private. Within three days, the chocolate was gone.

• • •

A WEEK AFTER Saw's disappearance, the 113th breasted a hill, and arrived at a settlement. Teltö still couldn't place it on the map, but he saw at once this was no ghost town. With its tidy streets, prim brick houses and rose gardens, abandonment had been a matter of several weeks, if not days ago. Keeker sent him and others scrounging for food. A crowbar made short work of the windows, and whatever reservations Teltö might have had soon vanished. *Decent food at last,* he thought on inspecting his third pantry. The bastards must have had a rationing exemption to afford all this. Sugar, pepper, pickles, pumpkins…

"Lieutenant, sir, they've found someone."

Teltö jumped, and dropped the gherkin jar. *Don't sneak up on me.* He grimaced at the broken glass. "What is it, Speer?"

The Sergeant shifted on his feet. "The New Chief, sir. He's found two Mnomo hiding in a cellar, and some women."

In truth, Groon's replacement had found the men who had found the women. That afternoon at court-martial, the fellow announced Ventiko's standing orders: the rapists and the Mnomo were to be burnt alive in the town square, together with some deserters he'd got his hands on.

"Traditional firing squad and cremation would have sufficed, but my hands, as they say, are tied." The New Chief knitted his magnificent caterpillar eyebrows. "I shall send my protests to the Marshal personally."

Teltö skipped the execution, suddenly remembering he needed to scrub pots for Keeker.

"They were howling, sir," said Speer later, referring to the Mnomo. Keeker had put him on potato duty again.

"I bet they were," said Teltö. "Green wood, was it?"

"Yes, sir. There was no other wood available. But that wasn't what they were howling about. They seemed to... enjoy it."

Teltö shrugged. "That's the Mnomo for you. Damn Imperials and their policy of toleration. Oh, and hurry up. There's another couple of bags waiting outside."

• • •

THE 113th HALTED for five more days, free to loot and pillage if not to rape. The morose skyline remained, variations of grey upon grey; Teltö almost felt at home. But it was nice to prepare food indoors again, and the extra bits and pieces he'd filched made life easier. Especially happy with his new razor, he spent much of his spare time scraping away surviving patches of ginger stubble.

"I never wanted to fight, sir," said Speer one

afternoon.

Keeker was away, and the pair of them had been tasked with getting the pea soup ready for dinner. The abandoned kitchen contained useful utensils, fresh eggs, and an eggbeater, all of which Teltö had promptly hidden. Some things were wasted on mere troops.

The Necromancer looked up from beside the regimental cauldron. "I don't think anyone does. Only lunatics want to fight, and you're hardly a lunatic, eh, Sergeant? Fetch me some pepper."

Speer rummaged around in the pantry shelves. "This, sir?"

Teltö pursed his lips. "No, Sergeant," he said gently. "That's salt. I'm after pepper."

He liked Speer. The blue-blood may have lacked the brains the Father gave an Unut, but the man was generous, polite, and honest to a fault. He was also the closest Teltö had to a friend since Saw disappeared.

Speer found the pepper. "My uncle forced me to fight, sir."

Teltö applied the spice to the cauldron. *Freshly ground black pepper. It's been too long.* "Your uncle being?"

"Count Speer's youngest brother, sir. My father was the middle brother, but he drowned in a yachting accident in the Straits. You remember, it made the papers? Anyway, being heir to the title, it was felt I had to do my duty, and champion the Speer name..."

Teltö waved his wooden spoon until the sergeant subsided. He resumed stirring the soup; the pea smell wafted pleasantly into the air. He suspected somehow Speer's uncle was motivated by more than family prestige.

●　●　●

THE MARCH RESTARTED. They cut across cultivated fields; despite objections from the more devout, Unut were slaughtered and devoured, and Teltö soaked his biscuits in dripping for days afterwards. But there was something soul-destroying about trudging through mud in eternal drizzle, with the humming of airships the only change. Teltö leant against a haystack, and pushed his damp hair back for the hundredth time. *What happened to summer?*

Then one evening in the kitchen tent, while Teltö and Speer scrubbed pots in the shelter of the Quartermaster's tarpaulin, and Keeker sat at a commandeered table with his dog-eared inventory notebook, a dull boom sounded in the distance. It came from the south.

"Lovely," muttered Teltö. "A thunderstorm. As if we weren't enjoying enough rain."

Keeker cackled. "That's no thunderstorm, Phuul. You're hearing the music of the Empire's anti-aircraft guns. The melody hasn't changed in forty years."

We're getting close to Mustanako. Teltö scoured the pot harder, transferring his panic to the scrubber. *Shit. I'd better get away soon.*

"Have you encountered this sort of thing before, sir?" Speer asked.

Keeker slapped him over the head with the notebook. "No, Sergeant. I know the sound from listening to you fart. But, since you ask, yes. I served on an airship the last time this happened. Not pleasant, my aristocratic little friend, not pleasant at all."

"How so, sir?"

Teltö cringed. *I wonder if Speer's related to Meerm.*

But the Quartermaster only laughed. "You'll find out soon enough."

Later, when Speer had buggered off to the latrine, or

wherever he went at night, Teltö prodded the old man for something more on the last war. Keeker resisted at first, before pulling out his tobacco and pipe with a grunt.

"A nightmare, lad." Keeker hunted around for a box of matches. "The Mad God in His maddest dreams could not have come up with something like that... I was in a team of three. Standard for the 42nd in those days. Still is, last I checked. Pilot, navigator, and me as maintenance man. I had the worst job, of course, since the fixer was also the monster who pushed the buttons."

Keeker found the matches: Proth & Proth white phosphorous standard. He broke two before getting one to spark. He lit his pipe, and puffed on it for a while in silence.

"We were east of Mustanako, low-flying to take out a railway bridge near some tinpot town. We did our job... then ran into the Empire's anti-aircraft guns. Imperials have always been good with those. One moment we're sitting pretty, the next, there's two man-sized holes in the compartment walls, and our navigator isn't there. Vanished without even a speck of blood. Pilot was crazy, screaming. He might've been trying to emergency land, for all the good that'd have done. I'll never know. I was panicking too. I pushed the button – white, not red."

Keeker smiled. "Red's standard, red's targeted and precise. White's special occasion. So in those days, white was *rulion*."

The rain of death. Teltö shivered, but kept his mouth shut. *Don't interrupt, Phuul.* It looked like Keeker was no longer even talking to him; the Quartermaster talked to himself, somehow, from across the years. Pungent pipe smoke hovered in the night-time air.

"Next thing I knew, I was sitting on a haystack with a

herd of Unut looking at me. Not accusingly, not like the unclean maggots of the Mad God, just brown and blank, the way those critters do. Just me too; the Mad God must've taken the pilot. Certainly took the airship wreckage over in the next paddock. Talk about pre-baked potatoes. But the *rulion*, ah, the *rulion*…"

Another minute-long pause. The Quartermaster's eyes were open, and his teeth still gripped the stem of his clay pipe; otherwise Teltö could have mistaken it for sleep. But Keeker hadn't finished. He blew a smoke ring.

"It'd landed smack-bang in the middle of that tinpot railway town. Lucky for me, the wind blew the fumes the other way, else I wouldn't be here, haystack or no. But the light, the piercing silver light… it outshone the Sun that afternoon. Bloody thing nearly cooked me too, from a good few furlongs away. I later heard they'd seen it from Mustanako. The rain of death, the Imperials call it. Funny thing about rain: the clouds don't feel guilty for flooding. They don't feel guilty for acting the monster. But I sure as anything do. I'm the one who dropped the *rulion* on someone's town, cooked entire families like so many pork chops. It stays with you, never lets you rest."

"Yet here you are, again," Teltö murmured.

"No." Keeker shook his head violently. "Not again. Not since the Prince banned it. Though if truth be told, I've relived that day in my dreams for forty years. I need an end. Death holds no terrors for the likes of me. It's you I feel sorry for. You and Speer. Now finish those god-sent pots or I'll skin you alive."

He stood and wandered out into the darkness.

Teltö stayed awake for a long while that night, staring at the tent roof. The shelling had started again.

Chapter Seventeen

T HEY HEARD MUSTANAKO before they saw it. The
thundering of the guns grew ever louder, and was
soon joined by other sounds: the explosion of bombs, the
humming of aircraft...

Teltö crested the final ridge, and looked down upon
the plain. Airships gathered over the Empire's great port
city like blowflies over an Unut carcass. The defenders had
razed the outlying buildings all the way to the old city
walls, and the northern plain had been reduced to wires,
mud, tunnels, and traps as far as the eye could see. *The
other regiments got here first.* Off to his right, where the
harbour bent inwards, Teltö spotted the broken hull of a
ship drifting on the waves. *Whose? Even squids aren't any use
against airships.* Myrstä Island loomed eternal on the
horizon.

So Ventiko had Mustanako besieged. *So much for the
maw of Kuolinako.* But the damage was done, and Teltö had
other concerns. *Is Rhea still there?* He imagined his sister,
trapped by Northern soldiers. No, it didn't bear thinking
about. *Please tell me someone with enough sense evacuated this place*

when the war started.

Next morning he went as normal to see Keeker at the kitchen tent. He found the Quartermaster hunched over some dirt-stained papers; he looked up, scowling.

"Sorry, Phuul. I've been given some other lads to help with the muck today. You and Speer are to grab some shovels and get digging, along with the rest of the 113th. Our friend the Marshal isn't happy with us missing the first few engagements. Groon's death was an inconvenience for His Skullface, though the New Chief's grovelled himself into permanent appointment."

Speer arrived, scarf on display. "What'll it be today, sir?"

"Spades, not spuds, Sergeant. Phuul will fill you in."

Teltö grimaced. "We're digging trenches."

"Eh?" said Speer, cocking his head.

"Are you deaf?" Keeker snapped. "We ain't getting any closer right now. The Imperials have probably laid mines everywhere. We missed their first wave of walking dead, but there'll be more. So start digging. Or are you worried you'll break a precious fingernail?"

• • •

THE SOFT GROUND made life easier, and a clearance in the weather even made the day remotely pleasant. Or it would have, were it not for the crashed airship in No Man's Land, barely six centifurlongs away. Teltö eyed the pilot's charred skull, and the dark rings where goggles had been. It didn't help to think this was the Empire's doing; it simply reminded him of Keeker's story. *I need to get out of here.* But how? Groon lay dead, and a literal war-zone stood between him and Mustanako. Teltö heaved out yet another load of waterlogged dirt and sighed.

For two days, the 113th added to the labyrinthine dug-outs, mostly in the eastern sector towards the Nhagivat. At last, the order came to rest. Teltö threw down his shovel and squatted in his underground shelter. Too tired to move, and sweating in his undershirt, he allowed himself mumbled curses. *If I liked tunnels, I'd have stayed in bloody Kuolinako.*

Poles and grubby beams supported the shelter's ceiling. Teltö pushed damp hair from his eyes, and imagined the thing collapsing, like the slamming of some giant's jaws. *If it does, it'll have me.* A lantern sat beside him in the dirt. It illuminated scuff marks and shovel ridges, and formed weird patterns where dark met light. This place, not fit for wetas, let alone people, had already trapped him. Either he'd escape or die.

Keeker brought food that evening: some biscuits and the dregs of the Unut-bone soup.

"Nice work, Phuul," he said. "Snali will be pleased."

Pleasing Snali Ventiko was the least of Teltö's concerns. He located a spoon and an enamel bowl from his pack, then tried the soup. He nearly spat it out. *Cold and foul.*

Teltö pushed the bowl away. "He's not coming to inspect them himself, is he? You know, to ensure that the 113th is pulling its weight?"

"Who, the Marshal?" Keeker chuckled. "A meet and greet would waste his time. We're the cogs in his machine. We do as we're told, but other than that he ignores us."

Teltö held up a biscuit. *No wetas, weevils or bite marks. Thank Father Life for small mercies.* He chewed it and considered his role in Ventiko's machine. It was likely larger than Keeker imagined.

Across the mud, Mustanako slept uneasily.

• • •

THE DAWN CAME, grey and humid. The dead came with it. Grey-faced, white-eyed, and relentless, their numbers were legion. Crouched behind the little mud wall, blue shirt sticking to his back, Teltö gripped his Rughvneer rifle, and waited. His mouth felt dry. All his life, he'd seen liches as nothing more than obedient servants, performing the role nature meant for them. They mined, they drove, they toiled in mills and factories. Harmless drudges who never complained or ate or rebelled. Now, things had changed. They were trying to kill him.

He steadied his tin helmet. *They haven't changed. I have.* Hova had plotted it, but the fat little Unut never took up arms against his country. Today, Teltö would wear an enemy uniform, and would do the enemy's work. *I swear I'm not a traitor, honest.* He doubted anyone back home would believe him, but, for once, home was the least of his concerns.

The liches stumbled through the cratered mud and waded through the man-made pits and bogs, some up to their necks in filth. They were now within…

"Fire!"

The Northern forces let loose. The orgy of bullets was deafening; like being trapped inside a thundercloud. The artillery shook the very earth. Explosions birthed geysers of mud and sent white smoke coursing over the field. But the dead did not flinch. They never once cried out or ceased shambling forward even as line after line was blown to pieces. Teltö hunched behind the bank and shuddered. *I can't shoot my own. I won't shoot my own…*

The man next to him frowned. "What's the problem?" he shouted.

"Sorry," Teltö shouted back. "Just checking my rifle."

Feeling his cheeks burn, Teltö swung around, and aimed into the air. Again and again, he sent the bullets flying over the heads of the liches and whatever living troops were back there bolstering the Imperial assault. Each bullet must come down eventually, he knew, but it was better than firing into bodies. *And it's not treason to waste enemy ammunition.*

Soon the surviving liches were within range to return fire. Teltö ducked, silently panicking while a maelstrom passed through the air less than a centifurlong above. *The Sämö-Sömö. Low calibre, ugly, and effective.* Screams came from nearby; others further down the line hadn't been so lucky. He saw Sergeant Speer bending over a casualty. Something rose up behind the Sergeant, knife in hand. Blue-uniformed and white-eyed: a freshly-risen lich. Teltö tried to reach out with his power, but couldn't. *Concentrate, Phuul, concentrate.* The blade swung down towards the exposed back.

A man came running from the right, levelled his rifle, and fired. The lich's head exploded like a watermelon; the corpse collapsed, a lifeless husk once more. The shooter wiped sweat from his sloping forehead, his simian face locked in a satisfied grin. *Keeker.* Teltö blinked. *The man's a crack shot.* He waved meekly at the Quartermaster, who delivered a forceful salute.

The Imperial liches closed in across No Man's Land. Off to both left and right, other Northern regiments fired flamethrowers until the dead burnt like candles. *Not the 113th though. Groon forbade everything but rifle and revolver. Father Life, bless that old romantic.* Corpse fat and hair alike ignited before Teltö's eyes. Holding his breath against the appalling reek, Teltö saw one lich, its face melting, trip on barbed wire and disappear into a mud pit. It did not emerge. By now, smoke clouds had blotted out the Sun itself, sending the battlefield into an unnatural twilight.

"So much for the Mustanakonian summer," Teltö muttered. "Next year, I'll go back to Dyrtölä." He looked over his shoulder, but there was no danger of anyone hearing him, not here, not with the racket of the guns and the thunder of the artillery. Overhead, the airships dropped their load on the Imperial positions, while the defenders took endless pot-shots.

Teltö fired shot after shot into the foul-smelling darkness, no longer caring if a regiment of liches was anywhere near his position. It became rhythmic, much like swimming strokes. And much like his swim in the Illuvian, his brain knew any break in the rhythm could prove fatal. His fingers grew numb from loading and reloading, but he kept at it for hour after hour, feeding little bits of lead into the ever-hungry Rughvneer M6941. *Aim. Fire.* Yes, you didn't need a living person for this. Animated corpses would work just fine.

Then he heard a siren, high pitched and blaring, audible even over the cacophony of the battlefield. Teltö stopped, and blinked. He lowered his rifle. *What's happening?* A figure in blue rushed past and pushed something into his hand. A gas-mask.

Do I look Kuolinakonian? Teltö shrugged and pulled the mask over his face. *Probably.*

Waiting was the worst. Waiting, the mind played tricks. The laboratories of the Empire had birthed lich squids of unimaginable size; Teltö wondered what else his homeland had concocted within the constraints of the old peace treaty. Safe and easily produced airship gases remained out of reach, but toxic gases? Child's play for a people raised on the air of Kuolinako.

Minute by minute, his dread grew. But he saw nothing: no classic green and yellow mist creeping over No Man's Land. *Perhaps a false alarm.* Finally, poking his head over the edge of the trench, he saw movement. Grey faces marching towards him, heedless of wire or crater. Teltö ducked down. *Yes. A false alarm.* He readied his rifle.

At the other end of the trench, he saw soldiers readying phosphorous grenades. *Burning destruction. How Northern.* A man pulled a pin…

Teltö never remembered a sound, but he knew what he saw. A river of orange flame rushed through the air. Those further along were engulfed; Teltö threw himself down face-first as the air above ignited. Pressing his body into the soft, welcoming mud until he was all but submerged, he felt the furnace heat of the burning gas at his back. *A moment later, and it'd have cooked me.* He didn't dare look up.

Even with the mask, Teltö became light-headed. The tempest of fire must have lasted mere seconds, but it seemed hours. At last the air grew cooler. He blinked, then sat up, disorientated.

"Father Life, what was that?" Teltö muttered. He pulled off the gas-mask, and breathed freely. *Is someone grilling pork?*

Strong arms pulled him to his feet. Someone thrust a rifle at him.

"They're coming, you idiot!"

•　•　•

BY THE END of the day, the skeleton in the airship had a glut of company, and Teltö was called back to the kitchen tent to prepare that evening's pea soup. Hands shaking, he dispensed muck into bowls, and tried to block out the sight, sounds, and most of all the smell of battle. *Father Life, I'll swear off meat for the rest of time.* The men he served weren't any more talkative. Someone tried to get a song going in the queue, but no one joined in. Another struck a match to light his pipe, and had his pipe-stem snapped for his trouble. The last fellow, gaunt with a big grey beard, looked up as the dregs of the soup sloshed into his bowl.

"Evening, Phuul," he said.

Welleorm.

*   *   *

THE CHAPLAIN'S UNIFORM and robe hung loosely about his frame; the paunch was still there, but his arms and legs had grown thin and brittle as twigs. Retreating to the dugout, Teltö brewed Northern tea in an upturned helmet, while Welleorm plonked himself on an empty sardine crate, and plucked burrs from his beard. He flicked them into the nearest water bucket.

"They're telling stories about you, you know."

Teltö froze. "What sort of stories?"

"The usual. Lieutenant Phuul, the master rifleman. I told them you're ex-Special Forces. Of course you're a bloody master rifleman."

Teltö grimaced. "Just doing my bit."

"From what they're saying, you were firing off a Rughvneer M6941 like it was an Imperial Sämö-Sömö. So much lead in the air, I'm surprised there's any bullet boxes left at all!"

"You're too kind." Teltö wondered how many of those bullets had hit anything. "Now, I want a story or two myself." *Or a change of subject.* "How did garrison duty go?"

"Pretty well," said Welleorm. "To start with."

He told of how the Northerners had cleared out the decay, turning the abandoned towns into functioning outposts. The railway ran again, and supplies of food, equipment, and other necessities trickled down from the Wall, ready to be sent on. But then…

"Like ghosts in the night," said Welleorm, shaking his head. "We never saw hide nor hair of a lich, but the men turned up dead one after another, and we knew something was out there. Major-General Rughvneer knew it too when he came to take a look."

"Sidewhiskers ventured down off the Wall? I am impressed."

"Don't leap to conclusions, Phuul. The man's an ambitious arse, true enough, but he isn't stupid. He doubled the number of scouts, and kept the fires burning round the clock. He even had me perform exorcisms to purge Him from the place, which says something. The Rughvneers may be renowned for rifles, but they aren't renowned for piety."

Teltö poured the contents of the helmet into a tin mug. He passed it to Welleorm. "Then what happened?"

"A scouting party returned. Said they'd spotted a division of Imperials – living and liches – heading south. Not coming towards us, mind you, though some of the other outposts were reporting skirmishes. Rughvneer thought this was the Empire's initial welcoming committee, sent out before they realised Ventiko was attacking by sea. They're coming to relieve Mustanako, and unless something's done soon, they'll catch Ventiko in the rear. Just the way Imperials like it, of course, but it's bad for us."

"Which is why you're here."

Welleorm sipped his tea. He didn't bother asking for

milk, which suited Teltö. He didn't have any.

"Pretty much. Rughvneer dragged down fresh forces – the ones Snali left behind in case the Empire had any bright ideas – and has them keeping the rail running. He's also grabbed every airship he can get his hands on, never mind bombing missions. The supply lines have to be kept open, he says, though I don't know how long they'll hold out. Meanwhile, he's booted us older chaps down here. Probably thinks we'd all have gone mad if we'd stayed." The cleric chuckled. "He's not far wrong."

*   *   *

TELTÖ STARED UP at the gloom as the shelling sang to him again. He'd become used to it as night followed night; the music of gunfire, Keeker had called it. Still, he'd have swapped this grim symphony for Private Saw's snoring in a heartbeat.

When at last it stopped, he burrowed his head into the greatcoat pillow. *Bloody Mustanako summer. Where's sleet when you need it?* Finally, he gave up on sleep and pushed back the blankets. He pulled on his shirt and trousers, grabbed the lantern from beside the driftwood support beam, and crawled out into the night.

Strong westerly gales had cleared the sky. Stars now shone over the war-cursed land, the same that looked down on his parents and Kyrmves. *The stars are shining down on Rhea too, wherever she is.* Teltö looked over his shoulder. The wind ran through his hair. *Sufael too. And Dyrstin.* He corrected himself. *No, not Dyrstin. Not in Kuolinako.*

Teltö strolled westwards, hoping the salt of the Illuvian would mask the charcoal odour of slaughter. It didn't. Edging around a puddle, he reached the end of his trench, and crawled through a connecting tunnel into the next. Yesterday, some ingenious fellows had dragged beach driftwood in here, for structural reinforcement; sea-shells ringed the tunnel exit.

Teltö was raising his lantern for a closer look when his ears pricked up. *Was that a scream?* Yes, muffled shouts and gunshots came from the front, where the last lot of ditches faced off against No Man's Land.

Teltö ran, boots squishing through the trench's ankle-deep mud. He tripped on a discarded crate, and went sprawling. Soft and cold, the ooze enveloped his fingers, reaching to his wrists. Grunting, he extracted his undamaged lantern, and ran on.

Another shot. Teltö turned a corner, and stopped. Centifurlongs from where he stood, a watch-fire burnt bright and yellow within an iron drum. Figures clustered around, in both blue and lime-green uniforms. *Either someone's fraternising, or it's a night raid.* Teltö doubted these Imperials were warming their hands. He shuttered his lantern and crept closer, grateful that liches had no better night vision than the living. Silent as the Mother Eternal, he crouched behind a line of full water buckets.

Three liches lay in the mud, skulls blown away by Messrs Rughvneer and Lono. A living Imperial, a woman, slumped against the drum. *Living, but not for much longer.* Blood coated the front of her uniform. Another casualty, this one Northern, lay face-down nearby. Three remained standing: two Northerners, and an Imperial. The latter had his back to the trench wall, and stared down the barrel of a Rughvneer M6969.

"Any last words, corpse-buggerer?" said the man with the rifle.

"Hold fire," said the other Northerner. Teltö blinked. *Father Life, that's Welleorm.* The Chaplain briefly looked over his shoulder. "What are you doing here, lad?"

Teltö opened his mouth, then stopped. *He hasn't seen me yet.* Welleorm meant the man in green. *No, the boy in green. That Imperial's younger than me.*

The prisoner spat. "Fighting you bastards, it seems to me."

"Why?" Welleorm's voice was full of sorrow.

"Because Mustanako's home. I know what you'll say. That I've been force-fed lies, that I'm fighting and dying, while the Governor, and the Lesser Council, and bloody Vaani Vyrellävek, and his big-nosed girlfriend run off to Tuonako at the first sign of trouble."

He's talking about Rhea. She got out. Teltö could have shouted. But the prisoner went on.

"I'm not fighting for them. Why would I? The Dragon took my Mam. I'm fighting for my home, you pellets of Unut shit. The one your bombs destroyed. And let me tell you this: I'm going to keep fighting."

Welleorm nodded. "Are you a Necromancer?"

The boy smiled.

Suddenly, both the face-down Northerner and the woman by the watch-fire were moving. *Necromancy.* Before Teltö could cry out, the liches leapt up, and tackled the fellow with the rifle. The man shouted, and fired harmlessly into the trench wall. Dead fingers wrapped around his throat, and a knife flashed in the firelight. There was a long gurgling scream. Meanwhile, the Imperial had drawn a revolver, and pointed it at Welleorm. The Chaplain raised his hands.

Teltö reached for his gunbelt. He'd forgotten his own Lono. *For the best. I'd only get myself killed.* But he could do one thing. He reached out to the brains of the murderous liches. *Release him, you bastards.*

The Imperial jumped, as though bitten. His child-like face peered wide-eyed into the shadows.

"You there," he shouted. "Come forward so we can see you."

No choice. Teltö scrambled up from behind the buckets, and shuffled towards the watch-fire. Still pointing his revolver at the Chaplain, the boy broke into a toothy grin.

"By Father Life, you're an Imperial Necromancer, aren't you? A karl or thereabouts."

Teltö felt ill. "Um…"

"A Necromancer?" Welleorm's face turned haggard. He might have aged twenty years in the past twenty seconds. "Tell me this isn't true, Phuul."

"Sorry…"

Welleorm blinked. "I saved one of His servants," he muttered. "I have betrayed my faith, and my nation. I shall burn for this…"

The boy shot him. Welleorm crumpled to the mud. Teltö couldn't move. *The man who saved my life, my friend.*

"You're an Inquisitorial agent, then?" The Imperial released his liches, nodding approval at their handiwork. He fired another shot into the dying rifleman.

"Something like that," said Teltö numbly. "I've been working behind enemy lines, but need to get back."

The boy stuffed the revolver back into his belt. "Come on, then."

"How is Mustanako managing?"

The boy shrugged. "I won't lie: it's pretty hairy right now. Lots of desperate people, and Kuolinako's been no bloody help. But it has its perks. Every girl in the city wants to lose her virginity before the Northerners arrive and rape everyone." He winked. "I haven't had a proper night's sleep in ages."

Teltö's mouth twisted. *Charming.* "Hold on, I need to get something." He went to the fallen cleric, and knelt. Blood still flowed from the wound in Welleorm's head; it'd splattered into his beard.

"Mother Eternal, keep him safe," Teltö whispered. *Wrong religion, Phuul. One day you'll get it right.* "Tes goor Yehi ognash." He pulled out the dead man's standard issue Lono revolver. *Necessity makes monsters of us all.*

"Sorry, lad," Teltö explained. "Just needing to arm myself."

The Imperial nodded. "Yes, yes. Let's hurry."

Nimble as a spider, the boy made to climb the dirt-and-sandbag wall. Teltö hung back, thinking of how he'd manage in Mustanako. The surviving authorities might draft him into the defending forces, putting him back where he started. *But I have to risk it.* He glanced back at Welleorm, sick to the stomach. *I can't stay here.*

Shouts sounded from further along the trench. Teltö looked over his shoulder, and blinked at the sudden lantern light. Eyes adjusting, he saw half a dozen blue uniforms.

"What sort of God-induced nonsense is going on here?" snapped one with a Sergeant's insignia.

Teltö Phuul did what he had to do. He cocked the Lono and pointed it at the Imperial, who still clung like a weta to the wall. He pulled the trigger. For a few seconds, nothing happened. Then the boy fell backwards, and dropped like a ripe plum into the mud. He lay there, arms stretched above his head, his eyes wide and glassy. One new corpse among many.

"What took you bastards so long?" Lieutenant Phuul barked at the Sergeant. *I murdered a boy. I avenged my friend. I murdered a boy.* "I've just finished cleaning up an Imperial incursion, no thanks to you lot."

"Oy, you shouldn't have killed him," said the new arrival. "We might have questioned him."

That's what I was afraid of. "Orders are orders. We keep liches and limes out of our trenches. Understood?"

"Yes, sir."

"Right, clear away the bodies, and make sure it doesn't happen again."

None of them saw Teltö creep into an empty dug-out and vomit up his dinner. *I have to get out,* he thought through the tears. Tomorrow, or else he'd truly go mad.

*   *   *

TELTÖ PEELED THE potatoes in silence. He'd managed some sleep, but it'd done little good. The reflection in the shaving mirror this morning had the ashen complexion of a lich. Or a Kuolinakonian. He'd lost another notch on the belt too.

Mustanako's a handful of furlongs away. If someone just called off this whole blasted thing, I'd be there within the hour. He allowed himself a grim smile. *If only. Why don't you ask for the Chancellorship while you're at it, Phuul?* The mud and pits of No Man's Land, the skeleton still sitting in its airship, the fires… those few furlongs were the stuff of nightmares, and he'd murdered the boy who could've guided him. Shot him in the back.

"I had to," Teltö muttered to himself. "They'd have killed him anyway. And me."

He finished flaying the skin from one potato, and reached for another. He squeezed the rough little thing between his fingers. *I'll try east, inland. There's perimeter guards, but if I can get out, I'd be safer than in Mustanako.* Certainly, he'd be less likely to suffer a return to battle, and he'd be spared the attentions of pubescent girls.

A soldier in a scarf burst into the dugout. Wide-eyed, and clawing at his hair, the fellow collapsed in a screaming heap at Teltö's feet. *Speer?*

"They're all over me!" The aristocrat gouged fingernails across his face. "Get them off…"

"Get what off?"

"The spiders."

Flecks of saliva ran down Speer's chin. He crawled into a corner between two bags of potatoes, and sat whimpering. Teltö dropped everything, and ran to fetch Keeker.

"There's no blasted spiders," said the Quartermaster when he arrived. He strode over and grabbed Speer's collar, hefting the Sergeant to his feet. "Do we look like Imperials to you?"

Speer's mouth opened and shut like a fish's. "They were all over me."

Keeker slapped him, firmly enough to make Teltö wince in sympathy. Speer gibbered something unintelligible.

"Look," said Teltö, trying to stay calm. "There were no spiders. There will be no spiders. Spiders are for games, not war. The creatures you can reanimate are useless for killing. Apart from bears, but under Nine Author edict, you can't use lich-bears for violence. And squids, of course, but they're new."

Keeker removed his spectacles, and wiped them with a dirty cloth. "And how come you know so much about necromancy, Phuul?"

That wasn't clever. "I have family in Mustanako. Or used to," Teltö added hurriedly, returning to the spuds. "Snali Ventiko had an Imperial soldier for a father. My loyalties are trustworthy as his."

• • •

THE SUN BEAT down brutally that afternoon, which cheered the Northerners no end. Some off-duty ones took to cards; the trenches rang with the cheering of little victories and the cursing of little defeats. Teltö passed a game across from the latrines, and caught a glimpse of one man's hand.

"Cheating bastard," he muttered. *If they're falling for that, I'd wipe the floor with them. They'd lose their bloody shirts to my old Great-granny. Even after she went blind.*

But for once, neither cards nor shirt-loss was important. Rather, the satchel Teltö slung over his shoulder held the key. Hour after furtive hour, he scavenged biscuits and stuffed them into the bag. His muscles tensed, the sweat beading beneath his uniform not just from the heat. But so far he was safe; Keeker sat in the kitchen tent scribbling notes about supply-lines, and Speer gibbered in the makeshift infirmary. The faceless hordes of the 113th never spared him a second glance.

He stopped when he'd stored enough to survive several weeks. Teltö hid the satchel behind an iron drum, and returned to the dugout to collect his razor and other necessities. Half-way through the trench-maze, someone heavy trod on his foot. Teltö hobbled about, and cursed loudly.

"Dreadfully sorry," said the perpetrator, without a tinge of regret. Then the man smiled from muttonchop to muttonchop. "Lieutenant Phuul."

You're here too. Teltö ignored his foot, and delivered an impeccable Northern salute to the flushed and heavily-medalled fellow. "Major-General."

Rughvneer nodded, and looked thoughtful. His breath reeked of liquor. *Not Asrak. Something classier.*

"Lieutenant, may I have a moment of your time?"

Teltö's heart sank. "If it were possible…"

"Now."

"Certainly, sir."

Still limping slightly, Teltö hurried after the man. Rughvneer moved at a cracking pace. They travelled back through the trenches; Teltö noticed copious *better you than me* looks from passing Northerners. Then it was up a ladder, across muddy wastes, over a ridge, and into a place where grass still grew. A spacious tent had been set up, well out of range of the sight or smell of the front line and the horrors of No Man's Land. *But not the sound. You can still hear the guns.*

"Make yourself at home, Lieutenant," said Rughvneer, pulling open the flap. "This is my field office. Close to the men, and all that. I have more permanent quarters elsewhere."

Inside, a portly pink-cheeked servant stroked a feather-duster large as his head. He wore some device on his cuffs. *Probably Rughvneer's House badge.* In the middle of the tent stood a table and twin chairs. Maps, papers, and a crystal vase with a white rose adorned the tabletop. There were also several glasses, two containing the dregs of amber liquid.

Rughvneer coughed. "Leave us, Kothro."

The servant shoved the duster under his jacket, and bowed. Rughvneer waved a fat finger. "Also, if you could be so kind, please put on more of those scrumptious venison sausages."

"Very good, sir," said Kothro. With jacket bulging and cheeks reddening, he hurried out.

Teltö sat at the table, whilst Rughvneer pulled a half-empty bottle from a travelling chest.

"Whiskey?" He held up a fresh glass. "Ten year-old single malt?"

Teltö locked his lips in a smile. *Teasing bastard.* "No thank you, sir."

Rughvneer shrugged, and poured himself a double. "Fine fellow, Kothro. Been in the family forever, and you couldn't ask for a better bosom chum on one of these excursions. Just don't leave him alone with poultry. Anyway, I have questions for you, Lieutenant. What do we know about this mysterious gas the Imperials are using? Until we figure it out, our flamethrowers and even our grenades are completely useless!"

"Pardon, sir?"

"You heard me. We've always countered Imperial necromancy with fire. Until now, that is. Now we can't do anything for fear of entire regiments going up in smoke. Each watch-fire needs a dozen water buckets apiece, just in case! What do you, and your skulking ilk, know about this? Else, what in damnation are you doing about it?"

Of course. Rughvneer still thinks I'm a spy. Being pumped by Ventiko in Skeevereet was bad enough, but this close to the front it was harder to bluff and get away with it...

"Sorry, sir. I report to the Marshal only. He insists."

The Major-General sipped his whiskey. "Really?" He looked intently at Teltö. "I haven't seen you around Ventiko's offices, even his field one. In fact, I asked him about you..."

Oh shit.

Rughvneer slid into the other chair. "He said you'd drowned in the squid attack, yet here you are behind our lines. What is your game, Lieutenant, if indeed you are who Ventiko says you are?"

"Um…"

"Perhaps I must drag you to Ventiko. I'll have the truth out of one of you, I swear it."

"Very well, sir." Teltö fought back the panic. "The perfect truth is that I have been avoiding the Marshal. I don't trust him."

"Don't trust Snali Ventiko? Most interesting. Tell me more." Rughvneer finished his glass, and poured himself another. The lack of ice wasn't bothering him one bit.

"I think he's secretly working for the enemy, sir."

"Ventiko an Imperial? I knew it. Blood always tells." Rughvneer leant forward, his medals clinking against the table glasses. "But do you have proof?"

"Regrettably, sir…" Rughvneer had put his hand atop Teltö's, which made Teltö vaguely uncomfortable. The man wasn't his type. "…much confidential and damning paperwork was destroyed in the ransacking of the Imperial Embassy. I am aware, however, that Ventiko potentially intends to betray the North by giving strategic advantages to the Empire."

"A dastard!" Rughvneer stood, and paced the ground. His face became a study in raw excitement.

"Indeed, sir. It would also explain your hitherto inexplicable banishment to logistics. A man of your skills and heritage should be organising the assault on Mustanako, not ferrying coats, helmets, and neeps." *Though I wouldn't have minded some more neeps.*

"Exactly. Now if you could write all this down…"

"I shall do it tonight, sir."

"Excellent." Rughvneer grinned. "Are you sure you don't fancy a whiskey, Lieutenant? Believe me, you feel the peat. A drink fresh from the marsh, as it were."

Teltö shook his head. "Quite sure, Major-General."

• • •

Teltö nibbled at a biscuit to settle his nerves, and nearly broke his teeth. *If I ever make it back to Qivunako, I'll never complain about rationing ever again.*

Beyond the trenches, the wire, the mud, the mangled unusable corpses, and the wrecks of lives and machinery, the airships swarmed over Mustanako. The city lay dark and wounded, illuminated only by the fires the bombs had started. The anti-aircraft guns boomed in reply, and while Teltö looked on, an artillery shell struck an airship. The craft ignited, a bright orange glow lighting up the night, and for a moment the contraption blazed like a comet as it tumbled down to crash into the Nhagivat. *Ammunition that burns on impact. Lovely.* Everything burnt around here, except the mud.

Time to go, time for his desperate escape attempt. The baking heat of the afternoon had given way to a cloudy evening; Teltö hoped the rain kept off. *For once.* He grabbed his satchel and edged towards the north-eastern perimeter, keeping to the shadows. Luckily, his path coincided with hastily erected structures, and even a few remaining wooded spots. He passed one maple, stunted and dead, with Mage's Beard dangling from an outstretched branch. The twisted vines resembled a noose.

Teltö stopped half a furlong from the sentries. Ahead lay an open patch of trampled grass. Someone had lit a watch-fire, but the soldiers he saw had their backs to him; no one looked in Teltö's direction. *I'll risk it.* Heart in mouth, he hobbled over to the thicket on the far side. *I'm going for a piss. That's what I'll say.*

Behind him, he heard a sharp intake of breath. *Shit.*

Teltö began to run, but managed no more than five paces before a sentry's tackle sent him face-first into the grass. The Northerner rolled Teltö over, and thrust a lantern into his face. Teltö glimpsed familiar features, and smelt a familiar musk.

"Where are you going?" *A woman's voice.*

The attacker recoiled in shock. "Teltö, is that you?"

"Sufael? What are you doing here?"

"More to the point, what are *you* doing here? I thought you were dead!"

She helped him up, and hugged him.

"Long story," said Teltö. He extricated himself from her embrace. "But with the Dragon dead, I can go home. Right now though, I'd settle for getting away from the war."

She grinned. "I did try to send you to the other bloody continent. How much more 'away' do you need?"

"Your nutcase Dad…"

She punched him hard in the gut. Teltö gasped, unable to breathe, and crumpled to the ground. He wriggled like a worm against the leaf litter. Sufael bent over him. She wore a mud-encrusted blue greatcoat. *Someone's on a mission.*

"Never speak of my father again," she said calmly.

Teltö's skin goosepimpled at her tone. He nodded. Still struggling for air, he climbed to his feet.

"What's that?" muttered Sufael.

"What's what?"

She held a finger to her lips, and pointed. A series of melancholy little gasps came from the thicket. *Someone's sobbing.*

Sufael crept over and parted a clump of flowering fireweed. Teltö held up the lantern. A dark shape curled foetus-like among the purple petals.

"I'm sorry. So sorry."

That's Speer's voice. Teltö squatted onto his haunches. "Sergeant, it's me. Lieutenant Phuul. What are you doing?"

It took a good ten minutes to coax the poor bastard out. Speer, Teltö learned, had panicked and fled the infirmary, only to collapse amid guilt.

"I'm worthless, absolutely worthless," whimpered the Sergeant. He scraped petals from his scarf. "Deserters are slime. I'll be disowned by the family…"

That's if the New Chief and Ventiko don't burn you first. "Look, have a nice cup of tea and a biscuit, and calm down. You'll be all right in the morning." Teltö patted him on the back.

"We haven't got time for this," hissed Sufael. "Leave him. Oh…"

"What's going on?"

Teltö jumped. A burly sentry had materialised in front of him, Rughvneer M6969 at the ready.

"Sorry for bothering you." Teltö's mind worked quickly. "I'm Lieutenant Phuul, serving with the Pastry Company of the 113th."

The sentry lowered his rifle. "One of Keeker's boys."

"Just so. Anyway, this here is one of our lads. Had an accident with the cooking wine, if you get my meaning. Could you escort him somewhere to sleep it off?"

The sentry chuckled. "I know just the place for him. Gives me something to do, anyway. Bloody guard duty makes you feel like you're turning into a tree."

He led Speer away, half-carrying the poor bastard.

Better this than Ventiko or the regulations.

Sufael nodded. "Impressive. Now let's go."

The pain lingering in his gut, Teltö followed the woman through the fireweed.

"I hope you've a better idea for a rescue this time," he muttered.

Sufael stopped. She turned, and cracked her knuckles. "What was that, Phuul?"

Teltö smiled. "Nothing."

After five minutes of wading through weeds, and dodging low-hanging branches, they came to open turf. *More mud. More sentries.* Sufael didn't hide. She headed straight for the lantern light, clearly uncaring about filth on her uniform. *Moth, flame.* Teltö followed. He picked through the mud, thanking Father Life for the Principality's line of indestructible army boots.

Beside the lantern, a grey-haired sentry sat on a tree-stump. Sufael reached into her pocket and handed over some papers.

The man squinted at the writing, and muttered something about 'no better than the Empire.' He jabbed a dirty forefinger into Teltö's chest. "Who's this then?"

Sufael stuffed the papers back into her greatcoat. "Lieutenant Phuul is with me."

•　•　•

TELTÖ AND SUFAEL arrived at a paddock. Figures in blue gathered around a fire, blasphemously roasting an Unut calf on a spit. *At least I hope that's an Unut.* Further afield, monstrous and shadowy, loomed three grounded airships. *So these are the bastards who're raining carnage on Mustanako. Can't say any of them look the baby-roasting sort.* Teltö looked over his shoulder. *But then, neither does Keeker.*

Sufael smiled. "Behold, the 42nd, reborn!"

She ran, boots squelching through the mud.

"Hold on!" called Teltö. "Where the blazes are you going?"

But Sufael was already beside the fire, shaking the hands of the flight crews. For an agent of the Inquisition, she acted damn familiar with the Northern military. *Mind you, I'm not exactly in a position to accuse anyone.* Teltö remained in the shadows.

At last, done with the well-wishing, Sufael waved him forward.

"This one, Teltö." She unlatched an airship door. "In here."

She climbed aboard the gondola. He followed, mouth hanging open. Any number of objections fought to be the first to get out.

"What?!" he barked, "you fly airships? You've been dropping bombs on Mustanako?"

She paused. "Yes and no. I fly the ship, and drop the load into the Illuvian."

"But you're working for us. Why don't you drop the bombs onto the Northern encampment?"

Sufael pulled a lever. The door clanged shut. "Teltö, I'm not describing the rest of my job to you. Suffice to say, I have no interest in blowing my cover or dropping bombs on my own misguided people. Now sit down, shut up, and let me think."

So she can't kill her own people. I can. Teltö found himself in a shadowy compartment. The rear wall sported a gas-light, which flickered with a strange and sickly green. The dim glow illuminated an adjoining door. *Probably the airship's bed and storage area.* Teltö glanced at the other green-lit walls. *No sabres.*

Sufael settled into the pilot's chair. The engines began humming.

Teltö grabbed a stray blanket off a seating bench, and wrapped himself in it. The knowledge he'd soon be far away from the war cancelled his discomfort at travelling on one of these bloody airships again. *Away from the war.* His eyes widened, and his fingers tightened on the woollen fabric. *I can do more than get away. She can take me home, just like this.*

His adoration and excitement were boundless. He'd shower her in kisses later, he promised himself. Yet what a tightrope Sufael walked. *How does her conscience square with her father? Dare I ask?* Pain returned, and he dismissed the thought.

But, really, it was about appreciating the people close to you. Teltö knew he could've poisoned the Northern food many times, but he hadn't, and it was more than fear of punishment or even pride in his own cooking. The Northerners he left behind had become his friends. Speer, Keeker, Groon, Saw, Welleorm… *let's not dwell there.* Even Major-General Rughvneer was far from the faceless enemy his teachers had told him about. Teltö sat back on the bench, and looked down upon the watch-fires that spread from here to the coast. Blood may be on his hands twice-over, but he could delight in one thing. He had escaped.

Chapter Eighteen

A KNOCK COMES from the door, a relentless thudding Teltö cannot ignore. He undoes the latch, and twists… the young Mustanakonian stands there in his green coat, blood dripping drop by drop onto the step, eyes full of accusation. There are no words, yet cries of murder and treason ring through Teltö's skull, tales of bloody-handed treachery. He blocks his ears and runs, but it is too late. He looks up, and sees Sufael's father, throat coated a savage crimson. Reqi, and Welleorm, and Phytek the physician surround him, each howling a screeching chorus. And then Alio Venomavat enters, a marmalade cat upon her shoulder, and she reads his confession even while the black hoods drag him to the Death Pool. Vyrellävek sits beside the cage, and his smile gets broader and broader…

Teltö woke with a start. He'd nodded off again, and the dreams weren't getting any sweeter. Rubbing his eyes, he peered out the window. The airship still drifted between dark earth and inky sky; the orchards and fields of the Ruvian Plains lay cloaked in murk below. Not a light to be seen from either homestead or town. Teltö tugged the blanket closer about his body and yawned. He shuffled over to the controls. Sufael turned. The dim glow from the controls and dials gave her face a grey complexion.

"Sorry, Teltö." Sufael pulled a lever. "I'll get you home, but we have to head a bit out the way. Anti-aircraft guns are everywhere, and it's bloody hard to judge locations without a navigator on board. Especially in a blackout. I'll say this for the Grand Council: they've organised a decent defence."

Apart from the attack on Mustanako catching them on the hop? Teltö yawned again, remembering what that boy had said. *Kuolinako's no help.* The high-ups probably all had their eyes on Vyrellävek's chair, and put politicking over the war effort. Or perhaps Meerm and Söstä were making desperate pleas, only to be ignored. *Söstä running things? The Imperial forces would have to fetch every last bullet afterwards.* Still, the anti-aircraft guns and ammunition, like the squids and the gas, kept the Empire afloat. The Dragon had been prepared.

"I think Ventiko's working for the other side," said Teltö.

Sufael chuckled. "Which other side? You've somehow become a Lieutenant in the Prince's Army."

The full story would've seen the woman throw him off the ship, romantic attachment or no. "I meant the North. I'm still an Imperial."

"Good to know. But what made you think the Marshal was anything other than a loyal servant of the Principality?"

"He told me."

Sufael's chuckle turned to full-scale laughter. "And you believed him? Thank goodness the Inquisition doesn't use you as an agent. Oh wait."

Teltö felt his cheeks flushing. "The Ambassador told

me too. He said I might be surprised."

"And have you been?"

"Not pleasantly."

He told her of his adventures adrift in the Illuvian. Sufael listened in silence. When he'd finished, she sighed.

"Let this be a lesson."

"Look, it's not as if I had a choice in dealing with Ventiko. I…"

"There's always a choice," she snapped. "And while I'm on the subject, I could tell you stories about your friends at the Embassy that'd turn your hair white. Every one of those bastards was there for a reason."

"Exile?"

"Exile's too nice a term. They're a rubbish heap of everything wrong with the Empire. But did you tell the Marshal about our activities, or about Imperial defences?"

"Of course not." Teltö ground his teeth. "Thinking Ventiko had Imperial sympathies, I persuaded him to take me on as a cook."

"For a cook, you've had some interesting conversations."

"I have a talent for being in the right place at the right time. And the fellow is mad."

Teltö resumed his seat. The gloom slowly faded from the hills of the Central Uplands, revealing precipitous green slopes that stretched to the horizon. No one lived here, save for the occasional recluse; under the Department of Agriculture, this was a world removed from civilisation. *And from anti-aircraft guns.* He watched the Unut grazing below. From this distance, the creatures appeared as little tufts of cotton wool.

Teltö pulled his satchel out from under the bench. "Fancy a biscuit?"

Sufael didn't turn round. "Please tell me they're not Army ones."

"Of course they're Army ones. Quite nice when soaked in lard."

She shook her head. "It's times like this I think the Church is right about Him. I'm not landing just so you can hack up an Unut."

"Me, hack up an Unut?" Teltö feigned outrage. "And deny our hard working officials their precious monthly quota? You must take me for some sort of criminal."

Their laughter was long and loud.

• • •

TELTÖ WOKE FROM another nap. *Must be midmorning.* The compartment had grown warm; he doffed his coat and rolled up his sleeves. Then he heard something. Sufael was singing, her voice strangely shrill.

> *"We travel the clouds, and float on the breeze*
> *The journey of lands, from mountains to seas*
> *Our ship and our skill shall keep us afloat…"*

"Is that a real song, or is it a quote?"

She turned. A wry smile crossed her face. "Ah, you're up again. Sorry for waking you. In my defence, it *was* one of my better efforts. I first sang it to my father after he took me up in an airship. He gave me a sweet, and I promised to add a new verse every time after."

"Did you?

"No." She shrugged. "I forgot, and never brought it up again in case I disappointed him."

Let her keep her illusions. If they are illusions. "How did your recent poem go?"

"The bear one? I burnt it. I couldn't…"

Teltö never heard the end of the sentence. A thunderous roar erupted from over his shoulder, and suddenly all was in tumult. The airship reeled. *What in blazes?* Thrown off his feet, Teltö went skidding across the floor. He thudded into a wall, ricocheted off, and grabbed hold of a bench just in time to steady himself.

"Shit." Sufael had fallen off the pilot's chair onto her arse. "We've been hit. The range of those bloody guns…"

"We're going to die. After all this, we're…"

"Not if I have anything to say about it."

Teltö shook his head. "The Empire's got flammable ammunition. I saw it over Mustanako."

There was a pause, pregnant and terrible. Sufael looked expectantly at the ceiling. "I know the stuff you're talking about. But no, not this time."

Teltö gripped the bench until his knuckles whitened. "How do you know?"

"Neither of us is dead yet." She stumbled to her feet. "Hold on."

Teltö Phuul didn't need telling. His fingers might have been glued to the wood. Not a centifurlong away, his blanket drifted back and forth like a drunken banshee. The satchel had become entangled just out of reach, but, thank Father Life, everything else in the compartment was screwed down.

Sufael punched buttons and flicked switches. A ghastly mechanical screech emerged, and the airship shuddered. For half a horrible moment, it sounded like the contraption was breaking up. *There'll be no swimming to safety this time.* Teltö imagined plummeting to earth, and repressed a scream.

But the airship kept together. Instead of a searing

explosion of heat and light, Teltö felt the airship descending, gradually at first, then steeper and steeper.

"Shit, shit, shit." Teltö shut his eyes and pressed his face to the bench. His ears ached, then popped. *We were so close.*

The floor shifted; there was a sharp jolt, then nothing. Teltö opened his eyes. *We've landed? That's it?* He stood, breathing deeply. At the controls, Sufael grinned like a mad woman; dark hair unbound, she thrust her arms in the air.

"Thus it shall always be," she sang, "the joyous happy few, who bring our cleansing flame, to purify the world. Thus it shall always be…"

The glazed look vanished. She smiled. "Sorry. Got carried away. But, yes, we've made it."

*   *   *

HE ROLLED OFF her and lay gasping and sated on the grass. Beside him, Sufael smiled up at the late morning Sun; Teltö's eyes drank in her breasts, her stomach, her legs… there was nothing like sex to celebrate being alive. A quarter-furlong away, atop the next hill, the airship sat busted and irreparable. Seeing it now, the successful landing had been a miracle. *A miracle worth celebrating.*

"If only we could stay here," Sufael murmured. She rested her hands behind her head. "You and me, and the Sun on the daisies. Away from the blood, and the mud, and the guns."

He ran a forefinger over her breast. "Stay with me in Qivunako."

"And spend winter nights nibbling on salty liquorice and frostbitten fingernails? Sorry, Teltö. I've a job. As you Imperials put it, duties must be carried out lest our last world crumble."

"Let it crumble."

"Blasphemy."

They kissed.

The world's as it should be. Teltö ran his hands down her, through her dark pubic hair. He felt himself stirring once more.

"I'm ready again if you are."

Sufael shook her head. "The Tower will be wondering where I am."

Teltö considered his clothes, heaped nearby. Something had nagged at him since he first boarded the airship. He groaned. *I'm an idiot.* "I haven't got any Imperial garb. In a blue uniform, they'll shoot me before I can open my mouth."

Sufael sat up. The dreaminess vanished from her face.

"True. Flying around the Empire in an airship is bad enough. Let's see… I've a change of clothes aboard for myself, but I don't think there's any male stuff. Let's check the hold."

• • •

THE BEST THEY found was a mufti shirt and a pair of pocket-less patchwork trousers. Neither looked remotely Imperial, let alone regulation, but at least it was non-military. Sufael dropped her own uniform in favour of tweed.

"Aren't you hot in that?" Teltö finished buttoning the shirt. *A bit big, but it'll do.*

"Hot? The Empire doesn't know the meaning of the word."

Teltö put his arm around her waist, and drew her close. "Oh, but we do."

Sufael laughed. She kissed him. "You know, that time you spent on the march did wonders for your figure. I like a man with lean muscle. Maybe I should take you back to Mustanako for another go."

Teltö pulled away. "Don't even joke about that."

They set out with a compass and map, as many water bottles as they could carry, and a satchel full of dry tinned food. Teltö hoped they wouldn't need the food, but better to be safe. *We'll come across a town, railway, or road eventually.* Or even Agriculture officials, there to tend to animals or weed out poachers.

The afternoon wore on. Teltö sweated in his thin shirt, but Sufael in her tweed remained unperturbed. *Let's see her in the Qivunako winter. Then we'll be even.* Furlong after furlong, up and down hill – it drove Teltö to distraction. There weren't even Unut around, just grass and boulders interspersed with pines and macrocarpa. A grey lizard sunned itself on a rock and watched them pass. Sufael stuck out her tongue at it.

Towards evening, a breeze blew in from the east. Appreciating the change, Teltö swigged some water and considered the monotonous run to the horizon.

"We are heading the right way?" he asked.

"South should be the right way," said Sufael. "I'm starting to think the coordinates on the airship were buggered up. Life's tough piloting without a navigator."

Something had been nibbling at Teltö's mind. "So you normally pilot with a navigator?"

"Pilot, navigator, and maintenance. It's standard."

"So your other two are Imperial agents too? If we've infiltrated the airships, why are bombs still dropping?"

She stood and looked at him. Her right hand twitched. "Teltö," she said calmly, "there are Northerners who hate this whole thing and want to go home. I should know: I am one. But I tell you now: if you ask me again about my job, I'll slit your bloody throat. Understand?"

"But we've…"

Her hand edged closer to her hip pocket. "Understand?"

There are tears in her eyes. "Understood."

"Sorry, Teltö." She smiled. "I didn't mean to get angry with you."

Teltö put his arm around her. "No worries."

They kissed, and suddenly all was right again.

Teltö grinned. "So we're lost?"

Sufael smiled back. "Not lost. I just don't know exactly where we are."

Three furlongs or so later, they crested a hill. Teltö pointed.

"Look!"

A group of Imperials rested in the shadow of the next hill. The lime-green of the uniform betrayed their purpose immediately. *Military, not Agriculture. Poor bastards. Patrolling this place must be like garrisoning the Moon. With extra Unut shit.*

"Hello!" Teltö shouted.

A bald and burly fellow looked up. Teltö waved. The man shouted something back.

Teltö cupped his hands to his mouth. "I can't hear you!"

This time the fellow didn't bother replying. He blew a whistle, ear-splitting even at a distance. Within moments, half a dozen soldiers swarmed up the slope towards Teltö and Sufael.

"Not sure that was wise," said Sufael. "Leave the explaining to me."

Teltö edged backwards, but too late. Two soldiers cut

off his escape, each with an ugly Sämö-Sömö and an even uglier scowl. Teltö counted seven total: four men, three women; all living. No ribbons or rings. *Ordinaries.*

A woman stepped forward. "Right, you bastards." Blonde and well-muscled, she wore a Captain's insignia on her collar. "Unload everything valuable, and we'll let you go."

"Pardon?" Sufael snapped. "We are agents of the Tower, and demand an escort to the nearest town. Do that, and I shall overlook this little unpleasantness."

On cue, she thrust her Inquisitorial paperwork under the Captain's nose.

"I see," said the other woman. "And you just happen to be hiking with a Northern civilian?"

"I'm not a Northerner," said Teltö. "I'm an Imperial Necromancer. An underkarl from Qivunako, to be precise."

The Captain's green eyes scanned him from shoes to hair. "Strange get-up for a Necro. Where's your ribbon?"

"I lost it."

"Papers? Exemptions?"

"Lost them too. Believe me, I can explain. My sister is engaged to the Dragon's nephew…"

"Hah. And my sister's the Inquisitor bloody General."

"No, really."

"Got a shred of evidence?"

"No, but…"

"I've heard enough. A shadow-stalker with obvious Northern ancestry – don't deny it – and an undocumented Necro with Northern clothing just happen to be hiking around in the Uplands in the middle of the Fifth Northern War. I'll believe that."

"Look," snapped Sufael. "If you doubt our story, hand

us over to the Inquisition, and no one will get hurt."

The Captain chuckled. "First time I've ever heard that. But this is where it gets funny. You see, I have a thing about shadow-stalkers. Drop your weapons. *Including knives.*"

With six Sämö-Sömo levelled at her head, Sufael shrugged. She pulled out two Iilno revolvers and a hunting knife. She placed them on the ground.

"You too, Necro!"

Sufael shook her head. "He doesn't have anything."

I left the Lono on the airship.

"We'll judge that. Reti, pat him down."

One of the men pawed at Teltö's shirt and trousers.

"Maybe later," said Teltö. But no one laughed. *Come on, no Northerner would joke about that.*

Reti nodded. "He's clean."

"Well, I do try." Teltö received a glare from Sufael and dropped the smile.

The Captain put her hands on her hips. "I said I have a thing about shadow-stalkers. I'm not lying either. It might be that they disappeared both my parents and my husband, but I can't stand 'em."

"What?!" Sufael barked. "What are you doing? I'll…"

"Reti, next time this one speaks, put a bullet where her brain ought to be."

The Captain pointed at Teltö. "So you're a Necro?"

Teltö's mouth was dry. He eyed the Sämö-Sömö barrels and nodded.

"Is she a Necro too? I wouldn't normally ask, but identification seems hard to come by today."

Teltö shook his head. *Father Life, what game is she playing?*

"Good. In that case, reanimate this one."

The woman drew an Iilno revolver from her belt.

With lightning speed, she cocked it and fired. Sufael bent for her weapons, but too late. Once, twice, three times, bullets slammed into her chest. Teltö's mouth hung open. *Father Life.* The Northerner slumped to the grass, coughing up blood. A red stain spread over the front of her tweed jacket.

"You bitch." Never had Teltö felt more numb and helpless. "You utter, utter bitch."

Sufael's brown eyes pleaded at him, terrified and strangely childlike. Teltö took a step towards her.

The Captain turned the revolver on him. "No, you stay put."

Teltö looked down the barrel, frozen where he stood. The seconds dragged like centuries. Sufael bled at his feet, and the deadly finger hovered on the trigger.

"Right," said the Captain. "I think she's dead enough. On the count of five, you reanimate her, or I'll blow your head off."

"Father Life, *please!*"

"One… Two…"

Tears ran down Teltö's cheeks. "No, please!"

"Three… Four…"

Forgive me, Sufael. Teltö reached out with his mind and felt Sufael's brain. Yes, she was dead, no doubt about that. He told her to rise, his command as gentle as the summer breeze. *They made me. Sometimes there is no choice.* The corpse's chest began to rise and fall. The soldiers edged back.

"It's rising!"

What had been Sufael jerked to its feet.

"The wrath of the Inquisition shall be upon you from the shores of the Illuvian to the Grey Ocean," said the lich. "From the Wall to the uttermost reaches of the Southern Fells, there will be no escape."

Teltö blinked through the tears. "Father Life, what the…"

The big burly chap turned pale. The Captain scowled at Teltö. Her revolver darted back and forth between the lich and the Necromancer.

"Don't threaten me, lad. Don't even think about threatening me."

Teltö shook his head. "Not me. Her. Residual memories. Accidental side-effect. Rare but can happen."

Another woman studied her boots and whistled tunelessly. But the Captain thrust the revolver back into her belt.

"So I'm being threatened by the dead? I'm terrified!"

"You're forgetting." Teltö tried to keep his voice steady. "I am a Necromancer. You'll scream for Mother Death by the time Kuolinako's finished with you."

"Please forgive me, oh mighty Grand Master. You won't tell anybody anything. I've as little time for you bastards as I have for shadow-stalkers – think yourselves so damn superior. My little brother was Drafted, and the likes of you getting ration exemptions while my mates starve makes me sick."

"I…"

"Shut it." Saliva flecked from the Captain's mouth. "Your garb declares you a foe of the Empire, and I have absolute authority to deal with you as I see fit. From where I'm standing, you're more an enemy than whichever poor bastard you swiped those rags off. I'll keep you alive for now, but once I'm bored…"

She smiled.

• • •

NICE WEATHER FOR *it*, Teltö thought, as they set off

through the Central Uplands. Behind him, the clouds on the horizon glowed pink in the light of the setting Sun. *I should have stayed in Mustanako.*

The binds on his wrists weren't cruel, but the rope scratched his skin, and made him want to gnaw it off. Not that he could gnaw anything; they'd stuffed a sock in his mouth as a gag. *Tastes like Army food.* One son of an Unut trailed behind to keep watch, and from time to time prodded a bayonet into his back to make him squeal.

He looked up the darkening slope, to where Sufael's lich kept an awkward pace in front of the troop. *If I hadn't asked her to take me home, she'd still be alive.*

Sharp metal bit Teltö in the arse.

"Keep walking."

*   *   *

THE BASTARDS USED an abandoned farm house as a headquarters; broken windows and a busted door looked out over a veranda. Outside, a rocking chair accumulated the grime of decades. *No one's lived here for years.* Teltö looked at his companions. *Correct that. No one decent's lived here for years.*

The Sun had dipped behind the horizon, but the long twilight of late summer dragged on. On the house's left side stood three rusting iron drums, and a paddock with a solitary dehorned Unut. The bovine grazed obliviously in knee-high grass. A pond lay to the right, waters dark and still beneath a cloud of dancing mosquitoes.

"Take him to the yard," said the Captain. "We'll have a little celebration tonight."

Securely shackled, and with that sock still lodged in his gullet, Teltö was marched around to the rear. The house had a back porch, where empty bottles peeked out from a rubbish bin. Teltö looked over at a clay square, flat and wide. A heap of broken bricks lay piled at one end.

"Sit, Necro bastard."

Teltö squatted beside the bricks. *Nothing to do but wait.* The bastard with the bayonet kept watch over his shoulder.

"No ideas, Necro."

The rest of the Imperials dragged crate after crate from the house, each full of bottles. *Asrak. Are they distilling it themselves, or did they stumble across a bootlegger?* Reti hacked up the remains of a bookshelf with a hatchet, while a woman emerged with bundles of newspapers. The soldiers set about starting a fire in the centre of the yard.

Once the flames were dancing, the Captain rolled up her sleeve. She pulled out a sliver of burning wood.

"This'll do nicely."

The woman bent down over Teltö, holding the brand not a millifurlong away from his nose. He blinked at the orange light, feeling the flame's hot breath against his face.

"Right, you big-nosed Necro arsehole, we're going to have some fun. Specifically, you'll treat us to some dancing."

He shook his head. "Ga…ga…mmf."

Cursing, the Captain pulled out the gag. Teltö rolled his tongue around his mouth in relief.

"Sorry," said Teltö. "You're asking the wrong man."

"I'm asking the right man. You see, it'll not be you dancing. It'll be your late lady friend." She nodded towards the farmhouse. Teltö had sent the lich inside so he didn't have to see it.

"No."

The flame crept closer. "Say that again and that pretty red hair of yours will burn all right."

"I've done nothing. Let me go. Please."

"How the mighty have fallen. Forgotten how to lord it over us? Forgotten about your precious natural order, where if you ain't a Necro, you're worthless Unut meat?" The woman spat. "Tonight you'll make her dance, just as we've danced for eight thousand years."

• • •

SO THIS IS what the Captain meant by entertainment. When the fun stops, so do I.

He sat back from the fire, and considered his binds. Not tight enough to cut off blood, they were still strong enough to render him helpless; Teltö felt like an Unut trussed up at the works. He wriggled to get comfortable. This earned him a kick from his guard, who sat biting his nails on a crate beside him.

The Necromancer smiled meekly, disappointed in more ways than one: the guard's high cheekbones, sandy hair, and blue eyes made him passably handsome. *In another time and place, I might have tried to bed him.* He returned his attention to the lich dancing around the fire. *A very different time and place.*

Her once beautiful brown skin turned grey, the thing that had been Sufael twisted and weaved. Teltö could hardly bear to look; when he did, he only saw the stain of congealed blood. *Like Dad like daughter. No, don't go there. You'll be begging them to shoot you.* He needed a drink, a strong drink, and if he never woke afterwards, all the better. But the soldiers weren't about to give him one.

Evening wore on, empty bottles clinked across the ground, and the Imperials grew ever louder. Someone slipped over amid raucous laughter. Teltö wondered whether he was ever this obnoxious when drunk. *Probably.*

"Smile, Master Necro." The Captain swayed. Dribble ran down her chin. "Smile, you bastard."

Teltö tried, and failed.

"Smile or I'll give you a red one. That's better…What did you do with my Dad, eh? And my Mam, and my poor sweet Asto? *Hic.* We'd only been married six months."

"Er, Captain, sir?" said the guard. "Any chance I can take a breather? I'm boring my arse off watching the Necro."

"You poor thing, I'd forgotten about you." She kissed the fellow on the cheek. "I'll give you a little reward. Hey, Dyrstin!"

Teltö jerked up. "Dyrstin?"

Not Venomavat, but an ugly man missing two front teeth. "Yes, sir?"

"Watch our big-nosed friend for a bit, will you?"

Nothing like the real Dyrstin. The man waddled across and sat on the crate in a huff worthy of Grand Master Meerm. The Captain and Teltö's previous guard disappeared over to the back porch, where they started tearing at each other's clothes in excited squeals.

"You know, I've a friend named Dyrstin," said Teltö.

"I'm not him." The man's tongue flicked out like a serpent's, and licked the gap in his gums.

"Why do you do it? Follow a bunch of thugs around, I mean. You're better than that…"

Dyrstin snorted. "This is where you tell me that you're closely connected to Grand Master so-and-so, and there'll be a reward if I smuggle you out."

Teltö's face fell.

"You probably think we're stupid serfs." Dyrstin stared into the fire. "That we'd be better as liches. But it's hard being an Ordinary. Everyone looks down at you; the major trades are blocked off… When I was growing up, my family got evicted. Twice. Dad was a small-town labourer and couldn't compete with the dead. Then I lost a sister to the Draft."

"I'm sorry."

"No, you're not. My uncle was a Necro, an underkarl, who actually worked for the Mustanako Draft Board. They took my sister away – standard operation. My father confronted him some weeks later. Turned out my uncle knew in advance, but never told his own brother."

"Of course not. If he'd told anyone, let alone tried to smuggle your sister out, the Inquisition would've disappeared the lot of you. Believe me, it happens."

"Disappeared by shadow-stalkers on orders from other Necros. Necros are scum, and the higher the Necro, the bigger the scum."

"So you hate the Necros." Teltö nodded. "Fair enough. But what good are you doing here? How will serving with this lot help things? This started as a bona fide patrol?"

Dyrstin shrugged. "Yes, and no. We're Imperial soldiers, right enough, all from the same town. We were to be shipped off to Mustanako – an interesting battle going on there, by all accounts. But a bombing raid destroyed the local registry. Suddenly, no one knew who we were."

"You deserted?"

"No. The Captain here, she approached the local brass and asked that they send a bunch of us out on patrol instead. Less chance of getting killed, she figured. The brass gave the go-ahead, and one thing led to another, so here we are."

And more feral by the hour. A metallic gleam caught Teltö's attention. A knife had slid out someone's pocket.

Sufael's hunting knife. They took it with them.

"No word from Kuolinako?" Teltö asked. Sufael's dancing grew grandiose and exaggerated.

"None," said Dyrstin. "The Last Capital's a mess though. Nobody wants any part of it."

The Captain cried out in pleasure.

"Keep it down," muttered Dyrstin, yawning. "I'll have a hangover in the morning, I just know it."

The hour grew late, and the lich danced on. Teltö sent Sufael tumbling and cartwheeling across the clay, to scattered drunken cheers. One of the women had passed out; her snoring drowned out even the noise of the sex. Teltö glanced at Dyrstin. The man was yawning again. *Go to sleep, you bastard. Do I have to sing you a lullaby?* Dyrstin closed his eyes. Teltö waited ten more minutes. He must be sure. He'd never get another chance. Finally, he heard it: the soft, steady breathing of a sleeping man.

The lich grasped the knife handle. *Here we go.* Teltö's heart pounded. One by one the soldiers died, their throats slit while they lay insensible or sleeping. None resisted or even cried out. *Like Mother Death herself.* This was worse than the Examination, much worse; but if this was murder, why did he feel nothing? *If the Masters at school could see this.*

The bloody-handed lich cut his bonds. Teltö grimaced as he rubbed life into his limbs. Dyrstin had fallen off the crate and slumped face-down, blood pooling dark and sticky across the clay. *Let's make an end.* Silent as the shadow of vengeance, Teltö stepped over the bodies and past the gentle crackle of the fire.

The Captain indeed died screaming.

Afterwards, the dead Imperials dug a single grave in the paddock, while the Unut looked on. Teltö sat on the grass, his back against an iron drum, barely paying attention. He cradled the woman he'd loved, his face warm and wet with tears. He whispered Sufael's airship poem, over and over, until it became an incantation.

When the grave was deep enough, Teltö laid Sufael in the earth. He kissed her cold lips and placed the hunting knife in her hands. *Sticky with blood. You've got your vengeance, Sufael. Sleep warm in the embrace of the Mother Eternal.* Teltö refilled the dirt himself, handful by handful.

"Tes goor Yehi ognash."

He piled on the last lot of dirt, and straightened up. *That time, I got it right.*

Then all through the night, he made them dance. Round and round the campfire, he hurled the dead soldiers ever faster, and they bobbed and weaved like grotesque marionettes while he gulped down bootleg Asrak and sang old songs to himself. When at last Teltö slept, his dreams were troubled by the sound of gunfire.

• • •

TELTÖ AWOKE WITH the Sun in his eyes, and his head pounding. His parched mouth demanded water. He blinked, and at once the horrors of the night flooded back. By his feet, the glazed eyes of the one who had been Dyrstin stared accusingly. Naked, the body of the Captain lay spread-eagled over the embers of the fire; the aroma of charred flesh reminded Teltö's nostrils of Mustanako. He looked over his shoulder at Sufael's resting place. The freshly-turned earth was stained dark, as if blood had gushed from her grave.

"Necessity makes monsters of us all!" he shouted. His victims weren't answering.

Teltö tried to vomit, but couldn't. *Need food, need water.*

He found his and Sufael's satchels on the farmhouse veranda. *No bloodstains. Good.* He drank a full water bottle before he stopped himself. *I have to get out of here.* He wandered back. The yard reeked like the battlefield, worse even. Teltö sniffed his hands. *A butcher's hands, red with slaughter.*

He stood, numb and sweating, beside the overflowing rubbish bin. *They're dead because of me. She's dead because of me.*

"Mother Eternal, take me," he whispered.

He kicked the bin. Empty bottles tumbling out, it rattled across the blood-dark clay, and came to rest against the outstretched arm of a corpse.

"She wanted to get me home!"

Yes, Phuul. She wanted to get you home. So you're going to get home. It's the least you can do.

Teltö blinked.

Somewhere out there his family waited. His parents. Sweet little Kyrmves. He still had something to live for. Something to give meaning to Sufael's sacrifice…

He rifled through the company's belongings. He found three marks and fifty-four bits, two boxes of matches, and three knives. With Sufael's compass, map, food, and the rest of the water, he still stood half a chance. A fully loaded revolver gave Teltö pause; he'd be happy if he never saw a bloody gun again. But he took it. *An Iilno X. Not the one that shot her though. Give me that.*

As the next task, he swapped into Imperial garb. Reti had been roughly Teltö's size, so he switched into the lime-green shirt and trousers, and bundled up the greatcoat for emergencies. Summer or no, the Uplands could get cold at night. He dumped his old clothes down a dry well on the far side of the paddock. He heaved the bodies after them. It was hard work, but it had to be this way. *No necromancy. Not now.*

With one look at the farmhouse, Teltö headed out in search of civilisation. He shuddered.

•   •   •

HE HIKED SOUTH some distance, trudging up and down endless hills. Three Unut, a bull and two cows, stared at him with brown bovine eyes. *Large, powerful, and harmless.* These ones still had their horns, but Unut hadn't invented warfare, which ranked them above humans. All Unut did was eat and shit. *Such a simple life. Bastards.*

He passed through forested thickets, half expecting another lot of bandits to leap out, but none did. Birdsong was his only companion. Doubts returned. *If I keep going, I'll eventually strike the Nhagivul, but eventually could mean a day or a week.* Sufael had sent the airship off-course, but Teltö didn't know how far. Should he try east? He might find a town on the perimeter of the Mää Wastes. Teltö sat beneath a lone pine, and swigged his water. Walking was thirsty work, and sunburn already blistered his skin. *Let's trust to chance.* He pulled a ten bit coin from his pocket; Emperor Gykäkkä's malformed head stared at him in profile.

"Heads, east, tails, keep going," he muttered. He tossed the coin into the air. It landed with the late Emperor's ugly mug dirtwards. "South it is."

South lay a weed-choked runnel, flanked by silver birches. The water ran off towards a hill before disappearing into a stone drain. A pretty place, home to dragonflies and flowering water hyacinth, but Teltö had no desire to look closer. *Stream's probably full of Unut urine. Thank you, Department of Agriculture.* He jumped atop a boulder, and thence to the far bank.

The Sun hung directly overhead as he crested the last hill. Before him, a plain of grass spread out like a green tablecloth into the distance. Beyond that stood the far-off outline of the Kullio Ranges. Vestiges of snow clung to the craggy peaks.

But there was an even more beautiful sight. For not a furlong away, metal glistened in the noon Sun: twin railway lines, running like a knife through the heart of the Empire. The Mustanako-Kuolinako connection.

He just had to follow the tracks east.

Teltö sank to his knees and wept.

*   *   *

TELTÖ'S BOOTS CRUNCHED the gravel and scuffed the sleepers. Hands in pockets, he drifted onwards, collar upturned against both Sun and the north-westerly. He saw not a single person, living or dead. No trains thundered past; no airships floated above. The tracks ran from horizon to horizon, vanishing into the afternoon haze. From time to time, the breeze strengthened, gusting clouds of dust across the plain.

The day wore on; shadows lengthened. A Full Moon crept into the sky. Teltö pulled on his greatcoat and studied the gloomy emptiness around him. *Perhaps the world's ended without me.* Another swig from the water bottle, and he resumed his trek. End of the world or no, he still had blood pumping through his veins. He'd follow the tracks if it meant walking all the way to the Last Capital.

At last, something black and uninviting crept into view ahead.

Buildings. Silent, yet not deserted: smoke rose from chimneys, and hung wraithlike in the moonlight. He'd found a town.

* * *

"SERVICES ARE CLOSED," said the dead Station Attendant. "Find your own way to Tuonako."

Wrapped in the greatcoat, Teltö rubbed his stubbled chin. Behind him waited the crush of Mustanakonian refugees. Necromancer, Guildling, or Ordinary, all with palpable desperation. Their breath steamed into the unseasonably chill midnight air. *Rhea a few weeks ago. Though getting out would be easier with Vaani Vyrellävek for company.*

"Why Tuonako?" Teltö blinked in the station's floodlight, the only light in town. "Why not the Capital?"

"You didn't read this morning's *Post*, did you?" snapped the woman behind him. "Out of the way, I've five children with me. And do you know you smell like an Unut?"

Teltö let the bitch be; he wanted a newspaper. He pushed back through the coated hordes, and tripped over suitcases.

"Queue-jumper!" snorted a yellow-scarfed man with a walrus moustache.

Teltö finally found what he wanted: a boy sitting on a bench with this morning's edition. No more than ten, the boy held the paper up to the light, squinting and chuckling. *The comics page, no doubt.*

Teltö leant over the back of the bench. "Hey, lad. Are you here by yourself?"

The pug-nosed thing looked much like Teltö's school bully. "With Dad. He's in the queue. He's been gone for ages."

"Good," said Teltö.

With a fluid motion, he ripped the newspaper away, and dashed into the crowd. The child's protest was lost amid the noise and bustle of the station.

• • •

EVEN AS A small railway town, with few streets and fewer shops, the blackout made navigation nasty as Kuolinako's tunnels. Teltö tripped on a loose cobblestone, and went sprawling. He levered himself up on an unlit lamppost and rubbed his shins, cursing ill luck. *Need somewhere to read. Isn't anywhere open?*

At an intersection, moonlight bathed a marble fountain in a cold glow. Grey in the dim light, water gushed from the carven lips of Mother Death. *Not the nicest omen.* Teltö looked closer. Copper bits lay strewn in the shallow water. Teltö smiled and rolled up his sleeve. Mam would scold him if she ever found out, but it couldn't be helped: he fished out a couple of coins, his skin goosepimpling in the chill water.

He was drying his hands on his greatcoat when he heard muffled singing. He looked around. Chimney smoke rose from the shuttered building across the way; a sliver of light poked through the curtains.

A pub.

Teltö picked up his paper, and hurried inside.

No Needle, that's for certain.

Beer puddles soaked the floor, and mugs with broken handles sat heaped on tables. The clientèle looked no better, and smelt even worse. Teltö sniffed under his own arms. *Perhaps I shouldn't pass judgement.* But odours or no, the place was warmer than the station, and there'd be no trains until morning. A solitary Mnoma danced atop a piano, waving a top hat and kicking violently. The alien was singing its green lungs out. *I almost miss the North.*

Teltö grabbed a watered-down Ruvian Bitter and a

bag of salted peanuts, as one of the Mnoma's buckled shoes landed toe-first in a beer jug. *Yes, the Church has a point.* Finding a table on the far side of the room, Teltö settled into the chair and unfolded the *Post*. This was his first look at Imperial news since the assassination of Vyrellävek.

Acting Chancellor Tyrtön makes an announcement? That fat arse is ruling us? The coverage from Mustanako was vague and sparse, which Teltö took as a bad sign. *Bombing raids continue, assaults thrown back. Help is on the way.* Then onto breathless adulation about the victory at sea, which in the *Post's* world somehow owed more to Admiralty officials than great bloody squids.

He saw no clear reason for avoiding Kuolinako. Tuonako had its mountain barrier, but the Last Capital sat underground, immune to airships. Teltö gulped Ruvian Bitter and scratched his head, deciding to ask the barman for further gossip. Then the seventh page caught his eye. *Inquisitor General announcement. So she's still there. Grand Masters come and go, but she remains.* Vöder had declared ... a crackdown on supporters of former Grand Master Rumi? Special emergency powers? Teltö sat up. In the midst of the Fifth Northern War, Kuolinako was turning itself inside-out in a hunt for traitors.

Teltö finished his beer and savoured the bad taste. Vöder's powers were getting expanded beyond even Dragon-era levels. *This'll be fun. How to get to Qivunako while avoiding the Capital.* This meant mountain crossings and...

He froze. *What about Dyrstin?* Had Venomavat fled back to Qivunako? Probably not; it'd be an admission of guilt. But staying would leave the poor bastard with a ringside seat to the insanity. Could Venomavat look after himself? Maybe, and Teltö would only endanger his own life by seeking him out. *Suicide is never right.* All through the dark days of the march, Teltö had known he was going home, back to library stamps and lost spider wars. Could he put this at risk, after the blood and sweat he'd shed? *And there's her blood too…*

He shook his head. *Cut the selfish Unut-shit, Phuul. You owe it to the people who got you here. You've destroyed enough lives, and it's time to make up for it.* Sufael may have died to get him home, but she'd done it for a reason. A gift to be passed on, not wasted. Foorit hadn't abandoned an enemy; how could Teltö abandon a friend? How could he rest at night without at least trying to find Venomavat? *I lost Welleorm. I lost Sufael. Bugger if I'm losing Dyrstin too, even if it means pissing away everything I've worked for. Some things are more important.*

That settled it. Teltö popped the last salted nut into his mouth and scrunched up the bag. He felt strangely energised. *I saved Vöder's life. What should I of all people have to fear?*

The Mnoma stopped singing, to no applause. Teltö was heading back to the bar when the alien leapt off the piano with an almighty thump. It ran across and seized his arm.

"It is you," said the Mnoma. It tapped long green fingers against his coat.

"Yes," snapped Teltö, pulling away. "It is I."

"Teltö Phuul."

Teltö stopped. "How…"

"I remember you from the boat. You strangled me."

The barkeep raised his eyebrows.

"Long story," said Teltö. He ushered the alien back to his table and ordered another beer, to be safe from awkward questions.

"What are you doing here?" asked Teltö. The Mnoma

had been heading to Mustanako. It might have news.

"Seeing the Empire by hot-air balloon. It is the only way to travel."

Teltö could have kissed the creature.

• • •

MORNING HAD BROKEN. Still yawning after a lengthy nap, Teltö peered over the side of the wicker basket. The lemon-yellow balloon floated a furlong or more above the ground; the world was once more at the young man's feet. To the north he saw green hills, from where he'd emerged with blood-red hands. *Somewhere out there is a farmhouse turned slaughterhouse.* To the south, the silver ribbon of the Nhagivat meandered its way through the Empire, oblivious to the machinations of humans and their wars.

"Aesthetically pleasing, no?" said the Mnoma, ensconced beside an array of chromium-plated tubes and levers. It fished an apple from a picnic hamper and polished the fruit on a velvet sleeve. "Rather like a painting, but with the perception all muddled."

"Very much so," said Teltö. Pleased no one on the ground could mistake the balloon for a Northern airship, he desperately hoped the basket held together. The pine floor felt solid enough, but one never knew with the Mnomo. It'd be just like them to sample the brief and unique sensation of falling horribly to one's death.

"Muddled perceptions are the best perceptions," said the Mnoma. "It enables us to see things as they truly are, rather than how we think they are."

Teltö frowned. "Pardon?"

The Mnoma threw the apple overboard, and reached for another. "Simple. We see things one way. But things are many ways at once. Thus, if we see things more than one way, our seeing is better, and more muddled. 'Tis the purpose of art."

Teltö's head hurt as he recalled his last conversation on art. *Poor Oym. He never wanted to rule, but we can't always get what we want. Hova wanted revolution, and look where that got him. And Vyrellävek wanted me dead, for all the good that did.* Teltö's gaze ran along the railway tracks. The connection ended at a bomb crater. *No trains to the Last Capital.* Hordes of Guild engineers, like black beetles at this distance, laboured in repair. Tangled heaps of iron and the skeleton wreckage of two airships littered the ground nearby.

"I want to thank you again for strangling me," said the Mnoma. "I have introduced it to four fellows now."

"Don't mention it." Teltö pushed his hair from his eyes. "Taking me to Kuolinako repays all debts."

The winds blew them ever more south-east. Just after midday, the balloon began crossing the Mää Wastes. A forest of tree skeletons, twisted and white, stretched away to the north. Teltö thought he saw a dark shape standing on one bald hilltop; when he squinted, it was gone. *The uleeveer walk here.*

"Time for gas masks," said Teltö, putting Sufael from his mind. The air had grown thick and foul; it was hard to believe they were still upwind from the city.

"What gas masks?" asked the Mnoma. It had finished the apples, and was devouring a dripping sandwich.

Teltö raised an eyebrow. "The masks that protect us from the chimneys," he snapped. "There must be some aboard."

The Mnoma chewed thoughtfully. "Ever since I hatched from the egg, I have delighted in the aroma of mighty Kuolinako. There is no need for masks."

All this way, only to choke to death. Teltö eyed the gas bag.

"How high can this thing go?"

"Many furlongs," squeaked the alien. "Where you wander through fields of cloud. Where vast mountains are islands in an ocean of mist. Alas that the sky is clear today. I curse you, Sun, I curse you." It shook its fist.

Teltö coughed. "Could you take us up anyway? We could pretend, and the view would be even more aesthetically pleasing."

The Mnoma beamed. It opened a valve, and the balloon drifted up into the fresher air.

· · ·

FOG SHROUDED THE Last Capital. Teltö spotted the Tower of the Emperors far below; the home of the Inquisition remained impervious to time, weather, or bombs, and somewhere in that monstrous pinnacle sat the dusty bones of Gykäkkä, untouched these past fifteen centuries. The Tower stood sheer and unyielding in the gathering twilight, and cast a long shadow over the surrounds, where chimneys belched green and brown vapours amid the old city ruins. The slag heaps of countless years lay piled around, twisted into man-made hills and crags. Kuolinako had not changed. *Nor can it.*

"We are here." The Mnoma's fingers quivered. "Let us descend."

Teltö drew his last lungfuls of wholesome air. The Mnoma tugged a cord, and they sank towards the city. The grim fog crept closer; Teltö covered his face with his greatcoat. *We're upwind. It can't be that bad.* When necessity forced a breath out of him, he realised how wrong he was.

· · ·

ABOVE GROUND, KUOLINAKO was a vaporous chemical

soup. Mustard blotches danced in the air like wraiths, then dissolved as swiftly as they'd appeared. Teltö Phuul didn't stop to look. His coat shielded his mouth and nose against the fog; his boots crunched against rock and rubble. His simple quest: follow the alien, or perish. Through the ruins he ran, on the trail of a mad creature, through the maze of chimneys and slag-hills. Over the stained remains of fallen statues, and across a bridge of quivering stone. Around yawning pits and ditches choked with industrial vomit. Through streets named only in the lost tongue of the Empire's youth. Everywhere, relics of the past crumbled, forgotten by all.

He spotted something, not ten centifurlongs away. A figure in a gas-mask limped around the base of a broken pedestal. Teltö waved. The figure vanished.

Teltö shook his head, and doubled his pace. *Probably an odd-shaped cloud. Father Life, seeing's hard as breathing.* In front, the alien pranced through Old Kuolinako as though the day were clear and the air filled with a fresh ocean breeze.

Then without warning, the Mnoma darted into a tunnel, like a rabbit into a burrow.

Heart hammering and lungs burning, Teltö almost lost his footing as he staggered to the entrance. Less than half a centifurlong high and mostly hidden by slag, the tunnel-mouth was well-camouflaged; he'd have missed it altogether had he not been in such close pursuit. Before him, stone steps led downward into darkness. Teltö wondered if the creature led him to a dead-end. *Your choice, Phuul: go on, or choke.* Spluttering into his greatcoat, Teltö began the descent.

He managed a dozen steps before he tripped and fell. He shouted, more in surprise than pain, and slid the rest of the way, tumbling into a heap on the landing.

"Shit."

Next he knew, the Mnoma's green face hovered over him, jovially tut-tutting.

"Clumsy, but amusing." The Mnoma prodded his cheek. "I must try that some time."

Cursing, Teltö sat up and dusted himself off. *No injuries, thank Father Life.* He'd stumbled into an empty chamber with corridors stretching out either side. *Lit by daylight, not lamps. We're still in the Old Empire.* The air, too, was breathable. Stale and dry, leaden with the weight of centuries, but hardly toxic. *Cleansing mechanisms?* He donned his greatcoat, and hurried after the Mnoma, which was already disappearing down the left corridor.

The creature ushered him into an abandoned hall, where webs draped the sloped ceiling like curtains. Spiders scuttled across lamps, as if feasting on the amber glow. Then through an open doorway and down steep and winding stairs. The stairs spiralled past a series of granite doors, each encrusted with unintelligible hieroglyphics. Teltö brushed the dust from one and sneezed.

At the bottom he found a rectangular cavern. No dust or cobwebs here, just Kuolinako rock. The Empire had smoothed the native stalagmites and stalactites into a succession of hexagonal pillars. Lamps shone from every side; flat dry rock though it was, the floor sparkled.

Teltö felt grateful for his greatcoat. Summer never penetrated these depths, and a draft was creeping in somewhere. On the far wall, a sheet of granite stood bathed in blue radiance. Teltö frowned. *A dead end?* No, a door, outlined in the stone. The source of the colouration, twin lamps hung on either side, and beneath the lights, two statues sat on little thrones. The Necromancer shuffled closer. *Father Life and Mother Death.* The statues barely reached Teltö's knee.

The Mnoma had hands on hips, and was squeaking at the shut door. Three shining bolts held the way shut.

"What is it?" Teltö asked.

What is it? asked the echo. *What is it? What is it?*

No sooner had the sound died than another came to Teltö's ears: a rumble from below, a noise like a thousand hands pattering away on the same drum.

"Who goes there?" a voice boomed. Deep as the ocean, old and unyielding, it seemed to come from the throned statues.

"A Necromancer and a Mnoma seek entry." Teltö's heart beat faster.

"Who goes there?"

This was no human, living or lich, but some devilry from the Old Empire, ancient even when Gykäkkä drooled upon the throne. Teltö hesitated, reluctant to declare his identity. *But this is old, very old. If it knows I'm lying...* Beside him, the Mnoma squeaked gibberish. It didn't look afraid, but it wasn't much help either.

Vöder's still there, and she likes me. "Teltö Phuul," he declared.

Again the rumble, and for a moment Teltö thought the bolts were sliding back. But it was not to be.

"Who goes there?"

Teltö knitted his eyebrows. "Teltö Phuul," he said, louder. "Necromancer, and underkarl of Qivunako."

"Who goes there?"

What? He turned to the Mnoma. "Is there another way?"

"No. But the gate has always stood open. I have never known it shut."

Teltö approached the statues. He knelt, and gingerly extended a blue-lit hand towards the head of Father Life. The stone was cold and rough, but he felt nothing untoward, nothing unnatural.

"Who are you?" His voice rang out, high and clear in this strange forgotten world of stone and lamp and echo. "Who in bloody blazes are you?"

"Who goes there?"

The voice had not changed. Eight thousand years distilled into sound, with all the weight of history, from Saari Ooks down to his great-grandmother, Keer and Vyrellävek…

Imagine a world without bowing and scraping to skeletons.

Suddenly Teltö was laughing, long and loud, while the warden demanded his identity over and over again. Even the Mnoma looked askance.

With a smile back at the alien, Teltö put his hand on the bolts. He pulled. Once, twice, thrice, he blasphemed against his heritage, yet no phantom came to claim him, not now when its threat had dispersed along with its purpose. *No Necromancer fears the dead. Why should we fear the past?* He gave the door a nudge. The stone swung back to reveal a cobblestone road, the way lit by the eternal lamps of Kuolinako.

Chapter Nineteen

TUNNELS BRANCHED LEFT and right, each indistinguishable from the next. Were it not for the Mnoma, Teltö might have taken a wrong turn and never known. He wondered how many people over the centuries had ventured into the Thousand Caves never to return, how many skeletons still grasped at the waterless dust of some forgotten grotto.

He looked over his shoulder. "So we continue this way?"

"That is not wrong," crooned the Mnoma. It flittered ahead. "Neither right nor left, but straight ahead. Is it not a fine day to be alive?"

"You ask that question in the Viiminian Empire? I'm here to find a friend, then get out." *I'm coming, Dyrstin.*

The path eased downwards. The tunnel walls grew narrower, the roof lower. Teltö sniffed at the stale air. He saw no living people, no liches, not even Unut shit. *I hope the Mnoma knows what it's doing.* The lamps burned dim and perpetual. That at least he found comforting. The calamities of war would never reach here, no more than anything else.

After half an hour – it felt half an hour, though time in Kuolinako was strange – something changed. His boots still scuffed the cobblestones, the rock still felt cool and glassy, and the gas-light flickered within crystalline cages. The air remained dry and sterile. But there was something wrong with the feeling. What had Oilio said about Kuolinako's hidden places? *Alien as the Moon. Yes.*

"The *uleeveer*," he muttered. *Sufael would hate this place. There's no poetry here.* Or perhaps there was, but only the sort that mouldered in attic drawers, awaiting some brave fool to pry.

The further they went, the worse it became. Teltö sweated, though it grew no warmer, and his ears strained for any sound at all. The insidious silence hushed even his own footfalls. He craved the crisp clop of hooves, or the creak of cab wheels. Or even the stench of roadside pellets. His fears mounted and his pulse quickened. Soon, every step became an act of will. He was about to suggest they turn back and find another route when the Mnoma suddenly vanished.

Teltö rubbed his eyes.

"Where have you gone, you blasted thing?"

No answer. Teltö pushed back damp hair. The alien had been not a dozen steps in front. *Bugger it. This isn't the time for games.* Then he froze. There was something else here, something that made his every hair stand on end. Something *alive.* He heard it call to him in an alien tongue, a wordless music more ancient than the Empire itself.

Teltö sunk to the ground and crawled forward on hands and knees. At last he saw: a gap in the tunnel floor, a crevice narrow as a knife slash.

The call persisted. Teltö edged closer. The buttons of

his greatcoat dragged against the stone. Part of him knew he'd be driven mad if he didn't look, and another part…

He peered into the crevice and saw light. Mist swirled, as if trying to take form. Teltö blinked, and it was gone. The music sang to him. *That which came before, and that which will be again. That which feeds us life in death, the toy of children.* The void reached out, ready to extinguish him with a thought. *No.*

Teltö lurched to his feet and ran. On and on, long after his lungs were heaving, and the stitch in his side grew unbearable. On and on through the corridors, on and on until his legs gave out.

He collapsed at the feet of a startled mine supervisor.

• • •

HE LAY IN a narrow bed in a narrow room. There was no carpet, little furniture, and only a single pillow, but he wouldn't have traded this sanctuary for all the marks in the Empire.

"Here, try this," said the supervisor. Young, blonde, and cheerful, she looked unnaturally ruddy for a Kuolinakonian. She handed him a flask. "I don't have any tea on hand. No solid food either, I'm afraid. Prices are rising faster than the rationing boards can deal with them."

Teltö drank the offering. Fermented Unut milk, home-brewed by the taste.

"Feeling better? You've been out for ages."

He nodded. He still felt lightheaded, but she'd tucked him up with a hot water bottle, and pampering made everything better. His freshly-pressed uniform hung over the back of a chair. *The uniform I stole from a man I murdered, but by Father Life, I'll make amends.*

"What were you doing in the mines?"

Teltö thought quickly. "My troop was shattered by an air raid and I took shelter below ground. I thought I could find my way through the tunnels. I was wrong."

"You were white as a sheet when I found you. You looked like you'd seen a ghost or something."

"Not something." He stared off into space. "Nothing."

She cocked her head at that, but asked no further questions. Later, after he'd had a bath and a shave, she gave him directions to the Central Railway Station. Moving a hand to her shirt buttons, she offered him something else too. *She wants to reward a war hero,* Teltö realised. He felt himself stiffening against his trousers.

"Sorry." He shook his head. *Too soon.*

•   •   •

AN ELDERLY UNDERKARL shook his hand. Then a jolly Shipper. Then a Tuonakonian with a wheezy cough and skin like sandpaper. At first, Teltö found it gratifying, but after signing an eight year-old's diary, he offered a feeble excuse and dashed through the Station crowds to the line of waiting cabs. The unearned glamour could wait until he got back to Qivunako. He needed to find Venomavat. *First stop, Keer's.*

Teltö snuggled into the travelling rug as the cab rattled through Kuolinako's tunnels. His first glimpse of the Last Capital in wartime, and he didn't like it. Civilians queued outside grocers and butchers; the lines stretched back into the street. Armed liches stood in the shadows, watching for rioters or looters. Teltö could almost smell the latent panic.

Then whole blocks passed without Teltö spotting a single person, living or dead. The door of what had been a physician's surgery hung off its hinges like a broken tooth. *Was the poor bastard a Northerner or a Rumi follower?* Teltö mulled it over as the cab entered an elevator. *Maybe it doesn't matter. Everyone's guilty in a purge.*

• • •

KEER'S GATES STOOD ajar.

Teltö slid open the rear hatch. "What's happened here?"

The corpse-driver stared. "Payment please."

Teltö shrugged. He stuffed bits into the cab's box, and hopped down.

No one toiled in the garden, and the blue lanterns had vanished from the tree-branches, rendering the night pines a formless ink-stain against the cavern wall. The front door lamp still shone, though, as did an interior light upstairs. Enough to guide him along the shadowed path. Teltö drew his Iilno X, but left it uncocked. Better to be safe.

He knocked, then tried the doorknob. No luck. *It only opens from the inside, Phuul.*

"Hello?"

He banged his fists on the shutters. Nothing. Keer's mighty fortress of underlings had no one to deal with visitors.

"Anyone?"

Teltö searched for a stone to fling at the upstairs window, but found nothing, even in the half-lit area. He looked over his shoulder, to where the fishpond lay, dark and still as the Mother Eternal. *It's shallow enough to reach the bottom. Perhaps I'll find a pebble or two.* About to test it, he paused. Had he heard something? Yes, footsteps… on the polished oak of Keer's entrance hall. Teltö heard scraping.

Someone was undoing the latches on the front door. He waited on the step and pushed his hair back. *About time.*

The door swung open. Teltö blinked at sudden lantern light. Too late, he realised that a revolver pointed at his chest.

"Right," said a woman, "I'll give you until the count of three to bugger off, or I'll pepper your liver full of lead."

The voice, the glasses, the strawberry blonde hair... He frowned.

"Tuvena?"

"Teltö!" she hissed, lowering the gun. "I thought you were dead!"

"Many people wish I were. What's happened? I came back for Dyrstin..."

"I can't chat out here. Hurry up and come inside."

• • •

THE HOUSE WAS a mess. Busted chairs mingled with upturned tables, and someone had knocked a hole in a bookshelf. Teltö bent to replace a fallen tome – Ooseman's anthropological collection of south-western folk traditions – but the pages spilt out and wafted to the floor.

"What are you doing?"

Teltö held up the book cover. "My Library Supervisor would have a bloody heart attack. Another one. This was a *first edition Ooseman.*"

"Leave it. There's nothing we can do."

Tuvena led him through to the parlour. She shoved aside a feather duster and popped her lantern on the table. Half a dozen dirty plates lay scattered around the room, each covered with fishbones and grease. There were enough bottles and glasses to supply half the 113th.

"Looks like an earthquake," said Teltö.

Tuvena slumped into a chair. "A political one."

She poured herself a drink. The lantern light did uncharitable things to her double chin. *I once loved that face,* Teltö realised, just as he'd loved her fondness for swimming and her cutting intelligence. Even after she'd shat on him, she remained the woman he knew best. Bedding another was like going right back to her, only to suffer again. *But now I know better. And so, it seems, does she.* He contented himself with a smile. It may have been Tuvena, but a defeated Tuvena, and he needed her help.

"I can't believe they got the Dragon." She grimaced. The Asrak clearly had sting. "The Tower took every precaution. Who knew it wouldn't be enough to defend a paranoid nut? Bloody Northerners."

"Oym didn't see it either. It was a rogue airship pilot who dropped the bomb – nothing to do with the officials."

"Interesting story, Phuul. Tell me more."

Teltö scooped up a small bottle from a shelf, and held it to the light. "I heard it from a mechanic." *Sleeping pills. Empty.*

"You really have the ear of the great and powerful, don't you?" Tuvena eyed his uniform. "But then you always survive. You're like a bloody weta."

Teltö replaced the pill bottle and helped himself to a glass. Tuvena didn't stop him. "Enough about me. Where's Dyrstin, and what happened here? What are *you* doing here?"

Tuvena giggled. "Dyrstin's gone. Keer's Housemaster denounced him."

"Oilio?"

"That's him. Bald chap, quick with the handkerchief. Denouncing is very popular right now; it's just behind hiding and bootlicking as Kuolinako's favourite pastime. I've no idea what he accused Dyrstin of, but I did hear Oilio had his eye on some paintings after Keer carked it."

Bootleg Asrak burned Teltö's throat. "Keer carked it? That'd explain the mess."

"Yes, he drifted into the Mother's embrace in his sleep, not long after Vyrellävek was blown up. The old man had no surviving relatives, and, it turned out, no will. Keer must have thought he'd live forever. Sadly, it turned free-for-all, and the Inquisition got involved…"

"The shadow-stalkers looted the place."

"Such an ugly word. I'll admit this wasn't one of the Tower's finest moments, but we did get lots of denunciations, which is always a plus in today's Kuolinako."

"If Dyrstin's been denounced, where is he?"

"The records are at the Tower."

"Can we go get them? Völder likes me well enough."

Tuvena shook her head. "Völder's not interfering in the round-up. With so many departmental underlings keen on promotions – plenty of positions to go round – even the bosses dance on a knife-edge. Völder wants to keep both her job and her life. In that order, knowing her."

"But you have connections; paperwork can get lost…"

"Hah."

Tuvena picked up an unused glass and threw it at a far wall. The vessel shattered.

"That's my career, Teltö. That's why I'm here, drowning my sorrows."

"With Dyrstin's Asrak? I recall you calling it downright foul."

Tuvena shrugged. "It is. But the looters overlooked it.

Thank Father Life for small mercies; the stuff's all I have. Well, that and raiding Keer's fishpond for dinner. Have you seen black market food prices?"

"So you've lost your job." It was not a question.

"Yes," she snapped. "I lost my job. Perceptive as ever, Phuul. But since you'll want to gloat, here's the sordid details."

"I…"

"Shut it, Phuul. Some underlings made it publicly known that Dyrstin Venomavat was my informant. The confessed criminal, Dyrstin Venomavat. Suddenly, there's an investigation into alleged corruption in my office."

"Alleged corruption in Kuolinako?"

"I know, right? Might as well investigate alleged breathing while you're at it. The report came back, doctored. My superiors sympathised, but said it was a matter of perception and public confidence. Bastards. So I wound up on indefinite suspension, which in Tower-speak is one rung up from indefinite disappearance. I lost the room I was renting, too. The landlord became paranoid he was next. Which I think answers your question as to why I'm haunting Keer's."

"I'm sorry."

"You're gloating, stop pretending. And get this: the person who got my job was the bastard who ratted on me. He looks a lot like you, actually: same nose and all. Except he's blond and Tuonakonian. Even took him to bed a couple of times. He was good so long as he kept his mouth shut."

Teltö repressed a retort. "So this rat will have Dyrstin's files?"

"Yes, and yours. Same office."

"Want to help me break Dyrstin out?"

"Do I look suicidal?"

Yes. Yes, you do. "It'll embarrass your backstabbing friend."

"If only. Good luck getting into the Tower."

"We're not going to the Tower."

Tuvena lowered her drink. "Eh?"

"Unless there's a spare wig of the right shade lying around here, we're going to the Theatre. Bring a bottle; we'll need it later."

* * *

TUVENA CLAIMED TO be skint, which may even have been true. Teltö grudgingly paid the cab fare and counted his remaining coins. Two marks, fifty seven bits. *Sounds good, up until I need it all for food, and what then? Tickets home aren't free.*

The Imperial Theatre House stood shuttered and barred; some wit had graffitied 'Closed, by Inquisitorial Appointment' and 'Dust: A Comedy Coming Soon' on the exterior walls. Assorted Mnomo, vagabonds, and unemployed actors milled around in fingerless gloves. *Half are probably shadow-stalkers, and the other half informants working for shadow-stalkers.*

But the place wasn't abandoned. Light peeped out from behind the shutters, and a security guard in grey hovered on the doorstep.

"We're closed," said the guard. A weedy fellow with glasses, nature hadn't cut him out for this role, but Teltö was relieved to find a live one. They'd never get past a lich.

"We need to see the Manager," said Teltö.

"Sorry."

Teltö puffed out his chest, and stood in the man's face.

"You wish to thwart the Imperial Inquisition?" *Take the hint, Tuvena.*

Snorting, Tuvena rummaged in her handbag, and handed over her identification card. Obsolete, of course, but the guard wasn't to know, and the Tower still hadn't got around to recalling it.

Sweat suddenly beaded on the man's forehead. "But of course, madam. And you, sir?"

Teltö glared, and flicked imaginary fluff from his lime-green coat.

"Oh, never mind. If you can't trust the troops, who can you trust?" The man giggled. "Come this way. The Theatre is always willing to cooperate with the Tower in all matters…"

The Theatre has fallen far. The guard unlocked the door and ushered them through to reception. Or what had been reception: neither desk nor chair nor even carpet remained. Only bare floorboards and dust. Tuvena sneezed violently.

"My bloody allergies," she snapped. "Would it kill you to clean?"

"I do apologise, madam, but Guild law prevents me from interfering. This Theatre only employs registered dusters, and since the closure it cannot afford to maintain full services."

In the corner, a busted typewriter lay buttons-downwards. Teltö turned it over with his boot.

"One writer didn't appreciate redundancy," said the guard. "Human, not Mnomo. I gather the Mnoman ones ate the typewriter ribbons before leaving. They seemed to enjoy it."

•　•　•

"YOU OWE ME," Tuvena whispered through her handkerchief.

Teltö grinned. "Of course, dear."

The guard opened a door, and stuck his head in.

"Sir, Inquisition here to see you."

Teltö's eyes widened. The Manager had relocated, and the new office… well, the place may have been less of a wreck than Keer's, but only because most of the remaining furniture was still upright. Empty liquor bottles manned one corner in best soldierly fashion, shoulder to shoulder with a well-used dartboard. Off to the side, a big black cat lapped at a saucer of milk. *At least I hope that's milk.*

The guard's footsteps faded. Teltö shut the door. "Sir?"

The Manager slumped shoeless and face-down on the desk. Covered in newspapers, he groaned incoherently.

"What is it now?"

"It's me, Teltö Phuul."

The Manager rolled onto the floor with a thud.

"Phuul, Phuul, Phuul? How do I know you?"

"I found the bombers in your toilet."

Tuvena coughed. Or laughed. Teltö couldn't tell which.

"And it has been the illest of ill winds." The Manager climbed to his feet. He smelt of sweat, Asrak, and dodgy meat pies. "Closed for an unspecified length of time? I've had to lay off staff. I can no longer afford mayonnaise with my daily salad. It's a tragedy, I tell you, but one entirely lacking catharsis. Thank goodness this Northern nonsense has distracted the Auditors, else I'd be out on the street. Me, a respected Guildling, out on the street, and living in a hole with only my Behemoth for company! It doesn't bear thinking about."

"Quite," said Teltö. "I was wondering…"

"Wondering if the Inquisition can squeeze me some more? Wondering if you could get another bit of flesh out of me? You walk in here, fresh from the slaughterhouse and the prison cells; you, who represent the worst in humanity, presume to destroy my livelihood? Others may bend and quake before the Tower, but not I. For there is still a man in this city with a dram of courage, sir. Go ahead, shoot me. Put me out of my misery, sir!"

Teltö bit his lip. This needed a rethink. "So you hate the Inquisition."

"With all my heart, sir. Or I would if the Inquisitor General had not already ripped it from my chest and danced the galliard upon it. A lifetime of service to the Grand Chancellor…"

Tuvena folded her arms. "Service that somehow involved staging *The Dragonbone Pipes*, a satiric commentary on our late Chancellor's efforts to preserve the old order. Is that how you repay your master? By taking his money, then mocking him in public?"

The man flushed. "It was an historical epic, damn you!"

"That's what they all say. At first."

"The Mnomo wrote it, not I."

"Whose name appears on the censor form? Now I recall, your play doesn't just feature Vyrellävek either. One of the other bigwigs plays the pipes, I believe."

The Manager's lower lip quivered. "Read into it what you will, but do not blame me!"

"Not my decision."

"I can give you names!"

"Stop!" Teltö barked. He looked at his former lover;

Tuvena's ability to concoct accusations impressed and terrified him in equal measure. "We're not actually from the Tower."

The Manager snorted. "A likely story."

"The truth." *Even if one of us would fit right back in.*

The Manager pushed aside papers, and sat on the desk edge. "You snare me with lies. I, who have been your most obedient servant, ill-used and ill-treated! 'Tis a scandal."

Teltö sighed. "Look, if we were Inquisitors, we'd have already shot you, correct?"

"Why else are you here, folk who wear the mask of Inquisitors?"

"We need props. Specifically, a blond wig, a red scarf, and a green ribbon."

The Manager shook his head. "You can't have them. They are not mine to give."

"But you are the Manager?"

"A Manager is merely the head of the great Theatre family. Its mouthpiece, or dare I say it, its brain. Such a thing would betray a sacred trust – can you imagine the Chancellor simply giving away Mustanako?"

The old Chancellor, or the new one? Yes, I can, actually. It'd get rid of Meerm.

"So you will not give us the props?"

"Not for all the salt in the Illuvian, nor all the tea in Klem."

Teltö held out a silver coin, flicked it up and caught it.

The Manager smiled, and rubbed his earring. "But that? That will do nicely."

•　•　•

THE ALLEY BETWEEN the fishmonger and the dentist was

perfect for perfidious designs. Teltö grinned. "How does it look?"

Tuvena looked up from her pocket mirror. She'd been rearranging her hair. "This'll never work. You could pass for him if no one looks too closely, but you're doomed the second you open your mouth. He's Tuonakonian, remember? Complete with accent?"

"I'm way ahead of you. You've still got that Asrak bottle in your handbag?"

"Bottle?" There was a pause, then Tuvena slapped her forehead. "You're insane, absolutely insane. This is an idea worthy of the Mnomo."

"It's the only way I can do the accent right. Vöder won't rescue us, you can't get it yourself, and you said it's this Kärytö fellow's day off."

"Teltö, this is suicide. Drunken suicide. Let's get out while we can. Head to Qivunako…"

Does the bitch want me back? Teltö shook his head. "I've lost people, Tuvena. Too many people, good and bad. I need to find Dyrstin for the sake of my own conscience. For the sake of my own sanity. Venomavat might be dead, but at least I can look myself in the mirror and tell myself I tried. That counts for something, doesn't it?"

"Are you doing this for Dyrstin or for yourself?"

"For Nelim Foorit, actually. For Sufael, Reqi, and another Dyrstin, for Private Saw, for Colonel Groon, for Welleorm, for physicians and ambassadors and princes. For friends and enemies. Even for a bloody Mnoma. Do you understand? Believe me, if I could run, I would. These past months I've done nothing but hunger for home, but I need to give it up." He shrugged. "Sometimes our most treasured dreams aren't that important."

Tuvena stared.

"You always were a fool, Teltö. But the best of fools."
She handed him the Asrak.

•   •   •

A BLOND YOUNG man strode into the Tower of the Emperors. A Tuonakonian by his scarf, a minister by the ribbon pinned to his breast, he swayed as he walked. The Inquisition held no terror for him. It was his livelihood. He was Kärytö Revenuta, a shadow-stalker with ambition, and at his elbow was the woman he'd replaced, Tuvena Sytöphin.

"Kärytö." An undermaster with slicked-back hair and spectacles elbowed through the masses, and shook the newcomer's hand. "Good to see you, and thank you again for your corrections to the Kovo file."

"A pleasurrrrre."

"But isn't this your day off?"

Teltö grinned toothily. "That it is, sirrrr, that it is. A fine day forrr a day off, is it not?"

The undermaster stepped back. "You're drunk."

"And you'rrrre ugly. *Hic*."

"Apologies, sir." Tuvena stepped between them. "I left something behind in my old office, so Kärytö's helping me collect it. He's a darling, isn't he? You're so lucky to have him."

"Sytöphin," said the official. "Still in Kuolinako, are we?"

"Oh yes," said Tuvena. "Doing this and that."

They collected Tuvena's key without trouble. Neither living staff nor liches had difficulty recognising Tuonako's latest rising star.

•   •   •

TUVENA TURNED SCARLET. "Look at this place. It's a mess. He's even chucked my precious bookshelf!"

"Neverrrr mind the bookshelf. We need to find Dyrrrrstin."

She pointed. "He's moved the filing cabinet too. Father Life, I hate change for the sake of change. There was nothing wrong with where it was."

Teltö couldn't see a difference, but nodded agreement. Tuvena rummaged through files.

"I remember this one." She pulled out a brown folder. "My second case…"

"We don't have time forrrr this."

Tuvena threw a look, and replaced the file. She thumbed through a few more. "Venomavat, Dyrstin… there's three of them. What's his date of birth again?"

"Firrst of Kuul, 7989. Thrree months afterrr me."

"Here he is. Let's see what the Tower has in store for the sleazy son of an Unut."

Tuvena's mouth drooped the more she read.

"What's wrrrong?"

"He's to be executed at midnight." She slapped the folder down on the desk, and glanced at the office clock. "That gives us just over five hours."

"Poorrr Dyrrrstin."

"Let's see… they'll have removed him from the cells. We'll have to free him from the cage directly. That'll be tough."

He gave her a one-armed hug. "We'll manage."

"Yes," she sighed, "I suppose we will."

• • •

THEY HEADED DOWNSTAIRS. Teltö's brain still swam in a swamp of heady intoxication, but a queasy sensation was developing in his stomach; he wanted to vomit. Suddenly, Tuvena shoved him back into the shadows.

"Take the wig off, Teltö," she hissed.

"What?"

She tugged it off herself. Teltö squawked. Strands of his real hair went with it.

"You're back to being you."

"Whateverrr you say, Tuvena."

"Keep your trap shut. The real Kärytö Revenuta is standing out there, and the last thing we need is a drunken doppelgänger."

Eyes down, Teltö allowed himself to be led through the crowd.

"Tuvena," said a male voice. "Fancy seeing you here."

"Kärytö." Tuvena was deader than deadpan. "I'm just leaving."

Teltö studied the Revenuta fellow. Yes, there was a similarity. Not like the bizarre undead twin he'd met previously, but were it not for the hair – the flowing locks were immaculate – one could think him a long-lost Phuul. *He even has the nose.*

"Who is this then? Your latest flame?"

"Look, it's complicated," said Tuvena. "But really—."
Can't hurt to say hello. "I'm Teltö."

Revenuta shook his hand. "Kärytö. Always good to meet a fellow Tuonakonian, and a minister to boot. We've got to stick together, right?"

"Rrright."

The man smiled. "Tuvena here can't resist Tuonako wood."

Tuvena glared. "Qivunako iron lasts longer."

"Until it gets old and rusty."

"No rrrust." said Teltö. "Not yet."

The man's face soured. "You're a south-westerner. One of those Lake Köömö types."

"That's rrrright."

"And you're drunk." Revenuta backed away. "Bloody inbred barbarians…"

"Good seeing you, Kärytö," said Tuvena cheerfully. "Now we *really* have to go."

She frogmarched Teltö outside, and before he knew it, they were flying down the street towards a cab.

Chapter Twenty

TELTÖ'S ELBOWS WERE on the table and his head in his hands. A glass or four of ice-cold water had sobered him up, but queasiness still gripped his gut.

"Father Life, how do we get in?"

Tuvena paced the parlour floor; she hadn't even complained when Teltö turned the light on.

"I'm thinking, Phuul. I've been to the drop-chamber during initiation. The way up is well-guarded. We'd be spotted and dealt with faster than a Mnoma in Skeevereet."

"Can we steal gas masks and cloaks, and trick our way through?"

She shook her head. "There's multiple gates with special passwords. Besides, no masks up there: only the pool area."

"Any windows or shafts?"

"There's a balcony, but it's a good decifurlong above the cobblestones, and the drop is sheer. I'm sorry, Teltö. I'd give you an outside shot of busting him out of the cells, but now he's been moved upstairs? I've cudgelled my brains, but I can't see a bloody sausage of a chance."

Teltö gulped down more water. "We're stuck then."

"Seems so."

"I've failed. In a few hours Dyrstin will be dissolving like thousands of others, and there's not a thing I can do." *When I catch Oilio, he'll think the Death Pool a bloody mercy.*

"Mother Death will take care of him. Think of all the good times you had together."

"I never told him, I never told him… never mind."

Teltö slumped, upending an empty bottle. *Think of good times.* The mutual Asrak fondness, the weakness for spider wars… who was left for Teltö to beat now?

Spider wars. He jerked up.

"Tuvena, do you have any Red Widows?"

The woman frowned. "Three. I won them off your sister in a bet. If you're after a game though, you're out of luck. I'm not in the mood, and frankly I'm not sure another defeat would help you."

Teltö grinned. "I'm not talking about games."

•　•　•

ARMS FOLDED, AND sporting a strained expression in the lantern light, Tuvena sent the massive arachnids scuttling up the cliff face. Red Widows had always made Teltö nervous. Their wine-red abdomen, their size, their diet of wetas and small birds…

But the species was strong. Tuvena had tied rope to their bodies with string.

"It's working!"

"Shut it, Teltö. I need to concentrate."

The spiders vanished into the overhead darkness, and millifurlong by millifurlong, the rope coil beside Teltö's feet grew smaller. Holding a lantern, he kept a lookout for trouble, but the alley was deserted, save for a rubbish bin he'd accidentally kicked over.

"Right," said Tuvena. "Almost there, I think. Now, you little bastards, tie a knot like you've never tied one before."

Teltö had no idea how she made calculations like that blind. *That's why she's a minister and I'm not.* The minutes ticked onwards. He fidgeted with his hair. The idea had sounded fool-proof back at Keer's, but here in the cramped and smelly darkness, faced with the monstrous wall, it seemed suicidal. Suppose he fell? Then it'd all be for nothing, and Dyrstin would never know how close rescue had been. Teltö drew a deep breath. *I must not fall.*

Tuvena tugged the rope. The knot held. "Do you want to go up first? I haven't done this sort of thing in years."

"Stealing prisoners out from under the noses of your former bosses?"

"Mucking around with ropes and cliffs."

"You've done more than me. But I'll go first."

"Don't expect me to catch you."

• • •

THANK FATHER LIFE he'd had the forethought to borrow gloves from Keer's. The Unut-leather made his palms sweat, but he'd never make it up barehanded.

Teltö edged up the wall at a snail's pace. He imagined some authority swooping through the alley, and swatting him like a fly. *Like I did to the young Mustanakonian.* But he heard no outcry, and soon Teltö breathed easier. Better still, the cliff proved full of bumps and recesses, enabling a foothold. An outcrop of stone took shape above, silhouetted against light from a window or door. Teltö climbed faster. *I'm nearly there.*

He looked over his shoulder, ready to wave at Tuvena. *Oh shit.* He saw neither her nor the lantern, nor even the streetlights. An abyss opened beneath his feet, and it called to him with the strange and horrible music of the crevice. If he let go of the rope, it'd have him. He'd fall for eternity. *Don't look down,* screamed his self-preservation instinct. *Let go,* whispered the other, *see what will happen.*

Teltö shut his eyes. Terror immobilised him, as he hung between the darkness above and the darkness below. Then he remembered Sufael mouldering in the ground. He thought of Welleorm, who'd saved his life. He owed a duty, and Saari Ooks had something to say about that.

"I'm coming, Dyrstin." He put one foot in front of the other. "I'm coming."

He repeated the mantra over and over, until finally he collapsed over a balcony railing. When he dared breathe, he realised music floated in the air. It came from inside.

•　•　•

SOMEONE SHOOK HIM. "Teltö, are you alive?"

He opened his eyes. Tuvena's bespectacled face swam into view.

"I'm fine."

He grabbed a railing and hauled himself upright. They were on the exterior balcony. A frosted glass door led to the drop chamber; yellow light shone within.

"You look like a bloody lich. What happened?"

"There's something there, Tuvena. Something that doesn't belong. Listen."

Tuvena frowned. "Music, yes. A bit strange. But we'll find out when we go in. I'm more worried about guards."

Can't you hear? But the music had changed. It no longer

called to him, no longer urged him towards destruction. *This is different.* A rustic imitation. *Like Meerm compared with Vyrellävek.*

Tuvena tried the door handle. "We'll have to break the glass. So much for silent entry."

"Did you bring anything we can use?"

"Your head?"

Teltö pulled off his gloves and stuffed them into his pocket. His fingers brushed against metal. He'd forgotten about the revolver.

"There's this." He pulled out the weapon. *We've come too far to turn back now.*

"Perfect." Tuvena grabbed it from him. "Keep back."

She cocked it and fired.

• • •

TELTÖ AND TUVENA ducked through the shattered door, crunching glass shards beneath their boots. They followed a corridor into a chamber some ten centifurlongs across. Hewn and smoothed long ago from Kuolinako's native granite, time had not been kind to the stonework; a crack ran through the floor, and the amber lamps illuminated every small crevice. Teltö paid it scant attention. He saw only the iron cage.

Dyrstin squatted within, clad in shit-stained shirt and trousers. The Inquisition had bound his wrists, but he wore no gas-mask, and beneath his matted hair, blood and sores covered his face. A hollow socket gaped forlornly. *They've taken his eye.* A chain ran from the top of the cage to an overhead wheel; twin levers jutted from the centre of the floor.

The music died.

"We have visitors."

Teltö turned. A throne stood against the left wall, fashioned from Myrstä Island obsidian and polished to a gleam. There lolled Yyrtön, Acting Chancellor of the Empire, in shirtsleeves and ill-fitting waistcoat. The man clutched a set of silver pipes in his pudgy fingers.

"I recall meeting you before," said Yyrtön. His eyes glistened with curiosity, green like a cat's. "You're that Qivunakonian nincompoop from the Council meeting. Hova's little Unut calf, unless I am mistaken, though it looks like you've joined the Army. I don't know your friend though…"

Teltö looked for guards, but saw none. On the far wall, the chamber door stood shut and bolted.

"Yes, Phuul, we are alone." Yyrtön smiled. "A quarter-millifurlong of oak and iron wards off the outside world. Thus I enjoy peace and quiet, away from those dead drudges who rule us. I'm now seeing why Vyrellävek went mad. Twenty-five years would send anyone dotty. Serves him right, of course."

"Release Venomavat, or you'll be dead as the Dragon," snapped Teltö. *Now let's see who can be rude, fat bastard.*

The Kuolinakonian boomed with laughter. "So that's why you're here. Well, if you'll let me speak, and if your charming companion will stop pointing her gun at my heart, you may take your friend. I will be delighted to hand him over."

Tuvena lowered the Iilno X. Teltö wondered if he'd blundered into some deadly trick.

"What's your game?"

"Mind your manners, Phuul. You Qivunakonians are all the same; I remember Master Reltvo blowing his nose on a tablecloth one year. But yes, your presence pleasantly surprises me."

"My presence?"

"Your daring rescue. No doubt you thought to overwhelm the tyrant, yours truly being the stand-in for that role. But, you see, I haven't the slightest interest in seeing this Venomavat fellow die. Nor, I suspect, does Vöder. Too many people do things because they think they have to, because some old duffer once said something. Duties must be carried out lest our last world crumble. Well, it's time our world did crumble. Crumbling is natural. This, Phuul, is where you come in."

Yyrtön grinned. Teltö edged back. *He's looking at me like I'm a cinnamon pastry.*

"You've disobeyed the system, the creaking, vile system. You've pointed a gun at the Grand Chancellor. You've thought for yourself without cowering and mouthing platitudes. In short, you are the man I have waited for throughout the long winter of Vyrellävek. Silly murderous old Unut, that one. Believed cleaning out the rust would rejuvenate us, not realising the Empire is nothing *but* rust. Only his determination kept us going, and when you think you alone can save the world, you become fanatical. Rumi's just as bad, wherever he is. He advocates radical reform. Yet our society is based off clear foundations. Remove those, and you lose what you're trying to save. Silly man wants to cook ice."

"Then what do you want?" Teltö asked.

Yyrtön raised an eyebrow. "I? I want the Empire gone, wiped clean away, as should have happened long ago. We must deanimate this monstrous rotting lich so our people can breathe free air again."

He held up the pipes. "I have a fondness for music, so I play the nearest humans can come to imitating the

Celestial Song, the melody of creation and destruction. A perfect rendition would destroy the world, but I merely wish for the destruction of our ancient prison. A farewell tune for Vöder's victims; it spites an Empire that can neither create nor destroy, only stagnate."

Teltö's head hurt. *He can tell us this with impunity because no one would believe us.* "But you wanted war to reclaim Skeevereet and the Lost Lands."

"Did I?" Yyrtön rose to his feet, leaving the pipes balanced on the throne's armrest. "I wore many a mask under Vyrellävek, and I was not alone. Better to be thought a fool than a threat. But in this case, yes, I desired war with the North. The flame of the battlefield may cleanse the decadence of our nation, and while excesses must always be deplored, suffering renders us better people."

Like a bucket of ice water in the face, the Acting Chancellor's final assertion broke the spell.

"Then you've Unut-shit for brains," Teltö shouted. "I've seen the flame of the battlefield first-hand. It damn near cooked me alive. There's nothing clean about war. It's blood, and filth, and nightmares, no matter what side you're on. Hova wanted revolution too, but he'd never stoop to thinking war was the way to do it!"

"Then you didn't know Hova. Yes, I knew his little secret, and your old master was bright enough to appreciate necessary sacrifices. Why run guns to people if you don't expect them to be used? Besides, war is the quickest way to send the Empire to its long overdue meeting with Mother Death, and that alone is enough to recommend it."

"Hurry up," Tuvena snapped. "We've come for Venomavat, not bloody philosophy."

Yyrtön shrugged. "Too much haste, too little thought. But since my wisdom is not required, here you go." He waddled over to the cage, patting his waistcoat pockets as if hunting for one last stick of liquorice.

"I'm sure I've got it somewhere."

Teltö frowned. "Got what?"

"Patience." Yyrtön smiled. He slid a shiny key from his pocket, and inserted it into the lock.

He swung the cage open, and dragged Dyrstin out by the shoulders. "You'll be pleased to know I put a stop to Vyrellävek's public executions. Never liked them – feeds an unhealthy mob mentality, and makes the onlooker the oppressor. Söstä was a most ethusiastic ally on the Council there. No more wasting masks on prisoners and spectators." He shoved Venomavat in Teltö's direction.

Dyrstin's shirt hung open, ragged and stripped of buttons. He stumbled into Teltö's arms. Mottled with bruises, the poor bastard looked positively skeletal, and smelt of vomit and urine. Blisters covered his bare feet.

Teltö clenched his teeth, and resisted staring at the eye wound. "What did you do to him?"

Yyrtön snorted. "Nothing. Vöder has an enthusiastic belief in duty, so look where that gets you. I believe your friend confessed to every imaginable crime while in custody. Very creative chap. Just keep him out of mischief."

Teltö pulled out a steak knife he'd nabbed from Keer's. Dyrstin flinched, but Teltö caught his arm, and cut away the ropes and gag. Venomavat slumped sobbing to the ground.

"Yes," said Yyrtön. He stretched out his hand, and let the key fall. It thunked against the granite floor, bounced twice, and lay still at his feet. "Blame Saari Ooks and his ilk. They provided inspiration. Blame that snivelling Housemaster. He set you on the path. Blame Vöder and those up-jumped…"

"Shut it," said Tuvena. "I won't shoot you. There's a better way." Lunging forward, she pushed the fat man into the cage. Yyrtön toppled backwards onto his arse.

"What are you doing?" His chins shook in disbelief.

Tuvena swooped on the key. Before Teltö could move, she'd inserted it into the lock, and twisted. "What better way to dissolve corrupt authority than literal dissolution?" She wound a clockwork mechanism at the cage's base. "You should be proud. Goodbye, you treacherous, warmongering, monologuing bastard."

Tuvena wrapped her hand around a lever. Gritting her teeth, she eased it back. A trap door opened. Dull crashing sounded from the outside the chamber. *The guards.* Teltö looked up. *They're coming.* The bolts rattled, but held. Tuvena pushed the second lever. The wheel began to spin, the chain grew taught, and the cage rose into the air.

"Let me out," Yyrtön bellowed. He pawed vainly at the mechanism through the bars. "I have a wife and children."

Tuvena pulled a dog-eared book from her hip pocket, blue with faded silver lettering.

"In accordance with my oath," said Tuvena, grinning maniacally, "I acknowledge your confession of treason against His Imperial Highness Gykäkkä IV. The penalty is death. Sorry, Acting Chancellor, but once an Inquisitor, always an Inquisitor. Bye bye." She waved at her prisoner, then pushed the lever to the floor.

Gunshots came from outside.

"Stop her, Phuul!" Yyrtön urged, as the trap door

swallowed the cage. "I have so much to live for, so much to do!"

Then he was gone. Teltö crawled to the brink and looked down. The cage sunk swiftly towards the Death Pool, jerking from side to side like a mad pendulum. Yyrtön's screams grew ever more shrill.

Behind them, the chamber door was giving way. A final scream from the Acting Chancellor – it sounded like nothing human – rang out just as the bolts snapped and the door broke off its hinges. Armed liches burst into the room. The leading one pointed its gun at Tuvena…

Splash.

As one, the liches froze. Far below, the cage sunk slowly into the deadly lake. Tuvena had given it too much chain.

Teltö shook his head. "You killed him."

Tuvena shrugged. "Perceptive, Phuul."

"But why? He may have been mad, but he'd have let us go."

"Duties must be carried out lest our last world crumble, and the thing about crumbling worlds," Tuvena put her book back in her pocket, "is they're hard to put back together. Are you all right, Dyrstin?"

Venomavat had curled into a ball, arms wrapped around his legs. He whimpered incomprehensibly.

Tuvena smiled. "In that case, let's get out of here before someone catches us."

Teltö stared at the corridor of broken glass, then at Dyrstin's bare and blistered feet. "We'll need to carry him."

* * *

DESCENT WAS EASIER. Teltö went first, the rope tied

around his waist and looped around the railing.

"Bugger," he said. Tuvena joined him. "What will we do about the rope? Between that, the glass, and the door, it'll be a dead giveaway how we got up there."

Tuvena glanced at Dyrstin. Venomavat had reacted badly to being winched down like a sack of potatoes, and huddled against the alley rubbish bin, biting his nails.

"Way ahead of you, Phuul."

The rope collapsed, and thudded to the ground by their feet.

Tuvena smiled. "I got our ever-helpful guards to undo it for us. I wouldn't worry about them telling anyone either. They'll have finished sweeping up the glass, and be jumping through the trap door about now…"

Dissolving the evidence. Yes, very smart. But can you look a little less smug? "Let's get back to Keer's. Once there, we can dose Dyrstin with your sleeping pills."

"Sleeping pills? What are you talking about? You know me – I've always slept like a log."

Teltö frowned. "Never mind. Let's take a cab."

"A cab for three?"

Teltö pulled the coins from his pocket, and counted. "I have enough."

Tuvena picked up the lantern. "Where did you steal it?"

"I didn't steal it!"

"No need to squeak like a bloody Mnoma. Anyone would think I'd accused you of murder."

Not that murder means anything to you.

· · ·

DYRSTIN PUT THE empty soup bowl on the bedside table. He burped.

"I can't believe I'm not dreaming." He pulled the quilted blankets about him. "Or woken from a horrible nightmare."

Teltö leant back in his chair and disguised a yawn. One of Keer's smaller guestrooms, this chamber had survived the looting, and seemed as good a place as any to nurse Venomavat back to health. The poor bastard could now talk coherently without screaming. But the gaunt and bruised body beneath the sheets still had a long way to go; his ribs stuck out like a toast-rack. *We're down to fishbone broth, too. Living on less than official rations: who'd have thought it?*

"My mind blanks the pain," said Dyrstin. "They managed so much with so little. By the end I was screaming when they hadn't even touched me. I told them everything I knew, and everything I didn't…"

"Stop dwelling on it. Revisiting horrors never helped anyone." *Why can't I take my own advice?* "We'll get you to Qivunako as soon as you're able to travel."

Teltö rubbed his eyes. His bloodshot, baggy eyes; he'd barely managed any sleep since the rescue. At first he'd hung around the bedside because he worried Venomavat might turn suicidal, but now Teltö enjoyed the company for its own sake.

His friend reclined among the pillows, and rested his hands on his narrow porcelain chest. "So you fought in the war?"

"I did. Not something I want to remember, but wants don't come into it."

"What happened to your gear?"

"I snuck into that smelter on the next level, and dropped it into a pot of molten aluminium. No more wars for me." Teltö straightened his cravat. "I prefer civilian clothes, even if they are looted from Keer's cupboards."

Dyrstin smiled. "We found out why you'd been sent North. The real reason, I mean."

Teltö was cut-off mid-yawn. "The Dragon tried to kill me."

"Yes, because you'd stumbled across his last and greatest atrocity. Vyrellävek was behind the Theatre bombing."

Teltö got up and closed the door. Not a mouse stirred in the corridor outside. "That's impossible," he hissed. "He'd have killed Vöder."

"Rather the point. Our draconic friend got it into his head that Vöder was plotting to seize power with Guild support. Maybe he thought Hova was in on it too, what with your master having other interests. A shame Vyrellävek only went after one at a time."

Teltö shook his head. "The Dragon didn't poison Hova. I mean, he probably had Hova marked, but I think he planned to smoke out other collaborators before arresting him. As it was, one of Hova's Northern friends suspected betrayal, and acted independently…"

"Really?" Dyrstin tried to rise from the pillow, only to fall back with gritted teeth. "I never heard that. If Vyrellävek already suspected the Tower of disloyalty, he must have had a heart attack when Hova turned up dead. Imagine how it must've looked: Vöder offing Grand Masters behind his back and ruining his pretty little show trial."

"But Vöder wasn't. And she doesn't strike me as imaginative enough to try."

Dyrstin chuckled. Another flinch of pain. "We're not concerned with the real Vöder. It's the Vöder in Vyrellävek's mind that matters. Paranoia is a wonderful thing."

It's not paranoia if people are out to get you. But you're second-guessing superiors. You must be getting better. "Back to the Theatre. When did this information come out?"

"Officially, it hasn't. Much easier to blame the North. Unofficially… an ashen-faced Vöder revealed it to the Council the day after the assassination news filtered in. You see, the shadow-stalkers caught the original perpetrators, and while they couldn't pin it on the Dragon directly, they implicated certain staff members. The Dragon had half the bloody Theatre in his pocket. Those staff members then implicated other staff members, and so on up the chain until every last bigwig from the Chancellor's Office was subjected to questioning…"

"And the Council? How did they take the news?"

"You should've seen the look on those old dears' faces, especially when Meerm of all people pointed out it was too late. Vyrellävek had become a martyr. The canny old bastard timed his death to perfection."

"But who would the Dragon blame for the bombing?"

"Anyone, and he certainly backed himself to navigate the firestorm. Vyrellävek never lacked for ego. But he couldn't accuse the North directly, not without war, and I'll say this for the Dragon: he was sincere about peace. I think he intended to blame domestic insurrection at home, then privately present Oym with stitched-up evidence for Northern involvement, to wheedle extra favours. He wiped the war reparations?"

"Yes," said Teltö. "Oym announced it at the Banquet, just before the massacre."

Dyrstin nodded. "So that bit worked. Vyrellävek just had to purge you to cover his other failure, and do it without the Inquisition knowing. But then a real Northern plot did him in."

"Nothing to do with the Principality."

"Really? You are full of surprises today, Teltö."

"The surprises chase me, I think." Teltö blinked, struggling to stay awake. "The knowledge killed Keer, didn't it?"

Dyrstin turned his head, and looked Teltö straight in the eye; the empty socket was unnerving. "What makes you say that?"

"Coincidence. Keer may have been old, but he was friends with the Dragon. Perhaps he died of grief, perhaps he realised what sort of monster he'd created. Conscience is a terrible thing for a Grand Master. Imagine realising your loyal service has been for nothing, and yet you can tell no one, just sit in your chair and stew. Perhaps he even sought help to end the pain, found a trusted assistant with a bottle of sleeping pills or something…"

"Out," said Dyrstin quietly.

Teltö took the soup bowl away without a word.

•   •   •

THE DEPARTMENT OF Energy had cut off the gas; its inevitability didn't make it any less annoying. Tuvena had vanished into the city for supplies, taking the kitchen lantern and the last of the money, so Teltö blundered around until he found a light of his own. He rummaged up a dirty oil-lamp and ate breakfast in its shuddering ambiance. But he'd needed more.

"Found some candles," he declared, checking a recess in the parlour. He pulled out a box containing a dozen. At the table, Dyrstin sat prodding his plate; he'd barely touched his dripping on toast. *I don't blame him. That toast is practically green.*

Teltö lit a candle and put it in an empty marmalade

jar. "These smell horrible. It's like something out of Great-granny's stories. If I didn't know better…"

"They're human fat, yes," said Dyrstin. Shadow shrouded his hollow socket, but that was all to the good. "Cheap, nasty, and Oilio's way of cutting costs. I bet the bastard was pocketing the difference. If only I'd taken a closer look at the accounts…"

"You have too many legs," says the centipede to the weta. Teltö bit his tongue. Just then, a door slammed, and a lantern-lit Tuvena entered, arms wrapped around a paper bag. Her smirk stretched from ear to ear.

"I bring presents and news," she said. "Yes, the bread's stolen, but I didn't have much choice, even with food prices dropping. Besides, the bitch had two loaves." She fished into the bag and dropped a newspaper and some fabric onto the table. "What's that smell?"

"Corpse candles," said Dyrstin. He poked the fabric. "What's this?"

"An eye-patch, Venomavat. Please wear it; I don't want to look at your face any longer than necessary. But see here," she unfolded a *Doomsday Post,* "Acting Chancellor Suphives Söstä and newest Grand Council member Eriva Völder blame Yyrtön's death on Rumi and the North."

Teltö read the headline. "Doesn't stop them chasing us privately."

Tuvena put the bag down. "Phuul, they'd only ever chase us publicly. Söstä and Völder owe their positions to our killing Yyrtön. With ready-made scapegoats, who cares?"

You killed Yyrtön, not me. "Völder will. It's her bloody job, remember."

"Bah. She's got a million things to worry about —

stopping food riots for a start – and the sweet stench of the Council will do its work. Power not only corrupts, it distracts. But time for my real announcement."

"Get on with it," growled Dyrstin. He donned the patch.

Tuvena's eyes glittered. "Whilst queuing for a new ration book, I bumped into my old superior Master Pale. A certain Kärytö Revenuta has been demoted for conduct unbecoming, so the Master offered me my position back."

She spread her arms, perhaps expecting applause.

"You'll excuse me if I don't jump with glee," said Dyrstin. "I can't jump at all."

"You're returning to an organisation of torturers?" said Teltö.

"Teltö, it's a bloody job. Job means money, and money means food. Yyrtön messed up the rationing, probably deliberately, and eating liches and rats is not an option. Plus the Imperial Inquisition is not about pointless cruelty…"

"Could have fooled me." Dyrstin scratched under his patch.

"Shut it, Venomavat. It's about a quest for higher truth."

Teltö shook his head. "A truth you decide, before sticking pins and pokers in someone until they sing the song you want. A truth born in the Council Chambers is no truth at all."

"You're missing the point," snapped Tuvena. "Facts are malleable, but truth is not. Truth is that which serves order. Yyrtön was wrong. The Viiminian Empire is more than the tottering monstrosity we all know and despise. It's also more than one person, Vyrellävek or Vöder, or the dusty bones of Gykäkkä. The Empire is us. Every man, woman, and child living from the Wall to the Fells, and their well-being is our only possible goal.

How would Yyrtön change things? With war, conquest, and famine. Even if the Northerners swept into Kuolinako without casualties, it'd mean their triple tyranny of Church, Army, and hereditary aristocracy, a world where balls and blood outrank brains. More books – more first edition Oosemans – would burn in an hour than the Inquisition has burnt in a thousand years. We cannot let eighty centuries crumble into dust, taking our people with it. That's the truth, Teltö. Chancellors come and go, but the Tower is the spine of the Empire. We are the last bastion against anarchy."

Dyrstin pulled up his patch. "How does this serve your precious truth, Tuvena?"

"I rescued you, didn't I? Also, have either of you railed against the Tower before?"

"Of course we have," snapped Teltö. "We just weren't in a position to do anything about it. Unlike yourself."

"So a pair of Native Assistants, with the ear of Grand Masters, and access to paperwork I never enjoyed, were helpless as kittens. Unut shit, Teltö. You and Dyrstin never cared about anything more than food and fucking. Disappearance was something that happened to other people, and who cared about them, so long as you had a full belly and a warm bed?"

Tuvena's recovered her poise. "Now that's unfair."

"It's perfectly fair. What makes you, or the people you love, any more special or worthy than those faceless thousands? Our entire society is based off the Death Draft. Ceremonial murder that's only legitimate because it keeps the Empire running. Every lich once had a Mam."

"That's different," said Teltö. "Necromancy is

natural, and…"

"And what? Ever stood on a street corner? Ever had an Ordinary walk past you, their eyes burning with bottomless hatred?"

"More than you'd know." Teltö's mouth twisted. "But nothing runs without the Death Draft, and it tries to be fair and painless. There's nothing natural, fair, or painless about tyranny."

"Necromancy and autocracy go together like potatoes and butter. Without tyranny, you'd have anarchy, and we all know about the age before the Toast, or even before Vyrellävek, back when Kuolinako changed its Chancellors like you change your socks. Again, you only care when your little circle suffers. You give no thought to the big picture."

Teltö shrugged. "The big picture is made of lots of little pictures, and love and affection are things of little pictures. You have to start somewhere. But tell me, since torturing Dyrstin somehow maintains the well-being of everyone in Kuolinako, why did you rescue him? He'd confessed, and was to be duly executed. Isn't that an affront to order? If not, why not free everyone from the Tower's dungeons?"

"You can build a house with a single brick missing. Try building a house with no bricks. Winter in a cave isn't pretty."

Teltö sat back. "Living in a cave is preferable to dying for a house."

Dyrstin slammed his fist down. The lantern and plates rattled. "Spare me your bloody metaphors and your bloody pity," he shouted. "Neither of you have any idea what you're talking about, and all I want is to leave Kuolinako on the next boat. I'm done with this crypt forever."

"You do sound better, Venomavat," said Tuvena. "But, alas, you'll have to scrounge up your own money for a ticket. My funds are going on food."

"How can I scrounge up money?" snapped Dyrstin. "I'm officially dead, remember? My aunt can fiddle the paperwork when I get back to Qivunako, but I need to get there first."

"I'll think of something," said Teltö. He drummed his fingers on the table. *How to get money in a hurry.* His eyes were drawn to the family of bottles on the nearby shelf. A broad grin spread across his face.

Chapter Twenty-One

"THE NEXT SHIP for Qivunako leaves in three and three-quarter hours," said the corpse. "There are spaces available in Fourth Class."

"Good," said Teltö, piling coinage in front of the counter window. He'd raised just enough money after flogging off the Asrak stockpile, together with a couple of Keer's unlooted knick-knacks. The clink of silver on copper was music to his ears. "Make it a one way."

He stroked the precious ticket with his thumb, and wandered out of the office, back to the gravel shore. The interior port bustled with refugees; children and Mnomo played hide and seek in the bushes, while adults huddled around looking fearful. Not Teltö though. This was the final leg of his long journey, and he yearned to be gone.

"Have a safe trip." Tuvena shaded her eyes, and stared about. "I'd forgotten how bright it gets up here."

"It's even brighter under the open sky. I can't entice you back to Qivunako?"

She shook her head. "Kuolinako's home now, and getting my position back means no more living on broth and dripping. Besides, Söstä's fixing Yyrtön's damage, and Meerm's muzzled."

"Anti-corruption campaigns are one thing. Going after the black market is quite another."

Tuvena smiled. "Yes, you sold that Asrak at an interesting time, didn't you? Anyway, here's a present." She pulled a newspaper from her handbag. "Yesterday's *Post*. I thought you might enjoy it."

Teltö grinned. "Nice."

Tuvena checked her pocket watch. "Oh bugger. I've a meeting in an hour. Farewell, Phuul. Don't do anything stupid, and when the war ends, I'll be sure to visit."

They shook hands. As she hurried away, Teltö realised he'd never told her about Sufael.

He sat on a bench and unfolded the paper. Some former Native Assistant had written a column urging all true patriots to avenge the tragic death of their late leader.

"Which?" Teltö muttered. He checked for signs of Inquisitorial vengeance. "The mad one who tried to kill me, or the even madder one who didn't?"

• • •

BESIDE THE GANGPLANK, a lich with a clipboard inspected luggage. Two more brought up the items, while those in the queue waited and waited. They'd be here some time; the line wound back around the rose beds. Teltö took his place. In front, a woman whined about her wife's backache and suspected infidelities, but Teltö ignored her. *Please let this work.*

After an hour came his turn. He peered over the shoulder of the clipboard corpse, his instincts readying him to run. The liches opened the travelling chest. Teltö held his breath. *Oh shit.* Dyrstin's kneecaps poked through the concealing coats, and the upper half of his face was uncovered from nose to forehead. Venomavat's solitary eye was wide with terror.

But there was no alert. The inspector replaced the lid, and ticked boxes on a form.

"No Asrak," it said. "No unregistered corpses or wanted Draftees. No unauthorised weapons or foodstuffs. You may board."

*   *   *

DYRSTIN WINCED AT what Teltö guessed were pins and needles, and collapsed onto the bunk.

"Don't do that again," he said. "For a while, I was back under the bloody Tower. The mind games, the waiting, it's worse than the actual knives. And I'm sure I told you to make the air holes bigger."

"If you have a better idea for smuggling someone aboard," said Teltö, "I'm all ears. One ticket, two people, remember?"

The Fourth Class cabin resembled a closet, with two sets of bunks jammed against the narrow walls. Clearly, someone sought profit from war-refugees. The beds themselves were small, and Dyrstin's feet dangled over the edge.

"Someone must've buggered up their supervisory instructions. The inspector saw me, but didn't do anything!"

"I read the wartime regulations." In truth, Teltö had skimmed the index, and hoped fate smiled on loophole seekers. "You're not a Draftee, and otherwise there's nothing about smuggling out *living* people."

Dyrstin laughed. "Father Life, bless literal liches. Where's the Asrak? We need a celebration."

"I sold it."

"Oh, right."

* * *

"PHEW," SAID THE big bearded man. "Good to get out of there." He dumped a satchel in the doorway. "Mind that, will you? I've more to come."

Our new travelling companion. Wordlessly, Teltö moved the satchel to the corner.

Moments later the fellow returned, wobbling under twin suitcases. His belly wobbled with them. "These too. Be especially careful with that one: there's precious stuff inside."

Teltö shrugged, and unceremoniously shoved the suitcases under the beds. A crushed spider lay smeared against the floorboards.

Another couple of suitcases arrived. Teltö relocated the satchel, and dumped them into the corner.

"Excuse me," he said. "But..."

"Sorry. More coming."

Another suitcase materialised; Teltö left it in the walkway. Then another appeared, and another. Within fifteen minutes, the cabin had suitcases stacked to the ceiling. The man climbed onto an unclaimed bunk and began unpacking books.

Teltö scratched his head. He knew he should put his foot down, but something held him back. "You would be..."

"Nieliini Giinovo, businessman and Ordinary. My card."

The Necromancer studied the pallid face. The man's beard hung white and wiry to his chest. *Nothing like the other Nieliini. I wouldn't sleep with this one even if I could reach the bloody bed.*

"I'm Teltö Phuul," he said. No need to specify rank; Keer's wardrobes had the right ribbons. "There's Dyrstin too, but he's at the toilet."

"So the three of us, then?" The Ordinary clapped his hands. "This ought to be cosy."

Teltö glanced at the door. "Not if I can help it."
"Pardon?"

Teltö smiled sweetly. "Sorry, just talking to myself."

That night, he broke out the spiders Tuvena had gifted him. Not for a game: Venomavat had gone to bed early, probably for fear he'd never reach his bunk again, and gentle snores rose from his blankets. No, Teltö wanted to see Giinovo's reaction to Red Widow-on-face. *After all we've been through, we deserve better than boating home in a glorified storeroom.* He considered the adult female in the arachnid collection. A body the size of two side-by-side matchboxes, a leg span the size of his hand, and terrifying hairy fangs? *If this doesn't scare the Unut calf away, nothing will.*

Giinovo woke just before dawn. Afterwards, when the cabin population had dropped back to two, and the clunk of fleeing suitcases had died, Teltö lay awake with a victorious smirk on his face. Giinovo's screaming had bordered on the symphonic. *Definitely an overreaction. Red Widows aren't even poisonous.* Teltö chuckled himself to sleep. Dyrstin snored through the entire thing.

* * *

GIINOVO HAD LEFT his wallet behind. Teltö upturned it; silver and copper coins rattled onto the floor. *A monetary melody.*

"Look, Dyrstin! The silly Unut left us a present. There's marks enough here for a black market binge when we get home, Söstä or no Söstä!"

A groan emanated from beneath the blankets. A head poked up, matted blond hair falling to bare shoulders. Dyrstin yawned and blinked. *Or winked. No difference now.* Either way, Teltö was grateful Venomavat slept with his eye-patch.

"Teltö, I need rest. Bugger off."

"I like sleep too, but we've got money."

"Excellent."

"Also, it's mealtime."

"Let me starve if only you let me sleep."

Teltö shrugged. "I've already missed breakfast. I'm not missing lunch too."

Teltö returned with two bowls of pea soup. He savoured the lukewarm, forgettable food slowly, musing on how fortune had swung in his favour. *I've rescued Venomavat from the Death Pool and crossed a continent. Now I'm going home with marks in my pocket.* It almost made up for the blood on his hands. Perhaps. He wished he had Tuvena's self-confidence in such matters.

• • •

THE MÄÄ WASTES drifted by. Teltö rarely left the cabin, save for meals, and spent successive afternoons on his bunk, retelling his Northern adventures. Dyrstin stretched out opposite, hands behind his head. Occasionally, Venomavat interjected comments and questions. Mostly good natured, some made Teltö squirm.

But the other Necromancer's face was losing its haggard look, and his clothes no longer hung off his body like scarecrow rags. He smiled more too, and as the days passed, his questions grew less concerned with war, and shifted towards Northern women and their habits. Sufael fascinated him.

"So she and her Dad were working for each other's worst enemies, and neither suspected?" he said one afternoon, when they'd tired of the cabin.

"Sufael wasn't stupid." *More than can be said for most of your women.* "She just couldn't admit what her Dad really was. She loved him, mad bastard or not. That's the thing about love: it's private and selfish and tells the rest of the world to go hang."

"Sufael's selfish emotion saved your hide."

Teltö shrugged. "You put someone else before yourself, but you also put that someone above everyone else. No one ever said love makes sense."

Dyrstin scratched under his eye-patch. "Here was me wondering about you getting Tuvena to rescue me."

"You know Tuvena." Teltö allowed himself the flicker of a smile. "She likes telling the world to go hang, especially if she *is* the hangman."

He leant against the railing. The Mää Wastes had finally vanished; the Nhagivat wormed through rocky foothills full of gorse and tussock. Soon, Teltö knew, they would come to the fertile areas north of Qivunako. He could almost smell home.

"I still can't believe you threw Ventiko into the Illuvian. What a priceless image."

Teltö's smile broadened. "You should've seen his face. His bald head bobbed around in the waves like a cork. Hold on… what's that?" He pointed at the northern horizon.

Dyrstin squinted. "No idea. My eyesight's still buggered. A cloud perhaps?"

Teltö stared. "That's no cloud. That's an airship." *What are they doing this far south?*

· · ·

THE SHIP STOPPED at a river village to collect supplies and drop off passengers. For those in Fourth Class, this meant fewer smelly bodies in the hold and a switch from pea soup to pickled cabbage. Teltö decided he and Dyrstin had earned an afternoon off, so with Giinovo's coins jingling in his pocket, he strolled down the gangplank in search of a pub. Dyrstin followed, munching an apple he'd found.

They located a tavern easily enough. Sporting a fresh paint job, the exterior was mostly black, save for a side-patch, which someone had painted dark brown. Adding to the gloomy aesthetic, the pub had both curtains and shutters closed, such that no light penetrated. *We're not in Kuolinako now. The Sun's in the sky, and people need drinks.* But despite appearances, the trio of female drunks on the front step testified to its ongoing trade.

"Mind you shut the door, lads," said one. "The publican doesn't want to breach the blackout even during the daytime."

"If she had her way, no one would go in at all," said a second. "I swear, this is the scariest lookin' pub this side of the Fells."

"Ah," said the third, "but there's rhyme and reason. Old Master Whatshisface left his door open, and next morning there's a great bloody bomb crater where his house was. Prudent woman is our publican."

"Aye," said the first. "Prudent and prudish. That's why we're outside."

· · ·

LIT BY GIANT iron candelabras, the common room was

strangely muted, its conversations hushed by curtains and nervousness. *Yes, I'm close to Qivunako. No one wants to stand out.* The air smelt of vinegar and mint, with not one whiff of tobacco. Two Mnomo huddled in the corner squeaking over cards, and two karls had a spider war going at a far table. A man in a Shipper's uniform sat weeping over a newspaper. He held his bulbous bald head in his hands.

Visions of Asrak dancing in his head, Teltö headed to the bar. The publican was a brown-haired woman, somewhere in her thirties. Her thin eyebrows contorted disapprovingly over black-rimmed spectacles.

"Yes?"

Teltö was lost for words. *I'm after a drink, not an appendectomy.* To buy time, he pretended an interest in the bar top. The unnaturally clean bar top, without a speck of dust.

He heard the door open behind him.

"Nobody move."

There were gasps, followed by the thud of Dyrstin's apple falling to the floor. Teltö turned. *What the…*

"Everyone keep your hands where we can see 'em. And keep away from those bloody candelabras."

"Everyone keep your hands where we can see 'em," barked the publican, "and keep away from those bloody candelabras, *please.*"

· · ·

THE PUBLICAN CHEWED her lip. "Look," she said, stepping out from behind the bar. "I serve beer and pies. I don't employ liches, and I'm not a Necromancer. So if you lot would take your airship, and go back to where you came from, it'd be much appreciated. We don't want trouble."

One of the Northerners relit his clay pipe. "Good. We don't want trouble either. So keep still until the Lieutenant arrives and we'll both be happy."

"I'm not happy. This is a non-smoking establishment."

The Northerner nodded. Paunchy and moustachioed, he had a scar across one cheek. "I'll pop outside then." He patted a colleague on the shoulder. "Otho, you're in charge. If anyone moves, kill the lot of 'em."

Otho nodded. The first soldier winked at the publican, then sauntered out. The remaining half a dozen didn't seem inclined to go anywhere.

Teltö eyed the array of rifles and revolvers. *Not just Rughvneers and Lonos either.*

"Any chance I can convince the rest of you to take up smoking too?"

Otho scowled. "Shut it, corpse-buggerer. And keep those hands up!"

Teltö looked for exits. Save for the front entrance and the too-distant back door, there were none. And the bloody publican had already boarded up the windows. *Don't panic. This isn't the 113th. They won't recognise me.*

"What in blazes is this?" hissed Dyrstin in his ear. "What are these blue bastards doing here?"

"Shut it, Venomavat. I have everything under control. I just have to…"

Gunfire. Teltö flinched, though it came from outside. Then the door opened again.

Short, and pasty for a Northerner, this one had a nose pink from either Sun or drink, and wore a Lieutenant's uniform. Teltö had never seen him before. *Thank Father Life for that.*

The new arrival climbed onto a table. "We will not

harm you," he bellowed, as if volume alone were convincing. "We seek valuables, specifically those manufactured from copper. Trinkets, coins, hand them over, and we'll be on our way."

So war had only increased Skeevereet's hunger for Imperial metals. *They should have thought of that beforehand.* But Teltö held his tongue.

"Did you not hear?" shouted the Lieutenant. "Copper!" He kicked a beer glass off the table; it shattered against the trunk of a candelabra. "We must have copper!"

"He must have copper," squeaked one of the Mnomo. "Did we not hear?"

"I think we did," said the other. "He was most insistent."

The Northerner blinked. "Creatures of the Mad God." He pulled a revolver from his belt.

Teltö dived to the floor, and huddled against the barstool as shots and screams rang out. A bluebottle settled on the remains of Dyrstin's apple.

Someone kicked Teltö in the ribs.

"He shot the Mnomo, you idiot." *Dyrstin. He's talking to me.* "Get up! Get up!"

"What's this?" shouted the Lieutenant.

Teltö looked up just as the little Northerner leapt down from the table. He clambered to his feet. "Nothing, sir. Nothing at all."

The Lieutenant shoved him up against a candelabra. Teltö felt the flame's heat, not far from the back of his head. He hadn't come this close to fire since… *Sufael.*

The Northerner scowled. "Not this sort of copper," he snapped. "Stupid bloody Imperials."

Fresh footsteps approached. Teltö dared not so much

as twist his head.

"Sir, come quickly. There's a problem with one of the propellers."

"There's a problem all right." The Lieutenant released Teltö. "It's that you were ever born."

He gestured to his men. "Take this lot to the back room. I'll deal with them later. Especially this one." He spat in Teltö's face.

A glob of spittle hung off the end of the Necromancer's nose.

• • •

THE ROOM PROVED too small to hold them all, so the Northerners relocated Teltö and Dyrstin to the cellar, together with the bald Shipper.

"You treacherous, murdering bastards," said Dyrstin. Otho shoved him down the stone steps at gunpoint. "Just who do you think you are?"

"Never you mind," said Otho. "But I see you've already lost an eye. Which makes your other one all the more precious, right? Put it like this. The more you talk, the more I come up with ideas for what to do with that other eye. And believe me, I'm *very* imaginative."

That silenced Venomavat, which pleased Teltö no end. *I've got everything under control. They don't know who I am, and they don't know I know about them. I'll get us out of this.* He looked at his sullen comrade. *So long as Dyrstin doesn't bugger things up.*

Spacious and clean, the cellar housed neatly-stacked barrels of depressingly legal alcohol. *And she calls herself a publican.* A table stood in the centre, sporting three stubby candles. There were no chairs, so Teltö and friends cowered with backs to the barrels as the Northerners bound their arms and legs. Teltö wriggled in his rope bonds, trying to blot out memories. *No. Don't go there. She's dead and you're not.*

Otho wiped his forehead with his sleeve. "Got anything to gag them with?"

"Not a sausage," said his companion. "And I'm not putting my socks in their mouths, if that's what you're thinking."

"I'm not touching your socks. Theirs neither. Never know where Imperials stick their feet." Otho kicked the Shipper's leg. "Looks like your lucky day, lads," he said. "No gag. But one peep out of you, and we'll be back to cut your tongues out. Understood?"

Teltö nodded. "Understood," he said, before Dyrstin could interject.

The soldiers disappeared up the steps, and shut the cellar door.

Teltö drew a deep breath. "It could be worse." *It has been worse.*

"How?" Dyrstin's remaining eye blinked in fury. "Those savages will kill us all!"

"Keep your bloody voice down," Teltö hissed. "They didn't shoot us on sight. That means they're not worried about liches. Which is pretty lucky, seeing as we're Necromancers, and there is a bloody war on."

Venomavat ground his teeth. "They haven't shot us yet because they want to have fun first. You just had to attract their attention, didn't you?"

"What, by ducking away from bullets? After what I've seen? Dyrstin, if I never see a gun again, I'll die happy. And if we're talking savages, it wasn't the North that took your eye." *Nor did they kill Sufael. Our savages are home grown.*

"Teltö, you saved my life in Kuolinako, but that

doesn't give you a monopoly on the truth, nor does it force me to nod like an idiot at everything you say. Those fellows? They're the enemy!"

"They're as human as we are. It doesn't matter whether you die for Vyrellävek or Yyrtön, Oym or Ventiko, Hova or Sösta: the pain is just as real, and the blood is just as red."

The Shipper laughed. "Well spoken, young man."

"Thank you," said Teltö. He'd nearly forgotten about their bald companion. "At least someone has some sense."

The Shipper nodded. "We must negotiate an armistice immediately."

"Hah." Teltö leant back against the barrel. "If only."

"I believe I'm the man to do it. Next time those fellows come down, I'll give myself up, and get to work. It's about time I stopped running. The people need me."

Teltö stared. "Negotiate a peace? You?"

Dyrstin laughed. "He's mad. Skeevereet and Kuolinako can fix their ways if only they'll listen to an old fool with even less brains than hair."

"Ventiko and Sösta won't listen to any old fool," said the Shipper. "But they might listen to once-and-future Grand Master Lolto Rumi of Tuonako."

It's him. Without the beard. Teltö's mouth hung open.

* * *

"THE FALL OF Yyrtön gave me hope," said Rumi. The man liked the sound of his own voice, but there was something soothing about the Tuonako trill. "It's about time something went my way. Too long has the Council ignored my abilities and shunned my ideas."

"A bloody good thing too." Dyrstin butted his head slowly against a barrel.

"Turning to me would've meant a new Spring for the Empire. At last we would give the people a voice, rather than terrorising them with dust, relics, and torture. But, alas, my colleagues hid her opportunism well, and we have suffered needlessly."

"Söstä claims you're aiding the North," said Teltö.

Rumi chuckled. "Lies, of course."

"Back to this plan for peace," said Teltö. "Ventiko will listen to you?"

"Naturally," said Rumi. "I am a voice of reason, and reason must always prevail: only a fool would permit further destruction of lives and property."

"I've met Ventiko. I'm not sure he's as reasonable as you think."

"Hah. I have met him too, three years ago. A more striking and decent man I have never encountered. Yet I say as much to the Grand Council, and they persecute me for it." Rumi shook his head. "This war is based on nothing more than hurt feelings and misunderstandings; with the right mediator, namely myself, we could end it in an afternoon. Ventiko will realise my offer is in the interests of Skeevereet, so one of his demands shall be my rehabilitation. Perhaps even my installation as Chancellor, though I hesitate to get ahead of myself. The key is convincing him not to claim war reparations. I will not let dragon's teeth curse the world again with dark and bitter fruit…"

The silly Unut might've been ensconced in Vyrellävek's chair, with Söstä, Ventiko, and the Fifth Northern War already dealt with. *I used to think him a dangerous radical. But he's utterly harmless. A man of ideas, with no bloody idea how to implement them. No wonder Vyrellävek kept him as opposition: the best puppets think they have minds of their own.*

Dyrstin sobbed in silence.

* * *

"RIGHT," SNAPPED THE Lieutenant. He stopped on a middle step. "I've wasted enough time. Where are your valuables?"

"In my head," said Rumi. "I'll give myself up if you'll take me to your Second Marshal."

The Lieutenant's face twisted in confusion. *Or perhaps admiration.* "You? See Rughvneer?"

Rumi frowned. "Ventiko. Why would I want to see Rughvneer?"

"Stupid bloody Imperials. They sent Ventiko to the firing squad last week for treason. Ereek Rughvneer's in charge, and we'll get our hands on Mustanako, just you wait."

Rughvneer had Ventiko shot? That must mean… Teltö kept his mouth shut. *My little lie of convenience had consequences. Still, I'd take Side-whiskers over Ball-bearing any day.*

"If it's Rughvneer, then take me to him." A touch of exasperation entered Rumi's voice. "I'm Grand Master Lolto Rumi of Tuonako. He'll want to see me."

The Lieutenant doffed his beaked cap, and ran his hand through thick curly hair. *Things are getting too big for him.*

"Very well," he said. "Come with me. Speer, look after these two in my absence. I'll be back."

Speer? Teltö barely suppressed a shout. He hadn't seen anyone he recognised, so all the Northerners blended into each other, but now he looked… yes, it was the Sergeant. He'd lost the scarf though. *This could go very badly, but if not, it's the lifeline of a lifetime.*

The Lieutenant untied Rumi's feet and marched him

up the steps. Only when the cellar door was safely shut did Teltö dare speak.

"Sergeant?" he hissed. "It's me. Lieutenant Phuul. From the 113th?"

The Northern aristocrat frowned. *He's growing a moustache, I think.* Suddenly, Speer gasped, and jumped back.

"It's you, sir. It is you."

"Yes, it's me."

"Lieutenant Phuul?" Dyrstin interjected. "What in blazes…"

"Shut it, Venomavat. Please."

Speer wrung his hands. "Sorry, sir, I've been dragged down from the airship. Repairs took forever: some god-sent gremlin got into the engines. Whatever are you doing here?"

"I'm not here because I want to be, Speer. I want to get home."

Speer nodded. "Dreadfully sorry, sir. I'll inform Lieutenant Pedeet. If I'd known you were trapped behind enemy lines, I'd have spoken up at once. Pedeet's a bit rough, low birth and all, but he'll give you a lift back to the encampment."

Teltö shook his head. *Poor, silly Speer. Thick as the day is long.*

"No, Sergeant, no."

"Pardon, sir?"

Teltö sighed. "I'm not behind enemy lines by accident. I'm an Imperial, Speer. An Imperial."

The Sergeant's eyes bulged. "But, but…"

"Worse, Speer. I'm a Necromancer, an underkarl. This garb is not a disguise."

"One mustn't lie," said Speer. "Mother always said

that lying helps the Mad God."

Teltö gritted his teeth. "This isn't a lie, Speer. I stole a Lieutenant's uniform, and pretended to be a Northerner. But believe me: I want no part in this war. All I want is home, and my home is Qivunako. And I need you to help me."

"Help a Necromancer, sir?"

"Speer, remember that night you tried to desert? When you quivered beneath the fireweed? That's me now. I need your help, like you needed mine…"

"And if you could kill that Lieutenant for us," said Dyrstin, "it'd be much appreciated."

Shut up, Dyrstin. Father Life, keep your bloody mouth shut.

Speer shook his head. "Kill Pedeet? Never. A Speer would never sink to such depths."

Pedeet materialised at the door.

"That's Rumi dealt with," he called. "Hopefully the Marshal can use him for bargaining when Kuolinako comes calling. This lot have anything?"

Please, Speer. I trusted you.

Speer looked over at Teltö. "Nothing, sir. Not a bit."

"We're getting out of here. Shoot 'em both, then meet us back at the ship."

The door swung shut. A mad smile crept across Speer's face.

Please. Teltö tried to shut his eyes. He wanted to scream. The Sergeant lifted his Lono revolver, cocked it…

And fired.

Once, twice, into the barrel in the corner. Brown froth pooled on the floor.

"See you later, sir." Speer winked. "Thank you for everything."

Teltö and Dyrstin sat for several minutes, jaws agape.

Dyrstin shook his head. "I don't know whether to hug or punch that Speer chap. The Mother Eternal will be bloody confused."

"I told you I'd everything under control. Sometimes being nice to people works, even if they were born north of the Wall."

"So what's this Lieutenant Phuul business? I don't think you were completely honest with those war stories…"

"I'll tell you later. The important thing is that we're alive, we're going home, and no one can stop us."

Dyrstin cackled dryly. "Not yet, Lieutenant Phuul."

"How so?"

Dyrstin held up his bound hands. "We're still tied up like a spaghetti accident at the Food Factory. And that beer, Ruvian Bitter unless I'm mistaken, is soaking through my trousers."

•　•　•

"SORRY, LADS," SAID the publican, sawing at the rope with a kitchen knife. "Awful business. I had to buy them off with trinkets. Thank goodness the candelabras are iron, else they'd have taken them too."

She leant back on her haunches. "There were three of you down here. What happened to that Shipper fellow? Killed?"

Teltö shook his head. "They took him away for questioning."

"Awful. He hadn't even paid for his drink yet."

It's Söstä's Empire now. Teltö smiled. "Do you need help cleaning up? It'll be hours before our boat leaves."

"Can you really?"

"Sure. And my friend will help too. Won't you,

Dyrstin?"

Dyrstin nodded, sullen as a sober sailor.

The publican patted Teltö on the shoulder. "Thank you ever so much. I mean, there's shattered glass upstairs and beer puddles down here. And the Inquisition will want a three-page report on those dead Mnomo. Awful. Utterly awful."

* * *

"FEELING ALL RIGHT, Teltö?" Dyrstin leant his mop against the cellar wall. "First you trust a bloody gun-wielding Northerner, and then you volunteer us for disposing of escaped alcohol. And not in the fun way."

Teltö drained the other mop into an iron bucket. "I think that's the last of it." He crinkled his nose. "Father Life, this place smells like a drunk's underpants, doesn't it?"

"Or my underpants. In case you haven't noticed, I have a massive wet patch on my trousers."

I've noticed all right. Looking after you needs some perks. "Sometimes volunteering pays off. You might try it some time. A bit of altruism goes a long way."

"Daring rescues from the teeth of the Inquisition is one thing. Offering help to a batty and unbeddable woman is quite another. You must be ill."

Teltö shrugged. "People change, Dyrstin. But if you must know: I was promised a little present while I was up there before. I'll even share it with you. Just stop whining. We're here to mop, not mope."

"Still there, lads? Excellent." The publican hurried down the steps. She clutched a cloth bag. "Here's your reward. Ooh, those wicks are almost done. Another half-hour and you'd have been cleaning in the dark. Poor things."

Teltö grinned. "Many, many thanks."

The publican replaced the candles. Sickly green substance drenched her apron. *Mnoman blood, unless I'm mistaken. Send it to Rhea's Research Unit after the war.*

"Keep it under your pillow, lad." The woman lowered her voice and glanced up at the cellar door. "This isn't cheap these days. Not with Söstä's hounds sniffing around."

"Still worth it," Teltö whispered. "I'll be prudent."

"Good lad. Now excuse me, I have candelabras to clean."

•   •   •

DYRSTIN PRODDED THE bag with a finger. "What is it?"

Teltö tugged the prize away. "Ah, Dyrstin. You put me in an interesting quandary. You see, the information is confidential, privy only to the Grand Council and Native Assistants."

"Hilarious, Phuul."

"It is, isn't it? How's it feel for the boot to be on the other foot?"

"Look, I'm sorry for playing with you back in Kuolinako. But that was ages ago, and people change, right? You said so yourself."

"People do change." Teltö pulled a bottle from the bag, and tapped it thoughtfully, admiring the familiar liquid therein. "But not that much."

•   •   •

WHEN THE CLOUD appeared on the horizon, Teltö Phuul was there to see it. He'd spent hours pacing the ship's deck, watching every millifurlong of the Nhagivat pass by.

Every last blade of grass, every last clump of dirt. When the wind came howling from the south-east, he'd nearly cheered.

"See that, Dyrstin?" He pointed. "See that?"

Dyrstin squinted. "Looks like a smudge to me. Insofar as I can see anything at this distance."

"It *is* a smudge. The best possible smudge. It's the smoke from the Qivunako Ironworks. We're nearly home!"

"I'm worried about you," said Dyrstin. He removed Teltö's plate with its remains of cold potato and pickled cabbage. "This obsession isn't healthy. You're missing meals."

"Don't worry about me. If happiness is unhealthy, I'd hate to be cured."

The cloud grew larger and more distinct, and next morning Teltö could even make out the chimneys, grey against the late summer sky. The smell of coal fires hung in the air, but not just any coal fires. *My soot, my home. Kuolinako can go hang.* His mind turned to thoughts of hearth and armchair.

The tussock exhausted itself as they reached the city outskirts. The Nhagivat had become the playground of water-wheels, engines, and steamboats with hungry boilers. Concrete lined the river's broad banks.

Then Teltö passed the steel processing centres, where liches fashioned rods, pistons and wheels. Drains vomited filth into the waterway. *The machinery that drives the Empire.* Teltö paused. *One type of machinery anyway.* War or no war, the government buildings loomed grey and eternal: the leaning steeple of the Lesser Council Chambers, the Undersecretariat, the Qivunako Public Art Gallery, and most joyous of all…

"Look, Dyrstin. The General Library!"

Dyrstin smiled, and shifted for a better view; Tuvena's luggage chest afforded seating for two. "And there's the Theatre. Do you think they'll reconsider me?"

Teltö patted his friend's shoulder. "After Kuolinako? When it comes to masks and pretending, you've learnt from the best."

Teltö untied the publican's bag. The Asrak remained untouched, for now.

"Giving into temptation, Teltö? You said you'd wait."

"I'm still waiting. A man can admire beauty, can't he?"

They rounded the last bend in the Nhagivat, and arrived at the riverside docks. Fluffy clouds drifted lazily across the sky.

Even on a weekend, this was the Qivunako Teltö remembered, a place of concrete, cobblestone, and grey brick. Liches carried boxes up gangplanks and unloaded crates. Shipping Necromancers chatted with Guildlings. Ordinaries waited for loved ones. *You'd have never thought that there's a war on.*

"No one here you recognise?" said Dyrstin.

"I recognise the city, not the people."

The skeletal ash tree was still there, spouting incongruously from the quayside concrete. It'd stood for long as anyone could remember, so the Lesser Council had resisted any calls for chopping it down. *The Imperial way. If it ain't broken, don't fix it; if it is broken, work around it.* A cloud of starlings swarmed in the tree's claw-like branches.

Teltö scanned the riverside. There was the distribution warehouse, a barber shop, a chemist's…

"Mind the bag." Teltö thrust the Asrak at Dyrstin. "Don't you dare drink any."

Teltö dashed across the deck. Past startled passengers, and down the gangplank, his boots thudding in a manic tattoo. A bale of Unut fur barred his way; he jumped over it in a single bound. Pigeons scrambled to safety like Grand Masters disturbed at dinner.

A lich with a clipboard hailed him. "Excuse me, sir."

He shoved the official in the chest, sending it sprawling. Teltö didn't care. There was a little girl leaning against a lamppost, directly opposite the chemist's. *It's her, isn't it? Please, let it be her.*

He'd got as far as the ash tree when the girl waved back. She ran across the quayside towards him, black pigtails flying in the breeze.

"Teltö!" she shouted. "It's you!"

She leapt into his arms. Or he leapt into hers: it was hard to tell. *Kyrmves.* He held his sister close, savouring the long-forgotten smell of her hair. *It's been too long.*

"I told Mam and Dad you'd be back." She snorted in delight. "And I was right!"

"Yes, Kyrmves," he whispered. Warm tears rolled down his cheeks and his ears rang with the chirping of countless starlings. *A celebration.* "You were right."

Dramatis Personae

The Phuuls:

Teltö Phuul: A Necromancer, from Qivunako.

Rhea Phuul: His elder sister, also a qualified Necromancer, now working in Mustanako.

Kyrmves Phuul: His younger sister, still in school.

Teltö's father: An employee of Qivunako Iron.

Teltö's mother: An employee of the Qivunako Food Factory.

Other Qivunakonians:

Dyrstin Venomavat: A long-time friend of Teltö, now working in Kuolinako.

Alio Venomavat: Dyrstin's aunt, the Undersecretary of the Qivunako Lesser Council.

Tuvena Sytöphin: Teltö's former girlfriend, now working in Kuolinako.

Metvet Otsola: Former friend of Teltö, now deceased.

Lumi Kloveio: Famous war-artist, now deceased.

The Grand Council/The Great Nine:

Peta Vyrellävek: His Excellency, the Grand Chancellor of the Viiminian Empire, originally from Tuonako, nicknamed the Dragon.

Suphives Söstä: Council representative from Mustanako, also Warden of the Imperial Mint.

Nhädiö Meerm: Council representative from Mustanako.

Hiisa Pliil: Council representative from Kuolinako.

Aarti Yyrtön: Council representative from Kuolinako.

Lolto Rumi: Council representative from Tuonako.

Mai Phermö: Council representative from Tuonako.

Kortek Keer: Council representative from Qivunako, the longest-serving member.

Hyät Hova: Council representative from Qivunako.

In Kuolinako:

Gykäkkä IV: Still-titular Emperor of the Viiminian Empire, dead these past fifteen centuries.

Eriva Vöder: Her Vigilance, the Inquisitor General.

Kärytö Revenuta: Tuvena's work colleague, from Tuonako.

Eriva Phytek: A Physician.

Kimi Sorko: Dean of the Guild of Skilled Labourers.

Rimives: Friend of Dyrstin Venomavat, in the Guild.

Telo Oilio: Housemaster to Grand Master Keer.

A Theatre Manager

Vaani: A security guard at the Theatre.

Nieliini Giinovo: A businessman.

In Mustanako:

Vaani Vyrellävek: The Grand Chancellor's nephew.

Aarti: Proprietor of The Cosy Needle.

Nieliini: A sailor.

Reni Kovo: A Guild member.

The Old Man: Entertainment at The Cosy Needle.

At the Skeevereet Embassy:

The Ambassador

Physsil: A receptionist.

Reqi: A security guard.

Northerners:

Sufael: A Northerner working in the Empire for Mustanako Fisheries.

Sufael's father: An airship pilot in the Northern military.

Prince Oym: The hereditary ruler of the Skeevereet Principality, Supreme Commander of the Northern military.

Second Marshal Snali Ventiko: Vice-Commander of the Northern military.

Count Sergev Rughvneer: Aristocrat

Colonel Ereek Rughvneer: Aristocrat in the Northern military, Sergev's younger brother.

Kothro: Family servant to the Rughvneers.

Count Thyorm: Aristocrat

Count Groon: Aristocrat, and café owner.

Colonel Frevorum Groon: Aristocrat, cousin of the Count, and Chief of the 113th regiment.

Keeker: Soldier and Quartermaster of the 113th regiment.

Sergeant Speer: Aristocrat, Soldier, and assistant to Keeker.

Lieutenant Pedeet: Soldier.

Otho: Soldier, serving under Pedeet.

Welleorm: Churchman and military chaplain.

Other:

A Mnoma: A tall green humanoid creature.

Acknowledgements

A book is a team effort, and as such, I would like to thank Sara-Jayne Slack, Rebecca Hall, and Venetia Jackson of Inspired Quill for their hard work in turning *Wise Phuul* from manuscript to reality. Thanks also to Neal Barber, Fiona Thomas, and Laura Cayuela for a last minute purge of rebellious typos.

I would like to thank those who read the earlier drafts and provided valuable feedback – Christopher Giles, Ursula Giles, Tina Shaw, Neal Barber, Mark Claborne, and Tim Forcella. You were right about the ending.

Also to Laura Heathcote, Tim Outshoorn, Jacob Manning, Joachim Torrano, and James Bull for their assistance and/or enthusiasm at various points. To Ellie Swann for the photo.

Finally, to my parents, Claire and Gareth Stride.

About the Author

Daniel Stride (also known as Dan) is a long-time fantasy reader and all-round geek, having fallen in love with *The Lord of the Rings* aged nine (he still thinks *The Silmarillion* is the best book ever written).

He spent far too long at University, where he accumulated multiple degrees in-between lobbying politicians and fighting for doomed causes. But he wasn't really a career student – honest – he even had a respectable nine years working for the local newspaper. And now he's pursuing a legal career...

Apart from reading, writing, and teaching himself foreign languages, he's a member of the Society for Creative Anachronism, with a taste for reconstructing medieval skaldic verse. His only true weakness is chocolate. And cats. But not chocolate cats, because the fur would get all sticky.

Dan lives in Dunedin, New Zealand and is currently working on a sequel to *Wise Phuul*.

www.ingramcontent.com/pod-product-compliance
Lightning Source LLC
Chambersburg PA
CBHW032156180726
48284CB00001B/68